Murder at
BARCLAY
MEADOW

Murder at
BARCLAY
MEADOW

WENDY SAND ECKEL

MINOTAUR BOOKS
A THOMAS DUNNE BOOK
NEW YORK

A THOMAS DUNNE BOOK FOR MINOTAUR BOOKS.
An imprint of St. Martin's Publishing Group.

MURDER AT BARCLAY MEADOW. Copyright © 2015 by Wendy Sand Eckel. All rights reserved. Printed in the United States of America. For information, address St. Martin's Press, 175 Fifth Avenue, New York, N.Y. 10010.

www.thomasdunnebooks.com
www.minotaurbooks.com

Designed by Omar Chapa

Library of Congress Cataloging-in-Publication Data

Eckel, Wendy Sand.
    Murder at Barclay Meadow: a mystery / Wendy Sand Eckel.—First edition.
        p. cm.
    ISBN 978-1-250-05860-7 (hardback)
    ISBN 978-1-4668-6293-7 (e-book)
    I. Title.
    PS3605.C553M87 2015
    813'.6—dc23

                                                        2015017010

Minotaur books may be purchased for educational, business, or promotional use. For information on bulk purchases, please contact the Macmillan Corporate and Premium Sales Department at 1-800-221-7945, extension 5442, or write to specialmarkets@macmillan.com.

First Edition: July 2015

10   9   8   7   6   5   4   3   2   1

For Mom, who savored a good mystery

Three things cannot be long hidden: the sun, the moon, and the truth.

—*Buddha*

Rosalie, come and dust some flour on your hands and drop the dough on the bread board. Now knead it with every part of your hands: fingers, palms, and fists. Don't think, just breathe through your young heart. Bread's very essence allows us to nurture those we love, and feel connected to the good solid earth. For me, baking bread is like coming home.

—*Charlotte Gardner*

Murder at
BARCLAY
MEADOW

ONE

Before my only child left for her first year of college, she suggested I create my own Facebook profile. Annie said we could "friend" one another, and chat online. That way she wouldn't have to tell me all the details of her life in a daily phone call or tedious texting. I could read all about what she was up to, who her new friends were, and what music she liked. The problem was, so could her other five hundred-plus friends. Ultimately, though, it was the private "chat" feature that sold me. So I created a profile, such that it was.

After two months, I had yet to post a picture or write what was on my mind. My profile didn't declare my relationship status or where I lived because those things had recently changed, rather abruptly, I should add.

Inspiration struck on a crisp, cool day in October when I posted my first status.

Rosalie Hart
Still reeling after discovering a dead girl floating in my marsh grasses.

• • •

Mr. Miele was delivered by UPS one day in late October. He was the first friend I'd made in the month since I moved into a two-hundred-year-old house bequeathed to me by my aunt Charlotte. Wedged between the bread box and my now diminished toaster, the coffee bistro's brushed steel sparkled in the low afternoon sun. Although my aunt's kitchen was large enough, with tall, white cabinets and a wall of windows that faced the south, much of the space was taken up by a stone hearth so massive I could stand up in it. Not everyone could stand in it, but at five foot four, my head barely brushed the flue.

Freshly ground coffee beans filled the room with a seductive, earthy aroma. I tucked *The Washington Post* under my arm and carried a double-shot mocha skim latte dusted with cinnamon out to the screened porch, sat down, and stretched my legs out on an old wicker ottoman. The scent of mildew lurked in the faded floral chintz cushions. This old house screamed for attention and at least a bucket of bleach. Later, I thought, and took a long sip of coffee.

I decided to begin with the back of the paper. I'd start with the crossword and Sudoku puzzles, peruse the advice columns, and eventually work my my way to the hard news. Lately I had the attention span of a goldfish.

As I folded the paper open to the crossword, I looked out at the Cardigan River rushing by at the end of the sloping lawn. I started to look down at the paper but stopped. A shock of color caught my eye. It stood out like a flower in a desert—the bright turquoise vivid and glaring against the gunmetal gray water. My nerve endings buzzed with foreboding. I set my cup down, swallowed hard against the dry lump in my throat, and steeled enough courage to stand up.

The sun warmed my skin as I walked. Innocent puffs of high clouds dotted the sky. An osprey glided by and settled into a twiggy nest. I shielded my eyes as I approached, my sneakers squeaking on the grass. I stopped abruptly and covered my nose and mouth when a putrid stench saturated the air. Despite the dread squeezing my heart, I continued.

And then I saw her—facedown in the river. She was cradled by marsh grasses, the lapping water rocked her gently. Grass reeds were tangled in her lifeless hair. Nausea roiled my stomach. Just before I threw up, I noticed what had caught my eye. Strapped to her back was a dainty cloth pack. I recognized the cheerful colors. A Vera Bradley pattern: doodle daisy.

A few hours later I paced through the kitchen waiting for the sheriff and his deputies to finish. Night had crept up the lawn, making shadows of the men as they worked. The lights on their vehicles bathed the house in manic red and blue flashes like a disco.

When they first arrived, Sheriff Joe Wilgus, a large, brooding man with inky black hair, asked me endless questions about the young woman who was now zipped into a thick, rubber bag. My teeth chattered when I spoke and I chewed every one of my nails down to the skin between questions. After I apologized for throwing up on the crime scene, the sheriff seemed to realize I had nothing helpful to say and sent me inside.

I noticed a stain on the white enamel of my sink as I made yet another pass. I dusted it with cleanser and scrubbed vigorously. I heard a throat clearing and spun around to see the sheriff standing in my kitchen. His broad shoulders and over six feet of height filled the small alcove.

"Sheriff?" I brushed my hair from my face with the back of my hand.

"Missus Hart."

"I'm sorry. I didn't hear you come in. Do you need to talk to me?"

He shifted his weight. His leather holster creaked. "Not unless you have something more to say."

"No," I said. "I'm sorry to be so useless."

His eyes took in my kitchen. They lingered on Mr. Miele. He gave his head a small shake.

"Would you like some coffee?"

"Is that what that thing is? Looks more like something out of *Star Wars*."

"I'll take that as a yes?"

He settled his bulk into my aunt's spindly antique chair. I filled two cups and set one on the table in front of him. "It's French roast," I said. "Extra bold."

He looked up. A deep scowl furrowed his brow. "You mind telling me why you're living out here?"

I stepped back from the table. This was my first time answering that question. "Well . . . um . . . I inherited this farm from my late aunt—Charlotte Gardner. You may have known her? And . . . well, my husband and I recently separated and . . ." Separated. Is that what I was now? No longer defined by my qualities, I was simply "separated"—like an egg white from yolk. I placed a hand over my stomach and prayed I wouldn't throw up again.

"I wondered if anyone would ever move into this old place," the sheriff said. "Seemed a shame to have so much good land go fallow." His eyes met mine. "You do intend to plant some crops, now, don't you?"

I swallowed hard. "Yes. Of course." I looked out the window. An ethereal fog was rising like a spirit from the dewy grass. I hadn't thought much about the fields. I didn't know how many there were or what, if anything, had ever grown in them. In truth, I hadn't decided how long I would even be living in this old house, let alone whether or not to plant a seed.

"Sheriff . . ." I said, anxious to move the subject away from my planting crops. I set some cream and sugar on the table cloth and sat across from him, tucking my leg underneath to boost my height.

He tapped the end of his nose. "You got some cleanser on your face."

"I do?" I snatched up a napkin and wiped my nose.

"You were saying."

I wadded the napkin in my fist. "What have you learned about the girl?"

"Seems she was a student." He stirred a heavy dose of cream into his coffee and set the spoon on a napkin. The coffee bled onto the white square. "Had a John Adams College ID."

"A student." I thought immediately of my Annie. "Have you told her parents yet?"

"We let the college handle that side of things. Our dispatcher is notifying President Carmichael." He took a long sip and set the cup back in the saucer, his thick fingers barely able to grasp the delicate handle of my aunt's Spode cup.

"But why aren't *you* telling them?"

"Well, you see, Missus Hart . . ."

"Please," I said. "Call me Rosalie." I smiled over at him.

"As I was saying, Missus Hart, colleges have to be careful about these things. If parents hear students are drowning in the Cardigan River, it can, well, let's just say it might keep people away."

"How can you be so certain she drowned?"

"Didn't you find her floating in the river?"

"Yes," I said. "But how do you know someone didn't put her there?"

He leaned forward, resting on his elbows. "Do you know the last time we had a murder in this county?"

"No, of course not," I said quietly.

"Sixteen years ago when old Percy Tate drank too much at Beeman's bar, went home and shot his wife because he thought she was an intruder." He finished his coffee in one gulp. "So, how many people would you figure drowned in the Cardigan this year?"

"I'm guessing more than one." I lowered my eyes.

"You live out here by the river," he said, tension tightening his voice, "and you think it's just a pretty view. But what you don't see is the current rushing underneath. Even the best swimmers can't stay above the water with it tugging at them, tiring them out, and then sucking them in." He leaned back. The chair complained. "We've had seven drown so far this year. And now Megan makes eight."

"Megan?" My eyes shot up. "Her name is Megan?"

"Now why is that so interesting?"

"I guess hearing her name makes it all the more real."

"Finding a dead body didn't make it real enough for you?"

"Yes, of course. But . . . well . . . now I'm thinking about the poor mother who chose such a pretty name for her daughter. She'll be devastated. It's the worst thing that can happen to a parent. Do you have children, Sheriff?"

He ignored my question, reinforcing my feeling of being considered an outsider. This was the Eastern Shore of Maryland, a flat stretch of land between the Chesapeake Bay and the Atlantic Ocean, dotted with farms and quaint little towns. It was known as "the land of pleasant living," a simple place where people prided themselves on being unguarded, friendly, and, beyond anything else, loyal. People like me from the other side of the Chesapeake Bay were viewed as interlopers who breezed through on their way to the coast, or, far worse, settled on the pristine land the locals believed belonged to them.

Two more officers shuffled into the room. "We're about done, Sheriff," the taller man said. "Body's on its way to the coroner."

"All right." The sheriff pushed himself up to a stand.

The other deputy twirled his hat in his hands. He was young—baby-faced; sweat bubbled along his hair line. "Boss?" he said. "With the way she was bloated, you figure she was in there a few days?"

"I'm guessing three."

"Probably from that college party we busted up down on the water Friday night," the taller deputy said. "Those dumb kids had the keg at the end of the dock. I'm surprised they all didn't fall in."

"But if she was at a party . . ." I stood quickly. "Wouldn't someone have noticed her missing?"

The sheriff looked over at me. "You ever go to college?"

"Yes."

"You ever stay out all night?"

My face warmed. "You said the party was three days ago. Surely someone has missed her by now."

"They didn't miss her enough to notify me."

"But—"

"You see, Missus Hart," the sheriff interrupted, "you can conjure up all kinds of theories, but in police work, we only know what we know." He fixed his hat on his head. "Now, I'd like you to put this whole incident behind you. It's no longer your business."

The taller deputy smirked. He elbowed the other one. "Sounds like somebody's been watching a few too many *Law and Order* marathons."

I frowned. Then I noticed Megan's backpack in his hand. The colors were muted by the muddy river and the cloth had dried. He held a Ziploc bag in his other hand. I looked closer, trying to make out the contents through the plastic. An accordion of condoms stood out among otherwise benign possessions—a lip gloss tube, a small brush, a Smartphone that couldn't possibly work anymore. So much for evidence. I looked harder. There was something in the back of the bag. An envelope with blurred, handwritten lettering. No address. No stamp. Maybe a name? I tried to read. Two words. Was the first letter an "I"?

"Hey . . ." The deputy ducked the bag behind his back. "What do you think you're looking at?"

"What does it say on that envelope?" I said.

I felt the sheriff's eyes on me. I stole a glance at him. A scarlet red flush was working its way up his neck.

"I believe I just told you this was no longer your business." He looked at the deputy and held out his hand. The young man knew to give him the evidence bag. Without another word, Sheriff Wilgus headed toward the front door. The deputies fell in behind, and the three officers walked through my adopted home in a slow, deliberate, almost possessive cadence. They glanced into rooms as they passed, their eyes traveling over the diminished wallpaper, the cut crystal in the corner cabinet, the sepia-enhanced photographs of my ancestors.

"Whatever happened to old Missus Gardner?" a deputy said. "She pass or what?"

Sheriff Wilgus stopped and appraised the woodwork around the front door. "Had a stroke or something, I think. Good thing Tyler'd been checking up on her. She could've been dead for weeks before somebody found her otherwise."

Two

The only place to buy a *Washington Post* in Cardigan was Birdie's shoe store. At first I missed not having my paper in the driveway every morning, but after just a week of isolation, the trip into town helped me establish a routine in my otherwise aimless days.

A bell clanked on the glass door as I stepped inside. I was met with the strong scent of shoe polish and a trace of lurking mildew. A card table had been set up in a corner, offering an array of handmade doll clothes with price tags pinned to them, while a long wall displayed a variety of magazines and comic books. And although a few pairs of sensible, outdated shoes sat on a low rack, the traffic in the store was almost entirely drawn by the candy, newspapers from several major cities, and the guaranteed source of local gossip.

Doris Bird had my paper ready. "Hello, Miss Rosalie," she said. Her wiry gray hair framed a kind face. Thick glasses magnified her eyes, giving her a look of perpetual wonderment. "So, I hear you've decided to farm your land."

I stared at her in disbelief. How could she know so soon? I had just said that to appease the sheriff. Now they expected me to actually follow through with it?

An impish grin appeared on her face. The idea seemed to please her.

"Out of curiosity," I said. "How did you hear?"

"Lila." Doris backed herself onto a tall stool and crossed her arms. Much-handled photos of a multitude of grandchildren were taped on the wall behind her. I had already learned the names and ages of each one.

"Lila?"

"She's the secretary over at the sheriff's department. Drives that pink Beetle with the eyelashes over the headlights."

"I've seen that car." I reached for a pack of spearmint gum and set it on top of my paper. "Sheriff Wilgus was out at my house the other night. That must be how she heard."

"Shame about that girl," she said. "It's in the paper."

"The *Post*?"

"I don't know about that," Doris said. "But it's in the *Devon County News*."

I selected one of the local weekly papers from the tiered rack next to the counter. "John Adams Psychology Professor Receives

Prestigious National Grant" spread across the top of the page. I glanced up at Doris. "I don't see it."

She opened the paper and tapped a stubby finger on an article on page three. "Here."

"Student dies in accidental drowning," I read. "So, they ruled it an accident. I wonder how they can be so certain."

Doris shrugged. "Lila said the girl must a been drunk and fell in the water."

"It just seems strange no one heard a splash."

"Maybe you should ask the sheriff about it."

"Oh, no." I shook my head. "He makes me nervous."

"Joe hasn't had an easy life," Doris said. "But he's a good law-man. Wrapped up this case pretty quick, don't you think?"

"Indeed," I said, thinking his swiftness was precisely the prob-lem. I looked back at the small black-and-white photo. The caption read: Megan Johnston, 21. Although the photo was blurry, it was clear she was stunning. Light hair, bright smile, round eyes that seemed to dare you to keep looking. "She's beautiful."

"Downright shame." Doris glanced at the photo. "Kids are too reckless these days. They think they're immortal is what it is."

"I agree. Our children may move away but the worry never leaves us."

The bell clanked again. More customers. After paying for my purchases I turned and almost tripped over two small children who had already crowded the candy case, dollar bills tight in their fists.

I hugged the papers and headed for my car. The convertible top was down and my hair was now a mass of windswept curls. This was a relatively new car. On my forty-third birthday, Ed had wrapped a bow around a cherry red Mercedes and parked it in the driveway. I had been happy driving a Prius. But Ed announced, "No wife of mine is going to be seen in a car preferred by senior citizens. Driv-ing this baby," he said as he dropped the keys in my palm, "will keep you young." The car was everything I'm not—flamboyant, pricey, and impractical. I stopped walking and took it in. Why hadn't I realized then Ed was in the market for a newer model?

I tucked my hair behind an ear and glanced in the window of Brower's cafe as I passed. The sheriff was seated at a table. Curious, I stepped closer to the window and peered in. He was talking intently to a man with salt-and-pepper hair, their heads dipped close together. Well, if you wanted to have a private conversation, Brower's would be the place to have it. I tried their coffee the other day and it tasted like a recently paved road.

The man slapped the table and pointed a finger in the sheriff's flushed face. Oh, I would never do that, I thought. He might bite it. I tried to get a better view, but all I could see was the back of the other man's head. My cheek was nearly touching the glass. I wondered who would have the guts to talk to him that way. The sheriff looked up at me. I panicked when his eyes narrowed in recognition.

I jumped back and slammed into a passerby. "Oh, I'm so sorry." I spun around. My gum slid onto the sidewalk.

"Whoa, there . . ." Tom Bestman said. Tom was the executor of Aunt Charlotte's estate and now my divorce lawyer. He was of average height and weight with brown eyes and a hairline that was taking its time to recede. He dressed casually for a lawyer and could be categorized as unremarkable. Until he smiled, that is. His was a smile so disarmingly warm and kind, it enabled one to trust him instantly. I was grateful to have him in my court. "You know, Rosalie . . ." There it was, that smile. "You can't really read the menu through the window."

"Did I hurt you?"

"Nope." He bent down, picked up my gum, and set it on the stack of papers. "I'm glad to run into you." He hesitated. "Literally, right?"

"I'm very sorry."

"No worries," he said. "Say, did you get my email?"

"No. Have you heard from Ed's attorney?"

He avoided my gaze.

"You have bad news." I clutched the papers tighter.

Tom rolled his shoulders back and shifted his weight. "It's not great news, but—"

"What?"

"Well, Rosalie, it seems Ed has frozen all of your accounts. ATM, checking, credit cards, the whole shebang."

"Can he do that?" I searched his face.

His eyes met mine. "Apparently so."

"But why? I haven't done anything to him. He's the one who—"

"Apparently he wants you to sell the farm."

"But I'm living there. What does he expect me to do?" I stared at the ground. "He's always hated the farm. He wanted me to sell it the day we read Aunt Charlotte's will." I looked up. "He said it was a money pit. And that he never wanted to own something on the . . ."

"On the what?" Tom said.

"You know what they say." I shook my head. "I'm sorry to be crude. He said he didn't want to own something on the 'shit house side of Maryland.'"

"It's nothing we Eastern Shore folk haven't heard before." Tom tucked his hands in the pockets of his khakis. "So, if he was so hot to sell it, why didn't you?"

"I was confused. I had recently lost my mother and then Aunt Charlotte and the last thing I wanted to do was hastily sell the last piece of history from Mother's family." I sunk my teeth into my lower lip. "But that was two years ago. Why would he force my hand now?"

"If you ask me . . . well, don't ask me what I think about it or I'll be the one sounding crude."

"Isn't there something I can do?"

"I don't know. He said he won't unfreeze the accounts until you list the place with a Realtor."

"I can't go back to Chevy Chase. Not yet."

"Rosalie," Tom said. "Charlotte left a small trust to help keep the place up." He patted my shoulder. "It may not put a whole lot of food on the table, but it should keep you warm."

"I have to do what he wants, then, don't I?" I said. "After everything he's done, now I have to sell my home."

"Hang on," Tom said gently. "Let me see what I can do."

"But you said . . ." I glanced over at the Mercedes and frowned. "Maybe I could sell my car. I've never liked that car."

Tom's brow furrowed. "Is the title in your name?"

"No, it was a birthday gift. But . . . oh, my goodness." I placed my palm over my heart. "I thought I was smarter than this. I never imagined I wouldn't be married."

Tom gave me a sad smile. "Of course you didn't."

The door to Brower's creaked open. Sheriff Wilgus hiked up his belt as the man with the salt-and-pepper hair followed him out. The sheriff looked over at us. Tom waved. I hesitated, then waved, too. After a short, disinterested nod, the sheriff continued down the sidewalk. The other man, who was in a tailored navy wool suit, walked next to him.

"The sheriff doesn't look too happy, does he?" Tom said.

"Happy doesn't seem to fall into his range of emotions. He seems to be in a perpetual state of annoyance," I said. "Who is the other gentleman?"

"That's David Carmichael."

"Are they friends?"

"They don't look to be all that friendly."

I watched them enter the next block. Their heads close, their bodies stiff with tension.

"Honestly," Tom continued. "I've never found the president to be all that affable."

"President?"

Tom turned to face me again. "He's the president of John Adams College."

"I wonder if they're talking about Megan."

"Megan? You mean the dead girl you found?" Tom said. "Why are you so curious, Rosalie?"

"Oh, not so curious." I tore open the pack of gum and offered him a piece. "I guess I'm just trying to learn the ropes of small-town living."

"Good for you," he said as he opened the wrapper. "Rosalie, don't make any decisions you'll regret later, okay?" He folded the gum into his mouth.

"Well, that's not a problem. I can barely decide what to eat for breakfast."

"Hey . . ." Tom stepped closer. "I heard you're going to plant some crops."

"You, too?"

"I hope it's true," he said. "You know, things happen for a reason." He cracked his gum. "I, for one, am glad to know you're settling in here. We need folks like you—folks with a history. Folks who want to keep the Eastern Shore the way it's always been."

As I drove home along the winding road that echoed the river's curves and bends, I felt a slow burning in my gut. I couldn't stop thinking about Ed. I felt as if I didn't even know him anymore. I wondered if our friends had been surprised by our separation or if perhaps they had seen the signs, the cracks in the foundation that I'd been blind to. Like with a Seurat painting, sometimes just a small step of distance can bring things into focus. I pushed harder on the accelerator. The wind restyled my hair.

The day my marriage shattered, I had been making plans for a trip to Napa Valley. We had recently delivered Annie to Duke University, and I thought a romantic getaway would be the perfect opportunity to acknowledge the next phase of our lives. As much as I would miss my girl, I was looking forward to our empty nest and hoped it would rekindle the romance that seemed to have cooled without my noticing.

It was a lovely Saturday afternoon, one of those pleasant weekend days when we each engaged in parallel, domestic activities. Ed was upstairs getting ready to clean out the gutters when his phone vibrated on the counter. It sat next to his keys, a receipt, and a mound of loose change.

"Ed . . ." I called as I clicked on a bed-and-breakfast website. It buzzed again. "Ed . . . your phone."

I was struck with the thought it might be Annie. Although she was more likely to text me with day-to-day issues, if it was an emergency, she knew her father's phone was always close to his heart. I glanced down at the screen. "Rebecca." The vibrating stopped.

Ed came into the kitchen while pulling a faded orange University of Virginia sweatshirt over his head.

"There you are," I said. "Hey—I just found this adorable bed-and-breakfast." I looked back at my computer and scrolled down the page.

"Bed-and-*breakfast?*"

"Yeah. It looks really cute. It has a package deal: bike rentals, wine and cheese every evening. Oh, and a hot-air balloon ride. Well, nix the balloon ride, but what do you think?" I looked up at him. When our eyes met my first thought was how handsome he was. His tortoiseshell glasses sat low on his nose and his graying sideburns seemed to deepen the tan of his skin. "I could try and find something nicer if you don't want to stay in a B-and-B."

"I don't care." He turned to fill a glass with water from the refrigerator dispenser.

I studied his back, trying not to feel hurt by his lack of interest. Maybe I should step outside my comfort zone and take that balloon ride. "Oh, Ed, someone named Rebecca just called. Is she the new—"

"Did you answer it?" He rushed to his phone and snatched it up. Water sloshed out of his glass.

"Ed?" I said, trying to subdue the tremble in my voice. "What's wrong?"

He stared down at the screen. "I can't do this anymore."

I tried to swallow. "Exactly what can't you do?"

"Rose . . ." He looked up at me. Pain etched his face. "I'm in love with someone else. I have been for several months."

A cloud blocked the sun, darkening the room. I couldn't move. I had always known I wouldn't last longer than the first bullet in a war. And I had just been shot through the heart. My head felt light and my joints had stiffened. How fast does rigor mortis set in, I wondered, after you've died?

Later that afternoon I brewed some Brazilian coffee—a nutty blend with a hint of cocoa—and sat at the kitchen table. Air breezed in the open window and I caught the scent of burning leaves. Halloween was in just a few days. I hadn't even bought a pumpkin.

I took a sip. No melancholy, I chastised. But the idleness of my new life was wrecking havoc on my nerves. The remoteness of this decaying house, the utter stillness, was as haunting as the humming golden calm before a tornado touched down.

I opened the local paper and read the entire article about Megan Johnston. There was nothing more about the cause of death, just the details of her life and surviving kin. My chest tightened at the memory of her bloated body, adorned with that cheerful, feminine backpack. After calling 911, I had gone back down to the shore and waited for the police to arrive. Although I kept a safe distance—at least enough to be able to breathe—I couldn't leave her alone in that cold, unfriendly water.

I looked back at the article. The funeral was to be held in Wilmington, Delaware. I was struck with an impulse to drive up there. Maybe it would help if I could just say good-bye—pay my respects. Besides, it would be good to take a road trip out of Cardigan.

I wrote the address on a scrap of paper. The furnace clanked and groaned, trying to come to life, but then nothing. I would have to call someone. Later, I thought, and flipped open my laptop to search the Wilmington papers for more information. I clicked on Facebook first to see if Annie was available for a chat.

> **Rosalie**   Hi!
> **Annie**   hi mom!

I typed quickly. I was particularly happy to chat with Annie today of all days. Ever since finding Megan, the mother lion in me was roaring.

> **Annie**   I still can't believe you found a dead body!
> **Rosalie**   I know!!!

I hesitated, not wanting to upset her. Mass shootings, suicides, and rapes were occurring on school campuses. All I wanted was for my girl to feel safe and loved, but even that had been disrupted now that her parents were getting divorced. I decided to spare her any details.

> **Rosalie**   I'm okay. And the police took care of everything.
>   How are you?
> **Annie**   I just did something rando
> **Rosalie**   Rando?

Annie	yeah, random
Rosalie	OK, I'll get this yet. So what did you do?
Annie	joined the rugby team!!!! :):)
Rosalie	What?!!
Annie	chill. it's fun. soccer is too competitive so my roomie talked me into it. we have a game parents' weekend.

Parents' weekend. I had made a hotel reservation in Durham for Ed and me the day Annie received her acceptance letter.

Annie	mom?
Rosalie	So, tell me everything. Are you walking with a buddy at night and staying away from fraternity houses?
Annie	**eye roll. you're the one who's getting into trouble. you need a hobby, ma. what are you doing with yourself?

I had to think for a moment.

Rosalie	I signed up for a memoir writing class at the local college.
Annie	now who's rando? what are you going to write about?

I stared at the screen. Until I found a job, I needed something to fill my time. I had scoured the continuing education classes offered by John Adams College. With a degree in creative writing, I was hoping for a journalism class, but they were filled. Memoir was the only course offering I could find that would allow me to hone my rusty writing skills. I had never thought about writing a memoir before, but who knew? Maybe I would come up with something.

> **Annie**   hello? jk!=) i'm sure you'll have tons to write about. make me look good!
>
> **Rosalie**   There's also a knitting class at the library. I could try that too.
>
> **Annie**   !!! mucho better. you could make me a scarf! i like blue. Haha g2g! xoxo ciao!

Before I could finish typing that I loved her, she had posted her new status:

Annie Hart

is in search of chocolate

Worry for Annie nagged at me. She never talked about the divorce. I wondered if she was pretending it never happened or maybe just hoping her father would come to his senses. That's how my friends reacted. "It's just a phase," my best friend Amy had said. "Ed will be begging you back in no time. Pull a Hillary," she added. "Forgive the man and get on with your life." But Ed wasn't asking for forgiveness. And I'd never seen him beg for anything.

I slapped my computer closed and stood. I needed to move.

After changing into a tank and jogging shorts, I snatched up my iPod and headed out the front door. Sunlight peeked through the rows of cedar trees, dappling the lane to the main road with shadow and light. Yes, I thought, vitamin D.

I surveyed the grounds as I walked. A mowing crew had kept up the lawn, but the rest of the property was a disordered mess. The fields were dotted with sweet gum saplings and an array of wildflowers—goldenrod, the scarlet tufts of Indian paintbrush—that bent to the demands of the autumn breeze. A sign at the start of the lane read BARCLAY MEADOW. Perhaps with my neglect, this property was living up to its name.

I inserted my ear buds and clicked my iPod on shuffle. I bent my neck from side to side, felt a satisfying crack, and broke into a run. This was good. Exercise activated endorphins. Endorphins elevated moods. Electric guitars started up. An organ ran the keys. A jazzy saxophone joined the mix. I picked up the pace, moving with the cadence of the music. Boy, did I need this.

I stopped abruptly, skidding in the gravel. I yanked on the ear buds and threw my iPod on the ground. "No!" I covered my mouth. Bruce Springsteen had begun the intro to "Rosalita." Ed and I danced to the song at our wedding. He used to call me that—Rosalita—when he was feeling affectionate. I pushed the heels of my hands over my eyelids. When had he stopped? My mind raced. When had he *stopped*?

"Ma'am?"

It took a few seconds before a sandy-haired man came into focus. "Who are you?" I brushed a tear from my cheek.

"Tyler Wells," he said as if I should already know.

He was tall with wide shoulders and wore a denim shirt, the rolled-up sleeves exposing muscular forearms. A chocolate Labrador with graying fur sat next to him. I glanced around, remembering how isolated I was. The nearest neighbor was a half mile down the road. There were no sounds of traffic, not even an airplane overhead. The only noise, other than my panting, was a red-winged blackbird sitting on a fence post clearly taken with the sound of his trilling.

"This is private property, Tyler." I looked up at him. His face was tan and slightly weathered. His vivid green eyes held my gaze.

He pulled a boxy cap lower on his head. "You running this place?"

"Yes." I shrugged. "Sort of. But why are you standing in my driveway?"

"Doris said you were finally putting this land back to work."

"Doris?"

"Doris Bird—Birdie's shoe store." He crossed his arms tight to his chest. Biceps bulged under his shirt. "Unless you've leased it to someone else."

"Honestly? I was kind of hoping everyone would forget about that."

He narrowed his laser-beam eyes. "Ma'am?"

"Why are you calling me 'ma'am'? I may be cresting the hill, but something tells me you are too. And just how did you get here? I don't see a vehicle. It's like *poof*, all of a sudden you and your dog are in front of me."

"My truck is at the end of the lane."

"Why didn't you drive up to the house?"

"You ask a lot of questions."

"Well, you took me by surprise."

He shifted his weight, kicking up a puff of dust. "And who are you, exactly?"

"I'm Rosalie Hart, Charlotte's niece." I put my hands on my hips. "Wait a minute . . . Tyler. I remember that name. You leased these fields from my aunt, didn't you?"

He gave his head one sharp nod.

"She used to talk about you." I stared down at the gravel. "She liked you very much." I huffed out a sigh and looked up at him, taking in his rugged good looks. "I don't suppose you'd like some coffee?"

"All right."

I started toward the house. Tyler followed with the dog trotting at his side. Gravel crackled under his boots. Why did the Marlboro Man have to show up when I was in spandex?

Once inside I pulled two mugs from the cabinet, filled them from the carafe, and held one out to him. He opened his fist. My iPod lay cradled in his wide palm. "You dropped this."

"Thank you." I wondered if it still worked.

"Actually," he said and accepted the mug, "I'm pretty sure you threw it."

"Yeah, well, it's a long and not very compelling story." I blew on my coffee to cool it. "Where's your dog?"

"The stoop."

"What's his name?"

"Dickens."

"Oh." I smiled. "He gets into trouble, does he? You can bring him inside if you're worried he'll run away."

"As in Charles Dickens. And he isn't going anywhere."

I took a sip of coffee. It scalded the tip of my tongue. I set the cup on the counter and looked up at Tyler. "So, how does this work exactly?"

"I lease the land from you and keep the profits," he said. "That's all you really need to know."

"Good grief. I take it you're not fond of tact?"

"Waste of time." He walked over to a drawer, removed a spoon, opened the sugar canister, and scooped several mounds of the fine white crystals into his coffee. His familiarity with my kitchen was unnerving.

"You've owned this place for two years." He turned to face me. "Why show up now?"

"Like I said . . ." I brushed a stray hair from my face. "It's a long story."

He leaned back against the counter and sipped his coffee. He looked down at it, paused for a moment, and took another sip. "You let a lot of good farmland go to waste."

"Haven't we already been over that?" I secured the lid back on the copper canister. "Were you close with my aunt?"

"Miss Charlotte was a classy lady."

"She was the best."

"Funny." He cocked his head. "I don't remember seeing you around here."

"I . . . well, we emailed almost every day, but I guess I didn't see her as much as I would have liked. I'm . . . well, I *was* very busy."

"And now you're not?"

"That's right. Now I'm not." I rolled my shoulders back and lifted my chin. "So, Tyler, what do you need from me? Do I have to buy you seeds? Do I even have any farm equipment? I never looked. I wonder if I have a tractor."

"You don't have to do anything." He drained his coffee and set the mug in the sink. I was still waiting for mine to cool. "Look, I'd like to get started right away. It's going to take some time to get these fields back in shape. But I could get some cover crops planted if I hustle."

"Do I need to get my lawyer to draw up a contract?"

"Lawyer?" He shook his head. "No need for one of them."

"So, there's no contract?"

"Your aunt kept a copy of the lease in a filing cabinet. It should be sufficient." He crossed his arms. "Unless you threw it away. You seem to like throwing things." I was pretty sure I detected a faint smile on his face.

"I haven't even opened the filing cabinet." I picked up a pen and looked around for a piece of paper. I wrote "find contract" on a napkin.

"There's one more thing. Miss Charlotte and I were farming organic—trying some experimental methods." Tyler cleared his throat. "I'd like to continue that."

"I didn't realize . . ."

"Look . . ." He started for the door. "You find the contract and I'll get a check to you tomorrow morning. I start early. Don't be surprised if you hear the plow before six."

"It all sounds so interesting," I said as I followed him through the house. "Planting things is optimistic, don't you think? Did you know Eleanor Roosevelt said, 'Where flowers bloom, so does hope'? And farming organic—that's so great."

He stopped and looked back at me. "So, now all of a sudden you're interested?"

"Yes," I said. "I'm a quick study. If you catch me up to speed, I—"

"The way I see it . . ." He picked his cap up from the antique demilune next to the door and secured it on his head. "You don't really need to study up. I'll just do my job and you do whatever it is that you do." He straightened his posture. "What exactly do you do?"

"Me? Well . . . I haven't quite figured that out yet."

Tyler opened the door.

"Wait, you never said if I have a tractor."

"I have my own."

"Okay." I extended my hand. "I guess we're partners now."

He reared back a little, hesitated, and then gave my hand a stiff shake.

As he turned to leave I noticed a paperback jutting from the rear pocket of his faded jeans. *The Heart Is a Lonely Hunter.*

"That's for damn sure," I whispered. The door closed with a heavy thud and I was alone again.

Rosalie Hart

will be planting winter wheat

Amy Pickering
Oh dear god! Come home!!!!!!!!!!!!!!!!!!

Annie Hart
you're scaring me mom : /

THREE

Megan Johnston's funeral was held in a large Episcopal church in an upscale area of Wilmington. After backing into a parking space, I killed the engine and watched as people arrived. The parking lot filled quickly. Several carloads of college students emptied out, each with a deer-in-the-headlights look about them. Their protective bubble of immortality had burst.

Megan's parents arrived in a black funeral home limousine. The mother was small and thin. She hurried toward the church steps, unsteady in her patent pumps. Her head dipped forward and she clutched a handkerchief to her nose. The father followed a few paces behind, his hands deep in his overcoat, his steps heavy. He was tall with broad, hunched shoulders and deep bags under his eyes.

I followed them inside, slid into a back pew, muted my cell phone, and folded my hands over my purse. The casket was sealed but photographs of Megan at various stages of her life had been placed on easels and on the altar. The largest was her high school graduation photo, the same one that had been in the paper, but in color. Flowing blonde hair graced her bare shoulders, a dainty string of pearls encircled her long neck, and those playful eyes were a piercing crystal blue. In one photo, she was dressed in a soccer uniform holding an enormous trophy. In another, she was being pulled by her father in a wooden sled, a fur-lined snow suit snug around her face. In every shot, she stared confidently back at the camera. This was a girl who loved life and had no interest in dying.

"Are you a friend of the family?" the woman next to me asked as we waited our turn to exit the church.

"No," I said. I smiled briefly and turned away. I was hoping to get out of there unnoticed. I felt a tap on my shoulder.

"So, who are you?"

I looked up. Her thin, penciled eyebrows had risen to expectant arches.

"I'm . . . well . . . I'm . . ."

"A stutterer?"

"No." I coughed out a laugh. "Not usually."

"Well, you'd never know it." She was still smiling, her lips coated in a rich, wine-colored lipstick.

"I found Megan," I said. "She was in my marsh grasses."

"Seriously? Oh my God." She placed a hand on my arm.

"Excuse me, ladies," said the man behind us. "The line is moving."

"Come on," she said. "Let's talk outside."

We walked into the too-bright sunlight. I followed her over to a clump of euonymus bushes, their leaves burning a vivid red. She slipped on a pair of owl-eyed sunglasses. I squinted up at her. "I'm Rosalie, by the way."

"Rhonda. Oh, and I *am* a friend of the family." She held a black Kate Spade clutch in both hands. "I can't believe you found Megan's body. How awful was it?"

"It was devastating. I will never forget it as long as I live."

"No, probably not." She frowned. "But why are you here?"

"Finding her has touched me deeply. I have a daughter in college, too. I can't imagine something like this happening to her. It's a mother's worst nightmare, right? I wanted—no, *needed*—to pay my respects. I would like to extend my sympathy to her parents, if that's possible."

"Nothing personal, but I seriously doubt they want to talk to you."

"You're right. I wouldn't want to talk to me, either. It would be much too painful." I hitched my bag higher up on my shoulder. "How are they holding up?"

"Not well."

"Of course not. How could they be?"

"I'll be surprised if the marriage survives this one. It wasn't exactly in great shape to begin with." She glanced around and lowered her voice. "Did you know Bill is Megan's stepfather?"

"No, I didn't. Where is Megan's father?"

"He was already married. When Corinne told him she was pregnant, he denied Megan was his child. I told Corinne to do the DNA thing, you know, make him get tested, but then she met Bill. After Bill adopted Megan she let it go. I still think she should have done it just to get some cash out of the bastard."

"You've known the family a long time?"

"My Chelsea and Megan were best friends since they were toddlers." She pulled a lipstick from her clutch and touched up her lips. "Sorry," she said and snapped the cap back on. "It's so dry this time of year."

"Your daughter must be crushed. Is she still in the church?"

"Actually, Chelsea couldn't make it." Rhonda's mouth twitched. "The University of Delaware soccer team had an important game and she couldn't get away. I know that must sound terrible, but . . . well, Chelsea was on the bench most of the time until Megan . . ." She waved her long, manicured fingers at me. "I shouldn't be getting into this now."

"Well, at least you're here. I'm sure the family will understand why Chelsea couldn't make it."

"You think?" She sounded skeptical.

"I've been to my share of funerals lately. The grieving family appreciates the people who show—I don't think they resent the ones who don't."

Rhonda gave me a crooked smile. "Do you really believe that?"

"Yes." I nodded. "I do."

"Are you always this nice?"

A loud sniffle distracted me and I looked over at two girls embraced in a tight hug, their faces tear-streaked and blotchy. A boy wrapped his arms around them and squeezed. A sob erupted from one of them. I looked back at Rhonda. "Can I ask you something?" I stepped closer. "What was your reaction when you heard she drowned?"

"I couldn't believe it. I can't imagine Megan ever going near a river."

"Why not?"

"She was terrified of the water. I know, a stellar athlete like her, but she had a bad experience. She fell in a pool and couldn't swim. I had to fish her out."

"Really?"

"We were at the club and, well, I didn't have to watch Chelsea because she was already jumping off the board. Anyway, after that, Megan hated the water. I don't think she ever learned to swim."

"Why . . ." I stared at the ground as this new information sunk in. I looked back up. "None of this makes any sense."

She frowned. "What are you getting at?"

"The police said Megan fell off a dock and drowned and you say she was terrified of the water. And she hadn't been swimming because her backpack was strapped on, and again, she wasn't a swimmer. So, how did she end up in the river? It's like you said; it wasn't voluntary. Did someone push her?"

"Wow." She crossed her arms. "You've really thought about this."

"Do you think I'm crazy for doubting the police?"

"Just between you and me . . ." Rhonda kept her voice low. "I think Megan could have easily been in some sort of trouble."

"Why?"

"You may have noticed she was rather pretty?"

"Stunning."

Rhonda rolled her eyes. "The girl was an attention magnet—always in the middle of some sort of predicament. It was like the television network, TNT: we know drama."

I bristled. How could she be saying such things about a young woman who just died? I hugged myself and rubbed my arms. Rhonda reminded me of the kind of person who might yank your chair away right before you sat down.

"What?" She frowned. "You look shocked."

"I'm just taking it all in."

"You might as well know . . ." She shrugged. "I tell it like it is."

"I'm not a big fan of secrets, either." A heavy, gray cloud shadowed the sun, instantly chilling the air. A breeze kicked up my skirt. I smoothed it down and looked up at Rhonda. "What sort of trouble could she have been in?"

"The latest drama was with a professor at John Adams." Rhonda pushed her sunglasses on top of her head. Her skin stretched tight across her cheekbones. "Megan was after this internship he was offering. I swear, she wanted to be the next Anna Freud. And apparently this guy is a big shot in the field—just got some fancy grant." She lowered her voice to a whisper. "Megan was sleeping with him."

"Oh." I reared back. "Did she report him?"

"What's to report? Sounds to me like it was her idea."

My mind went back to the headline: "Psychology Professor Receives Prestigious National Grant." "Do the police know about the professor?"

"The police? I don't think anyone knew except Chels."

"Why did she transfer from Delaware?"

Rhonda scowled. "How do you know about that?"

"You just told me, remember?" I smiled. "You said Megan played soccer with your daughter."

She studied me for a moment. "I have a feeling people underestimate you."

"I wouldn't know."

"Uh-huh." She gave me a wry smile. "Anyway, that's another story and, as always, full of drama." Rhonda glanced around. The mourners were dispersing. Cars were leaving and the limo idled nearby. Puffs of gray smoke billowed around the exhaust pipe. "I should get to the house. I promised Bill I'd pick up some Ketel One. I'm sure he could use the whole bottle right about now."

"Is Bill your husband?"

"I don't have one of those anymore." She wiggled the fingers of her left hand in front of my face. "Bill is Bill Johnston, Megan's stepdad. See? You don't remember everything I tell you."

"Rhonda, I don't suppose I could give you my number? Maybe we could stay in touch." I pulled an old gas receipt out of my purse and wrote my number on it. My pen made holes in the thin paper. I handed it to her. She creased it down the middle and placed it in her purse.

"Deal. I'd love to keep up with your nosing around. Make sure you tell me everything you find out. Oh, and here's my contact info." She handed me a colorful business card on which a younger-looking Rhonda smiled up at me, her head in that Realtor angle that made them all look as if they had an inner-ear disorder. "Okay, well, gotta run!" She turned and started for the parking lot, her stilettos clicking on the pavement. She stopped when Megan's stepfather emerged from the church. He walked over to her and spoke close to her ear.

They embraced for a noticeably long time. Then Rhonda brushed his cheek with a kiss, patted his arm, and walked away. He watched her go.

I startled when he looked my way. His gaze intensified. He studied me, as if trying to discern who I was. Unsure what to do, I smiled my most sympathetic smile and hurried to my car.

As I drove back to Cardigan, I reflected on my conversation with Rhonda. I felt energized that my suspicions were right—there was a lot more to this story than the sheriff's department was willing to uncover. My first conversation with someone who knew Megan and I already learned of a possible suspect: a psychology professor who sleeps with students. And what about Rhonda? She was completely irreverent about Megan's death. I wondered . . . was there an envy lurking, a jealousy of Megan's beauty and popularity? And what about her relationship with Bill? Their embrace revealed a shared intimacy that went way beyond friendship. And why did Megan transfer her senior year? Why would she leave the soccer team?

Maybe I should tell the sheriff what I learned. We could collaborate—brainstorm about some possibilities. He could reopen the case. No. Bad idea. He and his deputies already found me ridiculous. If I went to them with this, they would laugh about it for the next decade.

An unequivocal clarity heightened my senses. If Megan Johnston was murdered, then a killer was on the loose. The sun was dipping toward the horizon and the sky was streaked with indigo and vermillion. I pulled the visor down and hoped I would beat rush hour. I checked my mirror and merged onto I-95. "I'm going to figure this out, Megan," I said softly. "It might take some time, but I won't give up until I know the truth." I was sick to death of lies and secrets and betrayal. The turbo kicked in and I blew past a tractor trailer.

Megan Johnston came to me for a reason and it was up to me to find out how.

When I arrived home, I went straight to my computer without turning on a light. I sat down and noticed a check on the table. Tyler. I picked it up and studied it. Not so fast, Ed, I thought, and smiled. Maybe Tyler Wells was the Marlboro Man, after all.

I set the check down and hummed a little as my computer came to life. Ignoring my one hundred and thirty-seven new emails, I logged onto Facebook hoping to chat with Annie.

Rhonda Pendleton has sent you a friend request.

That was fast. I accepted her friendship and a message appeared in my inbox.

Hi Rosie! So glad we're "friends!" OK, well, the scene at the house after the funeral was positively dreadful. Corinne was on tranquilizers and Bill drank most of the Ketel One. He really leaned on me and I was so glad I was there. Guess what he told me? He's the one who told the police he didn't want an autopsy or investigation. He didn't say why but can you stand it? So dishy!

Sent from a mobile unit

I reread Rhonda's message and clicked my fingernails on the table. Why would a father not want to know how his daughter died? And how on earth did he get the police to close the investigation? There were so many unanswered questions.

I stared out the window. It was a black, moonless night. Somewhere in that darkness the Cardigan was racing by. No one rescued Megan from that cold, gray water. And with the recent events in my life, I had an idea how it must feel to drown. Struggling for breath, clawing to get your head above water.

I looked back at my computer screen and updated my status.

Rosalie Hart

Is wondering how a young college student, armed with athleticism, gorgeous looks, and a promising future, came to be facedown in the chilly currents of the Cardigan River.

FOUR

Introduction to Memoir Writing class was held on Thursday evenings in a drafty room with a high, stamped metal ceiling in the oldest building on the John Adams College campus. I arrived fifteen minutes early for class and purposely sat in the third and last row. This was our second of eight classes. The first night I had been surprised to learn we were supposed to have already written five pages of a memoir. And because it was such a small class, four students and one very young teacher, tonight we were each going to read what we had written aloud and receive feedback from our classmates.

Glenn Breckinridge was next to arrive. A little over seventy, he was dressed in a crisp, blue oxford shirt, professionally creased khaki pants, and a bow tie. I had been drawn to him immediately. Not only because he had such a kind, gentle demeanor, but because we were in similar circumstances. He also recently moved to Cardigan and, like me, was looking for ways to fill his time. I hoped Glenn was as desperate for friendship as me.

"Hello, Rosalie." The newspaper tucked under his arm was open to a crossword he was working on in pen. He slid into the seat and turned sideways to face me. "How did the writing assignment go?"

"Not so well, it turns out. Apparently you're supposed to have done something significant in order to write a memoir. Who knew?"

"I'm sure you'll have something compelling to say," Glenn said in his deep, sonorous voice.

"How about you? Any luck?"

"I already had one hundred pages. I just tidied the first few up a bit. I've intended to write a business memoir since I retired from IBM. I'm shooting for an airport read, the kind of book a businessperson can pick up and finish in one trip." Glenn nudged his wire-rimmed glasses higher up his nose. "Perhaps my plans are a bit grandiose."

"I would buy it," I said. "Can I preorder?"

"Ha ha. It's nice to have your confidence. So? What are *you* going to write about?"

"No clue. Do you know I've never even kept a journal?" I leaned in. "I might start now, though. Did I tell you I discovered a dead body in the river?"

"That was your place? Good heavens, I read about it in the paper. How dreadful for you."

"It was pretty horrific. She was a lovely young woman. Her death was such a tragedy. And all I can think about is my Annie away at college. So, well . . ." I hesitated.

"What?" he said, his tone encouraging me to continue.

"I think her death being ruled an accidental drowning is suspicious. There are some circumstances that don't add up. For instance, she switched schools in her senior year even though she was the star of the University of Delaware soccer team. She had only been at John Adams for a short time. And the biggest thing is she may have been having an affair with a professor." I searched Glenn's face, worried he would think I was past nuts.

"What are you saying, Rosalie?"

"The police have already closed the case. And I can't stop asking myself: What if it wasn't an accident? So, well, I've been looking into it a little."

"This is fascinating. The paper said she drowned, but you aren't buying it?"

I shook my head. "She was also terrified of the water. So . . ."

Tony Ricci bustled in the door. Although still in a sport coat, he looked as if the day had gotten the better of him. The top two buttons of his dress shirt were undone and part of his shirttail had loosened from his pants. He juggled a briefcase and a cup of coffee with a corrugated sleeve all while keeping a phone to his ear. He stopped and finished his conversation. "Yeah, Joe, I heard you the first time . . . No, I can't FedEx the report because I haven't finished it yet . . . Well, screw 'em . . ." Tony glanced up. We stared back. "Look, I have to go. I'll call you later."

After stowing the phone in his shirt pocket, he nodded to us and said, "How's everyone doing?" in a thick New England accent.

Tony was an attractive man with thick hair and wide brown eyes that drooped a little at the corner. He was of average height with a strong frame that he carried with a confident ease. When he gave me a quick wink, I looked away. Had I been staring? Good Lord. I was forty-five years old and had been married to the same man for the last twenty-three. He must think I'm pathetic. Or desperate. Isn't that what they say about divorced women?

Tony walked over and sat in the seat in front of me. He had been on the other side of the room the first night. "How you doin'?" he said again.

"Fine, thanks," I said. "And you?"

"I'm wondering if this class might be a bunch of crap. I don't think our fearless leader has one inkling about how to write a memoir." He rested his arm on the back of his chair. "You write anything yet?"

I shook my head. "Nothing."

Sue Ling hurried into the classroom. Sue was a lovely, twenty-something Korean-American. She gave us a shy smile and perched in the desk in front of the instructor's. After pulling a stylish pair of glasses from her bag, she slid them onto her nose and began perusing a stack of paper, making an occasional mark with a tightly held pen.

"Rosalie . . ." Glenn said. "I would like to hear more about—"

Our instructor's entrance interrupted him. Frazzled and haggard, Jillian dropped a stack of books on the desk and slumped into her seat. She had black, spiky hair dyed purple on the ends and a row of silver earrings climbing up her ear. She wore loose cotton clothing and a long hobo purse hung from her shoulder. A graduate student, she was working toward her master's in Fine Arts and was less than enthusiastic about teaching our memoir class to supplement her income. "Is everyone here?" she said as if she wasn't particularly interested in the answer.

"I certainly hope she can count to four," Tony whispered over his shoulder.

"Okay," Jillian said. "Who wants to read first?"

Sue raised her hand and began to read. Glenn pulled a small notepad from his shirt pocket and jotted something on it. He tore off the sheet and slipped it to me. *I am very interested in this murder. I would like to help you. I think we should start with this professor.* My eyes shot up. Glenn smiled broadly and faced the front of the classroom.

By the time the two-hour class ended, I felt completely inadequate. Glenn was a beautiful writer, his words as crisp as his starched shirt. Sue's writing was flowery and descriptive and touching. I could picture her mother and father huddled on a small boat, Sue swaddled in her mother's arms as they fled North Korea. Even Tony had a few compelling pages. He was framing his story around a love for baseball—the successes and failures in his life paralleling those of the Boston Red Sox.

When it came to me, I explained my dilemma. How does one write about a life lived for others? Who would be interested in my experiences as a PTA president or volunteer in a school library? I had joked that I could write about my driving finesse on the beltway or how I could rock a Sudoku puzzle, but the only person who smiled was Tony, and I think he was trying to look down my blouse at the time.

Everyone asked questions trying to steer me in some sort of direction. But the crux of it was this: How do I write about a life I thought was ideal—the envy of others—when in fact it was all a lie? It was as if a tsunami had rolled over my world, washing away everything I assumed was solid and constant and true.

Jillian frowned. "Surely there is something interesting. I mean, did your daughter have any sort of medical problem—like allergies or a learning disability?"

The only thing I could come up with was that Annie had been slow to potty train and wore a pullup until she was three.

I left the class feeling completely humiliated. I flinched when I felt Jillian's hand on my shoulder. "Look, Rosalie, you'll come up with something. Don't go jump off a bridge or anything."

FIVE

Annie Hart

Can't wait for parents' weekend. Mom promised retail therapy after the rugby match!

You and four others like this.

Annie was on the ground, arms over her head, while a mass of much taller and broader young women pushed and shoved and kicked above her. I watched in terror as she crawled out of the melee.

"Kill her," a voice shouted behind me. I looked over my shoulder. A group of very drunk college boys were lined up against a chainlink fence, each with one hand hooked in his jeans pocket and the other holding a plastic cup full of foamy beer.

I turned back to the match. Annie had gotten up. Dirt dotted her knees and strands of her silky brown hair were coming loose from the ponytail perched high on her head. A teammate tossed her the ball and she broke into a run. Get rid of it, I thought. Pass it! But another girl had already wrapped her arms around Annie's waist and slammed her to the ground. And there she was again, arms covering her head while the scrum continued.

The air was autumn crisp, just cool enough to invite wool sweaters and light jackets. Dried leaves dropped lazily from the trees and cirrus clouds streaked the turquoise sky. I was glad to see the sun. Last night's rain had been unending—the kind of night made for snuggling. But I was in my king-size hotel bed, feeling dwarfed and very alone. I had listened to heavy drops batter the window for hours, until they at last drummed me to sleep.

That morning, after three cups of weak hotel coffee, I had put some effort into my appearance. I wanted Annie to be proud when she introduced me to her friends. Although I was in a pair of jeans Annie had left behind, they were cut right and faded in places the designer intended. My hair was styled, my lips glossed, and I had looped a scarf around my neck. My only compromise was a pair of sensible shoes. I had wanted to wear a pair of high-heeled boots, not only to accent the outfit but to give me a little boost of height. But the rain-soaked grass was already turning to muck, so I settled on a pair of plain black flats.

I looked around at the crowd. Duke students and their parents dotted the sidelines. I thought of Megan's parents who probably never missed her soccer games. I wondered how they could possibly endure such a tremendous loss. I shrugged off a shiver and looked for Annie.

Two girls clutched the top of her shorts and lifted her into the air.

"Oh, my." I slapped my hand over my mouth. Annie caught the tossed ball and before I could discern what happened, there she was again on the ground in the fetal position.

"Slam her down," a voice called.

I turned around. "Why don't they wear helmets?" I asked one of the boys. "Or some sort of padding?"

"Because this is rugby, man," he said, slurring his words, eyelids at half mast. "Kill her!" Spittle sprayed from his mouth.

I turned back to the game. Annie was on the sidelines. She pulled her jersey over her head and handed it to a girl waiting to go out on the field. I gasped. Annie was in nothing but a small pair of navy rugby shorts and a sports bra. Surely Duke could afford an adequate number of jerseys.

"Hey, is that your daughter down there?" one of the boys said from behind me.

"Yes." I relaxed a little when I saw a girl hand Annie a T-shirt.

"She's awesome."

I looked back at him. He appeared to be more sober than the others and was the only one without a cap pulled low over his eyes. "Thanks." I smiled and faced the field again.

"Hello, Rose."

My mouth fell open as I stared into my husband's face.

"Quite a game." He was smiling, his teeth white against his tanned skin. He wore a brown suede jacket with elbow patches I had never seen before. A Ralph Lauren logo was stitched on the pocket. Apparently he still had access to the bank accounts.

A tall, thin blonde stood next to him. He brought her *here*? I stole another glance at her. She was the complete opposite of me—skinnier, blonder, and younger. Smooth, straight hair framed a pretty but expressionless face. She was dressed in a tweed blazer. A wool skirt hugged her ridiculously narrow figure and fell to a very expensive pair of chocolate brown boots with spiky, mudless heels. Well, of course she would be able to pull off the heels.

"Annie's playing great," Ed said. "She's definitely the one to pass to."

"It's a pretty brutal game," I said, fighting hard to keep my voice from quivering.

"She can handle it," Ed said. "Oh, Rose, this is Rebecca."

Rebecca finally meets the ghost wife. Our eyes locked—a flash of connection like flint igniting the ache burning in my gut. We both looked quickly away. He brought her here. She would meet my Annie. He really was in love with her.

I cleared my throat. "I didn't realize you were coming."

"Of course I came. Our daughter is going to Duke. I couldn't wait to get here." He was being overly enthusiastic. I wanted him to shut up. Yes, she got into Duke, something I helped her do while he was in our bed with his paramour.

The crowd roared. Annie was clutching the ball. She had scored a goal. Her much taller teammates pounded her back and smacked her head. Annie grinned while she tried to stay on her feet. I waved. She saw me and waved back. Then she saw her dad. For a brief moment the smile disappeared as she took in the undomesticated scene. But it returned and she trotted over to her team.

I looked back at Ed. I wanted to speak, but my larynx had locked up. This was all wrong. It was our only daughter's first parents' weekend and instead of meeting her roommates and getting to know the other parents, I was standing face-to-face with the woman my husband ended twenty-three years of marriage for. The ache rose into my throat. I wasn't up to this. Not yet. Not ever.

Rebecca examined her French manicure.

"So, how are you?" Ed said. "You look wonderful. Have you lost weight?"

"What did you say?"

"I said you look wonderful."

"Ed—are you kidding me?"

"Rose . . ." He shoved his hands in his jacket pockets. "I was giving you a compliment."

"First of all, I am anything but wonderful. And secondly . . ." I tried to breathe. My heart pounded. "You don't get to do that anymore."

"Do what?" He lowered his voice. "Pay you a compliment? Do you mind telling me what's so wrong about that?" He enunciated the 'T.' Staccato words. That was how Ed expressed anger. Snapping his consonants. No more. No less.

Rebecca placed a hand on his arm. A gesture of ownership. He glanced over at her and then back at me.

"I can't believe you're making a scene." He stepped back and shook his head. "I guess it was a mistake to say hello. I'm sorry—"

"Are you, Ed?" My voice cracked. "Are you really sorry?" No tears, no tears, no tears . . . I hugged myself, trying to hold them at bay.

"Rose . . ." His blue eyes were cool and narrowed with, what? Anger? Revulsion? Regret? "I'm sorry this couldn't have been a more civilized encounter." He turned away and guided Rebecca by her pointy elbow to the opposite end of the field.

My heart thudded harder against my rib cage. I couldn't breathe. "Oh, God." I pushed the heels of my hands against my temples. I can't faint, not here. I eased onto the ground and hugged my knees. I was trembling. I couldn't stop. I was going into shock. No, I can't. Not here. Not now. I can't do that to Annie. I rested my forehead on my knees. Breathe, Rosalie. Breathe.

I felt a hand on my back. I gasped. There. Air. I took in some air. I looked up. A boy crouched next to me. "You okay?" It was the boy without the cap.

"Yes. I mean, no. Not really."

"Who was that dude? He looked like a serious pant load."

"What? Did you just call my husband a 'pant load'?" I laughed. "Oh, my gosh," I said, still laughing. I don't know why or how, but it was the release I needed. I looked up at him. "God bless you . . . What's your name?"

"Connor O'Malley."

"That's a good name," I said. "I'm a Finnegan."

"Well, Mrs. Finnegan . . ." He held out his hand and helped me to stand up. "You look like you could use a beer."

Annie and I walked arm-in-arm back to her dorm. The scent of dust and drying sweat emanated from her clothes. "I didn't know, Mom, I swear. He never said he would be bringing her."

"I know, honey. I'm so sorry. It can't be too much fun for you, either." Our pace was brisk and I appreciated the chance to move. I pulled her closer to me.

"He wants to have dinner tonight, but I told him I already had plans with you."

"Oh, Annie." I brushed a stray hair from her face. I noticed a tear atop her dirty cheekbone. "This isn't fair. It's your first parents' weekend. We have no business putting you through this."

Lampposts popped on as it grew dark. Annie's cleats clicked on the sidewalk. "It totally sucks," she said. "I can't believe he's doing this to us." She brushed the tear away and wiped it on her shorts.

I wanted to side with her, align against Ed. After all, we were both victims. But I knew better. I'd seen too many divorces where the parents argued through their children, sucking them into the middle, dividing their loyalties and forcing them to make choices a child should never have to make.

"He didn't intend to hurt you."

"Are you actually defending him?" She stopped walking.

"God, no. But, well, I don't know. This is between us. Something went wrong, and I guess this is how it has to be now, as hard as it is."

"*Something*? You don't even know, do you?" She shook her head. "Why are you letting him do this? Mom, you always taught me to be strong—to stand up for myself. 'Annie,' you said, 'you have to go after what you want. Don't expect it to find you.'"

"And you are." I smiled.

"And you aren't," she said, her voice pleading. "Mom . . ."

"I'm trying. Honestly, I am." I studied her face. "I just don't want you to be in the middle. I want you to enjoy your first year of college and not worry about your parents. Can you do that?"

"It's hard. But the rugby is helping."

"Of course." I tucked my arm through hers. We started walking again. "You get to knock people down."

"Exactly."

"Annie . . ." I swallowed hard. "If you want, we can go to dinner with your father tonight. I can swing it if you can."

"No." She squeezed my arm. "I want you all to myself. Dad and I, and apparently that woman"—Annie made quotation marks in the air—"are having brunch tomorrow."

"I would go for you if I could."

"I'll be all right."

"Maybe you could accidentally tackle her."

"Mom!" Annie rubbed her arms. I noticed chill bumps on her legs.

I wrapped my arm around her shoulders and picked up the pace. "We need to get you out of those clothes."

"Okay." She leaned in close. "Hey, you know that guy you were talking to at the match? He asked for my number."

"You mean Connor O'Malley? He offered me a beer just when I needed it. Well? Did you give it to him?"

"No. But I told him he could friend me. I like to peruse the Facebook wall before I agree to a date."

"Smart girl," I said, pulling her closer, breathing her in, feeling grounded again for the first time in months. She was here with me. And she was alive.

SIX

The following Monday Glenn and I sat on a bench along a red-brick walkway that cut a diagonal path through the heart of the John Adams campus. Bright crimson leaves rustled in the Japanese maple above us, occasionally releasing one in an unhurried flight to the ground.

"I bought you a coffee," Glenn said. "From Brower's."

I popped off the lid and set the cup on the sidewalk.

"I've never known you to turn down coffee."

"Just letting it cool." I crossed my legs. "Okay, so what's my shtick?"

"You have decided to go back to college and pursue a degree in psychology."

I hugged my purse, nervous at the thought of encountering the mysterious professor—our first suspect. I had dressed up in an A-line black skirt and scarlet red blazer for our meeting. "Do you think he'll buy it?" I popped the heel of my pump off and on. "A forty-five-year-old woman returning to college?"

"It makes perfect sense. You've just emptied your nest." Glenn removed his notepad from his shirt pocket and studied it. "I've been looking into this man."

"Glenn," I said. "I believe you're getting as obsessed as me."

"I can get a little single-minded about things, I'm afraid. It served me well in business. But research is our best weapon."

"So, are you certain we have the right guy?"

A fresh gust of wind exposed Glenn's bald spot. He fixed his hair back in place and examined his notes. "Absolutely. Not only has he recently received a prestigious grant, he's the only professor teaching four hundred-level psychology courses. Oh, and all the other psychology professors are women."

"Well, that certainly narrows it down. Anything else?"

"Let's see." Glenn flipped a page. "He's forty-seven, married, and has two elementary school-age children." He peered over the top of his glasses. "Those are young children for a man that age. Maybe a second marriage?"

"If he sleeps with his students that wouldn't come as a surprise."

"Yes." Glenn nodded. "That's a good theory." He looked back at the spiral pad. "He's only been with the college three years. They hired him away from a small liberal arts college in New York."

"I wonder why he left." I picked up my coffee. "Glenn, how did you find all this out?"

"How else? I Googled him."

"Of course you did." I laughed.

The campus was dotted with students enjoying the sunny day. A pack of boys passed by kicking soccer balls and jostling one another, their cleats strung over their shoulders. One exceptionally tall and gangly boy kicked his ball into Glenn's shin. It thudded and ricocheted into the grass.

"Sorry, dude," the boy said and trotted away to fetch his ball.

Glenn rubbed his leg. "Did he just call me 'dude'?"

"He did. Are you okay?"

"I'm fine. Actually, I like being out here among these college students." He nudged his glasses back up his nose. "Waterside Village
is nice enough. My townhouse is adequate and I have a view of the
river. And I certainly don't miss mowing the lawn. But you know
the problem with living in an over-fifty-five community?"

I smiled at him. "What?"

"Everyone is the same age. It's not an accurate slice of the world.
I miss watching a child ride his bike down the street or a teenager
learning to parallel park. Sitting here with you is just what I needed."

"I never thought of it that way. You sure you're okay?"

"Couldn't be better."

"Back to Professor Angeles. Does he live in town?"

"One of those historic homes on the Cardigan. You can see it as
you cross the bridge into town."

"On the water?" I took a sip of coffee.

"Yes. Why?"

"Glenn . . ." I nibbled on my bottom lip. "What if the professor
has a boat?" I turned to face him. "If he does, then maybe he took
Megan out on it. What better way to keep an affair under wraps than
on a boat?"

"Of course. And if you want to end it, you toss her over the side.
Good thinking, Rosalie. In this business, what may seem trivial can
often be the most significant."

"I know, right? This is good. We're getting somewhere." A rare
feeling of elation tickled my neurotransmitters. I couldn't remember the last time I'd felt happy. "Glenn, do you think we might figure this out? I mean, look at us—you're a retired businessman, and
I'm a . . ." I frowned. "What exactly am I? A work-in-progress? A piece
of work?"

Glenn chuckled. "It's all in how you sell it. I would rather say
that I am an analyst and you are an exceptional observer of people.

Put those two together and you have the makings of a savvy detective."

"Ha! Nice spin." I jostled my shoe again. "I'm so glad you're helping me."

"It is I who should be thanking you."

Detecting a subtle change in his tone, I said, "Glenn, what happened to your wife?"

He tucked away his notepad and rubbed his palms on his corduroy pants. "She passed six years ago of breast cancer."

"I lost my mother to the same thing. I think it's an epidemic."

"Molly never knew she had it until it was too late." Glenn stared off. His voice was strained with emotion. "She found a lump. After three years of telling her it was nothing, the doctor told her it was something. She died three months later."

"That's awful. I'm so sorry."

He removed his glasses and wiped his eyes with the back of his hand. "I miss her every moment of every day."

"Of course you do." I patted his arm.

Once he had composed himself, Glenn said, "You should get annual mammograms, Rosalie."

"Believe me, I do." I gripped my cup with both hands. "Oh."

"Oh, what?"

"I just realized I'm going to need health insurance once my divorce is final. Gosh, I wish I could find a job."

"You don't believe your husband will impoverish you, do you?"

"He seems to be on that track. Let's just hope Tom Bestman's lawyering is as good as his smile." I took a sip of coffee, hoping it would taste better than the last sip. I grimaced.

Glenn eyed me. "Not enjoying the coffee?"

"Are you?"

"I haven't touched it since the first sip."

"I don't know how a restaurant can so consistently make bad

coffee." I set the cup down again. "Do you think searching for Megan's killer can help us with our grief?"

"It certainly could."

"I hope so." I smiled over at him. "I really enjoy your company, Glenn."

"And I yours." He returned my smile. "Maybe it wasn't a coincidence her body surfaced on your shoreline."

"I've had that thought, too."

Glenn tapped the face of his gold watch. "It's almost time for your appointment."

"Oh." I hopped up from the bench. "How do I look? Smart? Professional?"

"All of the above." Glenn frowned. "Um . . ."

"Yes?"

"Your buttons." He pointed to my blazer. "They're uneven."

"How embarrassing," I said as I fiddled with them.

"Perfect," Glenn said. "Are you sure you'll be all right?"

"Of course." I fluffed my hair. "I'm about to meet with a murder suspect. What could go wrong?"

Professor Nicholas Angeles was the best-looking man I'd ever seen.

I swallowed hard as I gazed into a pair of rich, chocolate eyes. His dark hair curled loosely around his head. He smiled when he opened the door and I detected the slightest gap between his front teeth.

"Dr. Angeles." I extended my hand. "I'm Rosalie Hart."

"Please come in." He gestured to the chair across from his desk. "Have a seat."

I sat down, crossed my legs, and glanced around the room. I started to pop my pump off and on again, but stopped myself. Be cool. Be a detective.

Shafts of light poured in through a large, paned window with a sweeping view of the campus. Dust motes danced in the beams. Several diplomas hung on the forest green plaster and a wall of bookshelves stretched behind him. I cocked my head and read the spines. There was an entire row of books by Alfred Kinsey.

A subtle smile appeared on the professor's face. I looked away and noticed a photograph of a strikingly thin woman flanked by two small boys on his desk. It was one of those professional photographs where everyone was dressed in beige, a golden retriever panting in the middle, a sandy beach in the background. She was pretty in the classic sense, a dark brown bob, manicured hands draped over each boy. I looked up at the professor. He was watching me closely.

"Your wife is lovely. Do you live here in town?"

"Yes." He hesitated. "We moved here a few years ago." He leaned back, straining the springs in the chair.

"Cardigan is such a nice place to raise a family. There's so much to do—outdoors, especially, not all that manufactured entertainment you have in the suburbs. I would imagine you have a boat?"

"I have a sailboat." He frowned. "Why would you ask me that?"

"It just seems everyone has a boat in Cardigan. Your children must love it."

"You ask a lot of questions." His eyes narrowed.

Slow down, I thought. He's getting suspicious.

"Perhaps you could tell me why we're meeting."

"Well," I cleared my throat. "I'm new to the area. I've recently separated from my husband and . . ." I stopped. Why did I just tell him that?

"I'm sorry," he said softly. "These things are never easy. So, you're new to the area . . ."

"Yes. I'm considering going back to school. I have a liberal arts degree from the University of Virginia and have already taken several psychology classes, including psychopathology." I chewed on the inside of my cheek. The closest I'd ever come to studying psychopathology was reading a Sylvia Plath poem.

"Why aren't you meeting with admissions?" he said. "Why a personal meeting with me?"

"Um, well, I saw the article in the paper about your research grant. If I enroll I want to make sure I study with the best."

"Rosalie . . ." He sat forward, narrowing the space between us. "Do you know what I'm researching?"

"It didn't say in the article. Just that it was a very prestigious grant for the college to receive."

"I'm studying human sexuality."

"Excuse me?" I pressed my lower back into the chair.

"So . . . are you still interested?" He formed a teepee with his fingers.

"Yes." I blinked a few times.

"Excellent." He smiled.

"How exactly does one go about studying sex?"

"Not like you might think. I hope that's not disappointing."

Disappointing? Was he coming on to me? He couldn't be. Get a grip, Rosalie. A trickle of sweat meandered down my spine. "What are you hoping to prove?"

"Primarily how our mating patterns are like that of animals— at least more than has previously been realized. There have been studies about pheromones and whether or not humans secrete them as much as other animals. But my research will delve a lot deeper. I'm focusing on the senses—particularly vision and smell— and the way they direct our desire." His eyes met mine. "Did you know that when a sexual connection is made, our irises dilate, ever so slightly?"

"Really?" I looked away. A rash of heat worked its way up from my neckline. Did he say *our* irises? I looked back at him, hoping mine were back to normal. "I've been told there's an internship."

"Yes. I have enlisted the help of some students—administering questionnaires, that sort of thing—but the internship is reserved for a senior."

"Do you already have someone?"

He looked surprised at my question. "No, I don't."

That's right, I thought. Because that student is no longer alive. Okay, Rosalie, get on task. I sat up a little straighter in my chair. "I hope I can help in some way. If I decide to sign up for classes, that is. How do you select your assistants? Is there a requirement?"

"You certainly are eager." He cocked his head. "Are you dating yet?"

"What?"

"You know, dating. Men." He smiled. "Didn't you say you were separated?"

"Oh, it's much too soon for that." The back of my blouse was drenched. Why are we talking about me again? I was really quite bad at this. "I won't take up any more of your time." I stood and straightened my blazer. "Thanks for meeting with me."

"Leaving? We were just getting acquainted." He rounded his desk and stood in front of me. "I've been admiring your jacket." His fingers grazed my elbow. "Did you know there have been studies about how men react to women in red?"

I tried to step back, but I bumped into a bookshelf. I cringed, waiting for a book to land on my head.

"Careful," he said. A trace of woodsy cologne belly-danced up my nose. "The color red draws men to women. They stand closer and are more likely to tell them a dirty joke." A wide grin spread across his face. "And they smile more."

"I honestly didn't know that. I've had this jacket forever. It's cool outside today and I—"

"Maybe we could have a drink sometime."

"A *drink*?" My mouth had dried. "But you're married." I glanced back at the photo.

"Not for long," he said.

"You're getting a divorce?"

"My wife left me a month ago. She's already filed. It looks like you and I have that in common."

"Just a month ago?" Right before Megan died, I thought.

"There you go with the questions again." He leaned in closer. "Think about that drink. And just so you know, your husband is a fool."

"Oh, no, he's actually very intelligent."

He chuckled softly. "I mean he's a fool for letting you go."

"Oh." I shrugged. "I guess there's some truth to that." I turned sideways and tried to edge past him. Our bodies brushed together. The points of contact sent a heat wave through my blood.

He reached around my waist and pulled the door open. "I hope you decide to enroll."

"Yes." I glanced back at him as I hurried out the door. "I'm very interested."

Oh, my, I thought, as my pumps clicked on the linoleum. Woozy, I grabbed the railing and descended the stairs. Dr. Angeles, I thought, your study was a waste of time. I could tell you right now humans are like animals—triggered by scents and attractive features. And I was a defenseless peahen who had just been done in by one hell of a set of plumage. I stopped halfway down the last flight of steps. I gripped the railing tighter. Good Lord. Is this how he seduced Megan?

SEVEN

Tyler Wells waited on my front stoop, hands in the back pockets of his jeans. He stood motionless as he watched me park my convertible and kill the engine. Dickens sat next to him focusing just as intently, his ears perked forward.

I picked up my bags, climbed ungracefully out of the car, and walked over to him. Two bottles of chardonnay clanked incessantly like tattling siblings. I looked up. His forehead was creased, his mouth pursed. He stared at me as if I'd grown a second head.

"What?" My voice was hoarse.

He took off a faded Baltimore Ravens cap and held it in both hands. His straw-colored hair tumbled onto his forehead. "It's not me I'm wondering about."

"Who then?"

His eyebrows rose a little higher and he cocked his head. "It probably isn't my place to say, but you look a little wild-eyed, is all."

I smoothed my hair. "Wild-eyed?"

"Just saying."

I walked up to the door. The bottles clanked again. I turned to face him. "If you must know, an Alanis Morissette song came on the radio while I was driving. It's one of her older songs and I was"—I avoided his eyes—"singing along."

He remained silent.

I looked up at him. "Did you need something, Tyler?"

"Coffee."

"You mean you liked my coffee?"

"I wouldn't be asking if I didn't."

"Of course I have coffee. I always have coffee." I opened the door and caught the scent of engine oil as he passed. A dirty rag hung from the back pocket of his jeans.

I set my bag on the counter and the bottles clanked yet again. "It's too quiet on the Eastern Shore. Does it ever get to you?" I looked over at him. A white stripe ran across the top of his otherwise tanned face. "No, I guess it wouldn't."

"Maybe some people like noise because it drowns out what's in their head," Tyler said.

"I never thought of it that way." I frowned. "Did you read that somewhere?"

"Nope."

A farmer and a philosopher, I thought as I filled a mug with steaming-hot coffee. I waited while he scrubbed his hands at the sink. "I'm so glad you like my coffee. I always have some ready. I keep it in this carafe to keep it fresh." I set the cup next to him and handed him a towel. "Today's brew is a dark-roast Moroccan—guaranteed to give you a swift kick in the shorts." I took a small step back. "I'm sorry. I've already had several cups. And I'm afraid after the third I tend to get a little loquacious."

He picked up his mug and carried it over to the row of canisters. I watched as he stirred a spoonful of sugar into his coffee. It was only our second shared coffee and I was already learning his routines. "Do you want something to eat? I'm not sure what I have, but . . ." I started over to the refrigerator.

"No thanks."

"Oh. Okay," I said. "So, how's it going out there?"

"It's a lot like work."

"At least the weather is good—lots of sun, not too cold."

"We could use some rain."

I leaned against the counter. I was working too hard. I crossed my arms. The pendulum of my aunt's grandfather clock ticked back and forth. Several cubes clunked out of the ice maker in the freezer. I waited, hoping he would say something. Tyler exuded strength and control. The absolute certitude in his every movement and minced word unnerved me. I was the complete antithesis of him in my current emotional state.

He finished his coffee, set the mug in the sink, and still said nothing.

"You know, Tyler, I prepare Mr. Miele every night before I go to bed. All you have to do is push the start button in the morning when you get here. You could help yourself."

He looked up at me. "Mr. *who*?"

"Oh, my goodness." Heat spread up my neck igniting my skin. "I didn't just say that."

A small, tight smile appeared on his face.

"My coffee bistro—it's a Miele and, oh my." I placed my hands over my cheeks.

His smile broadened. I had never seen him smile. Animation brightened his face and I was struck with the realization that he was actually very nice looking.

"So . . ." he said. "Where exactly is his start button?"

My mouth fell open. "It's . . ." I hesitated, trying to ignore his use of a personal pronoun. "It would be this one." I squared my shoulders and looked him in the eye. "The button that says S-T-A-R-T."

"You sure you don't mind me coming in your house?"

"Honestly, Tyler, this farm seems more yours than mine. I feel like the intruder, so yes, please, help yourself to anything."

He regarded me for a moment. "I should get back to work." He picked up his cap and headed for the door.

"The Ravens are having a good season so far. I watched the game last weekend."

He paused. "They're my team, no doubt." He reached for the door handle. "They're just a little too unpredictable for my liking."

I started to respond, but the latch clicked. Fading daylight washed the room in a dull gray. The kitchen felt cold and cavernous again. Tyler must be right about my need for noise because all the loneliness I fought to keep at bay rolled over me in the silence following his exit. I put his mug in the dishwasher, the chardonnay in the refrigerator—no, wait, the freezer, it would chill faster—and retreated to my computer, hoping Annie would be on Facebook and help fill the void that was now my life.

Rhonda Pendleton has posted on your wall.

Rhonda Pendleton
Hi, Rosie. Have you learned anything more? Let's have lunch. Meet ya halfway. xoxo

I replied an enthusiastic "yes!!!!" to the lunch invitation, then checked out the available chats. No Annie. She must be at dinner. I considered opening the wine, but decided it wouldn't be cold enough. I looked at Rhonda's profile picture. It was the same photo as the one on her business card—a much younger Rhonda with lots of air brushing and good lighting. Underneath was a quote: "No bird soars too high if *she* soars with *her* own wings.—William Blake." That didn't really sound like the Rhonda I had met at the funeral. Maybe Facebook profiles don't reveal as much about a person as I thought. Maybe it only exhibits how one wants to be perceived—controlled public relations—always in makeup, at an ideal weight, loved by so many "friends."

Feeling voyeuristic, I decided to snoop around her timeline. She had been tagged in a photo album labeled "Cougars' Night Out." The first picture was of a cake crowded with candles in the foreground, Rhonda and a group of arm-in-arm women in the back. The pictures that followed were quite different. I gasped when I saw the side view of a nearly naked man with bulging muscles straddling Rhonda. Her eyes were glossed in an alcohol haze, and she was stuffing a wad of money in what I hoped was the man's G-string. The caption read "Lap dance." So there it was: the completed Rhonda. Perhaps Facebook does, in the end, expose all.

Eight

Sue walked briskly into the room on the night of our third memoir class, settled into her desk, and checked her watch. She glanced over her shoulder. "I don't know why I rush to get here."

"You might want to switch to Jillian time," I said. "Save yourself the stress."

Sue smiled and reached into a red leather Michael Kors tote. She pulled out a fresh stack of papers and tapped them together on her desk.

The twilight sky glowed navy blue through the large paned windows. Tony arrived and flipped on a few more of the fluorescent lights. His BlackBerry clanged like a fire alarm as he settled into the seat in front of me. He glanced at the screen and let it fall back into his pocket. He turned to face me. "You write anything yet?"

"Nope," I said.

"You've got to chop up the writer's block. Just sit down and start writing. Here's your first sentence: I was born."

"Mm," I said. "Thanks for the help."

Tony's phone bleeped. He reached for it and started typing with his thumbs.

Glenn strolled in looking freshly pressed and confident. He sat in his usual seat next to mine and set his briefcase on the floor. "Tell me everything about your meeting with Dr. Angeles, Rosalie. I've been anxious to talk with you."

"I know," I said. "I'm so glad to finally see you."

"What was your impression of him?"

"For starters, he is very attractive."

"And?" Glenn said.

"And he's a terrible flirt."

"Did he make a pass at you?" Glenn said, sounding protective.

Tony stopped typing and drummed his fingers on the desk.

"I don't know. I can't remember the last time someone made a pass at me." I lowered my voice. "He asked me to have a drink with him. That's inappropriate, right?"

"I would say so." Glenn rested his arm on the back of his chair. "But that's good information. We suspected he comes on to his students and you've confirmed that he does."

"I know. I thought the same thing. That could be how he behaved with Megan. The man has the personal boundaries of a golden retriever."

Glenn chuckled.

"And listen to this," I said. "You know his prestigious grant?" I leaned in closer. "He's studying sex."

Tony spun around. "Who's studying sex?"

Glenn and I exchanged a furtive glance.

"Just someone," I said.

"Come on," Tony said. "Who are you two talking about?"

"If you must know, Rosalie found a dead body," Glenn said.

"No kidding?" Tony said. "Where?"

"Megan was in my marsh grasses." I glanced at Glenn. "I really don't think we should—"

"We're looking into how she died," Glenn said. "There is a professor at the college who is a suspect."

Sue placed her pen on the desk in a slow, deliberate movement. Her head was statue still.

"Maybe I could help," Tony said. "I've been living on my sailboat while my ex-wife is cozied up in our very expensive house in

Wilmington. When I'm not working, I'm bored out of my gourd. Other than you guys, I know a total of three people. Count 'em." He held up his hand and popped up his index finger. "The pizza delivery boy . . ." Another finger. "The liquor store owner, and three, the gal who takes my checks at the marina." Tony looked over at Sue. "Well, Susie Q? I know you're listening. You in?"

Sue turned to face us and tucked her shiny black hair behind an ear. "Do you have any other suspects?"

"Yeah," Tony said. "What do you know so far? And I want to hear more about this research. Sounds like he's going to study you."

"Everyone slow down," I said. "This is just something I'm doing and Glenn offered to help. I don't even know if she was murdered. It's just a hunch."

"The police closed the investigation," Glenn said. "Megan's father asked them to."

"Why would he do that?" Sue said.

"We're trying to find out," Glenn said. "But it certainly is suspicious."

"I agree." Sue leaned forward. "I think we should learn as much about this girl as possible. I can get us onto her Facebook page." Her cheeks had flushed a rosy pink. "Did you know that after the Virginia Tech shootings, people posted messages on the dead students' Facebook pages? It was a way to mourn. I would bet people are still posting on her wall. They do that now—keep people's Facebook pages up after they're deceased."

"Sue," I said. "Back up. Are you saying you can look at her entire page without being her friend? I thought that was private."

"It is." Sue shrugged. "But I have my ways. I can hack onto her page and figure out how to log on as Megan. If we need to, that is. And we might at some point. I really think the more we know about her, the better chance we have of discovering who killed her."

"*If* someone killed her," I interjected.

"Hang on," Tony said. "Sue, how the heck can you get on her Facebook page?"

Sue's hair slipped from behind her ear. She gathered it up and dropped it behind her back. "I can't really say."

"What's important is that you can do it," Glenn said. "There should be a wealth of information. For all we know the killer could have written on her wall."

Their eagerness was dizzying. I felt like Dorothy when her three new friends signed up to find the wizard. And like Dorothy, I needed to let them know there was a witch on my tail. "Slow down, everyone. I haven't told you about the sheriff."

"What about the sheriff?" Glenn said.

"He's scary," I said. "And he doesn't like me. In fact, I'm certain he despises me."

"He agreed to close the case very quickly," Glenn said. "Possibly prematurely. Perhaps he is a suspect, too."

Jillian strolled in, sat at her desk, and fished her cell phone out of her hobo bag.

"Sue," Glenn said. "I think you made a good point. We need to know our victim inside and out. Maybe we could divvy it up—each follow a different lead."

I looked from face to face. Maybe I wasn't as alone as I thought. Not only did they think I was right to look into Megan's death, they were going to help me. "So we're a team," I said. "I can't believe it."

"Hey," Jillian said into her phone. "'Sup?"

Sue glanced over her shoulder. "I don't think anyone should know what we're doing."

"We don't need to worry about Jillian," I said. "She barely listens to your memoirs."

"Sue's right again," Glenn said. "This is a very small community. We'll need a private place to meet."

"Is there such a thing in Cardigan?" Tony said. "I mean, heck, I went to the Acme the other day and the clerk asked if I was that guy from Wilmington living on his sailboat."

"We can form our own private group on Facebook," Sue said. "No one will be able to read our posts but us."

"That's it." Glenn slapped his palm on the desk. "My grandchildren keep asking me to get a Facebook account. This will be the push I need. All right, so if we form our own group, no one else can see our conversations?"

"That's correct," Sue said. "I'll set it up tonight and send you an invitation." She leaned back in her chair and looked down at her lap. "There's just one thing."

"What?" I watched her carefully.

"I won't be logged on as Sue Ling." She looked up at us, her eyes darting from face to face. "I'll friend you as Shelby Smith."

"I didn't know you could do that," I said. "Don't you have to be an authentic person?"

"There are a lot of things about Facebook people don't know," Sue said. "It's called catfishing. Anyway, if we have a private group we have to pick a name for it."

"Hm . . ." Glenn rubbed his chin. "To solve a problem you have to explore all possibilities. And as Rosalie said, we don't know for certain Megan was murdered. So we start with a question as you do in any valid research. All right, so what's our question?"

I thought for a moment. "What if Megan Johnston was murdered?"

"That's it," Glenn said. "Our Facebook group will be called the 'What Ifs.'" He lifted his notepad and a pen from his pocket. "Now, will someone please tell me how to get on Facebook?"

NINE

My stomach grumbled with hunger as I drove down the lane to my house. Afternoon sunlight peeked in and out of the rows of gnarled cypress trees. My papers and a pack of cinnamon gum were on the passenger seat. I gazed up at the house as it came into view. Built before the Civil War, Barclay Meadow was graced with two-story pillars and floor-to-ceiling, cross-paned windows. The lane ended in a loop that encircled a clump of mature, musky-scented boxwoods my aunt had tended as if they were her grandchildren.

Charlotte Barclay Gardner, who was ten years older than my mother, inherited Barclay Meadow from a long line of Barclays. As a child, I spent weeks here in the summer. I filled my days running through the fields, reading for hours on the dock, harvesting tomatoes from the garden, and kneading bread dough. She loved this house. It was the child she never had, the husband who died too soon. She ate the food it produced and nurtured the people who worked the fields.

Raised in Baltimore, Charlotte was the first of the Barclay clan in fifty years to make it a permanent home. But despite her kindness, her generosity to local charities and involvement in the community, she was always considered to be from "away." That was something else I inherited from her.

Tyler's tractor hummed in the distance. Dust billowed behind the large tires, seagulls dipping and rising in its wake. He had been working twelve-hour days. I envied his productive, structured life. The What Ifs were scheduled to chat for the first time later that night and I was excited to be moving forward with the investigation. I had my list of suspects all ready to go. Finding Megan had been traumatic. I will never erase the sight of her body from my mind. But now I felt a bond—a duty to find out how she died. In a way, my life ended, too. At least the life I had always known.

My skirt felt loose as I pushed open the front door. I'd gotten on the scale that morning only to find I'd lost five pounds. Of course Ed would have noticed that before me. He watched my waistline like a German pointer. Five pounds. Is that what he wanted? Five pounds less of me? Would that have made him happy?

I hadn't cooked a meal since I moved in. And yet, I loved to cook. It wasn't unusual for me to go to the market several times a week to secure fresh produce and ingredients for a new recipe. And on the rare times Ed, Annie, and I were all together for dinner, I would top the table with a cloth and a pair of tapers and cook a three-course meal. The candlelight encouraged conversation and lingering. Those were the happiest times for me—when Ed was engaged with Annie and we discussed everything from politics to rap music to the latest Nationals trade.

I set my bag on the counter and decided maybe a glass of wine would help motivate me to cook. A coffee mug sat in the sink. Tyler had taken me up on my offer and was helping himself to coffee throughout the day. I noticed his paperback on the kitchen table. *Dante's Inferno*. He certainly had unique literary tastes for a farmer.

After dropping a bouillon cube and a cup of brown rice into a pot of water, I sat at the table, combed my fingers through my hair, and allowed myself to think about Ed. I sipped my wine as the familiar ache of tears worked their way up my throat. I was still clinging to the belief that our marriage had been good. Ed always said I smoothed out his rough edges. His business aggression sometimes got in the way of his social encounters. It wasn't unusual for him to say what he thought before stopping to consider the effect it had on others. Some found him brusque and a little critical. And that's where I came in. My one skill—people liked me. Whenever I sensed Ed was about to blurt out a judgmental thought, I would simply tuck my arm through his and tell a funny story. I would feel his tensed muscles relax and later he would thank me. You know me so well, he would say.

"Yeah, right," I said and wiped a tear from my cheek.

"Come again?" I was startled to see Tyler standing in the kitchen. "Your rice is boiling over."

"Rats." I leapt up and flipped the burner knob. The bubbles immediately died away. I looked at him. "Are you finished for the day?"

"It's getting dark. I just came in for my lunch." He stared at the pot and frowned. "You're having brown rice for supper?"

"No," I said. "I mean, I haven't decided yet. I was thinking about a stir fry." I slid a finger under my lower lashes, wondering if my mascara had smeared.

Tyler walked over to the sink. I detected the scent of overturned earth and skin warm from the sun. I watched as he scrubbed the imbedded seams of dirt from his palms. He dried his hands, folded the towel, and hung it neatly on the oven door handle.

The odor of charring food filled the room. Tyler slid the pot to a different burner. He glanced up at me. "You might want to rethink the rice."

"My idea to cook a meal was a fleeting one. I'm already thinking cottage cheese."

He took me in. I wondered what he saw. Did he find me pathetic? I wanted to defend myself, tell him I used to be a pretty fun person, that I was active and generous, that my friends envied my life. Our eyes met. Despite the tightening in my throat, I held them steady with his. "My husband left me for another woman, Tyler. He had sex with her in our bed. That's why I'm here."

His chin lifted a little. "Okay."

"Okay," I said. I walked over to the pot, picked it up, and dumped the rice in the trash. I put the pot in the sink and filled it with water.

An acrid smell filled the room. Tyler watched as I poured out the water and dropped the pot in the trash with a loud thud.

Tyler picked up his book. "I'll see you tomorrow."

"Yeah, okay." I crossed my arms and stared at the floor.

"What are you going to eat?"

I looked up. "That all depends on the sell-by date on the cottage cheese."

He nodded and stuffed his paperback in his back pocket.

"How's the book?" I asked, realizing I wasn't ready for him to leave.

"A lot can happen when you learn you've chosen the wrong path."

My mouth fell open.

Tyler started for the door. He stopped and turned to face me. "I'm sorry," he said.

"It's all right. You weren't necessarily talking about me." I shrugged. "Although you probably were."

"Pardon?" He pulled his cap tight on his head. "I'm sorry about your *husband*. And what he did. That's rough."

"Oh. Thank you, Tyler. Thank you for saying that."

He hesitated a moment, then walked out the door.

At 8:00 p.m. I signed on to Facebook. The number one was on my friend icon. I clicked on it.

Nicholas Angeles has sent you a friend request.

Whoa. He's Facebook friends with his students? I hesitated, wondering if this was a good idea. But he was our first suspect. I might get some information that could help the investigation. I clicked accept and shuddered.

After following Sue's instructions, I joined our private group. The first post was from Glenn.

Glenn B	Everyone here?
Rosalie Hart	I am!
Shelby Smith	Me too!
Glenn B	All right. So how do we get started?
Tony Ricci	All present and accounted for.
Rosalie Hart	What do we do first?
Shelby Smith	Who are our suspects?

I stared at the screen. This was a disaster. We were all typing at the same time. Answers were popping up before anyone had a chance to read the last post.

Rosalie Hart	Hang on!!!! We need a system.
Glenn B	Good lord. Rosalie, take charge.
Rosalie Hart	Let's go in alphabetical order: Glenn, Sue, Tony. Each of you share a comment. I'll summarize and we can get assignments. Ready? Oh, wait, don't answer that. : / OK. I'll list our suspects. Suspect 1: Psychology professor. Motive: Hide sexual affair. Suspect 2: Rhonda Pendleton. Motive: Extreme jealousy of Megan. Possible relationship with M.'s stepfather. Suspect 3: Sheriff Wilgus. Motive: unknown. Suspicious behavior: Closed case prematurely. Other possible suspects: Family? Boyfriend?
Glenn B	Excellent work, Rosalie. The professor strikes me as the most plausible. I say we continue to focus on him. Tell us more about your meeting. You say he's studying human attraction?
Shelby Smith	Is he a psychology professor?
Tony Ricci	I can't believe you can get paid to study sex.

Rosalie Hart	Yes, he is a professor of psychology and he just received a very lucrative grant. He was not unattractive. I could see how, despite his age, he could easily seduce a student. Also, he has a sailboat. I think that's significant.
Glenn B	It's like you said. What better place to carry on a discreet affair than on a boat?
Shelby Smith	He could have pushed Megan off the boat into the river.
Tony Ricci	His boat must be bigger than mine.
Glenn B	Sorry, I'm typing out of order but let's keep this broad—look at all the angles, not just the professor. He almost seems too obvious. Philanderers aren't necessarily murderers. What about this Rhonda person? Even if she didn't do it, she may shed light on the family.
Rosalie Hart	I'm on it!

TEN

Rhonda and I agreed to meet at a small cafe halfway between Wilmington and Cardigan. With an Internet search, I had discovered a quaint little restaurant that served organic, local food. I was pleasantly surprised when I arrived. It had large, inviting windows, linen tablecloths, and was decorated in warm, earthy tones.

Once we were seated, I smoothed my napkin over my lap and looked over at Rhonda. "So," I said. "Tell me all about you."

"What's to tell?" She was dressed in a tailored business suit and pumps with three-inch heels. Her light brown hair had been professionally brightened with streaks of honey gold and her face displayed an array of expertly applied makeup: concealer under the eyes, neutral tones on her lids, tweezed and penciled eyebrows, and a soft peach blush on the hollow under her prominent cheekbones.

"Let's see . . ." She took a sip of ice water. "I've lived in Wilmington my whole life, got divorced seven years ago, and, forced to support myself and my children's expensive lives, got my real-estate license and have been working my butt off ever since." She rested her elbows on the table. "I have two kids, both in college, and well, I guess that's it. What about you?"

"I have a daughter who started college this fall. She's at Duke and loving it. And . . . well . . . I just moved into a very old house. My aunt left it to me in her will."

"How old?"

"Close to two hundred years. And the farm is huge. I have someone leasing it and—"

"How huge?" Her eyes narrowed. "Like how many acres are you sitting on?"

I shook my head. "I'm not really sure. Over a hundred, I think."

"Is it near the river?" She sipped more water.

"It's on the Cardigan. Remember? That's where I found Megan."

"Right." She gave me a sly smile. "If you ever want to sell it, I know a good Realtor." She winked. "So, why did you move? You don't strike me as an Eastern Shore–type of gal."

"It's complicated."

"I see a wedding ring but you haven't mentioned a husband."

I stuffed my hands in my lap. I still wasn't accustomed to admitting the truth about my marital status. Saying I was getting divorced felt like wearing ill-fitting shoes—it rubbed and squeezed and pinched at my heart. "He was having an affair. He still is," I added. "I moved out about a nanosecond after he confessed."

"So . . ." She folded her hands over the menu. "Dish—what happened?"

"Rebecca happened."

"Midlife crisis," she pronounced and leaned back in her chair. "Let me guess, he's around forty?"

"Forty-eight."

"How old is Rebecca?"

"Do I have to tell you?" I sipped my water. "Early thirties. And she weighs about thirty pounds, too."

"Don't do that." Rhonda glanced around for the waitress, impatience pursing her lips.

"Do what?"

She looked back at me. "Compare yourself to her. You're not the reason he strayed."

"How could you know that?"

"I just know." The waitress approached our table looking harried. "Finally," Rhonda said.

I smiled up at the young woman, trying to compensate for Rhonda's curt manner.

After ordering the butternut squash soup and a club sandwich, Rhonda slapped her menu closed and looked over at me. "How about a nice, juicy martini? It's Friday and I've had a bear of a week."

I shrugged. "Okay."

"Two Belvederes on the rocks, three olives."

I ordered the soup and a watercress salad and handed my menu to the waitress. I looked over at Rhonda. "You were about to explain why Ed left." I leaned in. "Please—enlighten me."

"It's totally and completely about him. You could be Angelina Jolie and he still would have had the affair."

I sat back and shook my head. "We both know that's not true."

"Oh, yes it is." She pulled a piece of bread from a basket and ripped it in two. "Let me guess, he's successful? Makes a lot of cash?"

"Only recently."

"So, here's the deal. The old four-oh comes around and he starts thinking, Am I only going to have sex with the same woman for the rest of my life? And here I am in my prime, good-looking, lots of dough. So he takes it all out for a test drive." She buttered the bread.

"That all sounds so trite."

"Honey, you aren't the first chick this has happened to."

I watched as the waitress set two sweating martinis on the table. Rhonda's comments were getting under my skin. Seeing Ed's actions as a midlife crisis seemed to trivialize our entire marriage. I picked up the glass and took a swig of vodka. Whoa, I thought. So that's what a martini tastes like.

Rhonda was eyeing me. "Divorce isn't so bad, Rosalie. It's not the end of the world."

"Then why does it feel like it?" My throat was tight from the alcohol.

She slid an olive off a hot pink plastic sword with her teeth. "Look at the bright side—being a divorcée is sort of exotic. You get to say dishy things like 'my *first* husband.' And no more dirty underwear on the bathroom floor, snoring in the middle of the night."

"Ed never did those things. He's neat as a pin."

"So . . ." she said, eyebrows raised. "Would you take him back?"

My fingers fluttered over my spoon. I avoided her eyes, glancing around at the other patrons. After a deep breath I said, "Yes." I centered my glass on the small napkin. I looked up at her. "How desperate do I sound?"

"You're practically an invertebrate. Well, if you do take him back, you better be damn sure because if the bastard did it once, he'll do it again. Either way, make sure you get a little action first."

My eyes widened. "I'm so not ready for that."

"You have to even the score. Otherwise you'll resent him. You'd be doing it for the marriage." She winked. "Besides, divorced sex is divine. It's not about obligation anymore. Just think, you have a fabulous dinner, a nice roll in the sack, and then he picks up his clothes and waits for *you* to call *him*."

"Oh. I haven't gotten that far. I still feel very married."

"You know what you are?"

I straightened my spine. "What?"

"You're the kind of woman who only plays her 'a' side. You know, the old records? There's an 'a' side and a 'b' side. You only play the sure thing—the song everyone likes. But sometimes the 'b' side can be more interesting." She took a long sip. "You getting this? Take some risks, girlfriend. We all have a dark side. And it's kind of fun to embrace it."

I studied her, the tiny lines tensing her eyes, the purse of her lips, all betraying the pain beneath her flippant facade. Would that be me in a few years? Hardened by my loneliness? "Well," I said. "It certainly sounds as if you've got it figured out."

"Divorced sex does have a *few* drawbacks. I'd forgotten how much you have to keep everything shaved and moisturized and wrinkle free." She studied me. "I suppose you did all that anyway."

I gripped my glass with both hands. "I really liked being married."

"Well . . ." She glanced around for the waitress again. "The man . . . what's his name?"

"Ed."

"Ed is a fool."

That was the second time someone had said that to me.

While the waitress delivered our soups, Rhonda ordered another round of drinks. I was surprised. I still had most of my first one, and the alcohol was already speeding through my veins like a snort of cocaine.

"Wait . . ." I said to the waitress as she turned to leave. "I'll just have some coffee. Black," I added. I avoided Rhonda's gaze and ladled a spoonful of soup. I was growing weary of discussing my marriage. "So, speaking of strain in a marriage, how are Megan's parents holding up?"

"Not good." She dabbed the corners of her mouth with her napkin, leaving a bright red smudge on the white linen.

"How could they be?" I tried to detect the spices in the soup. Cumin? Maybe a little curry?

"It's not like it was the perfect marriage before Megan died. I mean, Corinne is a complete mouse—plain, meek, and boring. Bill ruled that family, including Megan."

"Even as her stepfather?"

"Bill is the only father she ever knew, remember?" Rhonda dipped the corner of her sandwich into her soup. "And they were very close. He taught her to play soccer. In fact, Bill and I used to carpool and organize the other parents." She eyed me. "Did you happen to see Bill at the funeral?"

"Just from a distance."

"He's the best-looking man I've ever seen." She stared off. "He's deliciously tall."

"So, he adored Megan?"

Rhonda hesitated. "Something like that. I don't really know how to describe it." She leaned back in her chair. "It was more like he was obsessed with her."

"What do you mean?"

"Once she entered high school, it was as if he had to control everything she did." Rhonda looked down at her soup. Was that a tear in her eye? She took a deep breath and brought me back into focus. "Managing Megan's life took up so much of his time he abandoned everything else."

"How did Megan feel about that?"

Rhonda shrugged. "I don't really know. I never heard her complain. He spoiled her rotten, so why should she?"

"It sounds like he went a little overboard. Right when she was ready to launch, you know?" I paused. I'd just said "overboard." Was that a sign?

Rhonda finished chewing a bite of her sandwich. "She did get very rebellious there at the end. It was driving Bill crazy. He even reached out to me." Another smile, this one was softer. "I was so glad he thought I could be of help to him."

I watched Rhonda closely. Every time she mentioned Bill her eyelids fluttered and she stared off as if recalling a pleasant memory. She was in love with the man. I needed to keep her talking.

"Chelsea must miss Megan very much," I said.

"I wouldn't go that far. My poor Chels was sick to death of living in Megan's shadow." The waitress brought our beverages and as soon as she walked away, Rhonda picked up her glass and took a long drink. She closed her eyes for a moment, as if waiting for her blood-alcohol level to inch up another notch. She opened them and zeroed in on me. "Megan brought on her own problems." Another sip. "Bill was right to have her transfer to John Adams."

"Megan must have hated transferring."

"Of course she did. She was one of the most well known students on the entire campus. And once she got to John Adams, the drama got worse." Rhonda roller her eyes. "Bill regretted his decision almost immediately. It drove him crazy to have her so far away and out of his control. But if you ask me, the man was better off having the distance. He was past due to let her destroy her own life once and for all."

Rhonda's long fingers clutched her martini glass like talons. She watched me carefully, gauging my reaction like a predator sizing up her prey. Had she told me too much?

"So, Rhonda," I said. "It must have been very difficult for you being so close to the Johnstons when you disliked Megan so much."

Her eyes flashed. "I never said I disliked her."

I returned her gaze, the vodka boosting my height. "You didn't have to."

Rhonda wadded her napkin and set it on the table. She rolled
her shoulders back and said, "Bill adored her enough for all of us.
That's all that matters." She bit into another olive. "So, Rosie dear,
are you still interested in how she died?"

"I am."

"Why, exactly? You never knew her."

"I found her. She came to me and no one else seems to be interested in how such a lovely young girl had to die."

"Now who's the drama queen?"

"There is evidence indicating her death might not have been an
accident."

"Honey . . ." She reached over and patted my hand. "You're a
housewife, not a detective. Maybe you should stick to vacuuming."

I started to defend myself, to tell Rhonda how much I knew, but
stopped. She was warning me away. Despite her haughty veneer, it
struck me that Rhonda was a dilettante at the sophisticated persona.
Give her time and the real Rhonda comes through, and there she
was, claws bared.

"You're right." I folded my hands tight in my lap. "Maybe I should
focus on getting a date."

"Good girl." She raised her almost empty glass. "Here's to your
freedom." She started to sip but stopped. "And to a good roll in the
sack. God knows we could both use one."

ELEVEN

Janice Tilghman has sent you an event invitation.

I spent the morning following up on the applications I submitted
around town, but it was starting to feel futile. It was an unspoken
reality that any job opening would go to a local first. Maybe I could

do something over the phone. Telemarketing? I shuddered at the thought and went up to my room to find a sweater.

Earlier that day I had washed and refilled every one of Aunt Charlotte's spice bottles, adding a bottle of my favorite homemade seasoned salt and a bottle of garam masala. I scrubbed the cabinets and canisters and replaced the sugar, flour, and tea. A clean, fresh kitchen stirred my love for cooking. But since I didn't have anyone to cook for, I decided to bake.

My aunt's bread recipe was written on a yellowed index card in a crippled script. I hoped I got the proportions right. It was a complicated recipe with several types of flour, rolled oats, and honey. Not long before she died, Aunt Charlotte and I had made plans to get together once a week to make bread, just like the old days. She suggested I pick a day I didn't drive carpool, come to visit her, and we could immerse ourselves in the immensely therapeutic process of bread making. I was so looking forward to it. But it never happened. Life, or should I say death, got in the way.

My iPod played the original Broadway version of *Les Misérables*. Trumpeting songs urging men to revolution seemed to be the perfect accompaniment to kneading bread.

Once I had mixed the ingredients, I removed the sticky dough from the bowl and plopped it onto a wooden board. The scent of fermenting yeast met my nose, triggering warm, distant thoughts of family and home. After dusting my hands with flour, I pushed with the heels of my hands, putting my entire body weight into my efforts. I flipped and shoved, squeezed with both hands, dusted it with flour, and turned it again. The drums grew louder, the horns blared. I punched the dough with a fist. Then the other. I picked it up and flipped it again. As I worked to the music, the dough grew smoother. Muscle memory kicked in. I used to be pretty good at this.

The music softened. Sweet violins. Cosette began to sing in a crystal clear soprano, *"I saw him once . . ."* I froze. Oh, no. What was I thinking? Ed and I saw *Les Misérables* in three different cities, including London on our honeymoon. All three times he reached for my hand when this song began. It was our song. Marius sang, *"A heart full of love . . ."*

My knees weakened. I lowered myself into a chair and dropped my head on my arms. The ache in my chest squeezed my heart.

I don't know how long I sat there. The sleeves of my sweater were soaked with tears. The phone rang incessantly. The answering machine clicked on.

Janice Tilghman began leaving a message. "I know you're there, Rosalie. You're screening your calls. If you don't pick up, I'm coming over."

I lifted my head and brought the room into focus. I sniffled, walked over, and picked up the phone. "How do you know these things?"

"It's my business to know. What are you doing? Are you wallowing?"

I coughed out a laugh. "Maybe a little." I checked my reflection in the toaster. Mascara striped my cheeks. I dried my face with a dish towel covered with flour. Now that's really going to help.

"I knew it," Janice said in her trademark raspy voice. Although she had never smoked, she sounded as if she was up to three packs a day. "I sent you an invitation on Facebook. Did you even see it?"

Janice and I had been friends as children. She grew up on the farm next to Barclay Meadow. Her ancestors had lived on the Eastern Shore since before the Bay Bridge was built. And although she had attended boarding schools and now bopped up to New York to shop when the mood suited her, she was definitely a native.

She and her husband lived on a beautiful estate farther down the river. They farmed the land and hunted the Canada geese that drank from their pond. Although neither of them needed to work, they were both active in the community and always busy with one project or another. They had four children and raised them all with common sense and practicality.

"I saw it. I'm sorry, Janice. I'm doing my best. It's just . . . well, I was having a teeny little melt down."

"Hm. Bad?"

"Chernobyl?"

"Okay. That's why you have to come to my party—mix it up." Janice said. "I want you to meet some people."

"Thanks for thinking of me, but I'm not really up for a party." I propped the phone in the crook of my neck and picked up the bread. It had started to dry. I began to knead again.

"What are you listening to? I can hardly hear you."

"I was fighting the French Revolution. Only I lost."

"You're helpless." She laughed. "Almost."

I yanked my iPod out of the docking station. There was a paper-thin crack down the center of the screen. "Thanks for the invite, but—"

"You know me better than that, Rose Red. No one says no to Janice Tilghman. Besides, there's a very nice dentist I think you should meet."

"Absolutely not," I said. "No fix-ups. It's way too soon."

"Okay, okay. He'll be at the party, but I won't tell him about you. If you happen to meet, well, what can I say? We'll leave it to destiny."

Ha, I thought. Janice didn't believe in destiny unless she was the one predetermining it. "Are you sure you don't mean 'dentistry'?"

"Yeah." She laughed. "That, too."

Our banter brought back memories. When we were children, I was Rose Red and she was Snow White. We played endless pretend games with dress-up clothes and imaginary princes. But with a strong older brother and an innate need to please, I was easy prey for Janice's strong will. Whenever I insisted on contributing at least one idea to our game, she would say, "tit for tat," and add yet another of hers.

I thought for a moment and was struck with an idea. "Tit for tat," I said and flipped the dough. A light snowfall of flour sailed through the air. "I'll come to your party if you invite Sheriff Wilgus." My stomach tightened at the thought of talking with the man again, but I had an investigation to lead.

"He's already on my list," she said. "Hey, you just said you weren't ready."

"It's not about that."

"You sure? Because there's no judgment coming your way. He is kinda hot in a Rock Hudson sort of way. But remember, Rosie, you fart in this town and everyone smells it."

"*Rock Hudson?*"

"James Garner?" she said.

"Geez, Janice, what are you, seventy?"

"Wilgus is just sort of retro, you know?"

"I guess, but he's not really my type," I said.

"Good," she said. "Gives my dentist a fighting chance. By the way, what's that banging noise?"

"I'm kneading dough. I haven't made bread in years."

"You used to cook all the time."

"Ed was a carbophobic. No bread in the house. I think he was worried I'd get fat."

"Dumb jerk," Janice said. "Give the dough an extra sock for me."

I clicked off the phone, leaving a white thumb print on the talk button. After punching it one last time, I placed the abused dough in a bowl and covered it with a towel, tucking the edges underneath.

It was an unseasonably warm day and I had opened the windows.

Tyler's tractor hummed somewhere in the distance. I was learning a lot about his relationship with Aunt Charlotte. Not just from her files but from Doris Bird, as well. Tyler had been the one to find my aunt after an unexpected stroke. Unwilling to wait for an ambulance, he had picked her up, carried her out to his truck, and drove her to the emergency room. Although I was speeding to get to the hospital, it was a two-hour drive and by the time I got there, Aunt Charlotte was dead. Tyler had already gone home. I must remember to thank him for not letting her die alone.

Now that he was helping himself to coffee, I awoke every morning to an earthy smell of freshly ground beans. We were experimenting with different blends and concluded that the Italian roast was the best for early mornings. Lying in bed listening to his work boots on the floorboards below softened my loneliness. It was soothing to have another presence in this old house. He had gotten in the habit of sitting at the kitchen table and reading yesterday's *Washington Post* with his coffee. Crumbs from a slice of toast would be littered over the sports page, some of the print highlighted in darkened circles from his buttery fingers.

After scraping the dough from my fingers, I dried my hands and crossed "make dough" off my to-do list. I had also written "let dough rise" and "put bread in oven." It made me feel more accomplished.

Worry about my financial status was ever present, despite Tyler's checks. Ed and I had both come from humble beginnings. And while I embraced my modest roots, Ed had tried to sever his from the day he'd moved out of his family home in West Virginia. I had always worked. I always *had* to work. But when he sold his software company for a very large profit everything changed. He was suddenly status conscious and wanted to upgrade it all: the cars, the house, the private school, and a status wife, one who scheduled an active social calendar, squeezing in several philanthropies on the side.

Was it love at first sight like Marius and Cosette? Maybe. Although I found him attractive when we first met, it was more like a shifting—an acknowledgment settling in: this was someone I would know a very long time.

"Enough, Rosalie,'" I said softly. I felt something on my foot and looked under the table. Dickens had rested his head on my sneaker. I scratched his velvety ears. "Hi," I said, wondering how he had gotten in the house. His soft brown eyes smiled up at me. I petted him again.

A few hours later the room was filled with the toasty aroma of freshly baked bread. I was seated at the table buttering a slice when Tyler walked in. He stopped in his tracks when he saw Dickens eating his own very large chunk of bread. I looked over at Tyler and then down at Dickens. I patted his head. "I found someone to bake for."

TWELVE

After our first night of disorganized typing, the What Ifs had finally developed a rhythm to our discussions. We slowed down, for one, and did our best to direct questions to specific people. Most of the time, at least.

I began by filling them in on my lunch with Rhonda.

Glenn B	Interesting, Rosalie. Trust your gut. If you got a weird vibe about Rhonda and Bill, then we need to explore it. Would she meet with you again?
Rosalie Hart	I'm pretty sure. She wants to know what I know. And she tried to get me to stop the investigation. I think that's significant.
Tony Ricci	I got the creeps just reading what you wrote about

	her stepdad. I'll do some research on his business. Unless Sue can hack into his computer. Suzy Q?
Shelby Smith	I might be able to. But I'm better at Facebook. I'll see if he has a page.
Rosalie Hart	Anyone up for a party?
Tony Ricci	Always.
Glenn B	Are you hosting?
Rosalie Hart	An old friend. And there will be a very special guest.
Shelby Smith	Who?
Rosalie Hart	The one and only Sheriff Wilgus!
Tony Ricci	Nice going, Princess! I'm in!
Glenn B	You two should go as a couple. It will be a good cover. If we all traipse in together it could look a little suspect. I hope you can get some information from the sheriff. I've been trying to think of a way for us to see the police report. First and foremost I want to know if Megan was dead before she entered the water. There are very simple ways to know. Maybe you can get him to tell you. But be careful, Rosalie.
Shelby Smith	I agree, Glenn. Tony and Rosalie should go. I'm not very good at parties anyway. I'm on Megan's Facebook page btw. Let's meet soon, Rosalie, I need to show you some things.
Tony Ricci	Holy crap, Sue. How did you do that so fast?
Shelby Smith	Not a big deal. I'm just trying to be helpful.

"What's this?" Sue said.

"Lunch. I've been baking a lot of bread, so I brought you a fresh loaf and a bowl of minestrone." I set the bag on the floor next to Sue. "Lots of veggies and beans—good stuff."

"Rosalie, I'm a pescatarian."

"No worries. The soup is vegetarian."

"Soup rarely is. It's the—"

"I used vegetable broth. You're good to go."

"How did you know?"

I smiled. "I'm not really sure."

Sue was seated at a table in the John Adams library. She opened her laptop, logged onto the Wi-Fi, and waited for Safari to open.

"So, tell me, Sue, why do you live in Cardigan? I would think it awfully small for someone as young as you."

She looked over at me, her dark eyes perfectly lined, her high cheekbones framed by a heart-shaped face. "I like that it's small." She tucked her hair behind an ear. "My mother would really like me to come back to California."

"I would, too, if I were her," I said. "We moms like to be near our daughters."

"Actually, I miss California, but I can't move back right now."

I studied her. The realization that this young woman had many secrets was settling in. "It almost sounds as if you're hiding out."

Her eyes flashed. "Why would you say that? Rosalie, please don't ask me any more questions. I love this investigation. And I really want to help. For a lot of reasons. I just can't say what they are. Do you understand?"

"Not really, but I will respect your request." I patted her arm. "And I am very glad to have you onboard."

She checked her phone and set it on the table. "I have another new phone number, by the way." She looked back at the computer screen.

"Why are you using prepaid phones?" I said.

"Tight budget."

I glanced down at her cobalt blue Tory Burch handbag. "Okay,"

I said. "I know you have to get back to work. Let's see what you've discovered."

"I'll show you how to get onto Megan's Facebook page in a minute, but first I want you to see what came up in a Google search." Sue's small, rounded nails clicked on the keyboard. The Google home page appeared. "Did you know Megan was a student at the University of Delaware for three years before she came here?"

I nodded. "Rhonda's daughter played soccer with her there."

"Check this out." Sue typed "University Delaware Megan Johnston soccer" and we waited for the results.

"There are thousands of hits," I said. "Was there another Megan Johnston at Delaware?"

"No. The 'T' in Johnston narrowed it down." She scrolled down the page. "Every one of these links is our Megan." Sue moved her finger over the touchpad and tapped on one of the links. A page from the University of Delaware's website appeared. A photograph of Megan centered over the caption "Women's Soccer Team Division Champs." Megan is on the soccer field, one foot poised on the ball. Her arms are in the air and her University of Delaware jersey is in her hand. She's wearing a tight navy blue sports bra and her soccer shorts. It was a stunning picture. Her blue eyes stare straight into the camera, daring you to continue to look at her. With her arms in the air, a spot of cleavage dips into her bra, strands of her silky blonde hair loose in the wind. Her abs are defined, her waist small, curving in just above her shorts. The leg holding the ball in place is toned and shapely and the pose is completely feminine bordering on provocative.

"Wow, what a photo," I said. "She's gorgeous."

"I know. And it's not even photoshopped." Sue clicked on another link. "Look at this."

The link was to a sports blogger's page. The same picture of Megan appeared but with a different caption. This one read "Check out the best new thing to come out of Delaware. This chick is hotter than holy hell. Come to Papa, Meggie."

"After he posted this"—Sue clicked on another link—"the photo spread like a virus. Guys have it on their Facebook pages, blogs, porn sites, you name it."

"That's awful." I sat back in my chair. "What a violation."

Sue glanced over at me. "It got worse." She clicked on another link. "This is from the local newspaper. Apparently after the word spread that Megan was so beautiful, guys started showing up at her games with cameras and telephoto lenses. Everyone wanted to get a picture of her for their blogs. The stands would be crammed full of voyeurs."

"How could she possibly play?"

"That's the amazing part. The article says she never lost focus. They won the championship again last year."

"Rosalie?"

I turned around to see Professor Angeles standing behind us, a wide grin spread across his face. He was dressed in a blazer with a tight-fitting T-shirt underneath. He held a leather iPad case under his arm and his curls tumbled loose around his head.

"Professor Angeles." I stood quickly, positioning myself in front of the computer screen.

"Please, call me Nick. After all, we're Facebook friends now."

"Okay," I said. There was that cologne again. "How are you, *Nick*?"

"That's better." He stepped closer.

"Hi, Professor Nick." We turned to see a fresh-faced coed in a short denim skirt and fleece boots approaching. Her friend, dressed in similar boots, skin-tight leggings, and a snug sweater pulled down over her thighs, stood next to her. "Kaitlin and I were wondering if there is a movie in human sexuality class tonight." She clutched several books to her chest.

"I believe there is," he said.

"Okay." She grinned hard.

Nick waited. "Is there anything else, Ashley?"

"Nope." She giggled. "See you tonight."

Once she was out of earshot he said, "Mine is the only class where students *want* to attend when you show a video."

"Sex sells," I said.

"And what have you decided?" he said. "Are you going to enroll in one of my classes?"

"I'm definitely considering it. In fact, I was just looking at the application process."

"Really?" He peered around my shoulder. I followed his gaze. Sue was playing a game of hearts.

"Yes." I gripped the back of the chair. "Really."

"Rosalie," Sue said. "I'm sorry to interrupt, but I need to get back to work."

"I won't keep you." Nick handed me a business card. "Give me a call and let's have that drink."

I accepted the card. Should I do it? Maybe it would help the investigation. Maybe I would learn something. I looked up into those velvet brown eyes. "I would like that . . . Nick."

"I'll see you then."

I watched him go.

"Wow," Sue said. "He really is hot."

"I know." I sat down. "And he sure doesn't act like a murderer. He seems kind of nice."

"He likes you, Rosalie."

I rolled my eyes. "He likes everyone and anyone."

"Sooo . . ." She eyed me. "Are you really going to have a drink with him?"

"I'm considering it. I might get him to open up after a cocktail or two." I fanned myself. "How long do you think he'd been standing there?"

"I don't know."

"Do you think he saw what we were doing?"

"I sure hope not." Sue studied me. "Rosalie, you have to be careful."

"We all have to be careful."

She checked her watch. "Here's what you need to log onto Megan's Facebook page." She handed me a small piece of paper with an email address and password. "You have to log on from her email address. It's a Yahoo account and here's the password. Once on Facebook, the password is the same. Also, someone set up a memorial page. Anyone can go to it and write a post. Just type in her name while logged on as yourself and the memorial page will come up. There could be some clues there, as well." She closed her computer and tucked it into her tote. "Thank you so much for the soup and bread. I can't wait to eat it." She looked over at me. "Rosalie?"

"What, honey?"

"I am absolutely certain we will find who killed Megan somewhere on her wall."

Shelby Smith	Tony and Glenn: Click on this newspaper article about Megan.
Tony Ricci	Whoa! Good work, Suzy Q.
Glenn B	That bursts this investigation wide open. One of those gawkers could easily become a suspect.
Shelby Smith	I agree. And I'm on it. I sent Megan a friend request as Shelby Smith. Then I logged onto her page as Megan and accepted the request. So now I'm her "friend."

Rosalie Hart   Sue, won't that show up in the news feed that you and Megan are now friends? That could freak some people out.

Shelby Smith   I took care of that.

Tony Ricci   I'm not even going to ask how.

Shelby Smith   Anyway, now that I'm her friend, I've been friending her other friends. I even chatted with a few last night. There's one guy that jumps out at me.

Tony Ricci   Hey—went for a cruise in the dinghy. Tried to figure out where Megan went in based on the current. Could have been from the other bank—Queen Anne's side. You get a lot of debris around your dock, Princess?

I typed quickly.

Rosalie Hart   Yes, Tony, tons. Sue, are you sure that's a good idea? Don't put yourself in danger. He could be the killer.

Within two minutes Sue wrote:

Shelby Smith   Exactly.

THIRTEEN

The day of Janice's party I decided to get my hair styled and touch up my roots. The Curling Iron was the only salon with an opening on such short notice and a few hours later I sat perched in Brenda Baker's chair.

Brenda pumped her foot on the metal brace under the chair. I bounced around as if on a plane making a less-than-smooth land-ing. When I was at the desired height she stood behind me and looked critically at my hair, lifting layers, and letting them fall again. "You got a lot of hair, hon."

"Yes, I know." I gave her a friendly smile.

She continued to pick through my hair like a chimp. I noticed Brenda had a lot of hair, too, although hers was lacquered into a henna-colored bob with bangs that had been carefully sprayed into place. She had a pretty face accented with blue and green eye shadow and a plump set of lips. A petite diamond adorned her left hand and photos of a young boy and girl in soccer uniforms were tucked in the mirror.

"You want a trim, too?" Brenda asked.

"Maybe just the ends. I like the style. The layers seem to help calm down the volume a little."

"Yeah." Brenda cracked her gum. A puff of mint met my nose. "You go curly?"

"Wavy, I guess."

She fingered my hair some more, examining the cut. She frowned. "You get this cut here in town?"

"Bethesda. Quite a while ago, actually,"

She eyed me in the mirror. "The other side of the bridge?"

"Yes," I said. "I live, or I *used* to live, in Chevy Chase."

"It's a good cut. Somebody knew what they were doing. It falls nice, you know? And it's good around your face—brings out your big, brown eyes."

"Thanks," I said, feeling genuinely flattered. I thought I had just been dismissed when she realized I wasn't from Cardigan. But she probably knew that the moment she saw my name on the appoint-ment book.

She stretched a pair of gloves over her hands and I marveled at how her long, crimson nails didn't pierce the thin latex. After mix-ing the color, she pinned my hair up with several large clips. She slipped a piece of aluminum foil under a section and painted a dab of white goop onto my hair.

"So, where you living?" she said.

"Just outside of town on River Road. Do you know where Barclay Meadow is?"

"Hon, if your house has a name, then it ain't anywhere near mine." My scalp felt cool where she painted another section.

"Oh, I didn't name it. It's been in my family for—"

"Wait, is that the place where the dead girl washed up?"

I exhaled. "Yes. That's the place."

"No way," she said. "Did you find her?"

I nodded.

"Shut up." She stopped her work and regarded me with renewed interest. "What was it like?"

"Horrific," I said.

"So, how did she end up in the river?"

"They said it was an accident."

"How did she fall in? Did she trip? You know you don't just fall in a river."

"I guess she was at a college party and the keg was at the end of a dock."

"Well, then, someone would fish you out, right?" Brenda said.

"Maybe. It was at night."

"But you would still call the Coast Guard or the sheriff or someone. You should see what happens when someone gets caught in the river—they call in the freakin' cavalry—the river clogs with rescue boats and the choppers come with searchlights." Brenda clipped another section. "I'm not buying that no one even heard a splash."

"I find it hard to believe, too."

"So there must be some clues. Like what was she wearing?"

"Oh, that was hard to see. She'd been in the water a few days."

Brenda stopped painting. Her eyes narrowed. She listened hard.

"She was bloated," I continued. "Her clothes were stretched so tight they had started to rip."

"Get out of town."

Did she just say that to me?

"But you must have an idea," Brenda said. "Was she wearing jeans, skirt, top, bathing suit?"

"Come to think of it, she was in a dress. It was dark, black maybe, and above the knee."

"Like a cocktail dress?"

"Yes, now that you mention it, I think it was."

"That doesn't make sense. I thought you said she was at a college keg party. Who wears a cocktail dress to one of those?"

"Brenda, you ask some very good questions."

"I watch a lot of *CSI*. Miami and Las Vegas." She picked up another piece of foil and folded the end. "I'm not a big fan of the New York one, though. I don't like the chick. She's too smug."

"So, what do *you* think happened?" I said.

"Me? Geez, I don't know. Folks drown a lot around here because of the current. But that's usually when people are trying to swim. So who's going to go for a swim in a dress, especially in October?" She dipped the brush into the bowl. "But either way, don't you think the kids at the party would have said something?"

"Unless one of them was responsible."

"Yeah, like if he had something to hide. Kind of creepy, you know? To think somebody dropped a body in the Cardigan. They could be right on campus, for all we know."

"Well, I guess we'll never know. The police ruled it an accident plain and simple."

"Yo, Bren," a woman called from the front desk. "Your three o'clock is here."

"What are you taking out on your nails?" Brenda pumped the

chair back down. "Why don't you get a manicure while you process? Larissa's open."

Once I learned a manicure only cost ten dollars, I sat across from Larissa and extended my hands. She shook her head as she went to work on my cuticles. I looked over at Brenda. She was telling her three o'clock about my finding Megan. The woman was rapt and I could see by the animated expression on Brenda's face she was probably embellishing some of her own *CSI* details. The women on either side were wide-eyed and listening with "oh"s formed on their lips. Brenda held court while I felt like exhibit A. Larissa kept her head down, but her eyes darted around. I could tell she was listening, too, as she painted my nails with Plum Like It Hot.

After being out all day I was anxious to connect with Annie. Although Tony was due to pick me up in less than an hour, I had a mother's instinct she was upset about something. I tapped on my keyboard, careful not to smudge my nails.

Annie	Finally. Where have you been? Guess who sent me a friend request?
Rosalie	Who?
Annie	You know.
Rosalie	Rebecca?
Annie	Your friendly neighborhood home wrecker.
Rosalie	What are you going to do?
Annie	Ignore it, of course! I'm leaving her in limbo. It's the worst insult on Facebook.
Rosalie	Maybe that's not a good idea.
Annie	Mom!!!!!!!!!! WAKE UP!!!!
Rosalie	Please don't shout.
Annie	????

Rosalie	All caps—it feels like shouting to me.
Annie	I'm sorry. It's the chat. I was angry. I would never have said that to your face.
Rosalie	But you felt it just the same. Typing something as opposed to saying it doesn't make it less potent.
Annie	You're pretending this hasn't happened. But it has. Dad's ruining our family and you're just living in Siberia.
Rosalie	Ok. I get it. Have you heard from him lately?
Annie	You're doing it again.

FOURTEEN

A few days before Janice's party I had stood on the scale and was shocked to see I'd lost 4.2 more pounds. My body was a lot like my psyche—hating change. Welcome to the divorce diet, I thought.

The evening of the party I rifled through the dresses in my closet. Every one I tried on was loose and baggy. As if I didn't feel frumpy enough. I decided on black pants and a cream silk blouse. I stood in front of a cloudy antique mirror that made me look like I was in an Impressionist painting. I could hear Annie's voice . . . "You need a pop of color, Mom." But how? Ugh. I found a floral scarf and draped it around my neck. Nope. I decided to tie it. Way too eighties. Another ugh. Desperate, I wove it through my pant loops. Good enough. With my mother's pearls and my new hairdo, I was presentable. I slipped into my faithful black pumps and walked through a cloud of perfume.

"You look nice," Tony said as I slid into the front seat of his Mazda Miata.

I was relieved Tony agreed to come to the party. I secretly hoped he would be my fluoride to keep the dentist away. He shifted into gear and maneuvered the car down my narrow lane, an occasional cedar branch smacking against the window.

"Thanks," I said. "These clothes are ancient."

Tony downshifted and turned onto the main road. "Why do women do that?"

"Do what?"

"I say you look hot and you tell me how old your clothes are."

"Technically you didn't say 'hot.' You said I looked 'nice.'"

"Either way, all you have to say is, 'thank you, Tony.'"

"Thank you, Tony. You look very nice, also."

He glanced over at me. "But you didn't say 'hot,' either."

"Tony." I turned in my seat to face him. "Tell me more about you. Why do you live on a sailboat?"

"Divorced," he said. "Second time. My wife got the house." Tony shrugged. "I run my own consulting firm, so I figured I already had a place with a heater, head, and coffee pot. Why pay rent somewhere else?"

"Why Cardigan?"

"We lived in Wilmington and kept the boat here—came down on weekends. A lot of people from that area keep their boats in Devon County."

"Isn't it lonely?"

Tony looked over at me. "You already know the answer to that."

"Mm. There's some truth." I folded my hands in my lap. "So, why are you taking this memoir class?"

"It has a lot to do with the aforementioned marriages."

"I'm not sure I follow."

"My old man is on number five."

I thought for a moment. "Five? You mean he's been married *five* times?"

Tony nodded. "And the way this one is turning out, he may very well be on his way to number six. The guy has prenups down to a science."

"Okay. I think I understand. By writing a memoir you can figure out how to avoid being like your father." I smiled over at him. "Is that right?"

Tony downshifted. "You got it." The Mazda squealed onto the lane approaching Janice's estate. I peered out the window. The last slice of daylight hovered over the horizon. A small whistle escaped from Tony's lips. "Nice piece of acreage she's got here."

Janice stood in her immense two-story foyer under a dazzling crystal chandelier. The house was already humming with conversations and laughter. We brushed one another's cheeks, keeping our lipstick to ourselves, and Tony handed her a bottle of Moët. Janice had a round face framed with highlighted blonde hair and blue eyes that looked as if she was thinking up something mischievous. And most of the time she was.

"Snow White," I said.

"Rose Red," she replied.

"Your house is stunning."

"Come in, come in. There are so many people I want you to meet."

"This is Tony," I said. "I hope you don't mind I brought a friend."

"I didn't know there was a friend." She winked.

"No, it's nothing like that," I said. "We're in a writing class together."

Janice shook Tony's hand. "Are you from the Shore?"

"Boston—born and bred."

"Red Sox?"

"In good times and bad," Tony said. "Unlike a lot of their more recent fans."

"Yeah," Janice said and nodded in agreement. "I hate it when somebody roots for a team just because they're winning."

"Janice . . ." a voice squealed from behind me.

We stepped out of the way so that another cluster of guests could greet our hostess. When we reached the bar, I placed my hand on his arm. "Tony, thank you for coming with me. I'm new at going to parties without a husband."

"No problem," he said. "It's good to get out."

"Chardonnay," I said to a bartender dressed in a vest and crisp bow tie.

"I'll have a grounds for divorce," Tony said.

"That's a new one for me," the bartender said.

"Maker's Mark and a splash of coffee."

"That's a new one for me, too," I said.

"I made it up a few years ago," Tony said. "It did the trick when I needed it to and I've been drinking it ever since."

"Tony," I said. "You're vibrating."

He pulled his BlackBerry out of his shirt pocket. "Sorry. I gotta take this."

The bartender handed me my wine. I stepped out of the way and scanned the crowd while I sipped. Several other people were tapping away on their phones, others rapt in conversations. I didn't recognize anyone. But this was the Devon County elite—the families that sent their children to the private school on the river and owned the factories and chicken plants on streets named after them. Their farms lined the Cardigan River and their money floated the charities in town. It was as old as money can get in our young country.

I looked for Tony and spotted him still by the bar. He had stowed his phone and was in a conversation with another woman. That was fast, I thought. She was younger than Tony and on the plump side. Rubenesque, I decided. Her dress had a plunging neckline and her breasts bounced as she laughed. I looked away. And there he was— Sheriff Joe Wilgus. He wore a sport coat and a tie dotted with decoy ducks and was talking to a group of similarly dressed men.

I finished my wine in three gulps and set the glass on a passing tray filled with champagne flutes. I scooped one up and headed over to him before I lost my nerve.

"Sheriff Wilgus?" I said.

The other men stopped their conversation and looked at me with interest. "This is Missus Hart," the sheriff said. "She's living in Barclay Meadow."

"I know what you're thinking," I said. "And yes, it's true, I'm the one whose property that poor college girl washed up on."

"Welcome to Cardigan," a ruddy, redheaded man said and laughed.

"I was rather hoping my first guest would be alive."

He roared and slapped his thigh sheathed in madras plaid trousers.

"Sheriff," I said. "Could I talk with you for a moment?"

He faced me and the men closed their circle. The intensity in his gaze sent a shiver through me. I clutched my champagne glass with both hands. "I'm sorry to interrupt."

His eyes narrowed. He wasn't going to give me an inch.

"I've been wondering if you found anything else out about Megan."

"*Megan?*"

"The girl who drowned."

He sipped his drink. Ice cubes clanked against the glass. "I told you, it's none of your business." A cloud of whiskey wafted toward me.

"But why did you close the investigation so soon? You said you haven't had a murder in seven years. Maybe it would be kind of fun to investigate. You're probably a little rusty, right?"

"No one," he growled, "said anything about a murder."

"But there are so many things to look into. For instance, what was in that envelope? The one that was in her backpack? And was she dead when she went into the water or did she drown?"

"I don't have to tell you any of that."

"I know it was her parents who asked you to close the case. But why wouldn't they want to know how she died?" I looked up at him and batted my eyes.

"How in the hell do you know that?" His perpetually red face deepened to crimson. "What are you up to?"

"I'm just curious, is all." I took a small step back. "She was such a lovely girl with everything going for her—friends, a soccer career. She was smart, too." I hesitated, deciding whether or not to leak more information. But I could learn a lot from his reaction. "Did you know Megan had received a lot of interest from a psychology professor?"

His black eyes simmered, each burning with specks of gold that looked as if they were about to ignite into flames. He took a menacing step toward me. "I want you to get the hell out of my town."

"There you are." Janice slipped her arm through mine. "I've been looking all over for you. Hey, Joe," she added. "Having a good time?"

"Time of my life." He downed the rest of his whiskey.

"Looks like you're due for a refill." Janice tugged on my arm. "I hope you don't mind, but I'm stealing Rosalie." She kept me close as we walked away. "What are you up to, girlfriend?"

"Nothing."

"Don't piss on Joe Wilgus's grass. He is very well connected."

"Are you telling me Cardigan has a mob?"

"Every town big and small has a"—she made quotations marks with her fingers—"'mob.' Some people have more power than others. That's how the world works."

"The population of Cardigan is four thousand. I don't think it needs royalty."

"Don't be naive, Rose Red." She stopped and turned to face me.

"You're new to town. It's like learning to cross the street. Just stop, look, and listen."

"Or else get run over by the sheriff's cruiser?" I crossed my arms. "Janice, why do you invite him to your parties if he's such a bully?"

"That's exactly why. And a few other people, too. I invite them to my parties, and they leave me alone. Life can get very unpleasant around here if you don't follow the rules."

"You mean *their* rules."

"Every town has its decision makers. And Joe Wilgus just happens to be one of them. Did you know there's been a Wilgus in the sheriff's seat for three generations?"

"Last I checked I still live in a democracy."

"Rosalie, really?" She shook her head. "Sometimes I forget you grew up in the boonies. How did you survive so long in the city?"

"Did you just say 'boonies'?"

"You did and I did. Just stay out of Joe's way, got it? He's got a mean side and nothing good comes from him being pissed at you."

I looked up at her. The animation that usually lit up her eyes and rounded her cheeks was absent, her tone uncharacteristically serious. "Okay," I said. "I'll stay out of his way." A chill whispered down my spine.

"That's more like it." She tugged on my arm and led me through the crowd. "Let's lighten up and have some fun."

We arrived at a glossy black, grand piano. A young man looked up at Janice, his fingers poised over the keys. "How about some Beatles, Will?"

Without Tony as protection, I was growing suspicious Janice had made a point of including the dentist in the sing-along. As the crowd closed in, I slipped from her grip and backed away.

The room was thick with people and crescendoing conversations. I glanced around the room. No sign of Tony. I wondered where that waiter with the champagne flutes was hiding. My heart was still palpitating from my conversation with the sheriff. Not just because I had mustered the courage to talk to him, but also because the man sent pulsating waves of terror through me. It was as if he had a force field of menace around him. Maybe I should stop being so nosy. Maybe I should . . .

Janice belted out, *"Let it be . . ."*

Was that a sign?

"Why is that man glaring at you?" Tony sidled up to me.

"Finally. I've been looking all over for you." I looked out at the party-goers. "Who's glaring at me?"

"That guy over there by the window."

The sheriff's eyes were glassier than before. He was in an intense conversation with a distinguished-looking man. Salt-and-pepper hair. It was David Carmichael, the president of the college. Sheriff Wilgus nodded as David continued to speak, but his eyes were zeroed in on me. Chill bumps raised the hairs on my arms.

I stepped closer to Tony. He handed me a fresh chardonnay. "That's him," I said. "That's Sheriff Wilgus."

"Find out anything?"

"Nothing."

"It looks like you managed to piss him off."

"I'm afraid so." I sipped my wine. "That man he's talking to—he's the president of John Adams college. I saw them in Brower's together. Why would they be so chummy?"

"Good question. So, what do we do now?"

"Where's your new girlfriend?"

He frowned. "My who?"

"You know, Beverly Cleavage."

Tony shook his head. "Her name's Heather and she works at the marina where I live. She's got four kids and a tank for a husband. He's a guide—takes all the rich hunters from Philly and D.C. out goose hunting on Janice's farm for a nice fat fee."

"I'm sorry." I smiled over at him. "I'm just teasing you. I think it would be nice if you found someone." I started to drink my wine, but stopped midsip when I saw Professor Angeles. He stood by a window framed with long, plaid drapes. His dark curls were combed back and he wore a black silk shirt and a sleek pair of gray trousers. An empty champagne glass hung loosely in his hand. I stepped closer to get a better view.

"Now where are you going?" Tony said.

"That's the professor," I whispered

"No kidding? Everyone in town is at this party." Tony took a closer look. Professor Angeles was listening intently to a short, older woman with round, bottle-thick glasses. "Go say hi."

"No." I shook my head.

We watched as the woman fluffed her short curls. She gazed up at Nick, visibly enamored. Her irises were probably as wide as saucers.

"I know you said he was good lookin', but you never said he was *that* good lookin'," Tony said. "And he teaches sex? He must get laid all the time."

I glared over at him. "That's not a good thing."

"Depends on who you're asking."

"Behave." I elbowed him in the side.

"I didn't mean with his students. Oh, hey . . ." Tony tapped my arm. "He's waving."

I looked back. Nick was smiling at me. I gulped and gave him a tight little wave. Tony waved, too. Nick motioned toward the woman with a slight nod of his head and mouthed, *Help!*

"Look," Tony said. "He wants you to interrupt. Go on."

Just as I started over, Janice was at his side. "I know you can sing, Dr. Nick. Now come on over to the piano."

The woman looked deflated. The wind huffed out of my lungs, as well.

"Man, Janice is good," Tony said and sipped the last of his drink. "That's why everyone comes to her parties. She caught the SOS from the sex prof." Tony looked down at his glass. "And she buys the good stuff. You ready for a refill? I think the bartender is pouring Cakebread chardonnay. Doesn't that cost a bundle?"

"Yes," I said. "It does and I'm ready. But wait . . ." I grabbed his arm.

"Yeah?"

"There's David Carmichael again. Look how hard he's gripping the professor's bicep. He's angry with him." I looked over at Tony. "Why?"

"Maybe the short chick was his wife." Tony put his arm around my waist. "So, Nancy Drew, you coming to the bar or what?"

"The sheriff," I said as I followed Tony. "The sheriff told David Carmichael what I know. Don't you see? They're worried I'll expose the affair." I felt eyes on me and glanced over my shoulder. Sheriff Wilgus raised a fresh drink to his lips. He lifted his free hand and pointed his index finger at me, his thumb pointing up. He held my gaze as he slowly pulled the trigger and blew across his fingertip.

FIFTEEN

The following Monday I was idly waiting for Annie to sign on to Facebook when Tyler strode into the kitchen. The sun had set without my noticing and the room glowed in a warm amber hue from a small lamp on the counter. Dickens was at my feet again. The mouth-watering aroma of baking bread saturated the air.

"If he keeps coming in here, he's going to end up fat and ill-trained."

"He's old and happy," I said and scratched his ears. "You don't really mind him coming inside, do you?"

Tyler eyed my wineglass.

I stretched my back. "I know, drinking alone. It would taste better if you joined me."

"No judgement here," Tyler said. "Rosalie, I have an idea of what you're going through."

"You do?"

"I'm divorced. I'm surprised you didn't already know."

My eyes widened. Tyler had never revealed a personal fact. "That's probably the only thing I haven't learned at Birdie's."

He leaned back against the counter and folded his arms. "Cardigan must seem really small to you after living in the city."

"I grew up in the country, but yes, I miss Chevy Chase a lot. But I think the hardest part about living here is you aren't exactly a permeable crowd."

"You're not finding folks to be all that friendly?"

"Friendly enough, just not very welcoming. It feels like a gated community, only I don't have the pass code."

Tyler's lips set into a small frown. "You just need to understand where we're coming from. People move here thinking this is the perfect little town to settle into. They buy a house and join the country club. But what we've come to realize is most of you don't stay. Not for long. So we've learned to not get attached."

"Was your wife from away?"

Tyler walked over to the sink and picked up a bar of industrial-strength soap. It seemed I had crashed into that gate again. And here I thought we were getting to know one another. I wondered if the Eastern Shore had a rule book.

"You sure spend a lot of time on that computer," he said as he dried his hands. "You on Spacebook again?"

"It's Facebook. And yes, I'm waiting for my daughter to log on."

He folded the towel and looped it through the oven handle. "She doesn't have a cell phone?"

"Kids these days like to text and type."

"Sounds a little backward. Isn't that why they invented the phone?"

"Phones are outdated. I'm lucky if she listens to my voice-mails."

His eyebrows arched. "And that's *okay* with you?"

"I haven't really thought about it. But thanks to Facebook, I know every day that she is alive and well. I can see right here where she liked what someone posted. For instance, someone shared a photo from the SPCA. Annie liked it three hours ago. I just hope she hasn't adopted a kitten."

Tyler shrugged. "Seems to me you're the parent."

I snapped my computer shut and stood. I wasn't going to take the bait this time. "I look forward to you and Annie getting to know one another. She'll be here for Thanksgiving." I crossed my arms. "You actually have a lot in common."

He frowned as he rolled the sleeves of his work shirt down and buttoned the cuffs. "She's good looking, then?"

I smiled and shook my head. "Wait . . ." I said when he started to leave. "I have something for you." I picked up a foil-wrapped loaf of bread still warm from the oven.

He palmed it like a football. "I don't suppose this is Miss Charlotte's recipe?"

"Yes, I've been making a lot of it lately."

"Best damn bread I ever had."

"I hope it's as good as hers," I said.

Tyler brushed his hair off his forehead and picked up his empty lunch box. Dickens came to alert and trotted over to him. I glanced at the clock. It was nearing 8:00—time for the What Ifs.

"I've finished the planting," he said. "You won't see me for a while."

"So soon?" My heart sank at the thought of not having Tyler around. "What will you do?"

"Not sure. Maybe cut some deer or try and find where the rock-fish are hiding."

"Tyler, I noticed my aunt had you on a salary."

His posture stiffened. "I worked hard around here."

"I'm not questioning your work ethic. I just wondered what you did for her. I feel as if this house is disintegrating around me."

"You can't neglect a house this old."

"I'm doing the best I can."

Tyler's mouth curved into a small smile. "You're doing the best you can to neglect it?"

"No, I didn't mean that," I said, flustered. "I mean I'm trying my best to take care of it."

"You sure get defensive. Is that a city thing?"

"I think it's a Tyler Wells thing. Look, Tom Bestman said my aunt left some money in a trust account. I'm not sure how much is in it, but it's designated for the upkeep of the house. Would you be interested in staying on? If there's enough money to pay you, I mean."

"Beats going out on the water every day. I'll be here tomorrow. You see what you can do on your end."

"Wonderful. I'll have the coffee pot ready."

Tyler turned to leave, but stopped. "Don't you mean 'Mr. Miele'?"

Rosalie Hart   Sorry I'm late!

Tony and I filled the others in on the party.

Glenn B   Sounds like they want to keep you quiet, Rosalie.
Tony Ricci   Good luck with that, haha.
Rosalie Hart   Btw my hairdresser pointed out Megan was in a cocktail dress and didn't have a coat on. And it couldn't have fallen off because her backpack was still strapped on. So what student goes to an

outdoor college party in a cocktail dress and no coat but she has a backpack?

Glenn B So our theory that she was deliberately pushed into the water is holding up. And she didn't go in the river at that party.

Tony Ricci I'm wondering about the stepfather again. If Megan was sleeping with a professor she may have had daddy issues.

Glenn B I still want to see that police report. I wonder if it's on the Internet somewhere. It seems everything is these days. Also, what you learned at the party means the professor is still a viable suspect. I have an idea of what to do next.

Sixteen

Glenn and I waited on the dock while Tony untied his dinghy from the back of his sailboat. Sue had opted out of our mission, claiming her computer skills would be of more use to us.

With the absence of city lights, I was dazzled by the wall-to-wall stars strewn across the sky. A harvest moon illuminated surface ripples on the water. It was 1:00 a.m. I pulled my jacket tighter.

"All aboard," Tony called.

"Tony," I said as Glenn and I walked to the end of the dock. "Your sailboat is called *Honey Pot*?"

He shook his head and looked down. "It's a long story."

"Spill," I said, making no effort to suppress my grin.

"I got the boat right after we got married." He looked up. "I was feeling like I'd found my pot of honey, you know—new boat, new wife—life is good. I used to call her that, too—honey pot. So that's what I named the boat."

"Makes sense to me," Glenn said.

"Okay, Pooh Bear," I said.

"Cut with the Pooh Bear."

"You know," Glenn said. "Pooh is very Taoist."

"Yeah, well, he's also pudgy. And I'm a little sensitive these days." Tony patted his stomach. "Too many pizzas."

"When you put it that way, I will never call you Pooh again." I smiled over at him. "You're not pudgy. And I love that you were so in love. That's a rare thing these days."

"Are you two ready to get in the damn boat?" Tony stood and held my arm as I stepped into the dinghy. Once I was seated he reached for Glenn. The boat wobbled as Glenn hopped aboard in a pair of rubber-soled shoes.

Glenn sat next to me while Tony yanked on the cord. "This outboard is a lot like a woman," he said. "Only sparks up when the mood suits her." Tony gave it another hard tug. When it at last sputtered to life, Glenn untied the lines, dropped them into the boat, and shoved us off. The water was inky black. I wondered if Megan died on a night similar to this, swallowed up in the river, held down for days by what lay beneath. Was she pushed and left to drown? Was she aware she was dying?

"Most of the houses around the professor's have their own piers," Tony said, one hand on the rudder.

"I marked the professor's house from the street, but everything looks different from the water." Glenn peered hard at the shoreline, studying each house as we chugged along. "There." He pointed to a narrow white clapboard house. "It's that one. I'm sure of it."

Tony cut the motor and the current ferried us to the dock.

"I'm having second thoughts," I whispered. "How will we see anything? And even if there is some evidence, surely he would have gotten rid of it."

Glenn stared at the dock as if willing the boat to get there faster.

"We'll find something," he said. "The professor wasn't expecting three detectives to come looking around for clues."

"Detectives?" I said. "That's a bit of a stretch."

Glenn ignored me and looped a line over a weathered piling covered with bird droppings. He pulled the dinghy closer and hopped on the dock with a loud thud.

"Shush," I hissed.

The Angeles's sailboat was a few feet shorter than Tony's live aboard. A dome lined with small windows indicated a cabin. The sails had been secured and wrapped in a royal blue canvas. Halliards slapped against the metal mast like an eerie wind chime.

Glenn handed Tony and me small flashlights. "You'll need to conceal the light with your palm like this." He cupped his hand around the end. After stepping out of his shoes he boarded the sailboat.

Just as he reached for the cabin door, I said, "Glenn, wait." I pulled three pairs of garden gloves from my pocket and tossed him a set.

"Good thinking." He slipped on the gloves and tried the door. "It's locked," he called.

Tony finished securing the lines and looked over at me. "You just going to sit there?"

Every muscle in my body ached with tension. We were trespassing. I was about to commit a crime. I'd never so much as crossed a toe over the line of the law. I'd been that way since I was born. I was the teacher's pet five out of my six years of elementary school, and that was only because my fifth grade teacher thought I was too perfect and spent the entire year trying to find reasons to give me an A minus.

Tony continued to look my way. After a deep breath and a short prayer, I climbed onto the dock and crawled over to him on all fours. We had agreed to dress in dark clothing and I was wearing my black spandex running suit. "You look like Catwoman," he said.

"Don't call me Catwoman," I said. "She has too many issues."

I looked around the deck. "We're not going to find anything. I think we should go."

"Chill, Princess, you got us into this."

"I'm not a princess."

"Why don't you two look through the cabin windows and see if there's anything out of the ordinary," Glenn said. "I'll inspect the dock."

Tony shone his flashlight through the first window, shielding the light the way Glenn had instructed. We studied the objects appearing and disappearing in the concentrated beam. "What's that?" I said. Tony reversed the path of the light and settled it on a clean ashtray.

"Did Megan smoke?" he asked.

"I doubt it—she was a really good soccer player."

"What about the professor?"

"The only thing I smelled on him was some very nice cologne."

"Oh, really?" Tony shone the flashlight in my face.

"Stop it." I covered my eyes. "Someone will see."

"Quiet, you two," Glenn said. "I hear something."

We froze as a spotlight on the back of Nick's house blazed on.

"Oh my gosh," I whispered.

"Drop," Glenn said.

Tony and I flattened on the dock. I peered up at the house and watched as Nick creaked the back door open. He was in a pair of plaid boxers, his hair disheveled.

"This was such a bad idea," I said.

"Hush," Tony said.

Nick carried a small, fluffy white dog. He set it on the ground and waited as it sniffed the grass. The dog lifted its head, ears perked.

"Go wee wee, Alfred," Nick said. The dog looked back at him, lifted his leg, and waited to be picked up. Nick stared out at the dock.

"Freakin' full moon," Tony said and pressed harder into the wood.

After what seemed an eternity, Nick picked up the dog, and went inside. When the light at last flipped off, we inched over to the boat and fell inside.

Tony's sailboat rocked gently, the water lapping lazily against the hull. We huddled around the small table affixed to the floor. I took a sip of the single-malt whiskey Tony had poured. The smoky liquid burned my throat and instantly warmed me from the inside out, numbing my frazzled nerves like a welcomed shot of Novocain.

"That was terrifying," Tony said. He slugged back some whiskey. "And freaking awesome."

The evidence we collected lay on the table before us like a cadaver in an autopsy. Glenn had his notebook open and peered at it through the glasses he had fished from his pocket.

"So, what do we have, Pops?" Tony said.

"First, let's discuss what we observed."

"That sailboat was spotless," I said. "Someone had recently scrubbed it from stem to stern. It reeked of bleach. He already tried to erase any sign of a struggle."

"I don't know," Tony said. "Boaters are pretty anal. I've seen guys hosing down their rigs after a five-minute cruise to the fuel dock."

"Oh, really?" I glanced around Tony's disorderly cabin. A computer had been crammed onto the galley counter and books and papers were scattered on the floor. Dirty dishes sat in the sink and a laundry bag overflowing with clothes sat propped in a corner.

He shrugged. "*Most* boaters."

"I think Rosalie has a point," Glenn said. "The boat was spotless. What did you notice inside the cabin?"

"The ashtray," I said.

"Right," Glenn said. "Sailors don't smoke inside cabins because the fumes can build up. Either way, they don't need an ashtray because they can flick their ashes in the water."

"Unless you're cozied up in the cabin with a coed," Tony said.

Glenn made a note on his pad. "Did either of you see any evidence of alcohol?"

We shook our heads.

"He could have easily gotten rid of a bottle," Glenn said. "Or maybe he slipped her one of those new drugs the fraternity boys are using."

"Roofies," Tony said.

"So that leaves us with this," Glenn said.

We all stared down at three long blonde hairs Glenn had found wrapped around a cleat on the dock.

"The professor's wife has dark hair," I said. "And, of course, so does he."

"What about his kids?" Tony said.

"Well, one was a towhead, but there's no way his hair was that long."

"It could be a friend's," Tony said. "Or Megan's."

"Exactly," Glenn said. "Do you have a bag we could preserve these in? Because if we can get the police to pursue this case, they could test the DNA and prove it belonged to Megan."

"Do you think the police could admit it as evidence if we found it?" I asked.

"Don't be negative," Tony said.

"They could test it for DNA. It might be enough to get them to reopen the investigation. Besides, it's all we have," Glenn said. "Not much to hang your hat on, is it?"

"Did I ever tell you Nick's wife left him in October? That's the same month I found Megan."

"Maybe that's why she left," Glenn said. "Because of the affair."

"Exactly." I sipped my whiskey. "So let's be better detectives, set the scene a little. Say Megan tries to curtail the affair and he ends up forcing himself on her. Afterward he gets scared, strangles her with one of the lines, and drops her in the water."

"Now we're talking," Glenn said. "Did you two happen to notice one of the lines on his boat was brand new? It was soft as silk and white as a freshly bleached sheet."

"No way," Tony said. "Well, that would fit Rosalie's theory. He replaced the line because it was evidence. And good lines ain't cheap. You don't replace a line unless it's in bad shape."

"Surely the police checked to see if she'd been raped or drugged," Glenn said. "And what if there were marks on her neck? Did you happen to notice, Rosalie?"

"Oh, no. She was very bloated. Her skin was discolored and her clothes stretched tight. And, well . . ." I squeezed my eyes shut.

"What?" they said in unison.

I opened my eyes and noticed they were both several inches closer.

"I think maybe the fish had found her."

"Whoa, Princess." Tony recoiled. "I did *not* need to know that."

"And I did not need to see it. But if we're going to do this, we need to know everything."

"So very sad," Glenn said. "If this night produced anything, it's motivation to solve this crime. Some Neanderthal thinks he can commit murder at will and no one seems to care. We need to know what little evidence the sheriff's department collected."

"But how?" I said. "The sheriff has made it very clear he wants me to back off."

"Agreed. We won't be getting any information out of him," Glenn said. He took a slug of whiskey and smacked his lips. "Whomever

Megan's murderer is, he or she won't want you asking questions. Our killer thinks they've gotten away with it. That's our opportunity, right there."

"Unsuspecting," Tony said. "I agree, Pops."

"I just got goose bumps," I said. "You know, this detective work can leave you feeling a little paranoid. I mean, everything is a weapon, everyone is a suspect."

"Yes, that's true, isn't it?" Glenn said. "But the only things we can trust are the facts."

"That's right," I said. "Wasn't it John Adams who said, 'facts are stubborn things'?"

"Funny," Tony said. "You know, ironic? John Adams . . . John Adams College?"

Glenn frowned. "I still can't fathom why the police aren't pursuing this. Look how much we've already come up with and we're just writers."

I turned to Tony. "Why don't you top us off?"

Tony dropped a few more ice cubes in our glasses and filled them with whiskey. I raised mine. "Gentlemen—here's to knowing what we know."

Seventeen

I maneuvered my car down the lane and noticed Tyler had trimmed the cypress trees. It was a welcome change to not be accosted by branches. Tom Bestman would now be cutting checks from Aunt Charlotte's estate every month. There would be enough to pay Tyler and to keep me on the farm. At least for now. He worried I might still have to sell it in the divorce settlement, but I would think about that later.

I parked my car and noticed Tyler had cut the tree limbs and stacked them neatly for firewood. The smaller twigs were bundled for kindling. I wondered how he was with furnaces.

Later that evening I sat on my screened porch and ate a dinner of baby carrots, crackers, and cheddar cheese. I also poured a glass of wine so that I would have the four basic food groups covered. I settled in the chaise lounge and switched on the lamp. The chair had been part of the house as long as I could remember, the paint chipping off and littering the floor. It was covered with chintz cushions, the once vivid pinks and sage greens long since faded. I had memories of my aunt sitting on this chair, her knitting in her lap, as she watched me trap fireflies in a Mason jar or march through the grass in bare feet, a sparkler stick sizzling in my grip.

I kicked off my shoes and propped my legs up. It was times like these the loss of my mother swelled up like an unexpected storm. After her death three years ago, I reluctantly joined the ranks of motherless women. We're a recognizable lot, if you look for the signs. There's a sadness in our eyes, a hint of self-doubt in our movements, a cool breeze at our backs replacing the warmth from being unconditionally loved.

I closed my eyes. Ending my marriage would have been so much easier to bear if my mother was still there to support me, to wrap those arms around me and tell me I would be all right. Since her death I felt as if the Earth had turned away from the sun. Maybe that was part of what went wrong with Ed and me. He had no idea what to do when she died. He missed her, too, I know. But after a while he expected me to be better. "How long?" he would say when he found me crying. "Shouldn't you be better by now?"

I shook my head and opened my eyes. A partial moon was rising, casting light on the river, the rippling black water reflecting a distorted crescent. Dusk was setting in and the trees and shrubs were blending into the night.

"Enough," I said quietly and opened my laptop. I took a deep breath and thought about Megan. Sue's research had revealed another side to her—a young woman who had stood strong amid adversity. What determination and focus it must have taken for her to play soccer knowing she was surrounded by voyeurs.

Once on Facebook, I decided to go to Megan's memorial page. I waited for it to open and there she was—posing in a blue-and-white soccer uniform with long, windswept hair, a playful smile brightening her face. A girl named Petra Kurtz had written the introduction.

This memorial page is to honor the life of a dear friend, Megan Frances Johnston. Her life ended prematurely but her love and enthusiasm for life will never die. Megan was beyond gorgeous, but that's because her incredible spirit lit her up like a Christmas tree. She was talented, smart, and one of the best athletes to ever grace the soccer field of the University of Delaware. Her hardships came when she was objectified by a viral picture that flooded the Internet. Did the Internet kill her? In some way, yes. But we can fight back and keep her memory alive through our Facebook community. Please share your personal story of how you miss her, how your life will never be the same. For me, Megan was a gentle and kind spirit who graced this Earth with compassion, joy, and genuine love for her friends, family, animals, and God. My grief is gut wrenching. But I want her legacy to live on. Welcome to our memorial group!

Wow, I thought. And so it begins.

Barry Grossman
Megan Megan Megan. I miss her so much it hurts. The sky is less blue, the sun not as warm.

123 people like this

Jessica Martel

Omg! This is the worst thing that's ever happened! First she left UD and then this! The soccer team sucks without her. I can't believe I'll never see her again—laugh with her again!!! GOD!!!!!!!!!!!!!!!!!!!!!!

Chelsea Pendleton and 36 others like this

Beth Hazelton

Noah Kelly and I got engaged last night. Megan and I promised to be each other's maids of honor. She was going to wear a navy dress in my wedding and I was going to wear hunter green in hers because she always wanted a December wedding. Now what do I do? Why did she have to die???? I hate this. Nothing is the way it's supposed to be any more. I want her to give me a thumbs up on my new relationship status. I want her to throw my bachelorette party. I want her to help me pick out my dress. This sucks so bad. ; (

67 people like this

My stomach stitched into a tight knot. So many loved her. So many were grieving now. I looked back at that smiling, innocent face. I wanted to warn her, don't go near the river!

Unable to read more, I closed my computer, set it on the ottoman, and stood. After slipping into my shoes, I pushed open the screen door and stepped out onto the damp grass. A flock of Canada geese honked overhead, the V formation just visible in the evening light. Their haunting, out-of-sync honks faded as they flew away. I hadn't been to the river since the day I found Megan. But after reading the ragged pain and anguish caused by her death, I felt pulled toward the water.

The constant rush of the river grew louder as I started down the gentle slope. Muscle memory of the day I discovered Megan kicked in and I filled with nausea. I hesitated, but it was movement in a nearby shrub that stopped me cold. I spun around. A large, hulking man stood among the hydrangea bushes.

I froze. What should I do? Run, you idiot. But would I make it back to the house before he grabbed me? If only my legs would move. Okay, Rosalie, run into the house, lock the door, and call the police. The police . . . "Sheriff *Wilgus*?"

He stepped out of the shadows. His badge glinted in the moonlight, one hand on the pistol sagging his belt. His navy uniform shirt was open at the neck, several buttons unfastened, exposing his barrel-size chest. He wasn't smiling.

"Is there something I can do for you, Sheriff?" I pulled my sweater tighter around me.

"You wanna *help* me?" He crossed the distance between us in a few long strides. His heavy boot grazed my toe. "I'll tell you how to help me: quit sticking your nose where it don't belong." His words slurred. Sweat glistened on his face.

"I haven't broken any laws." I inched back toward the house.

He started toward me again. I backed up as quickly as I could, but he matched me step for step as if in a tango. I backed hard into the side of the house. He towered over me. "Why are you here?" His whiskey-saturated breath was hot on my face.

I was in suspended animation. Fear had tensed every muscle in my body. "I'm just trying to survive."

He leaned in close. Round peas of perspiration dotted his upper lip. "I told you to mind your own business and yet there you are, still asking about the dead girl."

I concluded at that moment this conversation could only end badly. I needed to break away. Sliding against the house I started to raise my leg over an azalea. In two steps I could . . .

His palm slammed against the house next to my head. I glanced in the other direction. Even if I could escape, I would be running *away* from the house. But if he was as drunk as I suspected . . . I started to move. His other palm slammed next to my ear. My hair was trapped. My scalp burned.

"This is your one and only warning." His black eyes sliced into me. "You continue snooping around, I can't guarantee your safety. And that's my job, remember?" His mouth twisted into a sarcastic smile. "Keeper of the peace?"

"This isn't right. You know as well as I do Megan was murdered. Who are you protecting?"

"You're not listening."

"Why are you doing this?" My eyes widened. "You know! Oh my gosh. You know who killed her."

"*Shut up!*" He slapped a sweaty palm over my mouth. His gun dug into my thigh. His badge poked through my sweater. "You're all alone out here," he whispered. "There's nobody to hear you scream."

I couldn't breathe.

"Go back to where you belong." His face was so close my vision blurred.

I squeezed my eyes shut.

"Well?" He pushed his palm harder over my mouth. "What's it gonna be?"

I wanted to run. I wanted to do what he asked. But I couldn't breathe. He's going to smother me.

He shoved his hand one last time and let go.

I gasped for air.

"Get the hell out of my town."

EIGHTEEN

Persistent banging roused me from a heavy sleep. I had been up most of the night listening for the sheriff. Although I locked my bedroom door, I startled awake countless times, certain I heard a creak on the stairs or the soft whine of the front door.

I sat up: 6:00 a.m. I pulled on my robe and hurried down the steps. "Who is it?" I called.

"Who do you think?"

Tyler. I fiddled with the dead bolt and pulled open the door. I squinted out at him. "Sorry."

He brushed past me, Dickens loping at his heels. "Since when do you lock the door?"

I tightened my robe and followed him. "It just seemed like a good idea."

"No one locks their doors in Devon County."

"Is that a law?"

Tyler ignored me and started up Mr. Miele. His cap was wedged into his jeans pocket and he wore a white thermal shirt beneath his usual dark green T.

"I would like a cup, too, please."

He glanced over at me. "Isn't it a little early for you to be up?"

"Yes," I said. "But someone was banging on my door."

"Because someone locked the darn door."

"I had no idea you were so grouchy before your coffee."

I watched as he slammed a few cabinets and shoved the silverware drawer shut with his hip. As much as I wanted to tell him about being threatened by Sheriff Wilgus, have him protect me, keep me safe, sleep on my sofa every night with a shotgun, I knew I couldn't. Tony, Glenn, Sue, and I agreed that we would keep this to ourselves. Although I trusted Tyler, I had to keep my word. If anyone accidentally found out what we were up to, it could endanger us all.

"I'll give you a key," I said.

"I already have one."

Once the coffee was ready, he filled the mugs, set them on the table, and sat down. Spreading yesterday's *Post* out on the table, he leaned on his elbows and studied the front page.

I sat across from him and patted my thigh. Dickens trotted over and rested his head on my leg. He gazed up at me with his droopy brown eyes. "Does it ever bother you to be a day behind all the time?" I sipped my coffee. "I mean, it doesn't do you any good to know yesterday was sunny with an afternoon breeze."

"I don't read the weather report." He continued to look down at the paper. "I don't need a paper or a phone, for that matter, to tell me what the weather is. I simply walk outside."

I eyed him over my coffee mug. "I don't suppose your horoscope will do you much good, either."

He exhaled. "Are you sure you don't need more sleep?"

"Nope. I'm picking up your check today, by the way. I'll pay you what Aunt Charlotte paid you with an adjustment for inflation."

He kept reading.

I finished my coffee and glanced around the room. "Do you want some eggs?"

He looked up. "Are you having some?"

"I'm in the mood."

"You won't burn them?"

"Ha ha. How was the bread?"

He hesitated. "Damn good."

I stood and walked over to the refrigerator. After rifling through the contents I realized I didn't have much to work with, just a half dozen eggs and a tub of feta cheese. "Any chance you planted herbs in any of the fields?"

Tyler looked over at me. "Miss Charlotte had an herb garden around the side of the house. You might find a few perennials still struggling in the weeds."

I opened the door and headed outside. Ten minutes later Tyler and I sat down to an omelet of feta cheese, fresh oregano, chives, and a few snips of rosemary. I added a thick slice of my bread, warmed and slathered with butter. When he finished, he stood, set his plate in the sink, and turned to face me. "How about I weed that garden out for you this afternoon?"

I watched him go. When he shut the door, I set my plate on the floor and Dickens licked it clean.

NINETEEN

With all of his resourcefulness, I was surprised Glenn had yet to discover Birdie's shoe store. When I told him about the array of newspapers, he wanted to see if he could get the Philly paper. Somehow *The Baltimore Sun*, a newspaper that was thinning faster than a receding hairline, wasn't fulfilling his daily news requirements.

Doris had my *Post* waiting. The bell tinkled as the door swung shut behind us. An older woman with fiery red hair sat perched in the chair closest to Doris. She wore large neon pink sneakers on feet that didn't quite touch the floor.

"Good morning, Doris," I said. "My friend was wondering if you could get *The Philadelphia Inquirer*."

I turned to introduce Glenn, but he was already bent over the tiered row of papers. "You have *The Wall Street Journal*?" He looked up at Doris.

"You bet," she said.

"Every day?"

Doris chuckled. "Every day it comes. And I get the *Inquirer*, but only on Sundays. The boaters from Philly like to read it."

"Madam, you have just returned a long-lost friend to me." Glenn's knees cracked as he stood. He extended his hand. "Glenn Breckinridge." Doris's eyes danced behind those thick glasses.

Glenn selected a *Wall Street Journal*, a *Post*, and the local weekly. He studied the headlines.

"You eat at the cafe?" Doris said while she collected my money.

I nodded. "Although the food is less than desirable. How do you burn French fries?"

Doris backed onto her stool. "Most people just go there for the coffee and doughnuts."

"I'll know better next time. There aren't many places in town where you can sit down for lunch. Oh, speaking of food, I brought you some bread." I removed a loaf wrapped in plastic from my tote.

"What kind of bread?" the woman in the chair said.

I turned to look at her. "It's multigrain. But it's pretty tasty, if I do say so myself. I have a small jar of fig marmalade and some plastic knives if you two want to try it."

"Rosalie, do you know Lila?"

"No, I don't believe I do." I smiled over at her.

"Well, I know you," she said, punctuating her words with a sharp nod. Her face powder was pancaked tight on her skin and she wore a vivid orange lipstick that matched her hair. "You're the one whose land that girl washed up on. Somebody Hart. Right?"

"Yes, that's me." I looked over at Doris. "I shouldn't be surprised, should I?"

Doris laughed. "Lila knows everything. She works over at the sheriff's department."

Glenn's head rose quickly. His eyes flashed to mine and then away.

"It's nice to meet you, formally." I walked over and shook her hand. "And the name's Rosalie."

"And I'm Glenn." He stretched his back. "Oof. Would you mind if I sat down? I would love to finish this article, but at my age it's hard to stand too long."

Lila patted the chair next to her. "Take a load off."

"Thank you," Glenn said and eased into the chair. He adjusted his bow tie. "Is it Lila?"

"As in *Dee*lilah."

"What exactly do you do at the sheriff's department?" Glenn settled in and crossed his legs.

"Oh, I do everything from answering the phone to typing reports into the computer to making the coffee."

"A jack-of-all-trades, then. Or should I say *Lila*-of-all-trades."

"That's me." She gave an exaggerated nod. "I could retire if I want, but I like it. Besides, Joe needs me."

"She also gets to spend a lot of time right here," Doris said.

"You got that right," Lila said. "But the way I look at it, when you got me around, who needs a newspaper."

"Indeed," Glenn said. He was grinning broadly.

TWENTY

After reading through more posts on Megan's wall, I signed off as Megan and back on as me. I could only get through a few of the messages at a time before the heartbreak expressed by her grieving friends overwhelmed me. Annie, I thought. Think about Annie. I clicked on my home page and checked to see if she had commented on my most recent status update.

Rosalie Hart
Is looking forward to seeing Annie over Thanksgiving and hosting dinner for my new friends.

Annie Hart
I can't wait, Mom!!!!! :)

Rhonda Pendleton
I hope one of those new friends is spending the night.

"Oh my gosh," I said and quickly hovered over the upper-right corner of Rhonda's comment, clicked "delete post," and prayed Annie hadn't seen it.

"He's letting her drive my car." Annie slammed a spoon down on the dining room table. "The Volvo is *my* car."

"I'm sorry, honey." I bathed the turkey with a baster full of juices. It wasn't in the All-Clad roaster I usually used. That was in Chevy Chase. This turkey was nestled in an aluminum-foil pan from the grocery store and I suspected it would tumble to the floor at some point.

A knife slapped down. I worried about Charlotte's antique cherry table. "Why doesn't she have her own stupid car?"

I closed the oven door and turned to face her. "Honey, I know you're upset, but—"

"Oh, Mom . . ." Annie slumped into a chair and buried her face in her hands. Her back heaved with sobs. I sat next to her and pulled her into my arms.

"I hate him," she said. "He's ruined everything."

We sat there, rocking, for what seemed like most of the afternoon. I petted her hair until the tears finally slowed. "I'm so sorry," I said. "Oh, baby, I'm so, so sorry."

Eventually she sat up and rubbed her eye with a knuckle. "So, who are these people coming to dinner?"

"Friends from my writing class."

"Mom, you aren't really going to stay here, are you? Aren't you going back home?"

"Probably. But not yet. Right now I'm just trying to survive."

"So . . . your friends?"

I walked over to the counter and began peeling a russet potato. I described Sue, Glenn, and Tony to Annie. They were all coming to my house for Thanksgiving dinner. Glenn's sons were visiting their in-laws and Sue couldn't afford a plane ticket to California. Or so she said. And Tony had a sister in Boston, but she was going to join friends in Cape Cod.

"We sound like the island of misfit toys," I said.

"Seriously, Mom, this is a little nuts. I mean, I'm sure your friends are fine, but, well . . ." Annie folded a napkin and sighed. "I just wish we were with Dad and Grandma."

Oh, how I wanted to fall apart right then and there—tell her how I had to buy a new turkey baster, how my mother had always taken out the giblets and innards that triggered my gag reflex, how my hands had grown chapped and icy because I hadn't thawed the turkey soon enough. I missed my dining room and the ivory linen tablecloth with the fall harvest inlay that I used every November. But I wouldn't. I couldn't. I had to be strong for Annie. This was our first holiday since Ed and I separated. "I think you'll like my friends," I said. "And you and I are together. That's what matters most."

Annie stood slowly and walked over to the china cabinet. "I can't believe my parents are getting divorced."

The delectable scents of Thanksgiving—roasted turkey, apple sausage dressing, pumpkin pie, baked rolls—permeated the air. We had finished dinner, but lingered in the candlelight, the sleepiness induced by our copious meal softening our voices. I had managed to successfully set my worries about the sheriff aside. If he showed up now, I would offer him some turkey and stuffing. Maybe I could win him over. Maybe I was going about this all wrong.

"More pie, anyone?" I asked.

"No, thank you," Glenn said. He groaned and patted his stomach. "I am beyond satiated."

"I wouldn't mind a little more of that wine," Tony said. "That's damn good wine."

"You mean the bottle you brought?" I said.

Tony laughed and walked over to the sideboard. He pulled the stopper from the bottle. "Anyone else?"

"Can I have some more, Mom?" Annie asked.

I started to speak but Tony said, "Absolutely." An impish grin appeared on Annie's face. Tony looked over at me. "Surely you don't think the kid has never had alcohol? I know you're naive, Princess, but come on."

"You think I'm naive?" I asked, feeling a little hurt.

"In a good way," Annie said and held her glass out to Tony. "You always think the best of people."

"Is there a lot of drinking at Duke?" Sue asked.

"Oh, yeah. It's college, right? The problems start when everyone hooks up. The drama is unbelievable."

"Hooks up?" Glenn said.

Annie sipped her wine and avoided Glenn's eyes. Her cheeks flushed a bright red.

"She means fooling around—casual sex," Tony said. "Or as the kids like to say, friends with benefits."

"Good Lord," Glenn said. "Now *I* feel naive."

"Hey, Pops," Tony said. "You never know, maybe there's some hooking up going on at Waterside after bingo. You could be missing out."

Glenn leveled his eyes at Tony. His bow tie was tight around his neck. Silence carpeted the table. Just when I was about to say something, a sound escaped from Glenn. His shoulders shook and a roar of laughter spilled out. "Ha!" he said. "Ha!"

Glenn's face reddened, his eyes squeezed shut. His laughter was as contagious as a yawn, and soon we were laughing along with him. Tears trickled from Sue's delicate eyes, and the width of Annie's smile soothed my heart.

After several more eruptions, Glenn removed his glasses and dabbed his eyes with his napkin. "Well, Mr. Ricci, you certainly know how to dumbfound a man, I'll grant you that."

"Whew," Tony said. "You had me worried there for a minute, Pops."

"I can't laugh anymore." Sue sipped some water. "My stomach is aching."

I watched Annie and my friends from my place at the head of the table. It felt strange to be seated there. I had taken over all of the tasks that were traditionally Ed's: carving the turkey, uncorking the wine, saying the blessing. I was relieved to see Annie's smile, her eyes dancing with delight at the recent outburst of frivolity. She was seated across from Sue and had been able to encourage Sue's shy but witty sense of humor. Tony was instantly enamored with Annie, calling her "Mini-Me" because the two of us were so similar. Their playful banter had kept the rest of us entertained. And Glenn treated her as a young lady. I suspected he was trying out his grandfather shoes again. It would be a Thanksgiving miracle if my Annie was the impetus for Glenn to reunite with his family.

"I'd like to make a toast," I said and lifted my glass. "To . . ." A crack sounded from the window behind me. Glass shattered and something whizzed by my ear, drilling into the wall behind Annie. Plaster sprayed through the room.

"What the . . ." Tony grabbed Sue around the waist and pulled her under the table.

"What *was* that?" Annie slapped her hands over her ears.

"A freaking bullet!" Tony cried. "Get down!" He reached up and pulled her under the table.

Glenn crouched over his plate, covering his head with his arms. His elbow bumped a glass. Red wine sloshed over the white table-cloth like a curling wave.

"Mom," Annie called from under the table. "Mom! Are you okay?"

I nodded slowly.

"Rosalie . . ." Glenn said. "Get under the table. There could be a second shot."

"Okay." I scooted out of my chair, feeling as if I were moving in slow motion. Tony grabbed my hand and pulled me down to the floor.

"What's happening?"Annie was trembling.

"I don't know," I said, trying to steady my voice.

We waited, motionless in our huddled positions for what seemed like a lifetime, anticipating a second shot. I stared at Glenn's shoes, noticing he must have shined them for our dinner. I reached up and touched my ear. I had felt the breeze . . . I could be dead.

"Maybe we should call the police," Sue said.

"Good idea." I was grateful for a task. I crawled out from under the table and stood. The candles flickered violently from the night air rushing through the punctured window pane. I looked over at Glenn. The thin strands of gray hair that stretched across his scalp had fallen into eyes. His glasses were askew and he had a dollop of whipped cream on his nose.

"Are you all right?" I handed him a napkin.

"Yes," he said in a quiet voice. "I believe I'm still in one piece."

He sat up and cleaned his glasses with the napkin. "Are you calling 9-1-1?"

"If I must." I fetched my cell phone from the kitchen. "Although I'm not sure the sheriff will be filled with concern."

Tony, Sue, and Annie emerged from under the table in various forms of disarray. "Mom," Annie said. "Mom . . ." She was still shaking.

Tony put his arm around her. "Hey, kiddo, we're okay."

She covered her face with her hands and began to cry. I hurried over and squeezed her arm. "Let's all go into the living room."

Glenn stood and went to where the bullet had landed in a milkmaid's cart on the toile wallpaper. "Looks like a high-speed rifle."

"Don't take it out," Tony said. "The police will want to see it."

Sue and Annie fell into the sofa, looking small and pale. Tony began pulling all the drapes closed. Glenn paced the floor. I focused on keeping my shivers at bay while I tapped on the three numbers. When I finished talking with the sheriff's department, I said, "They're sending a deputy right out." It occurred to me then that they said deputy, not sheriff. He wasn't coming because he was probably on my property right now with a rifle. "I'll make some tea," I said.

"To hell with that," Tony said. "You have something stronger?"

"Yes," I said. "Better idea." I went into the dining room, blew out the candles, and balled up the wine-soaked tablecloth.

"Rosalie," Glenn said in a lowered voice. "Do you think . . ."

"I don't know." I walked over to the china cabinet and removed several liqueur glasses. I turned to face him. "If it is what you're suggesting, then it only proves we're right." I handed him some of the glasses. Our eyes met. "I won't be intimidated," I said. "But I want the rest of you to back out. This is mine to handle."

"Slow down, Rosalie. Let's be rational."

"There is nothing rational about a gunshot through a dining room window. Glenn, please, I can't get out of this, but the rest of you can. No one knows you're involved."

"But you aren't locked into anything, either. No one will be hurt if you drop this investigation."

"Glenn . . ." I tried to stop my teeth from chattering. "Someone already has. A young woman was murdered." I walked into the kitchen, opened a bottle of port, and started filling the glasses. "I'm just so sick of injustice and selfishness. You may never understand why, but I have to make this right."

"My dear." Glenn peered over his glasses. "This is very serious."

I took a long sip of port and said, "So am I."

TWENTY-ONE

Tony Ricci
Ever figure out what son-of-a-bitch hunter took a shot at us? Other than that, it was a great dinner. Hope Annie got home okay.

Nick Angeles
My first visit to your wall and someone is shooting at you? You are full of surprises. Thank you for becoming my friend. What, no photo?

Tyler extended his measuring tape and held it up to the shattered window pane. "We'll have to special order a replacement—this house being in the historic trust and all."

I watched him through the wide archway separating the dining room from the kitchen. I looked down at the counter and carved a slice of turkey from what remained of Thursday's meal. "The police said it was just a rogue bullet from a deer hunter." I opened the refrigerator in search of condiments. I grabbed some cranberry preserves and kicked the door shut. "But why were they so close to the house?"

"Probably tracking a wounded deer."

"There's no sign of a deer out there." I spread the preserves on a thick slice of bread. "The police weren't even interested in finding out who it was. I mean, he could have killed one of us."

Tyler fit a piece of heavy plastic over my window and duct-taped it in place. "Did they look around outside?"

"For about a nanosecond." I sawed the mounding sandwich in half. "Do you know the deputies didn't even take the bullet with them? I have it. It's in a drawer."

Tyler stood in the dining room, a puzzled look on his face.

"What are you thinking?"

"How many people were here the other night?"

"Six, including me. Why? I still have plenty of turkey."

"That's not it. I just can't figure out how a stray bullet missed all six of you. It's not a big room."

I was suddenly very aware of my heart thudding in my chest. I was still reeling from the questions that had racked my brain all night. Had someone intended to miss our heads? Was this another warning or was someone actually trying to kill me? The plastic over the window snapped, looking like an expanded lung, and deflated again.

Tyler walked into the kitchen and stood next to me. "I've never asked you about your husband. He isn't one of those crazy guys, is he?"

"No." I shook my head. "Ed hates guns. And he isn't obsessed with me. He's obsessed with someone much younger than me."

Tyler nodded. "I'll go into town after lunch and order the glass."

"Do you think you could pick up a few 'no trespassing' signs?"

"That won't be too popular around here," Tyler said as he washed his hands vigorously. "Your woods are prime hunting grounds."

"Yes, well, I have zero interest in being their prey." I placed the sandwich on a plate and added some potato chips and a pickle. "Annie was totally freaked out. I'll be lucky if I can get her to come back for Christmas." I peered back into the dining room. The toile wallpaper's pastoral scene was now scarred by violence, as if war had fallen on the once carefree people.

"Do you want me to fix that hole in your wall when I get back?"

"Yes," I said. "That would help."

He eyed me. "I'll ask around when I'm in town—see if there were any drunk guys out hunting yesterday. Somebody might have seen him."

"Thank you, Tyler."

"You know you sure have run into some bad luck since you moved in, what with the dead body and now this."

"Do you think it's some kind of sign?" I crossed my arms in defiance.

"All I'm saying is . . ." He munched on a potato chip and stared out the window. "It used to be a whole lot quieter around here."

TWENTY-TWO

It was our final memoir class and we agreed to meet thirty minutes early to ensure we had time to discuss the investigation. Even Tony arrived on time.

I took a sip of the chai tea Sue brought for us. It was the perfect accompaniment to the maple and walnut scones I made.

Tony picked up a second scone. "Your husband must be fat."

"Ed? He has about five percent body fat."

"I knew I hated the guy."

"By the way, Tony . . ." I gave him a sideways glance. "How was that article you read. You know the one, '*Four Things You Do That Kill Her Sex Drive*'?"

Tony paled. "How the hell do you know about that?"

Sue dusted crumbs from her hands. "It was in the news feed on Facebook. You read it in *Men's Health*."

"It was in the news feed?" Tony's eyes widened. "You mean everyone *saw* that?"

"If you like something it goes in the news feed, too," Sue said. "You can change the settings. Do you want me to help you?"

"Heck, yeah," Tony said. He shook his head.

Glenn crossed his arms. "So, the World Wide Web knows who we like, what we read . . ."

"Who you date . . ." Sue said. "Where you live, what you buy, what you search, what songs you listen to. There are no more secrets. I mean, none."

"Not to change the subject, but can I ask you all something?" I leaned forward. "Are you certain you want to stay involved in this investigation? Because after Thanksgiving, I think we all know this has become dangerous."

"But it was just a hunter tracking a deer," Sue said. "It was very scary, but it was just an accident. Right?"

"What are you getting at, Princess?"

"Tyler mentioned that considering how many of us were seated in that small room, it's a miracle none of us got shot."

"Well, yes," Sue said, a trace of panic in her voice. "But that's a good thing."

"Princess?" Tony's eyes narrowed.

"What if it was deliberate? What if someone missed hitting us intentionally?"

"Like who?" Tony said.

"Someone who wanted us to stop looking into Megan's death."

I swallowed hard. "Don't you think it's odd that the sheriff didn't show up that night?"

"It was a holiday," Sue said. "He probably had the day off." Her voice had risen and I worried I was scaring her. But maybe that was what I should do—scare her enough to keep her safe.

"Rosalie," Glenn said, a stitch forming between his eyebrows. "Are you saying you think the sheriff shot that bullet through the window?"

"I don't know. But I think it's a definite possibility."

"Or the professor," Tony said.

"Nick?"

Tony rolled his eyes. "He may be hot, Princess, but he's still a suspect."

"No, he's not that hot," I said. "I just can't picture him with a high-speed rifle."

"Whoever it was," Glenn said, "it means we're on the right track."

"But someone could get hurt." I spun my cup around and avoided their eyes. "Or worse."

"You're not getting rid of me that easily." Tony leaned in. "We're in this together. And if someone wants to mess with me, I say bring it on."

"Tony, this is serious."

"And what makes you think I'm not?"

"I don't care, either," Sue said. "We have to see this through. And if someone wants to intimidate us, well . . . well . . ." She tossed her shiny black hair off her shoulder. "Then I'm with Tony. Bring it on."

"Sue," I said, astonished. "Listen to you."

"I know. I don't know why, but there's something about this investigation that's emboldening me. A girl was murdered. This is very serious and we're all she has." Sue pulled her phone out of her purse.

It was a different bag. This one was a Dooney & Bourke. Super-pricey. She glanced at her phone, set it down, and looked up. "So?"

"Why do you have such a cheap phone?" Tony said. "I thought everyone your age had an iPhone or a Samsung."

"Budget," she said.

"My point is," I continued, "I don't want anyone to get hurt. One life is enough."

"If you're trying to scare us off," Tony said, "you can see it isn't working."

I jumped when Jillian dropped her books on the desk. She scowled over her low glasses. I think it was the first time she had ever truly looked us in the eye.

"We can't do this again," Sue whispered. "Especially now. Facebook only."

"I have evaluation forms," Jillian said. "But before I hand them out, I want you to know that I need this job. It's part of my graduate assistantship and if I lose that I won't be able to afford school. You know, it's not my fault if you didn't get anything out of this class."

We exchanged guilty looks. "You've done a fine job, Jillian," I said. "I have learned a great deal by taking this class."

She picked up the papers. "You didn't write one word."

"That doesn't mean I didn't get anything out of the class."

"And what about you?" Her gaze shifted to Glenn. "You had one hundred pages when we started. And now you *still* have one hundred pages."

"And they are a better one hundred than they were."

Jillian rolled her eyes. "Why did you people even take this class?" When no one spoke, she stood and placed an evaluation on Sue's desk. "I hope you finish your memoir," she said. "It's very good."

"Thank you," Sue said. "I will. I've just been very busy lately. I have a big assignment I'm working on." She glanced over her shoulder and smiled.

Tony picked up his pencil as she set the form in front of him. "You really had something." She glared down at him.

"You know what, Miss Jillian? I haven't wasted a minute. I may not have finished my memoir, but I made the most excellent friends."

TWENTY-THREE

Janice Tilghman Christmas party, rose red. Small and intimate. You're coming.

Intimate? The dentist. But I was married. And as hard as it was for people to understand, my heart was still tied to Ed's.

Rosalie Hart Not really up for it but thanks. I'm hibernating this Christmas.

Janice Tilghman I've already printed the place cards.

Rosalie Hart Will the mob be there?

Janice Tilghman You realize we're on FB?

Rosalie Hart Shoot. I'll delete.

Janice Tilghman My dentist will be there, but I have you seated between a guy from the college, Nick Angeles, and Trevor. Good conversations. And the seat of honor.

Nick? I would be able to get some information from him at last. And without going out for a drink.

Rosalie Hart What's the dress code?

The night of the party I put on a simple above-the-knee black dress, my mother's pearls, and a pair of three-inch pumps Annie had grown tired of. As I wobbled down the narrow wooden stairs, I worried the heels would leave divots in the pine floors.

I was startled to see Tyler in the kitchen, reading the sports page and holding a steaming mug of coffee. "You're still here," I said.

He raised his head and sized me up. My stomach flipped a little. Tyler had never seen me dressed up.

"I'm going to a dinner party at Janice Tilghman's," I said.

"Ah, Janice," he said. "Always a good time."

"Do you know her?"

"She used to boss me around in elementary school."

"Me, too."

"Who's your date?"

"No one," I said quickly.

"Doesn't sound like Janice." He set his mug in the sink, closed the paper, and creased it along the fold.

"Actually . . ."

"I knew it." His green eyes danced. Dimples indented his cheeks.

"There's a guy named Dr. Laughlin. He's not my date. But she wants us to meet. Do you know him?"

"Of course I know him. It's Cardigan." He crossed his arms. "He seems like a nice enough guy."

"He doesn't have a chance with me. I'm married, plain and simple."

"She has good intentions. But I tend to avoid her just for that reason." Tyler picked up his cap and headed for the door. "Good luck."

The door clicked shut. I waited. It opened again. Dickens was at my feet. "Hey," Tyler called. "What do you think you're doing? Get over here."

Dickens didn't move.

Tyler shifted his weight. "I said come on, boy." He slapped his thigh. "We're going home." He looked over at me, visibly annoyed.

I smiled and patted Dickens's head. "Go on, baby. Time to go home." Dickens stood and trotted over to Tyler.

"Good night," I sang out as the door thudded shut.

Phillip Laughlin, DDS, was Poligripped to my side. I don't know how he knew who I was. Wait. Scratch that. I had to be the only unrecognizable person in the room. He approached as soon as I acquired my drink. He was shorter than me, especially in my heels, and was dressed in a yellow sweater vest and a Christmas tie with a repeated pattern of Santa sledding down a hill.

We were standing in Janice's spacious living room. A glowing fire popped and crackled in the wide fireplace next to us. The mantel was packed with pine roping and strings of sparkling white lights. The scent of burning firewood filled the air.

Janice walked over and literally pushed us together, a flat hand on each of our lower backs. "Now the party is getting started," she said. "How's your drink, Doc? You ready for a refill?"

"Yes, I believe I am."

"Vodka tonic, no lime?" Janice said.

"Yes," Phil said. "How do you remember these things?"

"It's my job," Janice winked. "So, Phil, did you know Rose Red is living in Barclay Meadow? Just moved in. You should drop in sometime." Janice looked back at me. "She's always making bread. I think she could use some company."

"That's a lovely home," he said. "I'm just two miles closer to town. We're practically neighbors."

"It used to be lovely," I said. "I'm afraid it's fallen into disrepair."

"But you're there now."

"Focus on the now." I sipped my wine. "I don't know how long I'll be staying."

"Rose Red isn't usually this negative, are you?" Janice gave me a meaningful look. "That's why she needed to come to a party." She cocked her head, took Phil's glass, and strode away.

Phil stared at me like a lost puppy. I filled with dread. I wasn't ready for this. Not with him or with anyone. I wanted to be home in bed in flannel pajamas and the remote. I drank my wine in small frequent sips as if it were a pacifier. This was my first Christmas without Ed. I was missing him more that ever. We loved Christmas parties and knew how to work a room like a couple of lobbyists. Now I was the yin without the yang. Hollowed out in the middle.

"So . . ." I forced a smile. "Is it an occupational hazard to check out people's teeth? I mean, I had some of the spanakopita. There was a lot of spinach."

"Your teeth are fine, Rose Red," he said.

"Oh, that's not my name," I said quickly.

"You don't want me to call you 'Rose Red'?" He looked crestfallen.

"I prefer Rosalie." I finished my wine and looked around the room for more. I spotted a server walking toward us, scooped up a glass from her tray, and took a sip. The wine was dry and buttery. Janice really did know how to pick a chardonnay. "You have very white teeth," I said.

"Yes, I know." He stared off. Crap. I hurt his feelings.

"I guess I shouldn't assume dentists want to talk about teeth." I tried to get him to look at me. "That's probably the last thing you want to talk about." He scanned the room. Probably wondering when Janice would return with his cocktail. "Phil," I said. "Were you ever married?"

He finally made eye contact again. "My wife died three and a half years ago."

"I'm sorry." I placed a hand on his arm. "How?"

"Heart attack." His eyes brimmed with tears. "She had it in her sleep. I couldn't save her."

"How tragic," I said.

He nodded. "I can't remember the last time I went to a party by myself." He sniffled and rubbed his nose with the back of his hand.

"Neither can I," I said. "Janice is right—we do have a lot in common."

"You're a widow?"

"No. But I'm going through a divorce."

He shook his head. "Not the same."

"Grief is grief, Phil."

"Your situation is much different." He straightened his spine and rolled his shoulders back. "If Lori were alive, we would still be married. We were going on thirty years." He lifted his chin. "I don't believe in divorce."

Neither do I, I thought. I studied him—his sudden arrogant stance. That's how I used to be. A flicker of judgment when I learned someone was divorced. I was like him—so certain it would never happen to me. I felt wretched. It was all I could do to not run out the door and go home.

Phil cleared his throat. "I think I'll go find my drink. Janice must have gotten lost in her own massive house." I watched him go.

An older gentleman in a tuxedo stepped into the center of the room and rang a delicate silver bell with a gloved hand. I followed my fellow party-goers to a set of heavy wooden doors, where a uniformed woman held a leather book with a seating chart. She asked for my name and pointed to my seat.

The table glowed from two large silver candelabras, casting the room in a soft gauzy light. A white linen tablecloth was topped with creamy dishes rimmed with gold. Small crystal vases filled with white roses were nestled among sprigs of pine and holly.

"Oh, Janice," I said. "It's so beautiful. I feel like I'm in Downton Abbey."

"Thank you," she said. "Now, go sit down and stay out of trouble."

Nick was in the seat next to mine, talking with the woman on his other side. Just as Janice had promised, I was seated to the right of Trevor, her husband, the seat of honor. A gold-embossed card listed the menu for the evening and the wine to accompany each course. A server had already begun to fill champagne flutes. Trevor pulled out my chair so that I could sit.

As I unfolded my linen napkin, Janice tapped a teaspoon against her champagne glass and stood. "Okay, everybody. Welcome! I want to make a toast to our guest of honor this evening." Her eyes zeroed in on me.

No, I mouthed.

"Some of you may not know that our newest neighbor is actually an old friend of mine. Rosalie has been spending summers in Cardigan since we were little girls and I'm thrilled to have her back. So if you could all join me in welcoming our newest friend and neighbor, Rosalie Hart."

Everyone raised their glasses. Janice knew exactly what she was doing. It was protocol for me to return the toast. So that's how it would be. Tit for tat. When the cheers and clanking died away, I hesitated. All eyes were on me. I pushed my chair back and stood. "Thank you, Janice, for the lovely toast and for including me in your elegant dinner. I look forward to getting to know all of you better and hope there are many future friends at this table." Janice watched me carefully. "I must say, for a small town, there is a lot to learn and a lot more excitement than I had ever imagined." I hesitated. What was I saying? Curse you Janice. I raised my glass. "Here's to Janice, her gracious hospitality, stunning home and her . . . unmatched wit."

I sat down quickly and pressed my napkin over my lap. The professor clinked his glass on mine. I looked over at him. His face was

close. "Hello, again." His cologne was a delicious mix of musk, vanilla, and a hint of citrus.

"Hi." I downed my champagne.

I spent the first three dinner courses talking with Trevor. His
family had lived on the Eastern Shore for generations and he de-
lighted in telling me lots of little-known history of the area. He talked
about his love of hunting and the outdoors and described in detail
how he had begun to build his very own skipjack, the classic Chesapeake Bay boat used for oyster dredging. The woman to his left
joined the conversation and knew a lot about the classic boats. With
nothing to add to the conversation, I looked down at my crabcake.

"I thought you would never stop talking to them," Nick said.

"They lost me at 'skipjack.'"

"Good." He winked. "I didn't realize you and Janice were such
good friends."

"Like she said . . ." I looked up at him. "We go way back."

"And is the man you were talking with earlier your date?"

"No." I held my wineglass by the stem and aligned it with my
spoon. "Janice is playing matchmaker. But this one was pretty much
a disaster." I shoved my hands in my lap. "That chemistry you're
studying? Dr. Phil and I came up short."

"Dr. Phil?" His face danced with delight.

"Oops." I placed my fingers over my mouth. "I didn't mean to
say that. I've been thinking it. I just didn't mean to say it aloud."

He rested his arm on the back of my chair. "I love it." He signaled to the waiter standing in the doorway. He approached and
leaned an ear toward Nick. "Bring me a vodka," Nick said. "Grey
Goose with a lime. Not too much ice." The man nodded and walked
away. Although most of the crabcake sat uneaten on his place, a trio
of empty glasses was before him—cocktail, wine, champagne. I
looked up into those Hershey's Kisses eyes. They were beginning

to droop. Maybe this was an opportunity. Get him to talk while he was well lubricated.

"Nick, I've been meaning to ask you about the study. How's it going?"

"Very well." He smiled. His arm was still on my chair. "Now that the grant is in place, my students are administering the questionnaires."

"Did you ever fill that internship?"

He frowned. "Why do you keep asking me about that?"

"I was interested in it, remember?"

"You're too late."

"You found someone?"

"President Carmichael found me a graduate student to run the statistics. No need for an intern."

"Really? What department is she in?"

"*He* is a math major." Nick sipped his water. "It will be better this way for a lot of reasons."

"What exactly are you asking in the questionnaires?"

"The first segment is designed to analyze visual triggers to sexual desire." He played with a strand of my hair. "We show our subjects a variety of photos and gauge their heart rates."

"To see if we're like animals, right?" I said. "The female bird picks the male with the most impressive display?"

"Ah—that she does. She wants the best genes for her babies."

"Yes," I said. "But too much plumage can make for a lousy husband."

He laughed heartily. "You're funny. Do you realize that?"

I sipped my wine. "I have my moments."

Our dinner plates were removed and replaced with dessert wine in small crystal glasses and a round of glazed crème brûlée.

"I'm also interested in the differences in sexual triggers according to age and time of life." His arm was still behind my chair. My scalp tingled as he continued to fondle my hair.

"I believe our triggers change over time," he continued. "Now that I'm no longer looking for the best mother for my children, I'm attracted to other things besides the traditional hip-to-waist ratio." He gave my body a once-over. "Although a lovely figure never goes unnoticed."

"Oh. . . ." My face warmed.

He leaned in and sniffed the lock of hair between his fingers. "Scent is an important trigger, too. Don't you think?"

I flattened my back against the chair. He was so close, I could smell the alcohol on his breath. The waiter returned with a tumbler of vodka.

"And let's not forget taste," he continued. "That's an important one, too, especially for men."

My mouth fell open.

Nick dipped a spoon into the crème brûlée and slid it into his mouth. I watched as he slowly removed it, seemingly savoring every flavor. He shut his eyes. "Mmm," he said.

I cleared my throat. "You were saying there are age differences in desire?"

He set his spoon on the tablecloth, looked over at me, and smiled. "Yes. But not just after child-bearing years. For instance, a girl who isn't in the market for a husband yet will be attracted to a different sort of boy. Doesn't every girl have to have at least one 'bad boy' in her life?"

"Of course," I said. "The guy in the leather jacket."

"They don't always wear leather jackets," he said.

"True. Some don't wear jackets at all." I eyed his silk shirt. "But mine wore a denim jacket and smoked unfiltered Camels. He had long, lovely hair and sang Cat Stevens songs to me."

"There you go. Funny again." He picked up his glass and took a long swig of vodka.

"Time for carols around the piano." Janice stood before us. "Rose Red? Dr. Nick? You think you can break it up long enough to sing?"

"Of course." I scooted my chair back.

Nick reached for my hand. "I have thoroughly enjoyed our conversation, Rosalie."

"Yes." I stood and pulled my hand from his. "I've enjoyed it, as well. I can't believe dinner is over so soon."

I followed Janice to the piano. "You go from one doc to the other," she hissed.

"They couldn't be any more different from one another." I tried to keep up in my heels. "Opposite ends of the man spectrum, if there is such a thing."

She stopped and turned around. I almost ran into her. "Dr. Nick is a womanizer," she said. "He has a reputation."

"What kind of reputation?" I said. "Married women? Younger women?" I hesitated. "Students?"

"All of the above."

"Really? *Students?*"

"Oh, yeah. But the college keeps it quiet. They're trying to rein him in."

"Good luck with that."

She started walking again. I tried to hide my giddiness at the information she had just disclosed. She stopped abruptly and turned to face me again. "You know your problem, Rose Red?"

"Which one? I have many."

"You have to stop reacting to everything. You're not a victim, you know? You've got to be *pro*active." I looked up at her. "If you're only reacting to things, you give away your power. Get it?"

"Janice, I'm really trying. It's just a rough time of year."

She rolled her eyes. "What am I going to do with you?"

After the first round of "Deck the Halls" I headed for the coat closet. I wondered if Janice would consider this being proactive. I looked back at the party. Dr. Phil was arm in arm with another woman. *Fa la la la la . . .* His teeth really were perfect.

I shut the door and headed to my car, concentrating hard on not twisting my ankle in the gravel.

"Oh." I stopped abruptly. Nick was leaning against my car, his ankles crossed, his hands in the pockets of his dark wool overcoat.

"That's my car."

"I know," he said.

"Of course you do." My breath crystalized in a puffy silver cloud. "There is no anonymity in Cardigan, Maryland."

"There's nothing anonymous about this car." He patted the door. "Something tells me a woman who drives a car the color of lipstick has another side. A side I think I would like."

My heart thudded in my chest. Why wouldn't he move? What was he doing? "Well . . ." I faked a yawn. "I'm really tired." I fished my keys out of my clutch.

"What's the rush?" Before I could speak, Nick slipped his hands into my coat, held my hips, and pulled me to him. His lips, cool from the December air, were on mine.

I pushed him away. "What are you doing?"

"What I've been thinking about doing all night."

I placed my hand on my forehead. "You were?"

He stepped closer. "You should button your coat. You'll catch a chill." His fingertips brushed against the wool as he slowly buttoned my coat. My nerve endings, on red alert, acknowledged every point of contact.

"There," he said. "All buttoned up. You okay to drive?"

"Yes," I said. "Are you?"

He cocked his head. His eyes glistened in the dim light of Janice's portico. "Shall I follow just to be sure?"

"No. I'm fine. Really." I waited for him to move.

"You're never going to take my class, are you?"

I shrugged. "I don't know. Why did you say that?"

"I don't think you ever intended to. I think you just wanted to meet me."

"No." I stepped back. My heels crunched the gravel. "I was interested."

"You," he chuckled, "are a lousy liar."

A small chime from my phone sounded in my purse, signaling my connection to the rest of the world. He stepped out of the way.

As I climbed into my car, he leaned in and nuzzled my ear, his breath hot against my skin. "You have secrets," he whispered. He backed away and I grabbed the door. "Till next time, *ma chérie*," he called. My hands trembled as I fumbled with my keys. At last the engine roared awake. I looked out at Nick. He was watching me, a thin, sly smile on his lips.

As I drove the short distance home, I tried to slow my heart rate. Maybe Janice was right. I've got to get some control. What if he had climbed in the car? What if he had followed me? I clicked on the blinker. As I started to turn onto the lane, a pair of headlights appeared in the rearview mirror. My nerves went into lockdown. No one traveled this road unless they had a good reason, especially this late at night. Nick? Oh my gosh, I lived alone. He could follow me into the house. He said I had secrets. He knows I know about Megan. I parked under a cypress tree and killed the lights. I waited in the moonless night. An owl shrieked and dipped low over the roof of my car. I instinctively hunched my shoulders. I waited, but the lights never reappeared.

TWENTY-FOUR

Nick Angeles	It was lovely to see you last night. Let me know the next time you need help buttoning your coat.
Glenn B	Birdie's shoe store is presenting me with a wealth of information. It seems our good sheriff and the college president are very well connected.
Tony Ricci	You're supposed to be hooking up with the bingo ladies. Not hanging out in a shoe store.
Rosalie Hart	I'm here. Keep talking. Remember I saw Carmichael and Wilgus having lunch one day and then they were talking at the party.
Tony Ricci	So why would the Pres and the cop be so chummy?
Glenn B	I believe the college is behind the sheriff's willing-ness to close the case so quickly. They want to keep their safe, idyllic image and they want their star professor's reputation to remain intact. Just think, if word leaked out that he was sleeping with students or, even worse, murdered one, the scandal could ruin the college. Especially if the president knew and covered it up.
Rosalie Hart	If Nick did it once, he could do it again. And how would that look? Not only did they cover something up, they allowed him to kill again.

I stopped typing. I just said "kill again." I remembered Nick's kiss, his breath hot on my neck, his hands on my coat. *You have secrets,* he'd said.

Tony Ricci Speaking of Nick, as it seems we're referring to our sleazy professor now, is he really a friend of yours on FB?

Rosalie Hart It's for the investigation. But I'm not so sure it's a good idea.

Shelby Smith Rosalie, did you remove your initial posts about Megan?

Shoot. How could I be so careless?

Rosalie Hart I had confirmation Saturday night that Nick sleeps with students. We had dinner together at Janice's.

Tony Ricci Whoa, Princess. Watch out for that guy.

Rosalie Hart I know. He scares me a little. But I'll keep this friendship going. Anything else?

Glenn B Lila also told me there's a possibility Megan committed suicide. That's why the parents dropped the investigation.

Shelby Smith Was there a note?

Glenn B Don't know. I'm treading carefully with Lila. And Doris Bird is well-named. She watches me like a hawk. But I'm hoping to get a little information about the police report. By the way, everyone loved your bread, Rosalie. She's hoping for more.

Shelby Smith Rosalie, remember Megan's post on Facebook the day she died? It read, "Independence Day." Maybe she really did commit suicide. I can't believe we never considered that before.

Rosalie Hart I don't buy it. My gut says no. And how on earth do you drown yourself? I know the river current is strong but there were no rocks in her purse. I saw the evidence bag. I think the stepfather is manipu-

	lating this too. What is he covering up? Did he do something? Is he protecting Rhonda? We have to keep the focus on him too.
Tony Ricci	I've been looking into Bill Johnston. He sells insurance. Maybe I could see if he wants to sell me a policy.
Rosalie Hart	I know, but Tony, he's grieving. He's lost his only child.
Tony Ricci	I'm just looking for a policy. I need to see this guy face to face. I'll find out if he's hiding something.
Rosalie Hart	Be gentle, ok? Anything else?
Shelby Smith	I've been chatting on FB with Tim Collier, the friend of Megan's that jumped out at me. His posts on her wall were creepy. So now he's starting to pour his heart out to me.
Tony Ricci	Nice going, Suzy Q. btw why did you pick the name Shelby Smith?
Shelby Smith	It's not gender specific.
Glenn B	Nice work, everyone. Oh, can someone help me hunt down a Ural liberation front contact in Mafia Wars?

As soon as I signed off I clicked on my profile, scrolled down to my original first two posts, and clicked "delete post." I stared at the screen for a long time. Had he looked? Did he know?

I logged out and signed on as Megan. I scrolled through her friend list and there he was—the gap in his front teeth, a subdued, studious smile on his face. Oh, how I wished I could have a conversation with Megan. Help me, I thought. Point me in the right direction.

TWENTY-FIVE

Annie Hart

See you Christmas AM Mom! Love you!!!!!!!!!

I clicked "like."

Amy Levengood

Carols and Nog! Meet at the gazebo at 6. Dinner to follow at my house.

10 people like this

My heart sank. Amy was my best friend in Chevy Chase. Every year our neighborhood caroled together Christmas night, begging for spiked egg nog and warm appetizers. After carols, we gathered at my house, where I would serve a buffet of ham, potatoes au gratin, corn bread, cranberries, my signature homemade Caesar salad. I had collected enough ornaments over the years to decorate two full-size trees and I filled every available space with poinsettias, white pine roping, twinkling lights, and velvet ribbon. Christmas had always been my absolute favorite time of year. I loved the warm fires, the baking, the scent of pine throughout the house, the shopping, and, more than anything, the giving. I prided myself on finding the perfect gift for everyone on my list, remembering the hints and wishes dropped throughout the year.

I imagined Ed escorting Becky to Amy's, laughing with *my* neighbors, *my* friends, on *my* favorite night of the year. Had they chosen him over me? Isn't that what happened when a couple divorced—divvy up the friends along with the assets?

I clicked out of Facebook. Sometimes I wondered if I was better off not knowing how everyone's life was more fabulous and exotic than mine. Reading their posts was like watching cruise ships sail by while I remained stranded on a deserted island.

I noticed a bright red "1" in the envelope icon of my email. I opened it. Ed had written, "Call me."

Was he serious? He emails me to call him? I can hear it now . . .

Hi, Siri. Not sure if you remember I have a wife. But could you email her to call me?

Hi, Ed. Are you sure you want to talk to her? Isn't she your ex-wife now? Aren't you in love with someone else?

Other than the brief encounter in Durham that brought me to my knees, Ed and I had not spoken since the day he helped me arrange my belongings in the small trunk of my car. What little communication we had was conducted through our lawyers or an occasional email. My heart was tight in my chest as I continued to stare at his message. What did he want? It must be serious or he wouldn't have asked me to call. What if . . . what if he wanted me back? Was that his Christmas wish? And what would I say? I chipped off every trace of the crimson nail polish on my thumb as I waited for him to answer his phone.

"Rose," he said. "Thanks for calling."

"Of course," I said. I placed my hand over my heart. I had forgotten the sound of his voice—that whispery, deep, velvety voice. I pictured him at his desk in the study I had decorated so meticulously: a wide Biedermeier desk, the thick silk rug that warmed the honey-colored wood floors, two leather reclining chairs sharing a soft floor lamp, built-in bookshelves surrounding the fireplace. I even bought him a small Bose stereo so he could listen to classical music while he worked. He would be sitting in the padded leather desk chair right now, his glasses off, maybe massaging the bridge of his nose. His gray sideburns would be neatly trimmed, a light trace of Burberry cologne lingering in the room. Did he think of me when he noticed those extra touches I was so devoted to adding? Making him feel comfortable, settled, undistracted?

"Annie is here," he said. "I thought you would want to know she arrived safe and sound."

"Thanks," I said. "But I already know. She texted me when—"

"Oh, right. How could I have forgotten? You're the better parent. Of course she would tell you first."

"What?" I couldn't catch my breath. It was as though he had just sucker punched me in the gut. Although Ed and I had our disagreements, we never quibbled about Annie. Never. "Ed, why did you say that?"

"I just wasn't a good enough parent for you, was I? I never did things exactly the way you wanted. It was just a matter of time before—"

"Ed." I was trembling. "*You* are divorcing *me*. Have you forgotten?"

"That doesn't mean you weren't part of the problem."

I walked over to the window and stared out at the setting sun. It was mirrored in the river like Narcissus—absorbed in his own glorious image. "Why did you want me to call?"

"Rose, you have to admit you played a part in this."

"No, actually I don't." Tears constricted my throat, but I willed them back. "I honestly thought our marriage was good. I still do. I was happy, Ed. I'm sorry you weren't."

He was trying to rationalize this. If he could affix at least some of the blame on me, he could assuage what little guilt he was feeling. *I was an adulterer because we were both unhappy.* Okay, Rosalie, keep your head on straight. And don't play his game. I remembered Rhonda and her confidence. Divorce is freeing, she said. Maybe I can make my own rules—drive the car for a change.

"Here's the 411," I said.

"The *what*?"

"Your infidelity is what ended this marriage. You are responsible for making that choice and only you. Now, why exactly did you want to talk to me?"

He hesitated. "I called to see if Annie could come to your place tomorrow night."

"You mean Christmas Eve?"

"Well, yes, tomorrow is Christmas Eve," he said as if I were six.

"But she told us she wants to be in her own bed, see her friends, see her Christmas ornaments on the tree, the stocking my mother knitted for her hanging from the mantel."

He cleared his throat. "I haven't exactly gotten a tree."

"Oh, no. You haven't, you aren't . . . you can't do this to her, Ed. You can divorce me, but Annie?" I rested my forehead against the cool glass and closed my eyes. "Of course she can come here. Have her drive out in the afternoon."

"Don't you want to know why?"

"Absolutely not," I said. "And you find that stocking."

I have never hung up on anyone in my entire life. And every ingrained trace of a conscience told me not to, but as the mother lion in me roared to the surface, I knew if I didn't fight for Annie no one would. So when I heard Ed start to rationalize his behavior and almost say the dreaded "Rebecca," I looked down at the flour-encrusted button and clicked it off. For the next hour I nursed a mug of coffee and stared at the ringing phone. He must have been totally baffled. I always answered the phone. I would talk to telemarketers for fifteen minutes before I could end the conversation without hurting any feelings. But this was my child. Nobody messed with my child.

TWENTY-SIX

Did you have to buy the biggest tree on the lot?" Tyler said as he watched me try to yank my new purchase through the front door. Needles sprayed like confetti. I gave it another tug and managed to wedge it solidly in the doorway.

I let go. My leather gloves were sticky with pine sap. "I thought it would look nice in the living room by the French doors."

Tyler sipped from a coffee mug. "Looks like it's gonna stay right where it is."

The frigid morning air whistled through the gaps in the doorway. "You could at least give me a hand."

He sipped again. "Do you have a tree stand?"

"Tree stand?" I stared at the wedged tree. "I didn't even think about it."

Tyler set his mug down and slipped his hands into his back pockets. "You could always string some lights around it right there. Might look kind of nice from the road."

"Ha ha." I glared over at him. "Now, get over here and help me."

After a few agonizing moments, he walked over to his jacket and pulled out a pair of heavy work gloves. He wrapped his hands around the base of the tree. I stood in front of him and grabbed on to a narrower part of the trunk.

"I have it," he said.

"You can't do this by yourself." I braced my legs. "On the count of three: one . . . two . . ."

Tyler heaved and the tree broke free. I lost my balance and tumbled into him. It took me a moment to realize I was in his lap.

"*Pfft,*" he said. "Your hair is in my mouth."

"You didn't wait until I said three."

"I told you I didn't need any help."

I was covered in needles. I started to brush them away when I felt Tyler's hands firm on my waist. "Ready?"

"No."

"One, two . . ." Tyler lifted me as if I were made of feathers and stood me upright on the floor.

"Thank you," I said, feeling breathless. "Do you have something against the number three?" His hands were still on my waist. "You can let go now."

"Yes, ma'am." Tyler dusted off his jeans and walked back to the tree. "Where did you say you wanted this?" He hoisted the trunk onto his shoulder.

"I'll show you." He followed me into the living room. Needles brittled like rain. "Something tells me this poor tree has been on the lot for a while," I said.

He propped it against the wall. "Maybe you should have thought of that before Christmas Eve."

"It's for Annie." I pulled off my gloves. "She and her dad always picked out the tree. They would go out the first weekend in December and chop it down themselves. I thought he was going to do that again."

Tyler studied me. "This isn't an easy holiday for you, is it?"

I was touched. So far all of Tyler's insight into me had been a series of comments highlighting my ignorance or naiveté. "No, it isn't," I said. "They say the first year is the hardest. But I can't think about that now. I've got to be okay for Annie."

"I have an idea of what you're going through."

"Your wife?"

He nodded. "It was pretty hard that first year after she left."

I looked up. His eyelids were at half mast. His green eyes glowed with a compassion I had never witnessed. I was deeply touched.

He turned and stood before the tree. "The attic."

"What?"

"You might find a tree stand in the attic. And some ornaments, too. Miss Charlotte always had a tree. And just so you know." He peered back over his shoulder. "She always put it right where you want to put this one."

I smiled. It tickled me to finally see beneath Tyler's veneer of indifference. It takes time, I thought, to build safety. Especially between two veterans decorated with purple hearts.

Tyler eyed the spindly limbs. "It's really not a bad tree."

"You sound like Linus." I stood next to him and brushed some needles from his shoulder. "But maybe you're right. Sometimes a few flaws, a few scars, add to the charm, don't you think?"

"Maybe so," he said.

"So, what will you do tonight?"

"I don't put a whole lot of merit in the holidays."

"Then stay here with Annie and me. We can have a little party. I bought some eggnog. You could help us decorate the tree."

"No thanks," he said. "I'll head over to my sister's house in the morning." He looked down at his boots. "In case you hadn't noticed . . . most times I prefer to be alone."

"Oh, wait. I almost forgot." I picked up a wrapped gift from the desk. "For you."

He stared down at it. "I can't accept this."

"You have to. I'm your boss, remember?"

"I don't have a gift for you."

"I wasn't expecting one." I smiled. "I want to thank you for everything you've done to help me." I placed it in his hands. "So? Open it."

Tyler carefully peeled back the gold foil paper and looked down at a yellowed copy of *East of Eden.*

"I saw you were reading your own copy a few weeks ago." I opened the cover. "This one is a first edition. See? And it's signed."

"Where did you find this?" He looked up at me, bewildered.

"I've been going through Charlotte's things. I found it on the shelf in my bedroom. I've always loved this book, too."

Pain tensed his eyes.

"She loved you very much, didn't she? I never thought about it before. She must have considered you to be family. Like a son." I studied his face. "The son she never had."

He continued to look at me, but said nothing. He clutched the book to his chest with one hand.

"These past two years couldn't have been easy for you." I touched his arm. "I'm sorry if I made it worse in any way. You must still miss her so very much."

"I do." His jaw clenched.

"I'm sorry if I'm slow to get things. I feel as if I'm climbing out of a musty cave after a long hibernation. But I see now how important this farm, this house, and, most importantly, Charlotte, have been to you." I stepped back and hugged myself. "And I'm really glad you're here now."

Tyler looked down at the book and then back up at me. His eyes searched my face. "Thank you, Rosalie," he said in a hoarse voice.

That was the first time he said my name.

TWENTY-SEVEN

Annie arrived that afternoon in a foul mood. She dropped her Vera Bradley duffle in the foyer with a solid thud and announced, "My father is the Grinch who stole Christmas."

"Oh, Annie." I pulled her into my arms. "I'm so sorry about all of this." I held her tight. When she stepped back I studied her face. Her eyes were red. She'd been crying. Annie loved the holidays as much as me. Seeing her Christmas sparkle tarnished for the first time in her young life made my heart ache.

"I have eggnog," I said.

"Only if you spike it with a lot of rum." Annie stuffed her hands into her coat pockets and looked around the house. I had just removed a batch of apple cinnamon cookies from the oven. The buttery cinnamon aroma saturated the air. Christmas carols sang out from the living room. *Dashing through the snow . . .*

Annie rolled her eyes. It was fifty-five degrees outside, the sun burning bright on a cloudless day. "I'm going to take a shower." She picked up her bag and started up the stairs.

"When you're finished, we have to decorate my tree," I called after her. The stairs were particularly squeaky, announcing the age of this isolated old house with each of Annie's footsteps. I nibbled on a fingernail. Damn you, Ed. When Annie reached the top I called out, "I'll find that rum!"

When Annie finally appeared in the living room, she was scrubbed clean and wearing sweatpants and a Duke University women's rugby hoodie. She slid her finger over her phone, turned it sideways, and typed with her thumbs. A loud whoosh signaled her email had entered cyberspace.

"Merry Christmas," I said and handed her a mug of eggnog.

"Spiked?"

"Rum," I said. "That was a good idea."

She dropped her phone into the front pocket of her sweatshirt and accepted the mug. I watched as she eyed the tree. It had begun to list to one side and a new layer of needles littered the floor.

I put my arm around her. "It's like Charlie Brown's tree. It just needs a little love."

"A *little*?" she said, but she was smiling.

"Let me show you what I found." I walked over to a stack of boxes and lifted the lid of one. "Look at these ornaments."

"Wow," she said. "They're so old and beautiful."

"Shall we?"

Tyler was right about the attic. Every box had been neatly labeled, and not only did I find a tree stand, but boxes of antique ornaments, the glass so thin Annie and I handled them gingerly as we secured them onto the spindly branches.

After we finished the tree, we sat down to dinner by candlelight. I had made her favorite: eggplant Parmesan (with extra sauce) and Caesar salad. We shared a bottle of chianti and her cheeks glowed with a tint of pink as we ate. She smiled more as she caught me up on all the events in her life, filling in the details that I could never glean through Facebook. As I listened and laughed along, my heart swelled with love and pride for her. She was beautiful. She was resilient. We would survive this.

After dinner we curled up in front of the fire with mugs of hot chocolate and watched *A Christmas Carol,* with George C. Scott. "Maybe Dad will get visited by some ghosts tonight," Annie said and we burst into giggles. While admiring the tree, we decided to end the evening with *A Charlie Brown Christmas.* We sang along with "Hark! The Herald Angels Sing," tears streaming down both our faces. Once we turned off the television, I presented Annie with her empty stocking. She hung it on the solitary hook Tyler had drilled into the mantel and, as was our family tradition, said, "Happy Birthday, Jesus."

We hugged good night and I warned her to not come downstairs until the following morning. When her door clicked shut, I poured a glass of port and went about the house playing Santa. As I reached for her stocking, I thought about Ed. It had always been his job to stuff Annie's stocking. He even made the purchases and prided himself on the practicality of his choices—pens, rolls of tape, a printer cartridge, lip balm, a thick pair of mittens, and of course a foil-wrapped chocolate orange for heft. I don't know what Annie enjoyed more, the chocolate or the tightly wound bundle of cash he always tucked in the toe.

I placed one of Annie's packages under the tree. Needles sprinkled on to it. I wondered if Ed was thinking about us—missing our traditions. Was our house as warm and cozy without his wife and daughter? Then I realized. He wasn't there. That's why he had Annie come to Cardigan. He was avoiding any of those emotions and focusing on that woman. Did he buy her something expensive? Something sparkly in a robin's egg blue box wrapped with white silk ribbon?

I huffed out a sigh and fell into the sofa. The room was lit by the dying fire and the sparse lights draped on the tree. I hummed "Silent Night." It had been my favorite carol as a child. I thought about my brother, Oliver, my partner in crime when we would search for the hidden presents. I longed for my mother. I went to all the sad places and cried and sang and sipped more port. Then I doused the fire and my tears, as well, combed my hands through my hair, and declared the wallowing was over. I was going to give Annie the Christmas vacation she deserved.

For the next six days I did exactly that. We took the candlelight tour of Cardigan's historic homes and ate at an inn along the water. We played in the woods and built a fort out of loose logs. We swam in the college pool and ran along the river every morning. Tyler taught us how to catch rockfish off the dock, but after four hours in the cold, we gave up and came inside. We watched movies and giggled by the fire. She beat me in a three-hour game of Scrabble and we lingered over every home-cooked dinner. On an unseasonably warm day, we packed an extravagant picnic lunch, piled onto Tony's sailboat, and explored the Cardigan from the water. "It's totally different from out here," I said, wind in my face.

"You have to get one of these, Mom," Annie called back.

On her last night, I topped the kitchen table with Charlotte's hand-tatted lace tablecloth and her floral Haviland china. Burning tapers painted the room in a soft, warm glow. Shadows danced on the walls as the flames flickered.

"Wow. New England clam chowder," Annie said. "My favorite." She scooped up a spoon full and tasted it. "Holy crap, Mom. This is amazing." She tore off a piece of bread, dipped it in the soup, and popped it in her mouth. "What kind of bread is this?"

"Pumpernickel. I added some coffee granules to make it richer."

"It's always about the coffee with you."

"Yeah, right?" I laughed.

"Geez, Mom, the food has been so great this week, I've probably gained five pounds." She took a long sip of water. "You know, if I were Dad, I would have stayed married to you just to eat your food." Annie's eyes widened. She stared down at her plate. "That was weird to say." She looked up at me with a sheepish expression, her shoulders hunched in worry about my reaction.

"A little bit weird," I said.

"Sorry."

I ignored the lurch in my stomach, reached over, and gave her back a quick scratch. "If we had a manual on how to do this, know what to say, what not to say, it might be a lot easier."

She smiled in relief.

"But just so you know . . ." I returned her smile. "I would have stayed married to me for that reason, too."

"Thanks for everything this week, Mom." She tore apart her last portion of bread. "I had fun and all, but it's been weird not seeing my friends at home. I've just finished my first semester away at college and haven't seen anyone. I mean, they have all been together for a week now. The stories have all been told, the reconnections made. By the time I get there everyone will have moved on." She dropped the bread onto her plate, wadded up her napkin, and tossed it on the table. "Is it always going to be like this? Me shuffling from one house to the other?"

"I don't know, sweetie. I came out here because I had to. I couldn't stay in our house and this one was here, sitting empty. I guess neither of us know what the future holds, if your dad will . . ." I stopped. "Your father has asked for a divorce. We both have lawyers, I don't know if you knew that. So . . . yes, you probably will be going to two houses for Christmas."

"But will you always be so far away?" She looked over at me with watery eyes. "I mean, I hate that Bay Bridge. It's so scary. And knowing I have to cross it in order to see you freaks me out. It's like this giant gulf between us."

My mouth fell open. "I had no idea, Annie. You hate the Bay Bridge?"

"Who doesn't? But more importantly, Mom, there's nothing to do here."

"I thought we had fun this week." I struggled to keep the defensiveness out of my voice.

"We did. I mean, you're like my best friend. But it's only you here." She stuffed her fists in her lap.

"At least you get to spend a few days with your dad before you go back to school."

"Mom? I hope it's okay to tell you this, but . . . well . . . I can't stand being in our house when she's there."

"Why? What does she do?"

Annie rolled her eyes. "What doesn't she do? She's totally cold and arrogant. And Dad is all tense and unnatural. He's always watching to make sure I'm nice to her. Then he tries to come up with things for us to do. He wanted us to get pedicures together. That's about the only thing we have in common."

"Liking pedicures?"

"No. We both have toes."

"Oh, Annie."

"The day after I got home, he suggested Rebecca and I go to Saks and get our makeup done. Since when have I been into makeup? Does he even know me? But then I started to think maybe he wants me to wear makeup, like I'm not pretty enough or something.

"Plus, I don't think she even knows how to cook. She leaves her stuff everywhere. And when I'm there she gives off this vibe, like, aren't you ever leaving? It's my house!"

"Is she always there?"

"She *lives* there. Mom! Hello?"

I placed my palm over my heart. "I didn't know."

She looked over at me, gauging my reaction.

I took a deep breath and exhaled slowly. "I'm okay," I said. "Back to you."

"I don't know. I just feel like it isn't even my house anymore— like *I'm* the guest. And when I come here you're so great, but it's *here*. Or should I say nowhere. There isn't even a Starbucks here."

"I'm so sorry, honey. I will keep all of that in mind while I figure out what I'm going to do. Okay?" I patted her back again. "But for now, I think this is a good place for me to be. I've made some friends, as you know. And I'm taking classes and cooking again. I'm getting the farm back in shape so that I can sell it. For now I feel I have a purpose here. I'm giving myself a year."

"A *year*? Really?"

"That's what I've decided. Why?"

"Well, what about the summer? Where will I be?"

"Here?" I said.

"No way." She shook her head. "Besides, I want to go back to my old job at the gym." She picked at the wax on one of the candlesticks. "Will you at least *consider* coming back to Chevy Chase?" She started to pile the dried drippings in the center of the table.

"Yes, of course. I've lived in Chevy Chase most of my life."

"Okay. I guess that's the best you can do." Annie gazed out the window as she took her last bite of bread. Outside the moon was low. A gauzy curtain of fog rose from the river. "Do you think about her much?" she said.

"Aunt Charlotte?"

"No." She looked over at me. "The girl you found. What was her name . . . Megan?"

I folded my hands and rested them on the table. "All the time."

"Did they ever figure out how she drowned?"

"Honestly, Annie? I'm not convinced she did."

"What the heck?"

I worried I would tell Annie more than she wanted to know. But I would never lie to my child. Never. "I've been looking into it." I hesitated. "Do you want to know more?"

While we ate our entree of Annie's second favorite dish: baked ziti (with extra sauce), I told her about the investigation. When I explained how Sue hacked into Megan's Facebook page, Annie's eyes widened.

"Can I see it? Maybe I could help."

"Absolutely." I hopped up and flipped on the light. I scooted my chair closer to Annie's and set my laptop on the table. Once on Facebook, I typed in Megan's password.

"Wow. She's so pretty," Annie said.

"Yes, she was. People are still writing on her wall. Even after all this time."

Annie reached over to the touch pad and scrolled through the endless posts of grief. "This is so sad."

"Heartbreaking."

"Click on her private messages, Mom. There might be something there to help you."

I stared over at her. "I never thought to do that. I wonder if Sue ever checked. She's been so busy friending all of Megan's contacts, maybe she didn't think of it."

"Doesn't sound like Sue," Annie said.

"I know. But she's uncovered so much already. Okay, let's see what we have." We opened the list of conversations.

"Do you recognize any of these people?" she asked.

I shook my head. "It all seems pretty benign."

"Go farther back," Annie said.

I browsed through the list until I saw Bill Johnston's photo. "This is her stepfather. He's a suspect."

Annie frowned. "Suspect, Mom? Really?"

"I'm serious," I said. "I'm going to figure this out."

"Okay." She shrugged. "Let's see what you have here."

We huddled over my computer, reading simultaneously. Annie's mouth fell open a few times. I gasped once or twice and when we finished, I fell back into my chair. Bill Johnston had just stepped boldly onto center stage and the entire six feet, four inches of him was front and center in the spotlight.

TWENTY-EIGHT

Bill Johnston	You're not returning my phone calls, texts, or emails so I have to write you here. This is unacceptable Megan. When I contact you I expect a response.
Megan Johnston	I'm busy with school, Daddy.
Bill Johnston	I want you to come home this weekend. I will come and get you. Your behavior is unacceptable. Transferring was supposed to help you get focused on your studies.
Megan Johnston	Please leave me alone. I'm not coming home. I'm spending the weekend with someone.
Bill Johnston	A boy? No. I won't allow it.

Megan Johnston I know you think you control me but you don't anymore. I'm actually glad you forced me to leave UD. I feel as if I can finally breathe without you telling me when or how. I'm going out tonight whether you like it or not. I'm not going to write to you anymore. I want you to leave me alone for once. I'm not opening any more messages from you.

"He wouldn't have left it at that," Annie said. "Go back to her wall."

I clicked out of the message chain and scrolled through the endless posts on Megan's wall that were written after she died. I had to hit "see earlier messages" at least a dozen times. And there it was.

Bill Johnston
I will be in Cardigan in a few hours.

Annie left early New Year's Eve. As I walked her to the car, I thought about how we had both benefited from our week in Cardigan. Our faces had been warmed by the sun, our lungs expanded to breathe in the crisp, clean air. We had laughed and frolicked and loved and were ready to start the New Year on a good note. As she closed the car door, it occurred to me that I was settling in here better than I ever expected to. I waved to Annie and crossed my arms. And yet Annie hated me living here. Oh, my girl. Who knows what the future holds for either of us?

Annie Hart
Just spent a fab week with my mom in Cardigan then rocked in the New Year with my homies from CC. Happy New Year everyone!!!!

17 people like this

Brittany Purcell

Back at ya Annie! It was awesome to see you! Love ya! xoxoxo

Jody Beckett

It was awesomesauce!!!

Connor O'Malley

Get back here to NC so we can bring in the NY the way it's meant to happen.

The comments went on and on and my heart warmed. I hit "like" and wanted to hit it several more times, but apparently you can only "like" something once. I wanted to write something, too, but thought better of it. I knew there were entire Web sites devoted to "Moms on Facebook." And although I was dying to know about her relationship with Connor O'Malley, the boy from the rugby game, I decided to let Annie have her privacy, such that it was.

I went to our private group and typed:

Rosalie Hart	Happy New Year, everyone! Welcome back to the Eastern Shore.
Glenn B	I can actually say I missed this town. Where are we in the investigation?
Shelby Smith	I still don't think we know everything we need to know about Megan. Now that the students are back from the holidays, I'm going to start talking to some of them who may have known Megan.
Rosalie Hart	Very good idea, Sue. OK, Annie and I looked at Megan's private messages. Bill Johnston threatened to cut off her cash flow the day she died. He said he was going to Cardigan that afternoon.

Rhonda is coming for lunch on Friday because I
think we need to take a closer look at Bill.

Tony Ricci   Good to have Mini-Me on the team.

Shelby Smith   Omg!!! I've been so busy engaging her friends I
never looked at her pm's. Annie is a genius. Btw,
Tim Collier is hooked. I am getting him to pour his
heart out to me and he is one creepy guy.

TWENTY-NINE

Rhonda rushed past me into the house, raincoat over her head.
She stomped her pumps on the mat. "Christ, what a day." She
handed me her raincoat. "I must look awful."

"Not a hair out of place."

She set her Chanel bag on the small table in the foyer and headed
for the living room. Her wide eyes took in my house. "Rosalie, you
never said . . ."

"Said what?" I hung up her coat and followed. I had started a fire
to take the damp chill out of the air and the living room was toasty
warm.

"How spectacular this place is." She surveyed the room.

"It's old," I said. "And on a day like this, it feels like it. I think a
log cabin would have fewer drafts."

"Are you serious?" She scowled back at me. "This is history.
Houses don't get much older in this country, so who cares about a
little breeze?"

"It's more than that. At night when I can't get to sleep I stare at
how the ceilings and the walls don't quite match up and it drives
me crazy."

Rhonda crossed her arms. "And why exactly are you living here?"

"I told you, my husband left me and—"

"Rosalie, please. I remember. Don't hash over all that again." She continued into the kitchen, stopped, and traced her fingers over the stonework surrounding the fireplace. "You could roast a pig in here."

"I haven't tried that yet."

She eyed Mr. Miele. "And what is that supposed to be?"

"It's a coffee pot," I said, making no effort to hide my defensiveness.

"It's the elephant in the living room."

"Well, maybe you should taste my coffee before you decide that."

"Rosalie, dear, do you know where I live?"

"Wilmington."

She turned to face me. "I live in a two-year-old house crammed onto about one eighth of an acre of land. If my neighbor coughs I know it and I probably will get his cold. It's perfectly nice, but it's got the history of a fart. You really have something here."

"It's just a house."

"If you ever think of selling, I know an excellent Realtor." Her penciled-in eyebrows rose into perfect arches. "You know, houses like these fall into a unique market."

"It's a farm. There are acres and acres of crops out there."

"Even better," she said.

"You know someone looking for a farm?"

"God, no. But with all that waterfront . . ."

"Yes?"

"Well . . ." she said in a honey-thick voice. She shot me a devious smile, peach lipstick glossed her lips. "Haven't you ever heard of a little thing called subdivision?" She continued to smile, waiting for my reaction. "You and I could become very wealthy women. Just picture it—Barclay Meadow homes. We would keep the original farmhouse and put the rest on big, spacious lots. They would have to be Colonial homes to fit with the whole feel of this place." She stared out at the river veiled by the heavy rain. "Each house could have its own pier. My God, we could lure all kinds of rich boaters here from Philly, Baltimore, D.C. And Cardigan is such a cute little town. So safe and pretty."

I stood next to her and stared out. Not so safe, I thought. Not always so safe. A cool rush of air snuck down my back. I felt as if the dead were trying to communicate with me. Megan? Aunt Charlotte? "How about some lunch," I said, "before we start bulldozing the soybeans?"

"All right." She smiled over at me. "I'm famished."

I grilled cheese and tomato sandwiches on slices of my homemade bread and topped them with a pesto mayonnaise. I tossed a mixed greens salad and placed a small mound next to each sandwich.

"Don't forget the wine," she said.

I popped open a crisp pinot grigio. Rain spattered against the window while we ate.

Ten minutes laster, Rhonda licked her fingers. There wasn't a crumb left on her plate. "This is the best sandwich I've ever eaten. You should start your own restaurant. I would definitely pay for that sandwich. Those thick slices of bread—I feel healthier just eating that stuff."

"Well, it's loaded with goodies. And I got the tomatoes at the farm stand in town."

"Who has tomatoes in January?"

"He gets his produce as locally as he can. I think these are from South Carolina. It's all part of the green movement—you know, the more local food you eat, the fewer emissions from trucking. Tyler and I are growing organic grains and . . ." I stopped. Rhonda was frowning. "Too much information?"

"Honey, I drive a Range Rover. My carbon footprint is more like a boot print."

I gathered our plates and carried them to the sink. After pouring coffee, I set a small plate of chocolate muffins on the table. Rhonda was gazing out at the river. I sat down again and tucked my legs beneath me.

She checked her bangs, ignored the coffee, and poured herself another glass of wine. "I hope you don't mind," she said. "I never used to drink during the day, but lately my nerves are jumping." She took a long sip, set her glass down, and eyed me. "So, Rosalie, are you still looking into Megan's death?"

I hesitated. "A little."

"Why? Megan is dead." She crossed her arms. "I told Bill about you."

"What did you say?"

"I said I'd met someone who thinks Megan was murdered and was looking into a bit." She shrugged.

"What was his reaction?"

"He was livid."

"So, why did you tell him?"

"That's my business. But the bottom line is this: Megan was distraught about having to leave Delaware and being stalked by a bunch of creepy guys. She committed suicide. As sad as that may be, it's reality. Everybody knows it but you. And you nosing around just stirs up all that pain."

I wrapped my hands around my coffee mug. "Don't you think telling him about me might have stirred up some pain?"

"Of course. Which is why you need to stop."

"But how do they know it was a suicide? Was there a note?"

Rhonda rolled her eyes. "There you go again."

"But Rhonda . . . what if we figured out it wasn't a suicide. Wouldn't her father want to know?"

"We?"

"Did I say 'we'? That was silly." I smiled sheepishly.

"Who else knows what you're doing?" She crossed her arms and flattened her back again the chair.

"Just you. And now Bill." I held my eyes steady with hers.

"I'm trying to tell you as nicely as I can, Rosalie, you need to stop." She shot me a stern look, one eyebrow a little higher than the other. "No more of this foolishness. Okay?"

"I would never want to hurt anyone."

"Good. Case closed." Rhonda puffed out some air, causing her carefully sprayed bangs to lift and fall. "Bill needs to get on with his life." She filled my wineglass, knocked hers against it, and drank the rest in one swallow. She slapped the glass back on the table and scrutinized my face. "Technically he could sue you."

I stared back. "I didn't realize you and Bill were such close friends."

She clicked her fingernails on the table. "Can I tell you something?"

"Of course."

"Bill and I? We had an affair. It lasted almost six years. It's why my marriage ended."

"Does Corinne know?"

She shrugged. "I sure didn't tell her."

"Why did it stop?" I said, trying to subdue my urgency to hear more.

More fingernail clicking. "I never really figured it out. He just ended it. I was heartbroken. I was hoping we would both leave our spouses and be together. He used to say that's what would happen. But when our girls hit high school he got very distracted. He broke dates and there were a few no-shows. But now, lately, he's been reaching out to me again. Ever since I told him about you." She looked over at me, a puzzled look on her face. "I have no idea why I'm telling you this."

"I'm glad you feel you can trust me." I smiled.

"Is that why?" She frowned. "Doesn't sound like me. Sometimes you look at me with those big brown eyes of yours and I start blabbing. How do you do that?"

"I just listen, is all." I started to fill her glass, but she covered it with her hand. "No. I think that's why I told you. The vino. It's the great truth serum." She stood. "Well, girlfriend, this has been delish, but I should head home before it gets dark." She glanced out the window. "Everything is one deadly shade of gray today, isn't it? I sure hope this rain doesn't freeze."

Tyler burst into the front door, rain dripping from a dark green poncho. He pulled it over his head and stomped his boots. He stopped abruptly when he saw Rhonda. "Oops," he said.

"No worries," I said. "Coffee?"

"I'm out of WD-40. I think there's another can in here." He pulled open a drawer. His sandy hair tumbled onto his forehead. His muscles were outlined through his thermal shirt. After rifling through the drawer, he picked up a blue-and-yellow canister. "That old table saw is a real bugger." He bumped the drawer closed with his hip, nodded to Rhonda, and walked back outside.

Rhonda's mouth hung open. "And who, my dear, was *that*?"

"My handyman."

"You have a handyman?" She grinned mischievously. "And what exactly is he handy at doing?"

I cocked my head. "Everything."

"How nice for you. I've always wanted a pool boy in a tight little Speedo. Funny thing about that is I don't have a pool." Rhonda picked up her purse and headed for the door. Before she left, she turned to look at me. She made a motion as if she were zipping her lips. "Let's make a deal. Between friends? I'll keep your hot handyman a secret if you don't tell anyone about my confession."

"Of course, Rhonda. It's not my secret to tell."

"Exactly. Besides, who would you tell? You're out here in the middle of nowhere rattling around in an old house. And I'm glad you agreed to stop all this detective nonsense. It's time, isn't it?"

"What can I say?" I said. "As usual, you are much wiser about these things than me."

After spending most of the day cooking for and entertaining Rhonda, I was anxious to check on Annie. I opened my computer and typed in my password. I was glad the What Ifs were scheduled to chat. Rhonda telling Bill about me was unsettling, to put it mildly. If he was the killer, he won't be happy to learn that I believe Megan was murdered. I glanced down at my exceptionally warm feet. Dickens. Tyler was still here. At least for now I was safe.

Annie Hart is in a relationship with Connor O'Malley

I went to Annie's profile. She had posted a new photo album. I clicked on the first one and then the next. Photo followed photo of Annie entwined with Connor. It was definitely him—the one from the rugby game. Had I brought them together? How weird was that? I paused at a photo of them in a very physical kiss. I clicked out of her album. Parents aren't supposed to see this stuff, but Facebook had changed everything.

Shelby Smith	I have news. I had coffee with a friend from John Adams who works in admissions. Long story short—she knew which room Megan was in so I managed to meet the roommate.
Rosalie Hart	OMG. How?
Shelby Smith	I found a photo of this girl in the yearbook, went to the dorm around dinner time, and waited outside. I told her I was an alum and wanted to see my old dorm room. When I said the number she said that

was her room and invited me up to see it. So we started to talk and when I asked how she ended up with a single she blurted out the whole story about Megan.

Tony Ricci I'm here. Wow. You're getting extremely good at this, Suzy Q.

Shelby Smith They only knew each other a short while. But she said Megan was super neat, kept to herself, and was in a relationship she was very secretive about. It wasn't unusual for her to go out on a Friday night and not come home until Sunday or Monday morning.

Rosalie Hart So that's why no one reported her missing.

Glenn B Did she say anything about the night Megan died? Was she particularly sad or acting strangely?

Shelby Smith She dressed up and said she was going to a restaurant in Queen Anne's County. She said she was going to end something once and for all.

Rosalie Hart I knew she didn't go to that party! Did she say anything about her dad coming down?

Shelby Smith No. But her dad came to their room the day after her body was found and cleaned out all of her stuff.

Tony Ricci He took her stuff? Maybe he wanted her computer. Evidence?

Glenn B As upsetting as all of this is, we have to remain rational. Ok. Queen Anne's County. That's significant. Whomever she was meeting didn't want to be recognized. We have to find out who.

Tony Ricci Hey! I was right about where she went in. I think I know exactly which restaurant it was. It's part of a marina.

Glenn B Excellent, Tony. And good work, Sue.

Rosalie Hart	Rhonda confessed to having an affair with Bill Johnston. She also said they were seeing each other again now that Megan was dead. Oh, she told Bill about my investigation.
Tony Ricci	Well that's not good. Why the heck did she do that?
Rosalie Hart	She didn't say. But she said they both want me to stop. She said Bill was angry. So it could have been any of our suspects: Tim Collier the FB friend, Bill, Nick, or even Rhonda for that matter. She certainly got what she wanted. Sue, any chance you could get onto Bill's FB page? I'll bet they have a message conversation going.
Shelby Smith	I'll work on that. This is all good! I was worried the trail was growing cold.
Tony Ricci	So if Megan went out to dinner with the killer, maybe we should show her picture around that restaurant. She was a real knockout. She would stand out.
Rosalie Hart	Great idea. Sue, did the roommate say anything about Nick?
Shelby Smith	She said a lot of girls have a crush on him. Oh, and he shows dirty movies in class.
Tony Ricci	Dirty movies????
Rosalie Hart	I saw it in his syllabus. It's in order to eliminate prejudice and desensitize inhibitions.
Tony Ricci	Ain't that a bunch of crappola.
Rosalie Hart	Maybe I should enroll after all. It would help the investigation.
Tony Ricci	Yeah, right. Take one for the team, there, Princess.

Thirty

Janice Tilghman
Girls night out, Rose Red! We're going to Joey's. Pick u up at 7 sat. Dress is cas. Won't take no for an answer.

I laughed when I read the last sentence. It wasn't really necessary.

I buckled my seat belt in the back of Janice's SUV. While getting ready I had originally slipped on my sensible boots and a pullover sweater. There was a sixty percent chance of a light snowfall. I looked in the mirror and changed my mind. This was Janice. She never missed an opportunity to step out in the latest fashion. So I kicked off the comfort and pulled on my nicest jeans, slipped into Annie's spiky heels, and the red cashmere sweater my brother Oliver sent me for Christmas.

Dede Morgan sat sideways in the front seat. "How do you like living in Barclay Meadow?" she said. "I've always loved that house."

"I'm adjusting," I said.

"So," Dede said brightly, "you're divorced?"

"Soon to be."

"We'll have to keep our eye out, then," Dede said to Janice. "We don't need another hot single chick around. I swear, the men in this town are about as monogamous as a rooster."

"Rose Red had it done to her," Janice said. "She won't be returning the favor anytime soon."

"Ah." Dede gave me a sympathetic smile.

"How do they get away with it?" I said. "I mean, Doris Bird would know two minutes after the guy rolled out of bed."

The car filled with laughter. I caught Janice's eye in the mirror. She winked.

"Janice said Tyler Wells is farming your land," Dede said. "Now, talk about hot."

"You think Tyler's hot?"

"Uh, yeah," she said. "I had the hugest crush on him in high school. I prayed he would ask me to prom. He ended up going with Janice."

"You never told me that, Janice."

"You never asked." Janice gripped the headrest and attempted to parallel park her SUV.

"What was he like in high school?" I leaned against the door to allow Janice a better view.

"He was quiet. Mysterious," Dede said as she refreshed her lipstick. "He was always reading and yet he was really good at sports. He's still got that tight butt. I saw him the other day at the hardware store."

"Every time I see him there's a book or a pair of gloves in his back pocket," I said as we climbed down from the truck. "I guess I never noticed his butt."

"Are you serious?" Dede said.

"Well, maybe once or twice."

"That's more like it," Dede said. She surveyed Janice's parking job. "That car in front of you will never get out."

"Too bad for them." Janice hit the remote lock. The headlights flashed. "I can't walk very far in these heels."

Joey's was named after the owner and bartender: Josephine. It seemed to be a theme in Caridgan: Birdie's, Joey's. When we first walked in I was disappointed. It was nothing more than a long, narrow bar with loud conversations and not much room to walk, let alone sit. But Janice strode past the bar and through an archway. We followed her into a large, candlelit room filled with groupings of upholstered chairs and a roaring fireplace.

Janice charged over to a circle of mismatched upholstered chairs close to the fire.

"Best table in the house," Dede said as we slipped out of our coats and settled into the comfortable seats. "How do you do it? You always get the best parking place, the best table. It's crazy."

"Joey knew I was coming." Janice unwound an exceptionally long wool scarf from her neck. "'Nuf said."

A waitress approached and we ordered drinks. She set a small bowl of mixed nuts on the table and Janice immediately scooped up a handful. "Hey, Dede," Janice said as she chewed. "Did you see Susie Clark all over Jack Peyton at the end of the bar?"

"That Jezebel." Dede turned to me. "Jack has three kids and while his wife was popping out the third, he was bopping Susie. His secretary! I mean, how cliché is that?"

I laughed—amazed how this town operated. Everyone knew everything about everyone, but they seemed to take it in stride. It was like the bumper sticker on most of the pickup trucks: SHIT HAPPENS. Maybe I should try and adopt their attitude. Our waitress set our drinks down. I took a long sip from my cosmopolitan. It felt good to be out.

A loud strum vibrated the microphone. I looked over at the stage. Three men were syncing their guitars.

"These guys are really good," Janice said.

"What's Trevor doing tonight?" I asked.

"He was out with the deer hunters at four this morning. He's probably already snoring."

"Are you married, Dede?" I said.

"Oh, yeah. Right out of college. Everyone knew Petey and I would get married. We started dating in high school and even though I went away to college, I came home every weekend to be with him."

"I thought you wanted to date Tyler?"

"That prom I mentioned? Petey asked me and the rest is history. You know, Petey and I probably couldn't have married anyone else in Cardigan. I did a family tree before the wedding to make sure we weren't cousins or something. Both our families are prebridge."

"Prebridge?"

"Yeah." She took a sip. "Before they built the Bay Bridge it was a little incestuous over here. No way to get across the bay and expand the gene pool." She set her drink down. "Don't worry. Everything checked out. And the babies came out okay. No extra fingers or toes."

It felt good to laugh. I liked Dede. I should definitely get out more.

"How's everything?" the waitress asked.

"Drink up, girlfriends," Janice said. "I'm driving tonight."

I looked over at Dede. We both shrugged. "Another round, please," I said.

The guitars strummed in unison and the sound fluttered through my chest. I sank deeper into my chair.

"Hey, Rose Red . . ."

"Yes, dear?" I said.

"Remember what I told you about Dr. Nick? He's here."

I sat up straighter and looked around the room. "Where?"

"In the corner." She gestured with her head. "With some serious jailbait."

I squinted at the spot Janice indicated. All I could make out were two shadows.

"He blew out his votive." Janice picked several cashews out of the bowl of nuts and popped one in her mouth. "He thinks no one can see him."

"How can *you* see him?" I said.

"Trevor calls me his aristocat." She sipped her Diet Coke. "Get it? 'Cause I can see in the dark."

The waitress brought our next round of drinks. The band began singing in earnest and overwhelmed our efforts at conversation. I looked back at the corner. Two heads were dipped close together. After another long sip of my cosmo, I stood and fluffed my hair.

Janice eyed me warily. "Where are you off to?"

"I'm going to say hi to Nick."

"No you're not." She shook her head back and forth. "No way am I going to let you do that."

Dede looked from me to Janice and back to me. "What's going on?"

"Oh, nothing," Janice said, her voice rich with sarcasm. "It just seems our friend Rose Red had a brainectomy."

"We made friends at your party. You sat us next to each other, remember?" I said. "It would be rude to not say hi."

"The chick's twelve, for God's sake," Janice said. "I think they want to be left alone."

"I won't be long." I steadied myself in my heels and started over to Nick. It occurred to me I would need a reason to be passing by his table—a table tucked in the most remote corner of the room. Or maybe not. Maybe it would be good to catch him off guard.

Nick was nuzzling the young woman's neck. Her eyelids, coated in baby blue eyeshadow, were closed. Her right hand was under the table.

"Hello, Nick," I said.

Their bliss disturbed, they looked up at me in unison."Rosalie," Nick said. "How? What—"

"I just wanted to say hi." I smiled. "Hi."

The young woman picked up her cocktail. Nick's glass was empty. He blinked a few times, as if trying to orient himself to the situation. "Excuse me," he said to her and buttoned his tweed blazer as he stood. "Shall we talk someplace where we don't have to shout?"

"Okay," I said and followed him out of the large room and into the bar.

He led me over to an idle foosball table in the corner. I flinched when he suddenly spun around. "What the hell are you doing?"

"I'm just saying hi. How have you been? How is the study?"

"Did you come here looking for me?"

"Nick," I said. "I'm here with Janice." I folded my hands together. "Why are you so upset?"

He took a deep breath and exhaled slowly. His eyes narrowed. "I haven't seen you. I assumed I was off your radar screen."

"Excuse me?" I stepped back. The intensity in his gaze was unnerving.

"I need to make a call," he said and removed his iPhone from his jacket pocket. "My being here tonight is none of your business. Understand?"

"No." I crossed my arms. "Not really."

He started to walk away, but stopped. "Look, Rosalie, it's nice to see you. But my life is complicated right now. Maybe we can get together in a few weeks." He seemed to have gained his composure. "Do you like to sail?"

"*Sail?*"

"I have a boat, remember? You were so interested that first time we met. I assume you like to sail."

"Of course I remember." I tried to smile. "I was just thinking it would have to warm up first, right?"

"Oh, it will be plenty warm." He leaned in and kissed my cheek. He stepped back. "Chanel Coco Mademoiselle?"

"Yes. That's my perfume."

"Memorable," he said. "Like you. Oh, and nice sweater."

I started to explain that my sweater was a gift, that I didn't deliberately wear red, but he was walking away. His phone was to his ear when he pushed the door open to go outside.

I returned to a scowling Janice.

"What did you just do, Rose Red? Have a quickie on the pool table?"

"Ha ha," I said and finished my drink.

While I listened to the strumming guitars and a newly added mandolin, I thought about Nick. He was angry with me. He was a lot of things with me—flirtatious, worried, perplexed. And who did he need to call all of a sudden?

The waitress approached with three glasses of a deep red wine. "These are for you, ladies," she said. "From a friend."

Janice picked up her wine as soon as the waitress set it on the table. "I can have one glass." She took a healthy sip. "You're driving me to drink, Rose Red."

After the second set, Janice jangled her keys. "Ready?"

Dede and I put our coats on and followed her. I glanced in the corner, but Nick and his youngster were gone. The new patrons had lit the candle.

"Coming?" Janice called from the door.

I hurried after her. Once outside, I skidded on a brand-new inch of snow. I grabbed on to the wall and righted myself. Janice's headlights illuminated a flurry of flakes. She stared ahead, but Dede looked at me with concern. I held up my hand to signal I was okay. I must have looked like a drunk, but I felt dreadfully sober. I started to walk again, treading carefully. When I was almost to the car, I noticed a police cruiser inching by. I glanced down the sidewalk and saw Nick getting ready to cross the street. I looked back at the cruiser, although I already knew who was behind the wheel.

THIRTY-ONE

Glenn and Lila sat in adjacent chairs, each with their feet extended, hands clasped over their stomachs.

"Good morning, Lila," I said. "Morning, Glenn."

"Morning," they said in unison.

I set a loaf of bread on the counter.

"How do you like the snow?" Doris said.

"Better now that I'm in practical shoes."

"Thanks for the bread," Doris said. "It won't last very long, though. People have been coming in here asking for it."

"Really?"

Doris perched on her stool and folded her arms. "I think you could sell it, if you want the truth. I think folks would buy it."

"Sell it here? Would you *do* that?"

She shrugged. "I sell just about everything else. Why not bread?"

"Okay," I said. "You take half of the proceeds."

"Not necessary."

"Oh, yes it is." I nodded.

"If you insist." Doris had a playful grin on her face. She was an entrepreneur at heart.

I glanced over at Glenn. He gave me a quick, surreptitious wink. I knew he wouldn't want me to linger because Lila was there. Glenn was so anxious to find out about the police report, he was spending a part of every day in Birdie's.

"I'll bring you several loaves tomorrow, Doris. But yours will be free."

"Deal," she said.

I waved good-bye and stepped back into the brightness of the day. After slipping on my sunglasses, I started for my car. A gust of wind tousled my hair. Maybe a warm front was coming in. I smoothed my hair away from my face. The snow was already melting under the rays of my precious Maryland sun. I stopped abruptly. Sheriff Wilgus was next to my car, an arm resting on the parking meter. I started to turn away, but he came to attention. I couldn't see his eyes behind his aviator sunglasses, but I knew they were zeroed on me.

"Sheriff," I said warily.

He touched the brim of his hat. "Missus Hart."

A ticket flapped under my windshield wiper.

"I guess I was in Birdie's longer than I expected."

He stepped to within inches of me. He hooked his thumbs in his belt and leaned in closer. "What makes you think you don't have to follow the rules?"

His breath was hot on my ear, making a whooshing sound as if he were speaking into a conch shell. It was heavy with mint and a trace of something else. Whiskey?

"I don't think that."

"You sure?"

I nodded.

"I'm not gonna warn you again, Hart. You got that?"

"I think so."

"You *think* so?" He was inches from my head. My eyes darted around, wondering if anyone was watching us, but the streets were quiet.

"Sheriff . . ." My voice quivered. "I'm not sure I know what I did wrong. I mean, besides not putting money in the meter."

"You want a list?" he growled.

"Okay." I made an attempt at a smile.

He grabbed my arm. "Mind who you keep company with."

"I can't go out with my friends? Is that it?"

He squeezed harder. "You know who I'm talking about."

"You're hurting me."

"I'm smarter than you, lady," he said through gritted teeth. "And don't you forget it." A wad of saliva landed on my lapel.

"Why do you care if I talk to Nick Angeles?"

"Shut *up*."

"What do they have on you?"

His grip tightened.

"You're hurting me." I tried to wrench my arm away. My fingers were growing numb.

"Scared?"

"Yes."

"Why don't you call a cop? Oh . . . wait. I am a cop." He shoved me into my car and walked away.

THIRTY-TWO

Bill Johnston has sent you a friend request.

I walked out to the shed with a fresh cup of Costa Rican blend for Tyler. He was measuring a piece of wood. Sawdust freckled his face.

"What are you up to?"

"I'm fixing the pier," he said without looking up. "Some of the boards have rotted. I thought I'd take advantage of the snow melting." He looked up at me. "That all right with you, boss?"

"Sounds lovely. Maybe we should get a boat."

"I'm still having trouble with Miss Charlotte's old power saw. It tends to jam up, but I think I can keep it going. If not I'll have to go back home and get mine, which would be a royal pain in my ass."

"How much does a new one cost?"

"No need to spend money on a new one," he said. "Not when I can fix this one."

"Feeling stubborn today?"

"'Frugal' is the word. We're both on a tight budget." He straightened and accepted the coffee. "You read my mind."

I returned to my desk. A breeze laden with the scent of freshly cut wood fluttered through the open windows. The struggling power saw occasionally broke the silence. I had already driven into town and dropped ten loaves of bread off at Birdie's shoe store. I printed labels, pale blue with a chocolate brown font that read ROSALIE'S HOME-BAKED GOODS. The list of ingredients was in a smaller font and I secured the plastic wrap with a blue-and-brown gingham ribbon.

I opened my computer and logged onto the Internet to check the What Ifs.

Shelby Smith	Tim Collier said he and Megan were engaged which of course couldn't be true. And her relationship status was single on her FB page. He's getting weirder by the day. Now he's asking me where I live and what I look like and saying some pretty creepy stuff. But that makes him even more suspect. Maybe he will confess. A confession on FB. That would be a first.
Rosalie Hart	Can't say it enough, Sue, don't take any risks. If he is a killer he managed to find Megan. Hey, I know what the college has on the sheriff.
Glenn B	What?
Rosalie Hart	He gave me a ticket today. He had whiskey on his breath and it was only 11:00 AM.
Tony Ricci	It's all falling into place.
Shelby Smith	I hacked into Bill's FB page. I'll copy/paste his private conversation with Rhonda. It's pretty juicy.
Rosalie Hart	Oh, great! I can't wait to

"Shit!"

Tyler. I jumped up and ran out the door and into the shed. He clutched his hand. Blood pulsed out.

"What happened?"

"I cut off my finger."

THIRTY-THREE

The entire index finger of his right hand was gone. I pulled my shirt over my head and wrapped it around the bleeding stump. "Put pressure on it. I'll get my keys."

I ran into the house. At the last minute, I realized I was in my bra. I pulled on a denim jacket and grabbed more towels. I opened the car door. "Get in," I said. "Keep it elevated. I'll be right back." I ran into the house and grabbed a small cooler, filled it with ice, and headed out to the shed. Every part of me screamed to shut my eyes and hide, but I forced myself to act. I found Tyler's finger in a pile of wood shaving. I wrapped it in a wet paper towel, put it into a plastic bag, and buried it in the ice. Tyler eyed the cooler as I climbed into the car and squealed out of the driveway. On the way to the hospital I called 911. "We need to helicopter him to Baltimore."

"You don't get to decide that, ma'am."

"Yes, I do," I said. "He needs to have his finger sewn on and I can guarantee no one at the local hospital has the skills or the equipment to do it. Call the helicopter. Stat."

The turbo kicked in. "Did I just say 'stat'?"

Tyler said nothing.

"Keep putting pressure on it." I sped through a red light. "Does it hurt?"

He gave me a short, stiff nod.

To my surprise, they met us at the ER door and a helicopter was on its way. I gave them the necessary information and pulled his wallet from his back pocket. "Can I ride along?" I asked.

"Are you the next of kin?" the nurse asked.

I hesitated. Tyler was watching me closely. "Yes," I said.

Among the many fears I confronted that day, blood and severed body parts being two, was an overwhelming fear of heights. As the helicopter lifted into the air, wobbling at first like the town drunk, I gripped the sides of my seat. Tyler was strapped on a gurney; the paramedic was starting an IV. Tyler's face was whiter than the sheet strapped over him, his eyes squeezed shut.

"His finger," I shouted over the noise. "It's in this cooler."

The paramedic nodded.

"Will there be a hand surgeon waiting?"

"Yes, ma'am," he said. "They've got an OR all set up."

I smiled. "Thank you for everything."

He smiled back. "It's our job." He injected Tyler with a heavy dose of morphine. He turned back to me. "Uh, ma'am . . ."

"Yes?"

He nodded toward my jacket. I looked down. I had never buttoned it.

"Oh, my gosh." I pulled it closed. "Thank you for telling me."

Once I buttoned up and recovered from my own injection of embarrassment, I looked out the window. We were flying over the Cardigan River. It was beautiful, pristine, almost innocent as it curved and snaked through the lush, green land. The river emptied into the wide, endless blue of the Chesapeake Bay. The beauty distracted me from my terror and, before I knew it, the tall buildings of Baltimore popped up like the Emerald City and the helicopter was easing itself onto the helipad.

•   •   •

Twelve hours later, Tyler's finger was reattached and he lay asleep in a private room. The surgeon said there was a chance the finger would survive and commended me for putting it on ice.

I stepped out into the cool, night air, my jacket buttoned up. The sounds and smells of inner-city Baltimore screeched and blared. I turned on my cell phone to see I had six missed calls from Janice.

"Geez, girl," she said. "You had us all freaking out over here."

"What do you mean?"

"I dropped by your place this afternoon and about passed out when I saw all that blood."

"Oh, my. It's Tyler, he—"

"I know all that now. But I didn't until after I called the sheriff and he came out and started looking around. He finally called the hospital and they told him the whole story."

"I'm so sorry. That must have been awful."

"How's he doing?"

"He hasn't woken up yet. I'll call you in the morning."

"You did right by him, didn't you, Rose Red?"

"I hope so," I said.

It was close to midnight when I realized Tyler's eyes were open.

"Hey," I said. "How are you?"

"It's throbbing."

I buzzed the nurse and brushed his hair off his forehead. "She'll bring you something."

"Well?"

"You have an index finger." I smiled down at him. "The surgeon said it actually may work."

An older woman came into the room carrying a small paper cup. She was dressed in scrubs, the top dotted with kittens in various states of play. "Hello there, sleepyhead."

"It's throbbing," I said.

"That's good." She handed him a cup of water with a straw. "We need to keep giving you these tranquilizers. It will help the blood flow."

"Okay by me."

After swallowing the pills, he laid his head back on the pillow. The nurse checked his hand. It was elevated in a sling. "The temperature is good," she said. "That means the blood is flowing into the finger."

"Amazing," I said.

"It is, isn't it?" She smiled over at me. "It takes two whole teams. One group works on the finger and the other on the hand. I watched it once."

"I chose not to," Tyler said.

"You mean you were awake?"

He nodded.

"Oof," I said. "I don't know if I could do that."

"Do you have children?" the nurse said.

"Yes," I said. "A daughter."

"Were you awake during her birth?"

"Wide awake."

"See? You could do it." She checked Tyler's dressing and looked back at me. "Do you need anything? I can bring you a pillow and blanket. Maybe some dinner?"

"That would be wonderful," I said. "But I don't think I'll need a blanket."

"We have to keep it warm in here. It's the most important thing right now—to get the blood flowing in that hand." She smiled. "I'll see if I can find some food."

Once she left, I looked back at Tyler. Pain etched his forehead. "Would you like to watch some television?"

"No," he said in a tight voice.

I looked around the sparse room, the pale green walls, the machines pumping and beeping. "Say, you wouldn't believe my day."

He turned toward me, a curious expression on his face.

"Well, first was that helicopter ride. Do you have any idea how terrified I am of heights?"

He shook his head.

"You wouldn't believe the people I saw in the ER." A small smile appeared on Tyler's face. "I had to stay with the paramedics until they did their transfer of care, you know, as next of kin." I smiled. "Well, you should have seen this one lady. She had cuts on her face and they had strapped her down—and she was very old. She kept yanking her gown open and the paramedics told her to stop. They were all shielding their eyes."

Tyler's smile widened.

"So, they asked her what happened and she said she fell out of bed. And then they asked her how much she had to drink today. Remember, this is two o'clock in the afternoon. And she said 'just one drink,' and they asked 'a drink of what,' and she said . . ." I waited.

"Well?" Tyler's voice was hoarse.

" 'Just one pint of Bacardi.' "

Tyler exhaled a laugh. "No way."

"Honest to God." I held up my hand as if to swear on it. "Welcome to Balmer."

I flinched when I felt his good hand on mine.

"I forgot to tell you," I said. "Janice took Dickens home with her. You worry I spoil him? We'll have to put him on a diet when we get home."

"Thank you," he said, his eyes moist.

"You're welcome."

As Tyler drifted off to sleep, I thought back over the day. I'd never been tested in that way before. I always wondered if I'd be brave. I smiled to myself and stroked Tyler's hand, grateful for his presence in my life. "Sweet dreams," I whispered.

THIRTY-FOUR

Tyler and I arrived back at Barclay Meadow a few days later. I had fixed up the guest room for him. He injured himself on my property and although his worker's compensation would pay for everything, I felt obligated to nurse him back to health. Once I had him settled in bed, I propped some pillows under his hand and dosed out his medications. He had to take blood thinners. "No salads," I said as I read the insert in the pharmacy bag. "Did you know that?"

"Know what?"

"Foods with vitamin K clot the blood. Anything dark green."

"I can manage fine without anything green," he said. "Hey, it doesn't say anything about coffee, does it?"

I scanned the orders. "Yes." I looked up at him. "I'm sorry—no caffeine—it restricts the blood flow."

His head fell back on the pillow. "That might kill me."

"I'll find something."

"Rosalie, you don't need to wait on me. It makes me tense."

"You can't take care of yourself and keep your hand elevated at the same time. Besides, I want to do this. I feel responsible."

I trotted downstairs in search of food. When I found some herbal tea, I put the kettle on the burner. I sorted through the mail while I waited. As I stood over the desk, the events of the previous days flashed through my mind: hearing Tyler scream, picking up his finger. One minute I was sitting at my desk, the next everything changed. There is a fine line between before and after, separating the two, demarcating who I was before and who I was now. I tried to remember exactly what I was doing before it happened. I had been on the Internet. Had I logged off? I jiggled the mouse, but my computer was powered down. Maybe Janice had turned it off. Our What Ifs group was private. No one had access but us. And yet, if my computer was open to that page, could the sheriff have seen it? I looked around, feeling as if someone was watching me. I jumped when the shrill whistle of the tea kettle filled the house.

"I feel ridiculous," Tyler said when I brought him dinner. "I am perfectly capable of moving around."

"You are not a very good patient." I set the tray on the side of the bed. "Besides, I won't have it any other way, so stop complaining. You need your finger to heal and it won't if you're walking around. Anyway, I'm being selfish. If you don't get better, who will work the farm?"

He pushed himself up in bed. "I'm bored out of my skull."

I opened the window and a warm breeze billowed the curtains. "It's really nice out this evening."

"That just makes me tenser," he said. "I should be out there getting the plow ready."

"You really are a bad patient."

"Yeah, well, I know what you're thinking," he said.

"Okay, what am I thinking?"

"You're thinking I should have let you buy a new saw."

"Wrong again."

"I don't believe you."

"I like your frugality. So," I said, "what are we going to do with you?" I glanced around the room. "Do you want me to try and bring the television up here?"

"No," he said. "I'm not a fan. Besides, watching television would only make me more depressed about sitting here on my ass."

"Well, we certainly don't need you to get any grumpier." I walked over to a bookshelf stuffed with my aunt's books. "I have an idea."

He eyed me. "You're making me nervous."

I selected a book and spun around. "I'm going to read to you. How about a little Harper Lee?"

His face softened. "Are you sure?"

I sat down next to him. "Just lean back and close your eyes."

The food started arriving the next day: casseroles, salads, desserts, and three different types of lasagna. Doris Bird had spread the word about what I had done for Tyler. I met the biggest smiles and friendliest faces I had ever seen since moving here. Everyone asked to see Tyler and would glance around the house as they made their way to the stairs. Women clutched my hands and thanked me. Some stayed for coffee and others said they wouldn't impose. But the biggest surprise was when two men showed up at the door in canvas coveralls and boxy caps and asked to speak to Tyler. The next thing I knew, they were firing up the tractor, the windows rattling from the clattering diesel engine.

Thirty-Five

Glenn B	I have news from Birdie's. It doesn't have anything to do with Megan but it's interesting.
Rosalie Hart	Come for breakfast tomorrow!
Shelby Smith	Does anyone have any news about the investigation?
Rosalie Hart	Not me. I've been too busy with Tyler. Anyone else?

Shelby Smith	We've been running this investigation for months and we haven't gotten anywhere. I'm worried we will fail.
Rosalie Hart	We know a lot, Sue. We'll figure this out.
Shelby Smith	When??? We have to step it up. We have to break something loose.

Glenn sat at my kitchen table reading the paper while I kneaded dough on the bread board my aunt had used, the wood dried with age and years of frequent use. My arms had become toned and strong, my fingers practiced and efficient as I squeezed and punched and flipped the pliable mound.

The sun streamed through the windows, bathing the kitchen in light, illuminating the paper for Glenn and warming the room. I had placed a basket of apple cinnamon muffins and chopped kiwi on the table. Mr. Miele was busy brewing us a Kenyan roast blend. The scents of freshly ground coffee and baked cinnamon stirred my morning hunger.

Glenn peered through his glasses at the financial page while he munched on an electric green kiwi slice. I was grateful for his presence in my life. I wondered if Sue was right—that we were abandoning the investigation. But lately I felt a surprising hint of contentment. I was happy caring for Tyler, baking for others, and enjoying my friendships. As much as I didn't want to give up on the investigation, I was relieved not to think about it as much. Even the sheriff seemed to be leaving me alone. I glanced over at Glenn and smiled. The absence of fear and violence in my everyday thoughts was refreshing—I felt lighter and a few steps closer to finding a new version of happy.

I covered the bread with a cloth towel, poured us coffee, and settled in across from Glenn. "So, what's your news from Birdie's?"

Glenn looked up and brushed the crumbs from his hands. "The college is going to raze those row houses across from campus on Church Street."

"Well, that will be an improvement."

"Not for the people living there." He helped himself to another muffin. "It will displace all those poor—and mostly black—families."

Tyler shuffled in, Dickens in close pursuit. "Sorry," he said. "I didn't realize anyone was here. I smelled the coffee and, well, I always seem to be to interrupting you."

"Tyler, you know Glenn, don't you?"

"Yes," Glenn said.

"I hope you don't mind if I skip the handshake."

"Of course not," Glenn said. "How's the finger?"

Tyler smiled. "It's there."

"Thank the Lord," Glenn said.

"Thank Rosalie." He removed a mug from the cabinet with his left hand and filled it with coffee.

"Join us," I said. "I'll get you a plate."

"That's the worst of it." Tyler sat next to Glenn. "She won't stop waiting on me."

"I think she enjoys it," Glenn said. "And you don't want to miss out on these muffins. I'm on my third."

"What have you been up to today?" I said as I set a plate down in front of Tyler.

"I've been on your computer all morning."

"Don't tell me you have a Facebook page?" I smiled. "We should be friends."

"Whatever you do, don't start that mafia wars nonsense," Glenn said. "It's as addicting as crack."

"No Facebook. I like to look a person in the eye when I'm speaking with him. Or her," he added.

"So, what have you been doing?" I said and sat down. "Solitaire? Hearts?"

"Research." Tyler sipped his coffee.

"You've lived in Cardigan a long time, Tyler," Glenn said.

"All my life and then some," Tyler replied.

Glenn smiled. "I might have stayed here, too, if I had been born in Cardigan." He leaned back in his chair. "Do you know the owner of those row houses across from the college?"

"Leroy Chalmers." Tyler was having difficulty unwrapping his muffin. I started to reach for it, but he shot me a warning look. After studying it for a moment, he finally peeled it off with his teeth. He looked over at Glenn. "Leroy's about as old as those places, too."

"Did you know the college is buying him out?"

"Good. Maybe Leroy can move to Florida and sit in a lounge chair for the rest of his life."

"He'll be lucky if he can find a place to live. They're paying him a pittance."

"How can they get away with that?" I said. "Can't he hire a lawyer?" I rolled up my napkin and placed it under Tyler's arm. "Keep it elevated."

"With what?" Glenn said. "They're living off the rent they receive and what crumbs Social Security throws their way. And believe me, they aren't getting a whole lot of rent."

"It's probably the only low-income housing left in this county, what with all the boaters and folks from the city moving in and . . ." Tyler glanced over at me. "Well, it's true." Tyler stood. "Mind if I use your computer a little longer?"

"Of course not," I said. "But keep your hand elevated. And put your feet up. You look pale."

Tyler carried his plate to the sink. As he walked out of the room he mumbled, "God, I hate this."

I smiled over at Glenn. "Bad patient."

"Anyone with drive and a will to work makes for a bad patient. Now, Rosalie, where did you learn to make these muffins?"

"I sort of made up the recipe. I've been experimenting. Annie loved cinnamon toast when she was little, so I thought, What better flavor for a muffin? Right? Besides, baking can be very healing." I smiled. "Tell me more about the houses."

Glenn leaned in. "The college wants to build two dormitories—state-of-the-art to keep those tuition dollars flowing. Kids expect that now, you know. They want private bathrooms and kitchenettes and maid service. No more cinder block cells with squeaky bunk beds."

"Can I ask why you're so interested?"

"It just doesn't seem right. I think the college should have to pay them their due. That land is valuable to them. And I don't understand the zoning. Something is fishy."

"It's all that time at Birdie's. You're getting attached to this town, aren't you?"

"This investigation appears to be uncovering more than just a potential murder. I'm starting to see how things operate here. It just doesn't seem kosher."

"Janice has led me to believe there are powers that be around here. Do you think that's true?"

"The sheriff doesn't follow his own laws. The college seems to have undue influence over things. Which makes me think it goes higher. Maybe a judge or a county commissioner. Or maybe the mayor."

"What are you going to do, Glenn?"

"I don't know yet. But I can't sit by and watch injustice. If those people can't advocate for themselves, then someone has to do it for them." Glenn's brow was deeply furrowed.

"Good luck with that." Tyler strode into the kitchen. He set his coffee cup on the counter and turned to face us, one hand on his hip. "Lots of people have tried to change the way things work here. Especially newcomers. But they soon learn it's like trying to change the direction of the Cardigan. Some things are just how they are."

•   •   •

After saying good-bye to Glenn, I scrubbed the kitchen clean and sat at my desk with yet another cup of coffee. As always, my first stop was Facebook.

Shelby Smith has tagged you in a photo.

Annie Hart
These are great, mom. Maybe you could pick one for your profile. That silhouette is creepy : /

Sue had joined Tyler and me for dinner a few days before. After eating my homemade cream of crab soup dusted with Old Bay Seasoning, corn bread, and a walnut and pear salad, the three of us lingered at the table and talked for hours.

The image was of me in my apron and oven mitts holding up the soup tureen. It was a flattering photo, which wasn't always the case when you're tagged on Facebook. Dim lighting is great for erasing crow's feet and the parentheses that seem to frame my mouth these days. Maybe I would actually have a face on Facebook.

I clicked on Sue's timeline in order to thank her. Three hours ago, she had posted the following status update.

Shelby Smith
Still in my P.J.s reading a can't-put-it-down mystery.

Thirty minutes later this was posted:

Tim Collier
I'm coming to you. I know where you are. Destiny has chosen this moment.

It was one o'clock.

"Call Sue Ling," I said into my phone as I ran out the door. I prayed to God she hadn't changed her number again. I got in my car and tore down the driveway. Gravel popped and ricocheted off the wheels and a cloud of dust mushroomed behind me. As I skidded onto the main road, my car fishtailed and I almost lost control. Answer, Sue. Come on. Voicemail. Damn. I ended the call and redialed. On the fifth ring, she finally picked up.

"Are you all right?" The turbo roared as I swerved around a tractor. I glanced in the rearview mirror. The driver gesticulated something offensive at me.

"I'm great," Sue said. "I'm in the middle of a Lee Child and didn't want to answer my phone. Reacher is kicking butt." She giggled. "I'm still in my pj's."

"Is your door locked?"

"I don't know. Geez, Rosalie. What the heck is wrong?"

"Lock your door." My heart was pounding. Please let me be in time. "Now!"

"Okay, okay." I could hear her muffled footsteps and finally a click. "There. It's locked. Are you going to tell me why you're freaking out?"

"Thank God." I exhaled a sigh of relief. "Oh, oops," I said as I avoided a cyclist. "Sorry, Sue. I almost got a new hood ornament."

"Rosalie, are you in your car? Hang up and call me when you're—"

"No! Go to your Facebook wall."

"Why?" Her voice was high and thin.

"Just do it."

"Okay. Hang on. Oh!"

"It's him, isn't it."

"Oh my gosh. Rosalie . . . it's exactly . . ."

"Exactly what he said to Megan the night she died. How did he find you?" She didn't respond. "Sue? Are you *there*?"

"I . . . I told him some things."

"Oh, no." Dread coursed through me. "Why would you do such a thing?"

"We were failing," she said. "The investigation was stuck and no one seemed to care. He wasn't writing to me as much and I wanted to keep him engaged. Oh, Rosalie. I had to do something. Don't you see? We were giving up on Megan."

"I'm almost to town. I'm just passing the country club." I tried to peer around the Lincoln Town Car that was snailing down the road in front of me. "Are you alive?" I said.

"*What?*" Sue said.

"Oh, gosh, I'm sorry. I was yelling at the car in front of me. Oh, good. He's turning. And you're right, honey. We were giving up on Megan. Okay . . . I'm almost to your street." After waiting at a light, I turned onto Sue's block. She lived in the upstairs of a house; the bottom flat was vacant, but Sue said she preferred it that way. It was a small clapboard house close to the street with a gravel driveway leading to the backyard. A rusty car sat in front of the house. Delaware license plates. He's already here. My heart fisted in my chest. "Sue, hang on, I'm going to put the phone down for a moment."

"Rosalie, no!"

I dropped my phone in my lap and tried to act nonchalant as I eased past. A pounding bass vibrated my car. Long strands of brown, stringy hair curtained the face of the young man in the driver's seat. He was staring at something in his lap.

I picked up my phone. "Sue?"

"Rosalie, *please* don't put your phone down again."

"Honey, he's here. He's sitting in a car in front of your house."

"Oh, my God," she screamed.

"I'm going to put you on hold while I call the sheriff. One sec."

"Don't call the sheriff."

"Why not? Sue!"

"Just please don't."

I drove around the block and parked behind the boy. The hard, angry rap thundering from the car increased in volume when he pushed the door open and climbed out. It muffled again when he slammed the rusty door shut. "Sue," I whispered. "He just got out of the car."

The boy's jeans were low on his hips. Plaid boxers billowed out of the top. He held his pants on with one hand as he walked to the sidewalk. I started to get out, although I had no clue what I would do. I stopped when he leaned against his car. He parted his hair with his hands and gazed up at Sue's window. I chewed on a fingernail. "He's a greasy boy. I don't think he's washed his hair in a month."

"Rosalie. What should we do?"

"We should call the sheriff, but barring that . . . I'm thinking. Hey, don't go to your window. He's staring up at your house. He must know you're on the second floor. How would he know that? Oh, wait." I squinted to try and see better. "He's reaching in his pocket."

He held a half-smoked joint tight in his fingers, sparked a lighter, and puffed it lit. He inhaled deeply, his eyes closed, and held it in. After a few seconds, he exhaled a long, steady stream of smoke. He paused, then took another hit. Tilting his head back, he studied the inertness of Sue's house with narrowed eyes.

"He's smoking a J," I said. "Isn't that what they're called? Or is it 'doobie'?"

After another toke, the boy knocked the ember onto the sidewalk and stepped on it. He licked his fingers, stubbed out the joint, and put it back in his pocket. As he walked around the back of his car, I kept the phone to my ear and pretended to be in an animated conversation. The door creaked shut. He picked something up off the passenger seat and hunched over it. The bass continued to thump like a heartbeat in a stethoscope. Clouds of dirty blue-gray smoke puffed out of the tailpipe and quickly dissipated.

"He won't try anything, right?" Sue said. "It's the middle of the day. Aren't there people around?"

"Well . . . there's a very old woman walking a ball of matted fur and another woman running by with one of those jogging strollers. I don't think they would be much help." I gripped the steering wheel and watched carefully. "Well, maybe the woman with the stroller. She's pretty buff."

After a few minutes, the boy climbed back out of the car and shoved his hands in the pockets of his hoodie. One of the pockets hung low, heavy with something bulky. What if it's a *gun*? I had to call the sheriff. I didn't know what Sue was hiding, but it wouldn't matter if she was dead.

He pulled the hood over his head and walked purposefully toward the house. His face was shrouded, causing him to look like the grim reaper incarnate. He strode past the front door and walked toward the driveway.

"I'm hanging up."

"Rosalie!"

I hopped out and hurried to the sidewalk. "Tim?" I called, slightly breathless. "Hey, Tim."

He spun around. "Who the hell are you?"

"Tim Collier, right?" I took a step closer, wobbling in my boots. Why was I in heels? "Aren't you Tim Collier?"

"Who wants to know?" His eyes darted around. The jogger had moved on. The older woman must have finally rounded the corner. We were alone.

"I'm friends with Shelby. I just dropped by to see her." I steeled my eyes into his. "I recognize you from Facebook."

"What the . . ." His voice was high in his throat. "Just leave me alone."

"I know, Tim." I took another step and crossed my arms. "I know you write threatening messages on young women's Facebook pages.

And then you find them, is that right?" I cocked my head. Adrenaline bolstered my courage.

"I don't have to listen to this. I don't have to listen to nobody. You got that?" He was yelling now. His eyes were wide, almost feral. "And I don't care what you say, 'cause none of it matters anymore." He jabbed a finger at me. "People suck."

My scalp tingled. This kid had probably posted a good-bye video on his Facebook wall trashing all the bullies of the world. He was going to kill me, Sue, and anybody else who got in the way.

He came closer. An ashy, herbal scent met my nose. He clutched the weight in his pocket.

THIRTY-SIX

"What do you want, Tim?" Sue sounded calm and unafraid. She stood on the sidewalk in front of her house in a pair of drawstring flannel pants and a pink tank top.

"Tim?" I said. His hand moved again. Perspiration trickled down my back. "I recognize you from Megan's wall, too."

His mouth dropped open.

"We've documented everything," Sue said.

Good one, I thought.

"And the police are on their way," she added. I prayed she meant it.

His eyes darted from Sue to me, then back to Sue. "You said you loved me." His voice was ragged.

"No," Sue said. "I didn't."

"We both loved Megan. Remember?" he pleaded. "We can all be together."

Sue crossed her arms. "I never knew Megan. I made it all up."

"Why . . . you lying bitch. You . . ."

A siren wailed. She did call the sheriff.

Tim hesitated, then ran to his car. The engine revved and he tore out, leaving a patchwork of black tire treads on the pavement.

Sue and I rushed to one another. "Thank God you're all right."

"You were amazing, Rosalie. So brave."

"What about you?" I stepped back and looked her in the eye. "And you called the sheriff."

She nodded. "I had to. He could have hurt you." The siren grew closer. Sue looked nervously in its direction. "I'm going upstairs. Call me down only if you need me, okay? But please, try not to mention my name."

"Honey, what are you *hiding*?"

"Rosalie, there's a lot you don't know about me." She glanced down the street. "Be careful. The sheriff hates you." She reached out and squeezed my hands. "You just saved my life." Her mouth twitched. "But I have to go."

She trotted around the house just as the sheriff's cruiser squealed around the corner, stopping within centimeters of my bumper. He killed the siren, but kept the lights on. The garish colors overwhelmed the cloudless blue sky.

My shoulders fell. I was completely enervated from the adrenaline that had just coursed through my body like a bullet train. "Sheriff Wilgus."

He eased his bulk out of the cruiser, making no effort to hurry. "I got a call someone was threatening a Shelby Smith."

"Someone was."

"So?" He stepped onto the sidewalk and adjusted his belt. "Where is she? And who's threatening her? You?"

"Not me. A young man was here, but he got away."

The sheriff rolled his eyes. "Why does that not surprise me?"

"He was stalking her on the Internet. And he showed up here this afternoon." I bit my lower lip. "I think he had a gun."

He scowled. "Did you actually *see* a gun?"

"No. But I'm ninety-nine percent certain he was carrying a pistol in his pocket."

"Maybe he was just happy to see you."

"I'm glad you find this so amusing, but the whole thing was pretty terrifying." I rubbed my arms.

"Well, you got no victim and no perp." He eyed the quaint, quiet street. "So, we don't have a crime. Oh, wait . . ." He looked over at my car. "Will you look at that. Someone forgot to put money in the meter again."

"Sheriff. I'm serious. This boy is dangerous. I have his license plate number. He's probably on his way to I-95. You could put out an APB."

"For what, exactly?" He rubbed his chin. "A guy I never saw?" He made quotations marks when he said "guy."

"He wrote a threatening note on my friend's wall," I said.

"He wrote on her wall? With what? A *crayon?*"

"No." This was futile, but I had to give it a shot. If Tim Collier was our killer, he could kill again. I looked up at the sheriff. How did this man always make me feel so inconsequential? "He wrote a threatening post on her *Facebook* wall."

"Oh, this is rich, Hart." He hoisted up his pants.

"He wrote on Megan Johnston's wall, too. The day she died." I paused, waiting for it to sink in. My eyes never left his. "If you actually investigated her death, you would already know that."

"You ever gonna shut up?" His face darkened. "I've had it with you and that girl."

"He could kill again." I lifted my chin. "And this time it will be your fault."

"*Again?*" His eyes smoldered.

"He stalks people on the Internet, then figures out where they live."

"You got a body?"

"No. I already told you. I scared him away with what I knew."

"You're certifiable, you know that? You should be in the loony bin." A terrifying smile curled up his lips. "I just had an idea."

I brushed my hair back from my face. "I know, Sheriff."

He was still smiling. "No, you don't."

"Yes, I do."

"I don't have time for your games, Hart."

"I know everything," I blurted out. "I know that Nick Angeles was sleeping with Megan. I know the college wanted you to drop the investigation to protect him. And I know why you were willing to do it." I stepped closer and lowered my voice. "I know what they have on you."

"You don't know *nothin'*." There it was. The whiskey-saturated breath.

"Then why are you harassing me?"

"You're freakin' nuts. Bonkers." He pointed up. "Elevator don't make it to the top."

I swallowed hard. "I have evidence."

"Ha! You know how much that matters?'" He towered over me. "You're nothing more than a drop in the Chesapeake Bay."

"I'd like to get in my car."

"You're out of warnings." He blocked my way with his girth.

I could feel the blood drain from my face. I had showed enough bravado for the one day. For one life. "I'm going home now."

I stepped around him and slid into the seat of my car. The lights continued to swirl. Vertigo spun in my head. I grabbed the steering wheel to steady myself and turned the key. I jumped when I heard a knock on the passenger window. After I buzzed it down, the sheriff rested his arms on the door and peered in. I had half a mind to put it back up. Maybe I would catch his head in the window.

"What?" I said.

"One more thing."

I waited. The car was in drive. I gripped the wheel tighter.

"I just wanted to tell you," he said in a slow drawl. "You'll be real easy to find when it's time."

THIRTY-SEVEN

Shelby Smith	Tim Collier canceled his FB account. I searched everything I knew about him. Of course his name isn't Tim Collier. That guy doesn't exist. What do we do next?
Rosalie Hart	It was a scary day. Tim was there with very bad intentions, I'm sure of it. And then I had a rough time with the sheriff. This is getting dangerous.
Tony Ricci	We can drop this any time, Princess. It ain't worth you getting hurt.
Rosalie Hart	No, I can't quit. We've come this far. Maybe if we rule out everyone else then we know it was Tim. Did he go to Delaware? Megan must have known him if she accepted his friendship. Sue, I have faith in your computer skills. Don't stop trying.
Glenn B	So let's get busy. What next?
Tony Ricci	I know her dad is nuts. I went to his office.
Rosalie Hart	Tony, was that a good idea?
Glenn B	What did you learn?
Tony Ricci	For starters he's arrogant and pompous and tried to sell me all kinds of stuff I don't need. He had pictures of himself all over the place with "celebs." He even framed his Delaware Blue Hens football jersey.
Rosalie Hart	Joe Flacco played for Delaware.

Tony Ricci	Princess . . . stay focused.
Shelby Smith	Did he mention Megan?
Tony Ricci	Not once. No sign of her anywhere.
Glenn B	So we've learned he's unlikable. Doesn't make him a killer. What else?
Rosalie Hart	I'm going to ask the professor out for a drink.
Tony Ricci	Princess?
Rosalie Hart	I'll be okay. We'll be in public. I just have to figure out what to say. But I need to provoke him into a confession of some sort.
Glenn B	In the meantime I'll go to the restaurant at the marina Tony mentioned and show Megan's picture around. Anyone care to join me for dinner? It's on me.
Shelby Smith	Yes!=)

Tony and I agreed to meet in town a few days later. Although I was worried I'd run into Sheriff Wilgus, it was a warm, sunny day and I was low on vitamin D.

"How's Sue?" Tony said as we strolled toward the small park in the center of Cardigan. We had purchased fountain sodas from the drugstore. Mine was a cherry cola and Tony had ordered a root beer float.

"Amazingly okay," I said.

We sat on a bench bathed in sunlight. A few stubborn leaves still clinging to the oak trees rustled above us. I took a loud sip from my drink.

"I wish you could have learned more from Bill Johnston," I said.

"Oh, I think I learned enough to know he could have done it. He screamed narcissist."

"Still . . ." I sipped again, disappointed my drink was almost gone. "We could use some more evidence."

"Hey . . ." Tony nudged my arm. "Isn't that Glenn?"

I looked up. Glenn was scurrying toward us, arms pumping as he speed-walked through the square. His hair was askew and his face was dotted with red blotches.

"Glenn?" I said. "Are you all right?"

"Better than all right." He flopped onto the bench between us. His chest heaved as he tried to catch his breath.

"Spill, Pops," Tony said.

"Lila has finally opened up about the police report." His chest rose and fell. "Megan"—he hesitated, seeming to want to savor his triumph—"did not drown."

I slapped my hand over my mouth.

"What did she say?" Tony said.

"There was no fluid in her lungs or air passages—none of that frothy foam from drowning."

"So, they did an autopsy after all?" I said.

"No." Glenn shook his head. "No, the family was adamant."

"So, how do they know?" Tony said.

"There was no foam."

"But . . ." I thought for a moment. "Then they should have had to do an autopsy. That means she was murdered."

"Well, it's not that simple. First of all, I think this town is so corrupt we are only scratching the surface. But also, the father said she had been depressed and that he found a suicide note."

"So, there *was* a note," I said. "You know, I did see an envelope in the evidence bag."

"Lila never saw a note. She checks in all the evidence. Someone must have intervened. Anyway, when the sheriff was getting ready to order an autopsy, something happened and he closed the investigation."

"The college," Tony said. "That's when the college put the kibosh on it to protect"—he made quotations marks with his fingers—"Nicky."

"And their reputation. So, yes, I believe that's exactly what happened."

"But if there was really a note," I said, "then she did commit suicide."

"Not so fast," Glenn said. "There are still facts that don't add up. No one ever saw a note. Bill just claimed there was one. And he said his wife was so distraught an investigation could do her in. But as we have learned, the man isn't overly concerned about his wife's well-being. So if there was an envelope, it wasn't necessarily a suicide note. Plus, Bill could have his own reasons to stop an autopsy from occurring. Didn't you say the college president notified the Johnstons? Bill could have skedaddled down there before the police had finished with the crime scene. It's all entirely possible." Glenn smoothed his hair back into place. His breathing had finally slowed. "There's another thing. According to Lila, the sheriff saw some things on the body, including some bruises on her neck. But even more important, he thought it odd she was dead before she went in the water. I mean, how do you die by suicide and end up in the water if you didn't drown? It would take an awful lot of jerry-rigging."

"That's true," I said.

"So this Lila chick told you all that?" Tony said.

"Yes." Glenn crossed his legs and hugged his knee. "The more interested I was, the more she talked. Funny thing is, she thinks she's protecting her sheriff, that he was unjustly prevented from doing his job. I don't think she realizes he could be incriminated, as well."

I fell back against the bench. "I was right," I said. "I was right all along. Megan was murdered."

"It's looking that way," Glenn said. "We have to keep up this investigation."

"Glenn," I said as I stared over at Birdie's. "Did Lila see you run over here?"

"No. She had already gone. I was finishing my paper and munching on one of those chocolate muffins you're selling and then I spotted you two. I folded up shop and got out of there."

"Do you think Doris is watching us right now?" I said.

We all looked over at the dark glass, the peeling letters that spelled BIRDIE'S SHOE STORE.

"Oh," Glenn said. "Perhaps I should have waited and told you in our private group."

THIRTY-EIGHT

I turned Nick's business card over in my hands and traced the raised lettering of his phone number. I had to do this. The trail was growing cold and we finally knew for certain that Megan had been murdered. I slid my finger over the screen of my iPhone, took a deep breath, and tapped out his number.

"Nicholas Angeles . . ."

Shoot. I was hoping for voicemail. "Uh, ahem. Hi, Nick. It's me. Rosalie."

Silence.

"How are you?" I said quickly.

"Busy, actually."

"Oh. Okay. I'm sorry to bother you. I—"

"You're not bothering me, Rosalie. I didn't mean that."

"I was just wondering if you wanted to get that drink we talked about. I've been doing a little better, you know, since my separation, and I think it would be good for me to get out. Is the offer still open?"

Another silence. I started to speak and then . . .

"I have a better idea. Let's take that sail. The weather is warming up. How does that sound?"

"A sail?" I bit my thumbnail. "I don't know a thing about sailing. I know I asked you about your boat, but—"

"Even better."

Better?

"Let me check my calendar and get back to you," he said. "It would be lovely to spend time with you. Are you in?"

"Yes," I said while my nerves bundled into a ball of terror. "I look forward to hearing from you."

"Rosalie?" he said. "I'm glad you're ready to get out and live again."

I ended the call and stared at the phone. I would need a planning session with the What Ifs, for sure. So many things could go wrong alone on a sailboat with Nicholas Angeles. I chewed on my thumbnail again. How on earth could I pull this off? I looked out the window. The sun was higher in the sky. Daylight Savings Time was finally over and I could adjust to the rhythms of the sun again. It cast a warm glow over the river, as if the tarnished gray had been brushed with a gilt of gold. The river. Megan. Yes, Megan, I hear you. I will do this. I trembled, feeling as if someone was sharpening a knife on my spinal cord.

I needed an Annie fix. I opened my computer and clicked on the blue F icon. Annie wasn't available for a chat, so I decided to go to her timeline to see what she'd been up to. She was taking her last midterm that afternoon and was scheduled to drive up to Chevy Chase tomorrow for spring break. After Thanksgiving, I insisted she get her car back and we secured a parking permit for the following semester.

I was surprised to see a different profile photo. This one was hard to make out. It looked like a dried-up flower—a rose maybe. I let out a small gasp as I read her post.

Annie Hart

Men are cruel selfish bastards who think with their #$^*.

• • •

I booked the first flight out to Raleigh-Durham. I would take a cab once I got there and go to my Annie. Janice agreed to stay with Tyler while I was gone. He was scheduled to start physical therapy in a few days, but until then, he needed to keep his finger motionless so the tendons had adequate time to reattach. Although he could do most things for himself, I worried about his state of mind. Tyler was a worker. He rarely stopped moving and I knew it must be hard on his psyche to be idle and unproductive for so long. An evening spent brooding alone was the last thing he needed.

She burst through the door with a magnum of wine, an extralarge pizza box, and a brown grocery bag looped over her arm. "Coming through," she said and charged into my kitchen

I dropped my overnight bag by the door and followed her. "I can't thank you enough."

"No problem." She wedged the wine onto a narrow space on the counter. She took in my coffee maker. "You know, you would have more counter space if you had a Mr. Coffee like everyone else."

"That, my friend, is Mr. Miele."

"Yeah, right."

"Don't be so quick to dismiss. He's the perfect man: he has no demands or expectations, he's a wonderful listener, and he perks right up with one touch of a button."

Janice rolled her eyes. "What time is your flight?"

"Nine."

"How's your girlie?"

"She's relieved I'm coming. We're going to drive back together tomorrow in her car."

"Is this her first bad breakup?"

I nodded. "She's never been in a serious relationship. She's always done the group thing. A few proms and homecomings, but never anything like this."

"Poor kid," Janice said. She set the pizza and bag on the table and slipped out of her coat. "Where's the patient?"

"In the living room. He's not pleased I called you. He thinks he's fine by himself."

"We'll have fun. Plus, it's good to get out of the house. Trevor can do the morning rush hour with the kids tomorrow."

"I left you a note with all of his medications and instructions. And make sure he keeps his hand elevated. He's come this far, I would hate to see him screw it up now." I pulled on my coat and hitched my purse on my shoulder. "What's in the bag?"

"I saw on Facebook you've been reading to Tyler, so I grabbed a bunch of old books off the shelves in our living room—anything with a lot of dust. I know he likes the classics." She lifted several books out of the bag. "I've got Dickens, Hemingway, Mark Twain . . ." She looked up. "How long is he staying here?"

"A while longer." I peered into the bag. "Janice . . ." I picked up one of the books. "What is this?"

"I don't know," she said. "I told you, I just grabbed all the books that were old." She looked down at the cover of *Lady Chatterley's Lover.*

"Janice!"

"Oh, crap." She barked out a laugh. "Maybe you should skip that one."

I found Annie curled up in a ball on the bottom bunk in her dorm room. Her roommate had already left for home. The room was dark, the blind pulled, and a stale smell had settled into the air. I hurried over and scooped her into my arms. The first sob sounded from deep within and I held tighter. She cried for most of the night.

The next morning, she tossed some clothes in a duffle, grabbed an overstuffed laundry bag, and we drove home in her car.

She slept the entire trip, exhausted from a tortured, sleepless night. Although I was tired, too, I made frequent stops for coffee and listened to talk radio. I had yet to learn the details of her breakup with Connor, but I would be patient. Annie would talk when she was ready. Although this wasn't a divorce, I did not underestimate her pain. A hurt like that can stir up older hurts and pile into one gigantic snowball that cuts off your breathing and swirls in your gut.

She spent the first day on the sofa watching back-to-back episodes of *Family Guy*, although she never laughed. The next day I sat next to her and handed her a mug of green tea.

"I thought you were all about the coffee," she said and accepted the mug. Her hair was back in a sloppy ponytail and the sheers were pulled across the windows. Oversize shadows haloed the objects in the room.

"Can we talk?"

She shrugged, clicked the power button, and the room fell silent. After a few moments, she looked over at me. "So?"

"Do you want to tell me what happened?"

"No."

"Are you hungry?"

"No."

"We could make a fire. Maybe watch a movie?"

"Uh, Ma, it's like fifty degrees." She stared back at the darkened screen. A tear escaped down her cheek and she quickly brushed it away.

"It would be good to get out."

"What the hell are we going to do? It's like the witness protection program here."

"Do you want me to call your dad? Maybe you could spend the end of the week in Chevy Chase."

"Mom?" She looked over at me. "How long is this going to go on?" Her voice was uneven and I knew she was fighting back another onslaught of tears. "Don't you see how crazy it is that you live here? You're not even trying to get back with Daddy. This is all as much your fault as it is his."

"Oh," I said and looked away.

"I can't do this anymore. I hate it more than you know."

I dried my palms on my jeans. "I'm so sorry, Annie. I wish—"

"I want us to be a family again." She slammed her mug down on an end table, picked up a throw pillow, and hugged it. "I want us to go home."

I faced her again. Another tear streaked her cheek. I reached up and wiped it away. "I understand how hard this is for you. And . . . well . . . I'll talk to your father. No, I'll do better than that. I'll meet with him."

"Really?"

"Yes. I'll go call him now."

"Okay," she said in a small voice.

I slapped my hands on my thighs and stood. I walked deliberately into the kitchen to find my phone and noticed Tyler at the kitchen table. He'd been trying to give Annie some space by lingering in the kitchen as much as possible.

"Hey," I said.

"How's the kid?"

"She's brokenhearted." I leaned against the counter. My head fell forward. "And it's killing me."

THIRTY-NINE

Clothes lay strewn on the floor and bed. I had no idea what to wear to my dinner with Ed. All I knew is I wanted to look good. Really good. I wanted him to regret his decision. I wanted him to want me again. And most of all, I wanted the three of us to be together. "Oof," I said and kicked off a strappy shoe.

After a frantic half hour, I stood before the mirror. I had decided on a short black skirt, sheer black stockings, and heels. My top was simple but elegant—a white knit with three-quarter-length sleeves and a scooped neckline, tight in all the right places. My hair was fluffed and I wore a lipstick Janice had brought me from New York—glossy and light, but with a detectable hue of red. It was the look I wanted: classy with a little bit of snug and hopefully a whole lot of sexy.

I spritzed my perfume onto my wrists and rubbed them together. It was my nighttime scent—vanilla, spices, and a hint of chocolate. Ed used to nibble my ear and tease that it made him hungry. How long ago was that? Well, I thought, scents trigger memories, so let's hope Ed still had some good ones.

Deciding there was nothing left to fluff, spray, or adjust, I grabbed onto the railing and teetered down the stairs.

Tyler and Annie were in the living room. Low streaks of light from the setting sun shone through the trees, dappling their faces.

She held his hand in hers and examined his finger. A sheet of physical therapy instructions lay unfolded in her lap. They both looked up when I cleared my throat.

"Whoa," Annie said. "You look clutch, Mom."

"I hope that's good," I said. "Don't you think it needs something, though?"

Annie studied me. "An accessory. A scarf maybe?" She looked over at Tyler.

"Nah," he said. "Why hide that neckline?"

My face warmed.

"Excellent point," Annie said. "We need to accentuate the assets." She placed Tyler's hand on a pillow and hopped up. "Be right back," she said and brushed past me.

"I take it you're meeting your husband."

"Yes," I said.

"You look nice."

"I'll probably break my neck in these shoes." I sat down across from him. "I guess I just wanted to feel taller."

"So," Tyler said, his eyes challenging me, "what will you say?"

"To what?"

"If he wants you back."

"Oh." I straightened my spine. "I guess that's the whole point. Annie needs us to be together."

He looked out at the river.

I followed his gaze. The small, windswept whitecaps shimmered in the evening light.

"But what do *you* want?" Tyler was looking over at me again.

"So much has happened. We're a family. We have a history together." I gripped the arms of the wing chair. "Well, you must know what I'm talking about. How long were you married?"

"You mean you haven't heard?"

"Heard what?"

"You need to hang out at the Curling Iron more often."

"Oh, thanks a million."

"To hear the gossip." He shifted on the sofa, propped a stockinged foot on the ottoman, and leveled his eyes with mine. "My wife ran off with the UPS man before our first anniversary."

"How? They run up the sidewalk and back so fast, I couldn't ID one of them in a lineup."

"Apparently this guy wasn't in such a hurry to deliver his packages."

I bit my lower lip and tried to keep a serious face.

"I know what you're thinking," he said. "And don't think it's a joke I haven't heard."

"I'm sorry, Tyler. I don't mean to be insensitive, it's just . . . well." My fingers fluttered over my mouth as I tried to stifle the laugh tickling me. "I'm sorry. Of course it's not funny."

"It's been almost twenty years. It's a little bit funny."

"There's just so much to work with. I mean, the jokes, oh, I just thought of another one."

Tyler shook his head.

I smiled at him. "What went wrong?"

"Everything. She was from Baltimore. Her parents kept a boat at a marina just outside of town. I used to work there and we dated a few summers while she was in college and once she graduated we got married. She started a business—a flower shop—thinking she could modernize the town, wake it up a bit, bring the city to us country folk. But the thing is, when you move to Cardigan, you either have to slow down or lose your mind."

"She didn't adjust to the pace?"

"Her business failed in a few months. I took a hard hit financially and lost my house. It was all a big fat mess and I'm better off without her. Besides . . ."

I tried to suppress the smile twitching my lips. "She liked things COD?"

"You couldn't stand it, could you? I pour my heart out and . . ." Tyler flashed me a rare, uninhibited smile.

"Got it," Annie said.

I went over to her.

"Good night, Rosalie," Tyler said.

I looked back at him. "Good night."

Annie and I went into the foyer and she clasped my mother's pearls around my neck. "Perfect," she said.

"Thanks, honey." I hugged her. "Will you and Tyler be all right?"

"Of course." I started to leave. "Mom . . ."

"Yes?"

"Um . . . well . . . have a nice time."

"I love you," I said. "With all of my heart."

• • •

Ed and I agreed to meet halfway. I made dinner reservations at a restaurant on Kent Island—a small strip of land on my side of the Bay Bridge packed with marinas, hotels, and restaurants. I arrived first and sat at a small table by the window that looked out at the Corsica River. A full moon perched large and low in the sky, spreading a deep tangerine cone of light over the water.

I spotted him from across the room. He was still in his suit—charcoal gray with a starched blue shirt that augmented his polar blue eyes. My mouth dried. He was still the most elegant man I had ever seen.

"I'm sorry," he said and brushed my cheek with a kiss. "The Severn River Bridge was backed up." He sat down and scooted in his chair. "I think Annapolis would have been closer to halfway. Or don't you cross the bridge anymore?" He smiled as he unrolled the silverware from his napkin.

"Actually, the bridge doesn't bother me anymore."

"Really?" Ed said, sounding skeptical. "Since when?"

"Oh, I don't know. Maybe since I flew over it in a helicopter."

Ed shook his head and laughed. "Will wonders never cease."

The waitress arrived and Ed ordered a Tanqueray martini on the rocks and a high-end chardonnay for me. A small candle flickered next to the salt and pepper shakers. A third shaker contained Old Bay Seasoning, as was the norm for restaurants on the Eastern Shore.

I tried to read his mood. I was glad he ordered drinks. At least he wasn't in a hurry to get dinner over with.

After the waitress filled our water glasses, Ed leaned forward, resting his forearms on the table. "So, how was *your* traffic?"

"Dreadful," I said. "There was this tractor—"

"Ha," Ed said. "Don't you own one now?"

"No, not yet, at least."

"Oh." Ed frowned. "Annie said you were farming."

"Tyler is farming. Tyler leases the land. He has his own equipment." I thought of another joke and smiled to myself.

"So, is this farmer of yours making any money?"

"Yes, as a matter of fact, he is. He farms organically and he got a great price for the winter wheat."

"God, Rose. Do you hear yourself? You went to the University of Virginia and now you're living in the middle of nowhere and talking about winter wheat."

"I was born in the middle of nowhere." I folded my hands over my menu. "Besides, I wasn't given much of a choice."

"I didn't tell you to leave the house." He flattened his back against the chair. "And I certainly didn't suggest you exile yourself to Elba Island."

The waitress returned and set our drinks down on flimsy square napkins. "Subject change," Ed said and took a long sip. "You said you wanted to talk about Annie."

"That's right."

"But why? She got a three-point-eight last semester. She seems absolutely fine."

"She's not." I shook my head. "She misses our family. She doesn't even know where to call home anymore."

Ed's jaw muscles tensed. "It's an adjustment, but she'll get used to it."

I watched him closely—the way he avoided my eyes no matter how hard I focused my gaze. He was flipping his spoon over and over, stopping only to check his expensive watch. I caught myself wanting to make it all better, to drop the subject and let him off the hook. I wondered if he was expecting me to do just that and was biding his time with his spoon until I offered to fix the problem. Not this time.

"Ed, our divorcing has been hard on Annie. And she just had a very bad breakup. She's devastated."

His eyes shot up. "Why didn't you tell me?"

"I texted you from the airport. I had to go to Durham and drive her home."

"That's right," he said. "I remember now." His shoulders rose and fell as he took a deep breath.

"Ed," I said. "I think you need to work a little harder with Annie now that you don't have me to manage your relationship." I braced myself for an angry retort.

He leaned forward. "You're right. I need to pay more attention. Why are you so smart about these things?"

I could smell the crisp, icy gin on his breath. "I just feel it, I guess."

"I'll try and do better this summer. I have more time on my hands these days."

"Doesn't sound like you," I said and sipped my wine.

"I sold the company."

"Ed." I gasped. "That's wonderful."

"Thank you," he said. "And I'm already working on the next one. I'm going to develop software. Retail businesses are always playing catchup when it comes to credit card security. I've got a couple of guys working on a program that is state-of-the-art. I don't know where this will end up, but I think we have something that will be very valuable."

"Wow." I smiled. "It sounds like a great idea."

"My guys are smart. They are already coming up with some models."

"I can't believe you sold another company. You are very good at what you do."

"I'm probably the only suit making money in this economy." He stretched his neck from side to side. "I forgot how much I like to talk to you about business."

"I like it, too."

"Rose? I'm glad you are having some success with the farm. Good for you."

"Thank you," I said, feeling truly touched.

"So, what will you do this summer?"

"Now that the crops are almost in, Tyler and I are looking into markets for the organic vegetables we're going to grow this summer. Oh, and I'm planting an herb garden in order to try some new recipes for my bread. I thought I would plant some dill and—"

"Your bread?"

"I'm selling it at the shoe store." I smiled, anticipating his reaction. He did not disappoint.

"*Shoe* store?"

"It's where I buy the *Post*. It's a version of Aunt Charlotte's recipe. I've sold over one hundred loaves. Now I'm trying out some muffin recipes."

"Well," he said and signaled the waitress for another drink, "you always were an excellent cook."

"Thank you."

The lights dimmed and the few lines that had been tooled into Ed's face by age were erased by the softened lighting and the warm glow of the candle.

"Annie said you've made some friends," he said.

"Yes, wonderful friends. I would trust them with my life."

He chuckled. "Sounds a bit dramatic."

Not really, I thought. "Ed? Do you realize Annie wants to live with you this summer?"

"With me?" He reared back. "*Really?*"

"She wants to be in her home. And she wants to keep her job at the gym." I studied him, worried I would push him too far. But this was about Annie. "Don't you want her there?"

"Honestly?" The waitress arrived with his drink and he took

another long sip. "I don't know if she's told you, but it's very tense between us. We can barely have a civil conversation. I think she's furious with me."

"She's told me a little, but you two need to have this discussion. Talk to her, Ed. You're her dad. She adores you." I smiled over at him. "And she admires you so." I reached out and patted his hand. "Give her time. And remember, your relationship can't improve if you're never together."

"I get that." He nodded. "She's always been my little Anna Banana."

I smoothed my napkin over my lap. "I'll really miss her, though. If I had it my way, she would spend the summer with me."

Ed stared down at the table for a moment. His head shot up. "Rose? I have an idea. And it's a good one." He flashed me a wide smile. "Now that I've sold the company, I'll be able to come up with a separation agreement for us. How about if I free up some money for you to rent a place in Chevy Chase? Then Annie could live with you and keep her job. What do you think?"

"I don't know." I stared over at him. "What about the farm?"

"As long as it's making money, we can keep it."

We? "But I thought you just said you were going to make an effort with Annie?"

"I will. I'll make a Herculean effort to spend time with her. And maybe she won't be so angry with me if she has you nearby. Maybe that's been part of the problem—that you moved so far away." He rolled his shoulder back and straightened his posture. "This is a good plan."

"I . . ."

"And Rose?"

My stomach flipped when he gazed over at me. His blue eyes sparkled. "If you move back to Chevy Chase, we can do this more often."

"Do what?" I asked tentatively.

"Have dinner together. I think this is going very well. Don't you?"

The waitress reappeared and we ordered dinner—steak topped with crab for Ed, a salad and cup of soup for me. Once she was out of earshot, Ed said, "You look stunning tonight. I don't think I've ever seen you dress so flirty." He reached over and lifted my necklace. "Your mother's pearls." His fingers brushed my skin. How is it that he could still excite me with the slightest touch? Why was he being so nice? Why did he do this to us?

He let go. The pearls dropped back to my chest.

I clutched the bottom of my wineglass. "I'm still the same old me."

"No." He shook his head. "Something has changed."

"Actually, you're right. A lot has changed." I hesitated. "I've undergone a lot lately and the thing is, well, I'm not afraid anymore."

He leaned back in his chair. "What exactly were you afraid of?"

"Everything. Change, maybe?"

"That's good," he said. "That's very good." His dimples framed a smile. "It shows through—that strength. It's lovely."

His words sifted slowly through my system, warming me, calming me. "Thank you, Ed. That's very sweet." I twirled my glass.

"Rose . . ." Ed reached out for my hand. "Do you hate me?"

"No," I said. "I miss you. I miss us—our family. But I could never hate you."

"No, of course you couldn't." He kept my hand in his and continued to gaze over at me. My stomach swirled with wine and the deep attraction I had always felt for this man. What would I say if he asked?

After dinner we walked outside to the parking lot. I started to say good night but Ed grabbed my arms and pulled me to him. A nearby trio of nautical flags rippled in the breeze, casting shadows across his face. "Can I kiss you good-bye?"

I flattened my hands on his chest. "Dinner was lovely."

He lifted my chin with his finger. "*You* are lovely."

I smiled up at him. "Wow."

His kiss sent an electric current through me. How long had it been since we shared such a sweet kiss? I opened my eyes. "Thanks for meeting me."

"Thanks for waking me up about Annie." His eyes shone like aquamarine gemstones.

"You're welcome." I couldn't believe I was in Ed's arms again.

"Okay. Till next time, kiddo. It's good to have a plan. Let me know if you need help finding a place." He let go and straightened his tie. "Have I told you how much I appreciate you being so reasonable through all this? It could have been a disaster. But you've been such a grown-up about everything. You're one classy lady. And you know? Maybe I sort of helped you. I mean, look how much you've grown."

My heart plummeted to the bottom of my belly. I placed my hand on my chest and tried to breathe. Had I really duped myself into believing he would want me back?

"Hey," Ed said. "You okay? Did you get a bad salad?"

I shook my head.

"Rose?"

I looked up at him. The breeze had died down. The flags went limp. "I'll be okay."

"You sure?" He smiled down at me.

"Ed? Can I ask you something?" I gripped my bag with two tight fists, steeling myself to be strong. "When did you stop loving me?"

His shoulders fell. "Please don't do this."

"Was it when I quit working?"

"I was relieved when you quit. Our lives had gotten too hectic." He looked around the parking lot as if in need of an exit.

"Did you lose respect for me at some point?"

"Of course not." He rubbed his temples. "You are the most ethical and kind person I know."

"So, what, then? Was it after my mother died?"

He shook his head. "I loved your mother more than my own."

"I couldn't have been easy to live with. I would understand if it was too much for you."

"Well, that would have been pretty rotten of me." He smacked his gloved hands together. "Okay, are we finished here? Because dinner was really great, but I'm not so into this conversation."

"I have a right to know what happened, Ed. It will help me to know."

"It wasn't you." He avoided my eyes. "I . . . I just fell in love with someone else."

I shook my head. "I thought we had a good marriage."

"I never stopped loving you, Rose."

"But you did, Ed. You stopped loving me enough." I turned to go. I heard him call my name, but at that moment I felt truly divorced from him.

Despite the cool air, I buzzed my convertible down and put my car in reverse. I turned in the seat and there was Ed, hands on the door of my car. "Rosalie," he said. "I'm sorry."

"I'm okay, I really am. Thank you for dinner." I started to back up.

"How can you be okay?"

I stopped. Our eyes met. "Maybe you underestimate me, Ed. Maybe you always have."

Forty

For the remainder of the week, Annie and I sank into a routine. We shared breakfast every morning on the back porch. I was trying some new recipes and prepared a different omelet each day. We decided the tomato, basil, and fresh mozzarella was our favorite. I worked hard to keep things on an even keel. She never asked how my dinner went with Ed and I never asked her again about the details of her breakup with Connor.

The rest of her time was spent with Tyler. She was fascinated by his finger. She had him tell her every detail of the surgery and examined it as if it were under a microscope. She researched finger reattachment and appointed herself his in-house physical therapist. After accompanying him to his physical therapy visit, she set up three sessions a day and posted the schedule on the refrigerator. While they worked, they chatted like best friends. They discussed books and movies but, most importantly, they talked about the farm. I had never heard Tyler talk so much, but Annie had a way that put others at ease.

On the last day we sat on the porch drinking coffee. "I always think about Megan when I look out at the river," she said. "I still can't believe you found a dead body." She looked over at me, her eyebrows arched in question. "Is that redundant? 'Dead body'?"

"I don't think so," I said and took a sip of coffee.

"Are you any closer to finding out if she was murdered?"

"We know she was murdered for certain now. But we still don't know who." I tucked her hair behind her ear. "I like that you care so much about her. That says a lot about you."

Annie smiled, then stood and said, "I should hit the road. I'll go get my bag."

"I think Tyler already carried it down for you."

"He's not supposed to be doing stuff like that. You need to make sure he does his exercises after I leave."

"I'm on it," I said and stood to follow her out.

After saying a warm good-bye to Tyler, Annie and I walked out to her car. A Vera Bradley duffle weighed heavy on her shoulder. She turned to face me. "Mom? I'm sorry I haven't been very understanding."

"What do you mean?" I smoothed my hand over her cheek.

"I've been pretty selfish this week. I made it all about me." She scratched her nose and tucked some hair behind an ear. "I understand that you didn't want this divorce any more than I did. And I know how hard you've tried to keep things good for me."

"Wow," I said. "Thanks for saying that. But I'm your mom. And I wouldn't have it any other way."

"I know what you did with Daddy and I appreciate you trying." She hitched the duffle higher on her shoulder. Doodle daisy, just like Megan's backpack. "So, what are you going to do?"

"I've decided to do what your dad suggested. I'll look for a place in Chevy Chase. Something small. An apartment maybe, but with two bedrooms. I'll live there this summer with you and I guess Tyler will hold down the fort here." I glanced at the house. "I haven't really discussed it with him yet, though."

"Are you sure you want to leave?"

I shrugged. "I haven't come up with any better ideas."

"So, should I try and get my job back?"

"Go for it." I pulled her into a bear hug. "I'm so sorry about Connor. Please take care of yourself." I stepped back. "Say, Annie, if you're going to get a job, maybe you should change your Facebook page."

"Good idea. I'll do some spring cleaning when I get back to school."

As I watched Annie disappear through the cedars, I realized I would have to start over again—reinvent myself yet again. Summer. I had until summer.

FORTY-ONE

After dropping off a delivery of double chocolate muffins at Birdie's, I popped a stick of wintergreen gum in my mouth and started toward my car.

"Rosalie . . ."

I looked over my shoulder. Nick was standing by Birdie's storefront window. He was in jeans and a blazer, his wavy dark hair tousled about. "Nick?" I shielded my eyes and looked up at him.

"I thought I might find you here."

I hugged my papers. "How did you know?"

"I've purchased a few of those muffins." He stepped closer. "Are you ready?"

"For what?" My instinct was to back away from him, but I held my ground.

"That sail we've been talking about." A gust of wind blew a tress of curls onto his forehead. "The weather is perfect these past few days."

I forced a smile. "Do you have a day in mind?"

"I was thinking Friday evening. I can pick you up at your dock."

"My dock?" I clutched my papers tighter, hoping to calm my trembling hands. How does he know I have a dock?

"I'll make us dinner. And I just got a delicious case of French muscadet. I'll bring a bottle." He winked. "Or two."

"Yes." I swallowed back the lump forming in my throat. "That sounds lovely."

"Excellent." His fingers tiptoed up my arm and brushed my neck. "It's good you're ready to get on with your life. At some point, we all have to allow the ghosts to exit the stage." He walked backward, still facing me. He was grinning hard. "Six o'clock," he said. "Don't be late." He turned and continued down the sidewalk.

I touched my neck. Was he trying to tell me something? I leaned back against my car to steady myself. Did he say "ghosts"?

Rosalie Hart	I'm going for a sail with the professor.
Tony Ricci	WTF????
Shelby Smith	Rosalie, you can't do that.
Glenn B	It's madness. That's the worst idea I've ever heard.
Rosalie Hart	These are all thoughts I've had myself but he asked so there must be a reason.
Tony Ricci	To drop you in the drink. That's the reason.
Rosalie Hart	He would never get away with it.
Glenn B	Maybe he has already. I've been doing some research on a possible profile of the killer. If the killer has gotten away with the crime, then it may give him or her a sense of invincibility. It also may have given him or her pleasure. So if the professor killed Megan without consequence, then why not kill you? Oh. That was awful to say. I forbid this, Rosalie. Good Lord. Now I sound like Henry the VIII.
Tony Ricci	You got yourself worked up there, Pops.
Rosalie Hart	What if we come up with a plan. Some way to protect me.
Shelby Smith	Tony could follow you in his dinghy.
Tony Ricci	I've always hated the word dinghy.

Glenn B	I'll go along. We could have cell phones and flares. You could text us if something is amiss.
Tony Ricci	I'm in. We can follow the boat from a safe distance.
Rosalie Hart	This is all sounding good. I am admittedly terrified. But whatever you do, don't call the sheriff. He would gladly help Nick secure the line around my neck.
Shelby Smith	So what will you say to him, Rosalie?
Rosalie Hart	I don't know. I hope he'll get a little tipsy and confess.
Shelby Smith	But why does he want to spend time with you?
Rosalie Hart	To learn how much I know? Do I tell him? Do I tease him with a few facts like I did the sheriff? Maybe I'll just use it as an opportunity to get a better read on him. If he threatens me in any way, well, then we know he has violent tendencies.
Glenn B	I think I need a Tums.

That Friday evening I stood in the kitchen and sliced an asiago baguette I had seasoned with oregano and sea salt. I agonized over what to wear for my night with the professor. I had no idea what message I wanted to send. I just knew I wanted him to talk. I was glad he was bringing wine. Maybe a little lubrication would loosen his lips. I finally decided on a pair of jeans and a slightly snug black sweater. Absolutely no red this time.

Tyler moseyed into the kitchen. "It sure is quiet around here without Annie."

"She enjoyed you, too, Tyler."

He shook the carafe to see if it held any more coffee. "There aren't too many kids like her."

"How's your finger?"

"This finger is a lot like your divorce. I don't welcome the attention nor the need to focus on myself."

"Does it still hurt?"

"You weren't listening."

I pressed my lips together, evening out the recently applied gloss, and checked my watch.

Tyler eyed me. "Where are you off to in that perfume?"

"Just a sail with a new acquaintance." I looked away. The room was still warm and aromatic from the bread. "There's some leftovers in the fridge," I said. "That lentil dish I made—"

"Rosalie," Tyler interrupted. "I can fend for myself."

I watched him go. Dickens uncharacteristically trotted after him. I stared at the spot where he had stood. The mug of coffee was cooling. I'd thought from the day Tyler strode down my lane that he could read my mind. I had no doubt he had done it again. I wanted to call after him—to tell him I wasn't interested in Nick. I wanted to blurt out the whole story about our investigation. I wanted to tell him how much I loved having him here, taking care of him . . .

Tyler's boots were heavy on the stairs, followed by the scritch-scratch of Dickens's nails. I would fix things with Tyler later. I needed to refocus. I had a mission. After looping the basket of bread over my arm, I grabbed a rain jacket and headed out the door.

Nick was already on my dock, tying a line around a piling. As I passed the spot where I found Megan, my stomach somersaulted and I had a massive urge to turn around and run back up the bank.

"Ahoy," Nick said.

I squared my shoulders. "Permission to come aboard?"

"An eager sailor," Nick said. "I like that." He climbed in first, took the bread from my hands, and helped me onto the boat. "How are you?"

"A little nervous." I sat on one of the cushions.

"Nervous?" He looked puzzled. "Why would that be?"

"I've only sailed once." I gripped the side of the boat. "Shall we go?"

I nonchalantly looked around until I spotted Tony and Glenn. They were hunched over fishing poles fifty yards away. I was ridiculously relieved to see them.

"Those guys will never catch anything at this time of night," Nick said as he busied himself around the boat. "Must be a couple of amateurs."

"What guys?" I said.

"Those guys over there in that tiny boat."

I thought briefly of what Tony's reaction would be if he heard Nick refer to his boat as "tiny." I looked back at them. Glenn had noticed my arrival. He tapped Tony's arm.

As Nick untied the bow line, I said, "Can I ask you something?"

He looked over at me. "Anything."

"Why did you invite me out tonight?"

"Seems to me, you were the one to ask." He tossed the line into the boat. The bow drifted away from the dock.

"That's true."

"You said you're ready to date. Am I your first?"

I avoided his eyes. "Yes."

"Are you working?" He turned a key and the small motor puttered awake.

"Let's just say I have a preoccupation."

"Intriguing." He paused. "So, I have a lot to learn, then."

"As do I." Our eyes met.

Nick freed the stern line and unfurled a sail. It filled instantly. I was shocked at how fast we were already moving. I glanced over my shoulder. Tony was trying to jerk the outboard motor awake. Hurry up, I thought.

After a breezy sail up the river, the boat clipped around a bend.

My hair was blasted against my skull. I hoped Nick didn't notice how many times I looked over my shoulder, but it was like a nervous tic I couldn't control. "Coming about," Nick called. I almost slid off the seat when he made a sharp turn. He pulled in the sail and let the motor ferry us into a secluded cove.

There were no houses, no docks, no sign of civilization, just marsh grasses and the squawk of a blue heron flying overhead, annoyed at the invasion. "Where are we?"

"My oasis."

"You've been here before?" I said.

"I love coming here." Nick killed the motor and dropped anchor. "It's the perfect spot for a date."

I glanced around. The water was motionless. The breeze had died. This place appeared utterly lifeless. "Did you bring wine?"

"Oui," Nick said and trotted down into the galley. I listened for Tony and Glenn. There. A motor. Yes. It grew louder and then . . . oh, no. They kept going. I searched my pocket for my phone.

"Rosalie?"

I looked up. Nick held a sweating bottle of French muscadet in one hand, two glasses in the other. "You look as if you've seen a ghost."

"I do?" I tried to smile. "I had a text, is all." I crossed my legs and smoothed my hair. "Parents never stop worrying, do we?"

Nick continued up the steps and sat next to me. "Is everything okay with your daughter?"

"I think so. Would you mind terribly if I texted her back? It will just take a second." I typed with my thumbs. *You passed us. We're anchored in a cove on the left.* I clicked send and stuffed my phone back into my jacket.

He filled the wineglasses and held one out to me. "You sure everything is all right?"

"It is now." I accepted the glass and started to sip.

"Slow down, mademoiselle. We need to toast."

"Oh. Sorry."

He held it up to mine. *"L'chaim."*

"To life," I said and took a long sip. Why did he just say *that*? I took another sip.

"Someone is thirsty." He tucked his arm around my shoulders. "Is this all right?" He squeezed my shoulder. Chills rippled down my arms.

"Sure." I finished my wine. "This is good wine."

"I'm glad I brought more than one bottle."

The sun hovered over the river shrouded in thin, wispy clouds. A cool breeze signaled the impending night. My nerves were completely frazzled. I needed to keep my wits about me, but I was losing focus. Why had I agreed to this? I held out my wineglass.

"So, tell me," Nick said as he poured, "why were you willing to go out with me now? What's changed?"

"Time?" Another sip. "Some time has passed since the initial shock of my divorce."

"There's more." He studied me. "I want to know."

Because I want to know if you are a murderer? I lowered my eyes. No. That won't work. I had to keep this real. I looked into his eyes and thought for a moment. "I had dinner with my husband a few weeks ago." I took a deep breath. "I haven't really talked about this with anyone. But you see, all this time, I've been holding on to the fantasy that Ed and I would reunite. I think I was assuming this was just a phase, you know? That he would grow tired of his girlfriend and want our life back."

"And now you know that isn't going to happen?"

"Yes." I sipped more wine. "It's like he left me all over again."

"I'm sorry." He stroked my hair. "That must be very difficult."

"You know what he said?" I shook my head remembering the

moment. "He thanked me for being such a good sport about the divorce."

"He's an idiot. I told you that the first time we met."

"So it's time, right?" I finished my second glass of wine.

Nick slipped my left hand into his. "I think I know something that might help." He looked up. "Are you ready?"

"What?" He placed his finger and thumb on my wedding ring. "What are you . . . ?"

It came off easily. The extra pounds, I thought. It had been loose for so long, I feared I would lose it. I sucked in my breath and stared down at my naked hand, so plain and unadorned. Age spots I'd never noticed before dotted my skin. I felt vulnerable without the talisman of my ring to protect me. My phone clanged.

"You have a text message."

"I don't care," I said. My throat was tight, but I spoke the truth. My tie to Ed severed, my veins coursing with wine, I didn't care about anything. I was spent.

After tucking my ring into the front pocket of my jeans, he looked into my eyes. "You seem sad."

"I'm sorry."

"Don't be sorry." He squeezed my hand. "You've been through so much." He stood and pulled me up next to him. "It's getting chilly. Why don't we go below?"

I picked up my jacket and followed him down into the cabin. It glistened with heavily varnished honey-colored wood. I had seen this cabin before, but by the light of a flashlight months ago. I sat at the small table and Nick twisted a corkscrew into another bottle of wine.

"What about you?" I said.

"What about me?"

"Your wife. What happened?"

"She left me in September." He pulled out the cork with a loud pop.

"Why?"

"I was having an affair."

"With who?"

He laughed. "I don't think that's really significant. It's over now, anyway."

"It's an epidemic," I said. "The infidelity."

He filled our glasses. "I was unhappy long before the affair. I don't think it was a surprise to her. And I think she's happier now without me." He set the bottle on the table and sat next to me. "It's true for most marriages, I think. The affairs come after trouble."

"I don't agree. I think that's what adulterers say after they've slept with someone to rationalize what they did."

"Ah, in vino veritas," he said.

"Well, it's true, so yes, in vino veritas."

"I like that we are being honest with one another."

"Me, too." I gave him a genuine smile. "You're easy to talk to, you know that?"

"Well . . ." He dipped his head. "It is my profession."

"So, in vino veritas. Who did you have an affair with? It helps me to know, Nick. I have been bowled over by my entire situation. Tell me how it came about for you."

"Although I had a few minor affairs before, this one was different." He took a long swig of wine. He had been matching me sip for sip so far. "She was beautiful and passionate and pursued me relentlessly. She was—"

"A student?"

His eyes flashed. "Yes. But over twenty-one."

"This cove," I said. "Is this where you carried on your affair?"

He leveled his eyes with mine. "Sometimes."

"Is that how your wife knew?"

"Rosalie . . ."

"I told you about Ed. And you just removed my wedding ring from my finger. I believe it's your turn."

He took another long sip. Keep it up, Nick, I thought.

"Okay," he said. "Fair enough. But that's not how my wife learned of our affair. The girl? She emailed my wife. And she copied President Carmichael."

"That would put an end to things pretty quickly." I held his gaze.

He filled my glass again and I immediately took a sip. The wine was empowering me to go for it. I cleared my throat. "Why didn't Carmichael fire you?"

"Because I'm a rock star. My study is going to make me the next Kinsey." He set his glass on the table and rolled his shoulders back. "I'll be speaking all over the country and bringing in a hell of a lot of money. Do you think they would fire me because a student overstepped her bounds?"

"How did you get her to leave you alone? Or did you keep seeing her after that?"

A loud boom resounded through the cabin.

"What the hell is that?" He bolted up the ladder. I followed. The sky glowed with a large red flame. "It's a flare," he said. "A boater must be stranded."

"We should help them," I said. "Isn't that in the boaters' code of ethics?"

Nick shook his head.

"What if they're sinking?"

"You can see that flare for miles. Someone will call it in."

The wind had picked up, carrying a metallic scent. "Is there a bathroom?" I said. "I need to pee."

"Of course. I'll show you how to flush."

"Isn't there just a pedal thing?"

"That's right."

I felt immediately woozy as I descended back into the cabin. We still hadn't eaten. Nick followed and watched as I walked into the head and clicked the door closed. When I stepped out, he was standing before me, my phone gripped tightly in his palm.

"Nick?"

"You weren't texting your daughter." His eyes smoldered under heavy lids.

I stepped back. "No."

"Your friends are signaling you. They want you to answer their flare." He shook his head. "Is that the best you could come up with?"

I crossed my arms. "I want to go home."

"But you didn't learn what you were hoping to. You might as well ask. What have you got to lose?"

I looked up at him. "Did you sleep with Megan Johnston?"

"Many times," he said.

"Why did she tell your wife? I thought she pursued you."

"Because I wouldn't give her the internship. What else would you like to know?"

"How did she die?"

"She killed herself." He didn't even flinch.

"I thought we were being honest."

"What makes you think I'm not?"

"Because she didn't drown, that's why."

He took a menacing step toward me. "Nobody cares about that anymore."

I avoided his eyes.

"So, why do you?" he asked.

I looked up, his lids were at half mast. "Maybe I don't anymore, either."

"Now who's lying?" He cocked his head.

"I'd like my phone back."

He dropped it in my hand. He had powered it down. "Do those clowns in the boat know anything?"

"They know I'm here with you."

"Accidents happen, my dear."

The wine swirled in my gut. I placed my hands over my stomach. "I need some air."

"Be my guest."

I squeezed past him and hurried up the ladder. Cold wind blasted my face. A roll of thunder vibrated the hull. I looked for an escape, but all I could see was darkness—sky, land, and water bleeding into one solid black. I noticed a boat hook tucked under the bench. I dropped to my knees and tried to free it. A good jab and I could shove him right into the water.

"Stop. It's secured."

I sat back on my knees. "There's a storm coming."

Nick wore a yellow windbreaker over his sweater. He held a chunk of my bread in one hand and clutched a small joint in the other. After taking a long hit, he exhaled a thin stream of smoke. The ashtray, I thought. The prestigious professor smokes dope.

I stood, keeping as much distance as I could between us. I gripped the side of the boat behind my back. "I want to go home."

His eyes darkened. "I'm sorry."

Terror constricted my throat. I wanted to scream, but no one would hear. Is this how he killed Megan?

"You found her," he said. "Didn't you?"

I nodded.

He held the joint out for me.

"No."

He took another toke. "What to do?"

"My friends?" I said quickly. "They know about you."

"I'm getting bored." His eyes darted around the deck. He walked over to a loose line and picked it up.

My teeth chattered. I was losing control. He was going to strangle me with that line. I had to do something. "My friends won't let the sheriff overlook it another time, no matter how much of a rock star you are." I waited a moment before showing my best weapon. "You wrote on my Facebook wall that we would be together tonight. If I die, everyone will know it was you."

He was deep in thought. I watched him closely. If I had to, I would dive into the water. I thought about all the warnings I'd heard about the Cardigan's current. The number of drownings. I wasn't a strong swimmer. I looked out at the blackness. Where was the shore? I jumped when he started to move. He squared his shoulders, walked past me, and raised the anchor. The small motor sputtered to life, the boat jerked, we were under way at last.

I sat as far away from Nick as I could. He never took his eyes off me. His face glowed from the embers every time he took a toke. I clutched the side of the boat, willing it to go faster. Lightning flashed around us like strobe lights at a rock concert.

When we reached my dock, I jumped up. If he thought he was going to toss me in the water where Megan washed up, he had another thing coming. "Nick," I said. "Let me past."

"Not yet." His windbreaker flapped in a gust of wind. Thunder bowled across the water. He grabbed my arms and shook. "Why are you messing with me?"

I steeled my eyes into his. "It's a preoccupation. Remember?"

"This isn't even close to being over." His face was inches from mine. His breath smelled of herbs and smoke. Suddenly, he shoved me hard and I fell onto the bench. My head snapped back against the teak. "Get the hell off my boat."

I clambered over the side of the boat and onto my dock at last. My hair whipped around my face. Huge drops of water fell out of the sky. I stood, relishing the solid footing. "She was trying to break free," I called as I backed away. "The night she died. She was trying to break free from all of you. But she didn't get to, did she, Nick?"

"Shut up . . ." he roared. He slid his hand in the pocket of his windbreaker. He was holding something.

"Oh . . . Nick, no!" I turned and ran up the bank, fully anticipating a bullet ending my life. Rain pelted down on my skin. I stumbled and felt the cold mud soak through my jeans. I stood and continued running without looking back. My heart pounded as I burst through the back door. I turned the dead bolt and tried to catch my breath. A note on the table caught my eye. I snatched it up.

Dear Rosalie,

   Thank you for all of your kindness but I have overstayed my welcome. I am feeling much better and will get back to work on Monday. I can never repay you for your generosity or for saving my finger. Your aunt was lucky to have you for a niece.

Fondly,
Tyler Wells

I clutched it to my chest. He's not here. I whirled around. Nick's sailboat glowed in the darkness. I turned off the lights in the kitchen and ran to the front door. It was unlocked. Tyler—he forgot. I flipped the dead bolt, hurried back to the living room, and switched off the table lamp. Standing behind the drapes, I peered out of the window from the darkened house. He was still there—the green and red lights of his boat staring back at me like a lurking ogre. My legs trembled. I pulled my phone from my pocket and turned it on. Nick had texted Tony from my phone. *I'm fine. Everything is good here. We're having fun so no worries. You guys can head back.* I screamed when a burst of lightning flashed. I looked back out into the night. He was gone.

FORTY-TWO

I awoke the next morning, passed Tyler's empty room and perfectly made bed, and showered until the hot water grew cold. I pulled on my jeans, slipped a sweatshirt over my head, and wandered aimlessly through the house. The post-Tyler silence screamed at me—I was alone once more. I went into the kitchen, glanced down at my computer, but didn't turn it on. The room was spotless. Tyler had cleaned before he left. There wasn't even a dirty coffee mug in the sink. After putting Mr. Miele to work, I fished my wedding ring out of the pocket of my jeans and raised the diamond-studded band up to the morning light, noting how the delicate stones reflected the colors of the spectrum: green, indigo, rose. Rose. That's what Ed called me now. The only person in my life to leave off the whimsical endings to my name: Rosalie, Rose Red, or simply Rosie.

I set the ring on the counter and realized I needed an occupation and began to clean. I scrubbed, scoured, and swept the entire house. I opened every window and moved every piece of furniture. I washed the wood floors and beat the rugs with a broom and didn't stop until there was nothing left to clean.

Next, I decided to empty out Charlotte's files. Although I had gone through everything about the farm, there was a lot more I hadn't sifted through. If I was going to leave this place at the end of May and move into an apartment, it would all need to go anyway.

I filled four grocery sacks with recycling. Aunt Charlotte was a true Depression baby and saved everything. She had receipts from twenty years before. I slowed when I came to a thick file labeled: History of Barclay Meadow.

The sun had set and a cool breeze blew up from the river. I closed all the windows and blinds and lit a fire. After brewing a cup of tea,

I carried the file over to the sofa, snuggled under an afghan knitted by my mother, and began to read.

I was startled to see a handwritten note to me on top of the papers.

> *Dear Rosalie,*
>
> *If for some reason I don't get around to putting this all in some sort of order, I hope you will. Barclay Meadow is a treasure and I hope you find it to be, as well. If not, here is a key to a safety deposit box. Tom Bestman can tell you where it is located if he hasn't already. Thank you for taking care of our family's home.*
>
> *All my love,*
> *Charlotte*

I pulled the key from the yellowed paper and turned it over in my hands. I set it on the end table next to me and began to read the documents—family trees, old deeds, house plans, and crop histories.

As I read, I learned the Barclay clan sailed over from Scotland in the late 1700s. They bought the land and planted tobacco. The original house was torn down in 1810 and this house was built in its place. During the Civil War when many of the farmers in Devon County wanted to keep their slaves, Fuller S. Barclay set his free. He was threatened and harassed, but held true to his convictions and sent his sons to fight for the Union while other county residents were sneaking off to fight for the South. Due to their education, all were officers and Fuller lost only one. The other two went on to become professionals in Baltimore. Fuller was the last Barclay to live in the house and died in 1895. After his death, the house was used as a summer resort and the farmland leased by locals. I was shocked to learn Tyler's family had been leasing these lands for three generations.

Charlotte moved in after the Second World War, which had taken her new husband. She was young and widowed, but brought the house back to its original splendor. She restored the antiques and hung the portraits that had been stored in the attic. In the 1990s, she enlarged the kitchen and installed new cabinetry and countertops that didn't detract from the original decor, but made it inviting and livable.

I looked up from my reading and rubbed my forehead. It took a few moments for my eyes to adjust, but eventually I took in the clock. It was after ten. Other than one lamp, the house was dark, the fire only glowing embers. I walked out to the kitchen and flipped on the spotlight I had asked Tyler to install after my encounter with the sheriff. It was triggered by motion, so after a few seconds it clicked off again. I readied Mr. Miele and made my way up to bed. In the middle of the night I jolted up. The lawn was illuminated. The spotlight had been activated. I counted—it stayed lit for twelve minutes.

FORTY-THREE

Corrine Johnston has sent you a friend request.

Glenn and I sat on a bench on the pristine John Adams campus. New spring grass, thick with nitrogen, glowed a neon green. Sweet, redolent cherry trees stood behind us, heavy with plush pink blossoms. Velvety petals swirled around us as a cool breeze carried the last remnants of the fading winter.

Glenn and I gazed across the street at a row of dilapidated houses. The paint had loosened from the wooden planks and the front porches sagged as if the houses were too tired to hold them up anymore. Odd pieces of furniture with exposed batting and rusty springs lounged on the porches. The contrast in settings was not lost on us.

"How are you, Rosalie?"

"Me? Oh, I'm good."

Glenn glanced over at me. "Really?"

"A little jumpy, is all."

"I can only imagine. Have you heard from Professor Angeles?"

"No, thank goodness." Another gust of wind tousled our hair. More petals pirouetted onto the grass.

"Good." Glenn crossed his legs, cupping a knee with both hands. "You've been through so much. I am impressed at your resilience."

"You think I'm resilient?" I looked at Glenn.

"Rosalie, do you realize how many things could have gone wrong Friday night?"

"I believe I've imagined every horrific scenario."

"My point is, I think you should focus on what you did right. How you got out of there alive still baffles me. But whatever you did, it was smart and savvy and thank the Lord you are sitting next to me right now."

"This probably won't come as a surprise to you, but I never looked at it that way." I smiled over at him. "Thank you for that perspective. I guess I did do all right. And we learned something, right?"

"Oh, yes. That man is hiding something and we will have to be very careful with our next move. I don't think you meeting with him again is the answer. I think it has to be more subtle." He rubbed his chin and frowned. "But what?"

"Facebook?" I said.

His head shot up. He looked over at me, eyes dancing. "Of course! We can lure him out on Facebook. Maybe Sue will have an idea. She really seems to understand social media way beyond any of our capabilities."

"The What Ifs are scheduled for Monday night. We can both noodle some ideas before then."

"Yes, yes, yes," Glenn said.

I tucked my hands into my jacket pockets and looked back out at the houses. "They aren't the most elegant homes I've ever seen."

"No." Glenn exhaled. "But that's not really the point. The property is worth a lot of money. And that old couple has roots here. Their families have lived in this county for generations."

"Prebridge?"

"Most definitely."

A few weeks earlier I emailed a friend at the *Washington Post*. He had been a neighbor of ours for many years. He'd won a Pulitzer Prize for his investigative journalism and I hoped to tempt him with a juicy story about a sleepy little town on the Eastern Shore with a well-endowed liberal arts college.

"So, if John Adams kicks them off," I said, "those families will lose their homes and the owners their income?"

"Exactly. I have no idea how the college has evaded paying them more, but maybe that is what your friend will discover."

I checked my watch. "He said he'd meet us here at two."

"Is he interested?"

"He's beyond excited. He's thinking another Pulitzer."

"I like the sounds of that." Glenn looked over at me. "Rosalie, are you still thinking of moving back to Chevy Chase?"

"Yes," I said. "I need to find a place before Annie's semester is over."

"I don't mean to be critical, but I really don't understand your decision."

"Annie needs more stability—some semblance of family life. Her parents live in two different towns. She doesn't know where to call home. I shouldn't be making it so difficult for her."

"Annie needs you, most definitely." Glenn looked back across the street. "But maybe not quite in the way you think."

I listened hard to Glenn. He was a wise friend and never failed to surprise me with his insights. But this time I wasn't seeing it. "Annie has been deeply hurt by our separation. I don't mind making sacrifices for her."

"I admire that about you. I just . . . well, I think she may learn to like it here. And what have you learned, really? About yourself, I mean. Putting aside your needs again might put you right back where you started." He shrugged his shoulders. "But what do I know? I'm not exactly the expert on getting along with one's children."

"Glenn, you lost your wife whom you loved very much. And your sons have lost their mother. A family is a delicate system and yours has been thrown completely out of whack." I placed my hand on his arm. "You will regroup, and then I'm sure you will reconnect with your sons."

"Well, that was very well said." Glenn clasped my hand. "I guess we've both learned something today."

"We have?"

"We're much more astute about what the other should do with their families than with our own." Glenn squinted in the direction of the street. "Look," he said as a slightly disheveled man hurried over to us. "This must be your friend."

A few hours later, I started my car and buzzed the convertible top down. The sun warmed my face and softened the leather seats. Once out of town I picked up speed and pushed on the radio. An Adele song was on the radio and I sang along with her throaty, passionate voice.

Woop . . . woop.

I glanced in the rearview mirror. Circling red-and-blue lights seared my corneas. I flipped on my blinker, hoping the cruiser would pass. I hadn't been speeding. At least I didn't think so. I eased the car onto the shoulder. Loose stones crunched under the tires. I watched with foreboding as the sheriff did the same. I turned off the radio, opened the glove box, and fished my registration out of the owner's manual. The sheriff remained in the car. I could see someone beside him. I chewed on my thumbnail, what was left of it, that is, and waited.

When he climbed out of the cruiser, I stiffened. The man was like the scary clown that ruined birthday parties. He walked around to the passenger side and stared down at me through his sunglasses. My eyes were level with his belt. I looked away. "I wasn't speeding," I said and gripped the steering wheel. "It just looks like I am in this car."

The sheriff reached inside, unlocked the door, and opened it wide. "Get out, Hart."

"Why?"

"I said get the hell out of the car."

I gripped tighter in an attempt to control my terror. "You have to tell me why."

"I'm hauling your ass to jail. That a good enough explanation?"

My eyes widened. "You can't do that."

"Looks like I'll be adding resisting arrest to your charges."

"Charges?" I combed my hands through my hair and sunk my teeth into my lower lip. *Charges?*

Once I got out of the car, the sheriff lumbered over to me. "Put your hands behind your back."

"No!"

"Jesus effing Christ, do what I tell you the first time."

I put my hands behind my back and he slapped on a pair of cuffs. I tried to look at him over my shoulder. "That hurts."

He guided me to the car via my elbow, tucked my head down, although it wasn't necessary, and shoved me into the backseat. I tried to sit up, but I kept falling forward. The deputy in the front seat stared ahead. I recognized him from the night I found Megan. He was the one who dangled the evidence bag in front of me. He was the reason this whole mess started.

The sheriff eased into the car, slammed the door, and fired up the engine.

"My car," I said. "You can't leave it here. It's supposed to rain. And my purse is still in there."

The sheriff eyed the deputy. "The keys are in the ignition." He winked. "Enjoy your ride." Sheriff Wilgus glanced over his shoulder at me and back at the deputy. "If you think of it, put that fancy convertible top up when you get back."

So, this is what a jail cell was like. I sat on a spindly cot and scooted back into the corner. I clutched my knees and tried to make myself as small as possible. A drop of water fell from a lime-encrusted spigot every seven seconds. It was oddly reassuring in its predictability. *Plop.* One thousand one . . .

Sickly fluorescent lights buzzed above me. A brighter light shone through a crack at the bottom of the door leading to the office. I noticed a second cell when the sheriff ushered me in, but it appeared to be empty. At least for now. I had no idea what time it was. The sheriff had taken all my jewelry. Even the belt from my jeans. He snapped my mug shots, front and profile, and read me my Miranda rights. It all seemed so surreal. I never broke a rule in a game, let alone a law. I loved rules and laws. They kept order and civility. And yet here I was. You've hit bottom, Hart. This is your bottom. At least I prayed it was. I had full knowledge that things could very well get worse from here.

When we had arrived at the station, the sheriff read me the

charges with relish. I was breaking Maryland law by selling food not prepared in a commercial kitchen. I had risked the public's health. According to him, I could have killed someone. He read me a litany of regulations I failed to meet. In his twisted mind, I was a potential murderer. More irony. I hugged my knees tighter. Cardigan had no Saturday court. Or night court, for that matter. And Tom Bestman was on the golf course when I used my one phone call. I hoped he would get here and fix this whole mess. Surely you can't arrest someone for making muffins.

Plop.

Tyler wouldn't notice I was gone. It was Saturday. He never worked weekends. At least he hadn't for a long time. I should have called Glenn. He would have done something. I wondered if Annie was worried about me. I never missed a day without communicating with her in some way.

A loud clank sounded and the cell door slid open. The tall deputy came through the door carrying a McDonald's bag. His hair was windblown, his face red.

"What time is it?" I said timidly.

"Eight. Why, you going somewhere?" He chuckled at his own apparent wit.

His boots were heavy on the floor as he walked in the cell and dropped the grease-stained bag on the end of the bed. He set a waxy cup on the floor. "Sheriff said you seemed like a Diet Coke kind of girl."

"Is anyone coming for me?"

"Sheriff wants you in here all night."

"All *night*?"

He shifted his weight. "Can I get you anything else?"

I looked at him, trying to read his face. Was he being sincere? "I don't suppose you have any coffee."

"Lila made a pot this afternoon."

"Never mind," I said.

"I can make a new pot."

"Really? That would be very sweet of you."

He stared down at his extremely large black boots.

"What is it?" I said.

"I'm sorry," he said and looked up again. "I'm sorry you're in here. You want anything else besides coffee?"

"Do you have anything to read?"

A sheepish grin appeared on his face. "We got some *Playboys* in the john."

I shook my head quickly. "No, thank you."

"Let me check the ladies' room. Shari might have left something in there. She moved to Seattle after she got married. She was one of those crunchies. You know, granola types? I don't really know why she ever became a cop in the first place."

"Fix the world's ills from the inside?"

"Yeah, maybe. Anyway, she was the last female we had on the force. She might have left a magazine. Or maybe Lila has something in there other than a ginormous can of hair spray." He smiled. "Anyway, I'll be right back."

I watched him go, touched by his kindness. He even left the cell door open. After a few minutes he returned, the smell of freshly brewing coffee wafted in after him. "Found something." He handed me a *People* magazine. Tom Cruise and Katie Holmes were on the cover holding their new baby. "It ain't exactly breaking news."

"It's better than nothing." I looked up at him. "Thank you."

He nodded. "Coffee should be about done." He started to leave.

"Deputy?"

"You can call me Jason, ma'am."

"Jason, what time do you turn the lights out?"

"Ten." He hesitated. "Tell you what. Seeing as you are the

only one in here, you tell me when you're ready for me to turn 'em out and that's when I will. You want 'em on all night, that's okay by me. And if you need anything, you just holler." He turned to go, but stopped. "By the way, that's a nice car you got there, ma'am."

"It's Rosalie. And thanks. It's fun to zip around in, isn't it?"

He tucked his thumbs in his belt. "I didn't go joy riding. I brought it back here stat, put the top up, and locked it tight."

"Wow," I said. "You're a good guy, Jason."

He walked out and the automatic door clanged shut. I was encaged again. The scent of greasy food permeated the cell. I tossed the magazine onto the end of the bed. My reading glasses were in my purse.

Plop.

I looked up at the ceiling. "Okay," I said aloud. "Message received. I'm done. Kaput. I'll go home like a good little girl."

I took a deep breath and glanced around at the sparse room. I hoped Jason would remember to bring me the coffee. I intended to drink the entire pot. There was no chance in hell I was going to sleep one second in this lair.

Forty-four

I awoke to raised voices. I jumped up and splashed cold water on my face.

"Enough already, Joe. Get her the hell out of here."

Doris?

"Don't go getting your shorts in a knot, Doris Bird. What do you care, anyway?"

The sheriff was back.

"Enough," Doris said. "You act like you don't have to answer to no one."

I dried my face, smoothed my hair, and listened closely.

"I checked the laws you are supposedly upholding," Doris said. "It's a bunch of bunk. All those ideas about a commercial kitchen—those laws are liberal for baked goods, particularly in the low volume she was selling."

Wow. You go, girl, I thought.

"I got the state law right here," she said. "I printed it out on the computer." I heard a hand smack on paper. "You got no right to keep her here a minute longer."

"I was going to let her go this morning. Stop your bellyaching."

"What's happened to you?" Doris's voice dropped in volume. "You used to be a good man."

After a long silence, the door opened. Blinded by the bright light, I shielded my eyes.

"Seems you finally have someone to bail you out, Hart."

"That's enough, Joe," Doris shouted from behind him.

I rubbed my arms and waited for him to unlock the door.

"This ain't over, little lady," he whispered. "You got that?"

"Yes." I nodded. "Message received. You don't have to worry about me anymore. Your work here is done."

He frowned. "That for real?"

"Yes," I said. "I'm going home. I'll be out of Cardigan by the beginning of May."

When I entered the main office, Doris stood in the middle of the room clutching a handful of papers. She hurried over to me and scooped me into a bear hug. I closed my eyes and breathed in her scent. Tabu. My grandmother's perfume. Every one of my muscles relaxed as she held me in her arms. It was a mother's embrace full of love and protection.

I stepped back. "Thank you, Doris."

"You all right?"

"I am now. How did you know I was here?"

She smiled that warm smile, her thick glasses askew from the hug. "Lila, of course. She called me first thing this morning."

The sheriff shifted his weight. "Who's selling your shoes while you're out rescuing the world?"

Doris looked over at the sheriff with a deep-set frown. "I have the 'be back in ten minutes' sign up."

"Shouldn't you be getting back? Somebody might be wanting a Snickers bar."

She crossed her arms. "Not without Rosalie."

"Calm down, woman. I never said she couldn't go."

I looked back at the sheriff. "Isn't there some sort of paperwork?"

He lumbered over to his desk and tapped a stack of papers with his finger. "Sign here."

"What am I signing? I refuse to admit I broke the law."

"It just says I released you, okay?"

I walked over to the desk. "I'll need my glasses. They're in my purse."

The sheriff unlocked a drawer and removed my things. He set an evidence bag on the desk and I fished out my glasses. After slipping them on my nose, I read through the document. "I want a copy of this for my lawyer."

"Just sign the damn thing and I'll give you your copy."

Once I had gathered my belongings, Doris wrapped a protective arm around my shoulder and we headed for the door.

"Hart?" the sheriff said.

My head fell forward. "Yes?"

"You remember what you told me back there?"

I nodded.

"And?"

"I meant what I said."

When we stepped out into the daylight, I immediately dug through my purse for my sunglasses. It was a gloriously sunny day. I breathed in the fresh, dew-laden air. "Freedom," I said. "I will never take it for granted again." I faced Doris. "I can't thank you enough."

"He had no right doing what he did." She studied me. "So, why did he? Why is he always picking on you?"

"I'm not really sure." I shook my head. "Because I'm an outsider?"

"No. That ain't it." She continued to study me. "Does this have anything to do with that girl you found?"

I avoided Doris's gaze. "It doesn't matter now. He has no reason to be concerned about me anymore."

She looked down the street toward her store. "I'm going to have a riot on my hands if I stop selling your baked goods."

I smiled over at her. "We'll figure something out." I patted her back. "You'd better go mind the store. You probably have a line outside."

She chuckled. "Let 'em wait."

I peered up into her kind face. "Why did you help me, Doris?"

"Because I know a good egg when I know one." She glanced back at the sheriff's headquarters. "I swear, someone has eaten that man's soul and spit it back out."

FORTY-FIVE

How was your golf game?" I asked Tom Bestman.

"Three under. Almost had a hole in one on a par three," he said from behind his very tidy desk. "Missed the hole by this much." He held his finger and thumb up just inches apart.

"Why didn't you call me?"

"I did. Didn't you see all the missed calls on your phone?"

"The sheriff confiscated my phone." I narrowed my eyes. "You were supposed to call the station."

"Problem with that, Rosalie, is you never said where you were."

"What?" I stared over at him in disbelief. "I never told you I was in jail?"

Tom shook his head adamantly. "You just said to call as soon as possible. I thought you wanted to talk about Ed unfreezing your accounts."

"I can't believe I didn't tell you I'd been arrested." I shook my head. "I was just so upset."

"I'm sorry, Rosalie. But it's over now." He wiggled his Cross pen between his fingers. "The sheriff dropped all charges. Even the re-sisting arrest. Hey, how did he come up with that one, by the way?" Tom smiled.

"There's nothing funny about any of this." I hugged my purse. "How does the sheriff get away with it? It's as if he can do whatever he wants to whomever he wants."

"He hasn't always been this bad." Tom frowned. "Something weird is definitely going on with him."

"So, everyone ignores it?"

"It isn't that simple. In a small town, people go through bad stretches and then they come around. I think everyone is waiting for Joe Wilgus to get his head on straight again."

"You don't know everything he's done to me." I glanced out the window. Tom's full name and title were painted on it in gold letters. I looked back at him. "I feel like I'm in a bad Western."

"I straightened it out, okay? Your record is expunged." He leaned back in his chair. "So the next time you have to fill out a form and it asks if you've ever been arrested, you can still check the 'no' box."

"I don't suppose you could expunge my memory of Saturday night."

"I'm very sorry this happened. And I agree that Joe Wilgus is overstepping his bounds. I don't like a damn thing he's doing lately, but I can't just go in like the calvary and boot him out. His family has lived in Devon County for generations. And ironically, that's what I love about Cardigan, that people look at you as a real person with flaws and good points, too. It's not like politics where your career ends because of one slipup."

"I see that," I said. "I really do." I set my purse on the floor and folded my hands in my lap. "I guess it won't matter in a few weeks."

"Why is that?"

I avoided his eyes. "I've decided to go back to Chevy Chase."

"Will you come back?"

"After Saturday night, I honestly don't know. That's why I need the number of the safety deposit box."

"I'm sorry." Tom shook his head. "I thought you would stay. I was so happy when you started to work the land. Barclay Meadow is a treasure. I honestly hoped you would bring it back to life."

"I'm really confused. The only thing I know is I want to do right by my daughter. Since the separation . . ." My head shot up. "Wait, what did you say about Ed earlier?"

"Your accounts are unlocked—credit card, ATM, savings."

"But why now?" I said.

"I was going to ask you the same question."

I thought for a moment. "It's because I'm doing what he wants—getting a place in Chevy Chase. It was his idea."

"Sounds like he wants to get back together."

"No, he wants his life to be easier. He's done a lousy job spending time with Annie since the separation. And when his girlfriend is there, Annie feels like an outsider. Having me nearby will give Annie somewhere to go."

"At least you'll have some cash." He forced a smile.

"I don't want his money." I fell back into my seat.

"Don't say that to him. I plan on getting you a good settlement."

"Thank you." I smiled. "Thank you for everything you've done for me."

"You look tired, Rosalie."

"I'm exhausted. I never thought small-town living would be so stressful. I came here to escape my problems, not create more."

"Maybe that's where you went wrong." Tom clicked his pen and wrote the number of the safety deposit box on the back of his business card. He slid it across the desk. "Here you go."

"Why didn't you tell me about this before?"

"She didn't want you to know right away. She hoped you would fall in love with the farm first."

"I haven't told anyone else about my plans. I dread telling Tyler." I stared down at the number. "And now I'm letting Charlotte down."

Tom leaned back in his char. The taut springs creaked. "You're going to have to tell Tyler eventually."

"I know."

"I wish you'd give yourself more time. Cardigan is a great place to live."

I gazed over at the framed diplomas on his wall. SUNY, Columbia Law School. "Did you grow up here, Tom?"

"Not even close. Born and beat up in Brooklyn."

"How have you adjusted so well?"

"It took a while. When Paula and I first moved here, I was always anticipating that edginess in people. You know, primed for a fight. But I never found it. So I relaxed for the first time in my life. What's better than that?"

"Maybe I just got off to a rough start."

"I'll give you that. Between the dead girl and the divorce, I don't think you could be happy anywhere this past year. So maybe give it more time. I mean, I love knowing the people I meet on the street. And I can give my kids a couple of bucks and they can walk by themselves to Birdie's and get a bag of Swedish fish. How cool is that?" He flashed me a wide grin. "Plus, it's beautiful here. Have you spent any time on the water? It could change your mind."

I thought hard about what he said, about how nice everyone was, people like Doris and Janice. He was right. There was a sense of place here. It was impossible to be anonymous so you had to connect, to engage. I thought of Glenn and the houses that were about to be unfairly razed. He was right to take on this problem. And then I had a brilliant idea. "Tom . . . if I heard you correctly, you are just as upset as I am with what Joe Wilgus is getting away with."

"More or less. But like I said, I think it's a phase that will pass."

"But would you agree there is some serious corruption going on around here?"

"Where are you headed, Rosalie?"

"Do you do any work for the college? Or the county commissioners, for that matter?"

"Why?" he asked warily.

"Well . . ." I leaned forward. "Do you?"

"I have several clients that work for the college, but no, the county commissioners and I just see each other at parties."

"Do you ever do any pro bono work?"

He laughed. "Not if I can help it. You can take a guy out of the city . . ."

"What if you could get your name in the *Washington Post* as someone who has done something wonderful for this town?"

He set his pen down for the first time since I arrived. "I'm listening."

When the bank clerk shut the door, I turned the key in door 103 and
slid out the long, metal box. It was stuffed with a pack of trifolded
papers. I hadn't expected to find anything of value. My aunt had been
buried with her wedding ring and I had already received my grandmother's and great-grandmother's jewelry. It was all locked in my
own safety deposit box in Chevy Chase for Annie.

I unfolded the papers. It was the deed to Barclay Meadow. Some
of the documents were over one hundred years old. I handled them
delicately and was surprised to see a handwritten note to me paper
clipped to the top.

> *Dearest Rosalie,*
>
> *It seems you have decided to sell Barclay Meadow. As much
> as I hoped you would find a way to keep it in the family, I am
> sure you have a very good reason to sell it. I hope I have not
> burdened you in any way. I remember how much you loved it
> here as a little girl. I remember you growing so tan from your
> time outdoors your mother would tease that she didn't recognize
> you. Remember picking blackberries and then washing them in
> the sink? They would be so juicy we had to hold napkins under
> our chins.*
>
> *But now you are a mature woman with a lovely family and
> so Barclay Meadow must go. I have one request, although I know
> I have probably worn out my welcome when it comes to favors. I
> hope by now you have met Tyler Wells. His family has been with
> Barclay Meadow for generations and they are a lovely, hard-
> working family. I have asked Tom Bestman to try to find a way to
> sell the farm to him. If this in any way compromises your finan-
> cial stability, then pretend you never saw this letter. But if there*

is some way his lease payment could go toward buying the house,
then maybe he could make a go of it.

Thank you for all that you have done. You were the daughter
I never had and I loved you more than I ever thought possible.

Charlotte

I clutched the papers to my chest. I looked up at the ceiling. "I'm so sorry, Aunt Charlotte." I put the papers back into the box, slid it back into place, and locked it.

"You were out all night Saturday," Tyler said from behind me.

I minimized my computer screen so he wouldn't see I was looking for apartments. The nutty, rich scent of brewing coffee filled the kitchen. "That smells divine," I said and walked over to him.

He stood with his hands on his hips waiting for Mr. Miele to press out a fresh batch of Gold Coast blend. "Things seem to be going well with your new acquaintance," he said.

"No. That's not what I was doing." I pulled two mugs from the cabinet as the last burst of steam spat out of the coffeemaker. "Tyler, I need to talk to you about something."

"I want to talk to you about something, too." He crossed his arms and leaned back against the counter.

"You first," I said.

He filled our mugs and handed me one. I slid the sugar canister over to him. "I've been doing some research—about the farm, I mean. That's why I was borrowing your computer so much."

"What about the farm?"

"There's something called sustainable. It's a higher rating than farming organic. It's complicated, but I think we could pull it off."

I gripped my coffee with both hands. He said "we" now when referring to the farm.

"We would have to get some livestock," he continued. "I was thinking we could start with chickens."

"*Chickens?*"

"Yeah, you know, they have feathers . . . lay eggs."

"Aren't they an awful lot of work?"

He stared at me, hard.

"I'm sorry, Tyler. I really am. I'm just so tired lately." I brushed my hair back from my face. I hadn't combed it yet. "I didn't mean to dismiss your idea. It sounds very interesting. If you could refer me to some information I could read up on it."

Tyler dumped his coffee in the sink and wordlessly left the room.

I stared at the spot where he had stood. What was I doing? The distance growing between us would need the Bay Bridge to connect us again. I would tell him the next time I see him. I had to give him time to make arrangements.

I walked back to the table, flopped into my seat, and stared out the window. I had propped the windows open earlier and the sweet scent of peonies drifted toward me. Goldfinches were fluttering around the feeder, their feathers already turning a bright marigold. At the end of the sloping lawn the river sped by, an occasional log caught in its current. I only had a few weeks and what had I accomplished?

I brought my computer back to life. I had to see this investigation through. We were close and yet miles away. I thought about my conversation with Glenn. We were underutilizing our best weapon—Facebook. Maybe I could lure the killer out—whomever he or she may be. I rolled my shoulders back and logged onto Facebook as Megan. After clicking on the box "what's on your mind?" I typed:

Megan Johnston
I didn't want to die. Why did you kill me?

FORTY-SIX

I was surprised how quickly I reverted back to the person I had once been. It started on the Capital Beltway. I darted in and out among the best of the aggressive drivers, squeezing into nonexistent spaces, and took the curves toward the Wisconsin Avenue exit as well as any NASCAR driver. As I drove into Bethesda where I was to look at apartments, I checked my hair and decided I was due for a new style. Yes, I thought as I hit the gas. Time for a change. Maybe I would cut it all off, dye it red.

The first apartment was in an elegant high-rise just north of Western Avenue. It was beautifully lush, and there was a Saks Fifth Avenue a few doors down, but I barely looked around. I could never live somewhere that required an elevator to get outside. And a window box does not a garden make.

I was already enervated and it was only one o'clock. I spotted a coffee shop and went in. I watched as a young woman manipulated the coffee machine. I could do that job, I thought. Mr. Miele and I should hit the road.

Outside, the sky had filled with an unending line of gray clouds, heavy with rain, anxious to unload their burden. Daffodils bloomed down the median of Wisconsin Avenue while Jags, sporty Mercedes, and glossy black BMWs sped down the busy road.

"Rosalie!"

I turned and saw my dear friend Amy charging toward me, dressed in yoga pants and a tight sweatshirt.

"Amy—it's wonderful to see you."

She brushed my cheek with a kiss. "You look incredible. I love your hair longer. And . . . have you lost weight? Look at you. My God, I positively hate you."

"It's the divorce diet and I don't recommend it," I said. "Tell me what's new with you."

"I miss you." She flashed me a little pout. "I got stuck with the Cancer Society golf tournament. It's totally stressing me out."

"I left notes."

"I know. But that doesn't mean you're doing it."

I sipped my latte through the small hole in the plastic lid. "Do you have any help?"

"A little. But enough about that. What brings you into the city? I thought you were living on a farm." She gave me a once-over. "You don't look like you've been living on a farm. Where did you get those jeans? Damn, they look good."

"I am grateful for Annie's hand-me-downs."

"Walk with me. I'm on my way to Saks. We're going to the opera with Jay's boss and I need a killer dress." Amy walked in long strides and I hurried to keep up with her. She was short and physical with a cute angled haircut that bounced as she walked. "So, spill. Why are you here?"

"I'm looking for a place to live."

"Really?" She stopped. "That's awesome news!" After embracing me with another quick hug, she started walking again. "Oh, Rosie, I've missed you so much. You don't know what it's like around here since you left. Everything has changed."

"I'm sorry, Amy."

"I just want you and Ed to be together again. That woman has changed everything."

"I've only seen her once," I said. "What's she like?"

Amy glanced over at me. "You really want to know?"

"It can't be any worse than my imagination." My latte bounced out of the hole as we walked. Caramel rings were polka-dotting the sleeve of my white top.

"She just kind of floats around batting her eyes."

"She bats her *eyes?*"

"Well, sort of. Jay thinks she's hot. I can't believe my husband is lusting after a thirty-year-old home wrecker. I mean, seriously," Amy said. "Since when is tall and bone-thin hot?"

"Since forever."

She rolled her eyes. "But she's not all that beautiful. It's more how she flirts, in subtle ways. I mean, at parties she's always with the men and she'll wear blouses that are cut low, you know the style? The ones where if she turns a certain way a guy could peek inside? So all the men in the room are watching her every move to see if they'll catch some eye candy."

"Wow." I stepped out of the way of an oncoming pedestrian who was unwilling to yield the right of way. I caught up to Amy again. "She sounds like she's pretty good at it."

"The thing is, she's changed everything. Our parties used to be a lot of fun, remember? We all got along and laughed and enjoyed each other. Now there's this competitive thing going on and everyone is tense and stiff and the women are mad at their husbands and oh . . . Rosalie, come home." She gave me a sad smile.

"I'm sorry Ed has done this."

"I think he's enjoying it. I think Ed loves that every guy in the room wants to go to bed with his girlfriend." She checked my reaction. "Sorry to be so harsh."

"Sometimes reality is pretty darn harsh." I tossed my cup into a wrought-iron trash bin.

Amy looked at her watch. "Rosalie, I have got to get into Saks. Come with me?"

"I have another apartment to see. But I would much rather shop with you."

We hugged. "Let me know the minute you move back. I'm throwing a big old party and I'm not inviting Ed." She stuck out her tongue a little and laughed. "'Bye—I love you!"

Just as Amy disappeared through the revolving brass doors, the rain began. There were no warning drops, no prelude of rain-scented wind. It started right with the main course as if the bottom had fallen out of the clouds.

I ran to my car, where my umbrella was tucked neatly under the seat. Amy and I had walked over two blocks and by the time I leapt inside I was drenched. I shivered as I started the engine. How could I tour an apartment when I was completely sodden? I glanced down at the digital clock. Maybe I could swing by my house and grab some clothes. Ed wouldn't be there in the middle of the afternoon and I still had my key. I put the car into gear and merged onto Wisconsin Avenue. My house was less than a mile away and I needed some spring clothes anyway.

I parked in front and stared up the steps. I had lived there for close to ten years. It was still beautiful—with white cedar siding and floor-to-ceiling windows. Narcissus and grape hyacinths filled the flower beds and two dogwoods rich with white, velvety blooms graced the lawn. I hurried up the steps, wrung out my shirt, and went inside.

So little had changed—the table by the door still held my silk flower arrangement, although it needed dusting. An umbrella with a carved wooden handle was still in the blue-and-white ceramic stand. My mother's grandfather clock stood in the corner, the pendulum stationary.

I gazed into the living room—a still life of the beautiful decor I had worked to get just right. Up until then, I thought I would claim some of this furniture for my new apartment. But as I scanned the room, I thought better of it. This was Annie's home and I couldn't divide up yet another part of her world. I had been in houses where the couples were divorcing, one wing chair instead of two, no kitchen table, indentations in the rug where a coffee table had once been. They looked sad and diminished. No, I would hit up Pottery Barn instead.

I dropped my keys in the rattan tray, my wet clothes sapping the warmth from my body. I walked down the hall to the kitchen. A pungent smell hung in the air. An orange, I thought. An orange is moldy. A box of clementines sat on the counter. I knew if I dug through to the bottom I would find the source of the smell. But this kitchen was no longer mine to maintain.

The thought struck a deep and very sad chord in my heart and I realized instantly it had been a mistake to come here. A scarf that was not mine was draped over the back of a chair. Two wineglasses sat in the sink with drying burgundy circles in the bottom, one with a distinct lipstick print. A sugar bowl had been placed next to the coffeemaker. Ed and I drank our coffee black. I glanced over at the pine hutch that held my good dishes. It was painted white. *White?* Ed loved that hutch. He would never paint it. We had discovered it together at an antiques show at the D.C. armory. Our first apartment had no cabinet space so we splurged our budget and brought it home.

I jumped when I saw a figure in the archway. "What are you doing here?" I said.

Rebecca folded her arms. "Better question, what are you doing here?"

"I needed some dry clothes. I got caught in the rain. I didn't expect anyone to be home." I hesitated. "Why are you here?"

"*Seriously?* I live here." Her hair was in a high ponytail and without her expertly applied makeup she looked surprisingly plain and very young. She was dressed in a loose blouse over a pair of skinny jeans.

"I forgot." I held her gaze. "But now I remember. Annie told me you lived here."

"What else did she say?" Rebecca pursed her lips. "Is she your little spy?"

"Spy? Annie? I would never do that to my child. Don't tell me you're threatened by her?"

"I barely even know her."

My eyes narrowed. "Then shame on you."

"Spare me," Rebecca said. "Oh, your clothes are in garbage bags in the cellar if you're looking for them."

I had to clench my teeth to stop them from chattering. I felt invaded and foreign at the same time. "No," I said. "I'll buy new." I walked past her. I stopped when I reached the door. I took a deep breath and turned around. She was standing in the hallway with a smirk on her face. "You need to keep your bony little hands off my things. Don't you dare paint or move another thing until the divorce is final, do you understand? And you'll be stripping my hutch."

Her mouth dropped open. "Who do you—"

I grabbed my keys and pulled the door open. "Oh, and Rebecca?" She cocked her head.

"Button up," I said, and strode out the door.

It took me over two hours to get home. I think I hyperventilated at one point on the beltway, but since it was gridlocked in rush-hour traffic no one noticed. It was Friday and the Western Shore folks were crowding to get to their boats and beaches. I waited forty-five minutes in an inching line for the Bay Bridge even in the EZ Pass lane and, with the heater on full blast, I eventually dried out. The clouds parted as I crested the bridge and prisms of light shafted through with biblical drama. I felt surprisingly calm. That was the end of it, I thought. I was getting a divorce. The next chapter of my life was starting now. Relief soothed my nerves and I felt as if the rain had washed away the last of my old life.

When I finally reached the quiet, two-lane road that led to Cardigan, I pulled over, turned off *All Things Considered,* and buzzed the convertible top down. I could smell the scent of spring onions from a freshly mowed lawn. The setting sun was completely unveiled and the birds were singing their lullaby songs. I took three, yoga-depth breaths, eased the car back on the road, and drove fifty-five miles per hour the rest of the way.

Birdie's was on my way home so I stopped in for my papers. "Good afternoon," I said to Doris. "It's a beautiful day, isn't it?"

"It's about over, now. But it was all I could do to not close up shop and go sit on a bench out there in the park."

"I have something for you." I reached in my tote and pulled out a package wrapped in foil. "The sheriff hasn't been around here today, has he?" I glanced out the window.

"Nope. Just Lila. She's mad at Joe for forcing you to stop selling stuff."

I placed the parcel on the counter. "He can't stop me from giving gifts, right?" I hesitated. "At least I don't think he can. Anyway, these are for you."

She unfolded the foil to reveal four freshly baked muffins. She picked one up, peeled back the paper, and took a bite. "Mm," she said and chewed. "Is that lemon?"

"And rosemary," I said.

"Rosemary? Well, who woulda thought of that?" She took another bite, set the muffin down, and brushed the crumbs off her fingers. "These would sell out in a heartbeat." She bent over and picked up my papers. After setting them on the glass counter, she folded her arms and looked over at me. "You okay?"

"I think so. I haven't seen the sheriff around. Maybe he's finally going to leave me alone."

"He needs to pay attention to all the drugs the high school kids are selling in the park."

"That would be a better use of his time." I smiled over at her. "Thank you, again, for what you did. I think I'll tell you that every day I come in here."

She studied me over her glasses. "I don't suppose you heard the news?"

"News?"

"Brower's is closing."

"The cafe? That's too bad."

"Maybe it is and maybe it isn't."

I cocked my head. "You didn't like their coffee, either?"

"I think maybe your baked goods put them out of business."

"Really? That wasn't my intention."

Doris's eyes twinkled. "Those folks are going back to Philly. They weren't from here."

"Another one bites the dust. No wonder the population in Cardigan has stayed the same for so long." I set my money on the counter and picked up my papers. "I'll see you tomorrow. I hope you get a chance to enjoy the sunshine."

Doris watched me closely. She pursed her lips and scratched her nose. "You know, Miss Rosalie . . ." She folded her arms again. "That space next door will be vacant. This town is short on restaurants as it is."

I turned to face her. Was she suggesting that I . . . no. That was madness. And yet I was deeply moved by the sentiment.

"Thank you, Doris." I waved good-bye and walked out the door. As I passed the diner, I stood close to the glass and peered into the empty restaurant. The window fogged. I cleared it with my sleeve and looked closer. It was a small space, but with wide, welcoming windows. I wondered how it would look with Tuscan orange walls and blue-and-white tablecloths—maybe yellow daylilies on each table in small crystal vases.

I shook my head. Get a grip, Rosalie. You're leaving, remember?

When I arrived home, Tyler was nowhere to be found. He had finished for the day and the kitchen was spotless. His absence was palpable. I filled a glass with water and walked out onto the porch. Staring out at the river, I realized I would have to make Tyler understand. My leaving could be temporary. I could be back here before we knew it. I caught the scent of overturned earth on a light breeze. I had grown to love this farm—the smells, the sun, the quiet, slower pace of life.

Needing to stretch my legs, I decided to fetch the mail. I trotted down the front steps and noticed at least a dozen flats of herbs along the shed. The herb garden. We were going to start an herb garden for my baking. They hadn't been watered. The dill was already starting to yellow and droop.

I headed down the long lane to the mailbox. The spring peepers had begun their trilling and the peace and beauty of Barclay Meadow warmed my heart. The intoxicating scent of lilacs in bloom caught my nose. I didn't know I had lilacs. I would have to bring some inside. My mother had carried lilacs in her wedding bouquet.

When I reached the road, I pushed up my sleeves and opened the large, dented mailbox, wondering how many times the poor thing had been a victim of a drive-by baseball bat. Maybe Tyler could replace it. Tyler. I had to find a way to repair the damage with Tyler.

After removing several envelopes and a heavy load of catalogs, I turned and noticed a car parked across the road. A large man sat at the wheel. Probably another gawker, I thought. After all this time, people are still trying to get a view of where the dead girl was found.

I looked again. Our eyes locked. Did I know this man? Recognition hit us at the same moment. Oh my gosh. He looked as shocked as I did. I could see him putting things together as he stared, his brow knitted in thought, his lips parting as he reached a conclusion. I held the mail close to my chest. I could see the blue-gray bags under his eyes. Clueless as to what I should do, I gave him a small wave. His eyes narrowed to two small slits of loathing. He started the car and revved the accelerator. Gravel spat out from under the tires and dust rose in a cloud behind the car as he drove away. I coughed and tried to wave away the smoke, but Bill Johnston was gone.

FORTY-SEVEN

Corinne Johnston   Thank you for accepting my friend request. I would very much like to meet with you. Could you come to my house Friday afternoon?

I hesitated before responding. Why would this poor grieving woman want to meet with me? As much as I had been driven to solve this crime, I never wanted to intrude on Corrine's unimaginable pain. I started to decline, but stopped. Bill had been at the end of my driveway. But why? Then I remembered the post I put up as Megan: *I didn't want to die. Why did you kill me?* I typed quickly.

Rosalie Hart   Yes, of course.

Even with the help of my GPS, I made several wrong turns trying to find the Johnston home, arriving in cul-de-sac after cul-de-sac. There appeared to be four basic designs to the houses in their community, all variations on the same themes. The Johnstons' house had a brick front with beige vinyl siding. But unlike the other fertilized lawns and well-planned landscapes, their front yard was mostly crabgrass and clover with two spindly, undernourished azalea bushes flanking the stoop.

I had to wait a few minutes before Corinne opened the door. She peered out through a narrow crack.

"I'm Rosalie," I said.

She sized me up before opening the door the rest of the way. Her face was pinched and pale and the dark roots of her hair hadn't been colored in months. I followed her into the living room. The room was dark, the blinds closed, allowing only thin strips of light to illuminate the small space.

"Can I get you something?" she said, her tone making it clear she hoped I would say no.

"No, thanks." I clenched my fist around my purse strap. I had no idea what she wanted from me or what I should or could say. This must be how a witness feels being called to the stand. Answer only what she asks, I thought. Don't offer any more. And yet, as I looked into this woman's sad, lost eyes, I felt a responsibility to tell her more.

She brushed a loose strand of hair from her face, which was void of makeup. Her eyes darted around the room as if she were unsure what to do next.

"Maybe we should sit down," I said.

Corinne perched on a burgundy leather love seat and clutched her hands together, the knuckles stretched white. I sat stiffly in an identical one across from her. A large photograph hung over the mantel of the Johnston family as they had once been. Bill was seated in the center of the photo, the king, the lord of the castle, while Corinne and Megan stood behind the chair, each with a hand on his shoulder. My eyes were drawn immediately to Megan. Bright white teeth glowed from a wide smile. Next to Megan's beauty, her mother looked tired and small. Outdone. Outshone.

"I'm sorry for your loss." I looked back at Corinne. "I can only imagine what you are going through."

"No, you can't." She tugged her skirt over her knees. I noticed an idle cell phone next to her on the table—the twenty-first-century umbilical cord to our children. But Corrine never even glanced at it. Her cord had been severed.

"Corinne," I said. "Why did you want to meet?"

"I want to know everything."

"Okay," I said. "Let's start with what Rhonda has already told you."

"She's told me very little. Basically that you had been looking into what happened to Megan. I still don't understand why." She looked at me pointedly. "After she told me about you, I went to her Facebook page and found you on her friend list."

"Of course," I said. "You and Rhonda are friends."

"Friends? *Rhonda* and me?"

"I mean on Facebook."

"We nose into each other's business. That's what it means to be friends on Facebook."

"Why do you think she told you about me? I would have preferred to let you grieve in peace." I tried to convey the empathy I felt for her in my gaze. "I just don't know what purpose it serves. I mean, Rhonda telling you."

"The only purpose it could possibly serve is to benefit Rhonda in some way. It certainly wasn't because she was being thoughtful or virtuous." She picked at the hem of her skirt. "I don't know how well you know Rhonda Pendleton, but FYI . . . she doesn't have an honest bone in her body." Corrine's voice had grown ragged. "Rhonda spent her life being jealous of my daughter and lusting after my husband. Did she tell you she was having an affair with him?" She shot me a challenging look, her chin lifted.

I remained silent.

"She ruined her marriage and it drove her crazy that Bill didn't end ours." She tugged on the thread again, unintentionally unraveling the hem. She looked up at me. "They don't know it, but I saw them. I didn't always go to Megan's soccer games. I'm not really fond of open spaces." She wrapped the thread tight around her finger. "But one afternoon, I had a particularly good therapy session, so I popped a Xanax and decided to go. I know it was hard for Megan, my condition. But I really wanted to see her play. She was in middle school, but already getting noticed." Corinne's eyes welled with tears at the memory. "She was so beautiful. And understanding." She stared off. "Megan never complained when I couldn't go to her games. She would just sit next to me when she got home and tell me all about it." Corinne wiped her nose with the back of her hand. "She could describe it all in such vivid details. It was as if I were there. I always told her she should be a writer." Corinne looked back at me. Tears escaped down her cheeks. "I think she wanted to study psychology to help me. To try and cure my agoraphobia."

"That's so sweet." My chest filled with a ballooning ache. "What an incredible child."

Corinne's expression hardened. "Back to that afternoon." The tears stopped abruptly. "I got stuck in traffic on my way to the game. When I arrived, it was over. I saw Bill's car, so I got out. That's when I saw them." Her bottom lip trembled.

"You *saw* them?"

"They were in the backseat of Bill's car. I could hear him grunting like a pig." She closed her eyes, held them shut for a moment as if recalling the memory, and opened them again. "And I saw Rhonda underneath him through the window. They never knew I was there."

"I'm sorry. I have an idea of how—"

"Tell me everything you know," she interrupted.

"Okay." I jumped when I felt a tail weave through my legs. I looked down to see a large Maine Coon cat rubbing my calf with the side of its face. I scooped him into my lap. His motor kicked in and he began to knead my skirt. "What a beautiful cat," I said.

"I could care less if he lived or died."

My eyes shot up. "But—"

"Bill gave him to Megan for her sixteenth birthday. She named him Sweetie Pie. But now that she's gone, I can't look at him. I barely remember to feed him."

I put the cat back on the floor and recrossed my legs. Foreboding pulsed through me. It felt as if the air were a mass of static electricity prickling my skin, lifting my hair at the ends. "I will help you in any way I can." I tried to gauge what she was ready to know. Her pupils were unusually large. I suspected she had taken some sort of prescription meds. "First of all, please know it was never about being nosy. I have asked questions because I could see your daughter was a kind and sweet girl. I have a daughter of my own. And the more I discovered, well, things just didn't add up."

"Like what?" She scooted forward in her seat, barely perched on the edge.

"Let me ask you this. Don't you and your husband believe Megan committed suicide?"

"I did." Her brow furrowed. "At first."

"Why?"

"There was a note among her things. Bill read it and asked the police if he could keep it."

"Did he show it to you?"

She shook her head. "I was on tranquilizers. He knew I was fragile. I couldn't bear to see it. And then David Carmichael urged us to remain quiet. He said it would allow us to keep our dignity if Megan's death was ruled an accident and not suicide. The sheriff wanted to look into it. He wanted an autopsy or to at least find out what was in her stomach, but David and Bill somehow convinced him to let us grieve in peace."

"And you've never seen the note?"

She shook her head. "My daughter was dead. Bill said she took her own life. That's all I could bear to hear. I mean . . ." She choked back a sob. "She had been through so much. Megan had to leave Delaware to get away from the gawkers. She didn't want to leave, but Bill insisted. They had horrible arguments before she left for school." Corinne dragged her hands through her hair. "After she died, I didn't want anyone to know I was such a horrible mother, my only child would kill herself." She dropped her face into her hands. "Oh, God. What have I done?" She gasped out a sob. It caught in her throat and an animal cry of pain spilled out of her. She fell forward, clutching her stomach with both arms.

I started over to her, but her head shot up.

"No," she said in a tight voice. "Stay where you are." The muscles in her neck bulged. Her eyes were red, the lids swollen. "I'll be all right. I do this all the time."

"Corinne," I said as I sat back down. "I have been blind to many things myself. Sometimes we only see what we think we can endure. But I do believe we do the best we possibly can at the time. A mother's road is never straight nor easy."

She stuffed her hands in her lap. "Why do you think my daughter was murdered?"

"Like I said, too many things don't add up. But Corinne, if you want me to stop asking questions, I will."

"What if you're right? If she didn't commit suicide, I want to know. I'm ready to know. And if someone murdered my daughter, I want that bastard to die in the chair."

"Do you still have the note?"

"Maybe. And if Bill hasn't destroyed it, I know exactly where it is." She stood quickly and had to steady herself.

"Are you sure you're ready?"

"I should have done this months ago." She started to walk and I hurried after her.

We entered a dark-paneled room lined with shelves and hardcover books. Corinne walked over to a filing cabinet, opened the top drawer, and felt underneath. "Bill thinks I don't know where this is." She removed a small key that was taped to the bottom. "He's always taken me for a fool."

She opened a cabinet door and inserted the key into a glossy black safe. We peered inside. The first thing I noticed was a gun. I froze when she picked it up. But she just moved it aside and rifled through a stack of documents—birth certificates, insurance policies, passports.

"There," I said when I saw a water-stained envelope. "That's it. It was in her backpack. I saw it in the evidence bag the night I found her."

Corinne picked it up. "Independence Day." She shoved it into my hands. "Read it to me?"

"Of course." I lifted the flap and pulled out a creased sheet of paper. Megan had typed it on her computer. The ink hadn't smeared in the river water. I cleared my throat. "Ready?"

"Just read."

Dear Predators,

This includes my stepfather, my professor, and every one of you creeps who stalks me at soccer games and on the Internet. It includes the women and friends who can only feel envy and hatred toward me instead of getting to know me as a real human being. I no longer belong to any of you. I am starting anew. None of you will ever see or hear from me again. I am finally taking control of my own life.

To the people I love, especially you, Mommy, know that I am

alive and searching for happiness at last. When I am ready, I will
bring you to me and find you the help you need.

I swallowed back the emotion overwhelming me and continued
to read.

Today is my Independence Day.

Signed,
The phoenix who was once Megan Johnston

I looked up. Corinne was staring hard at the floor. I folded the
letter back into the envelope. "This isn't a suicide note."

"No." She raised her head and looked at me, her eyes questioning. "Why would Bill hide this from me? I've been going through
hell all these months thinking she killed herself."

"I don't know," I said. "Maybe because of how she refers to him?"

Corinne took the letter from my hands, tucked it into the safe,
and started to close the door. She hesitated and reached for something. I watched as she removed an aged, leather-bound book.

She turned it over in her hands. "Megan's diary." Corinne perched
gingerly onto a plaid upholstered chair. "Bill never told me he found
this. It must have been in her dorm room."

The clasp had been pried open. Every muscle in my body tensed
as Corinne flipped through the pages until she came to the last
entry.

"Corinne?" I said. "Are you sure . . ."

" 'Dear Diary,' " she read.

I placed a hand on her arm. She shook it away and continued.
" 'This will be my last day at John Adams University. I've packed my
bags and have an escape plan. No one knows what I am going to do
and I feel as if a thousand weights have been lifted from me.' "

"Oh my gosh," I said. "This is the day—the day she . . ."

"Her writing is sloppier here," Corinne said quietly. "And she pressed hard with her pen." She lifted the diary closer to her face and continued to read. " 'My stepfather is coming here today. I told him to stay away. I don't want him to know my plans. But he should know it's because of him. I can't take his controlling me anymore. He is like a noose around my neck. I hate him with every fiber of my being. I wish my mother had never married him. But this is it. This is the last time I will ever have to see him and before I go, I will tell him how I feel.' "

She closed the book and held it over her heart, clutching it tightly, as if she were holding the last remnant of Megan.

"Corinne," I said. "Can I get you something? A glass of water?"

"No. I'd rather just sit here alone."

"I can't let you do that."

"You're very stubborn." She smiled weakly. "But I would like you to leave now."

"What will you do?"

She shook her head and said in a barely audible whisper, "I don't really know."

I startled when I felt a tail on my legs. I looked down. Sweetie Pie wove between my ankles.

Corinne looked over at me. "Rosalie . . ."

"Yes?"

"You really want to help me?"

"Any way I can."

"Take him."

"The *cat*?"

"Yes."

"But . . . all right." I picked him up. Sweetie bumped his chin against mine. His claws pierced my shoulder.

"Now, thank you for all that you've done, but I can handle things from here."

I fetched my purse from the living room and returned to Corinne. She hadn't moved. I wasn't sure what to do. I was turning to leave when the front door latch clicked. Corinne and I waited, motionless, as we listened to Bill's heavy footsteps draw nearer.

"There you are," he said. He flinched when he saw me. "What in the hell are you doing here?" His mouth fell open when he eyed the open safe. He looked back at Corinne. "What's that you're holding?"

"Nothing," Corinne said. She stood slowly and walked back to the safe.

I set Sweetie Pie gently on the floor. He let out a soft mew and trotted away. With Bill intent on Corinne, I slid my phone out of my purse. I clicked on the emergency icon so that I didn't need to take the time to type in my pass code.

"What's going on here?" Bill demanded.

I tucked my phone behind my back and glanced up.

Bill looked over at me. "What did you tell her?"

"I don't know what you mean," I said.

"I invited her," Corinne said and faced him.

"No!" I gasped.

Bill spun around and stared into the barrel of a gun. He held up his hands instinctively. "Honey, what are you doing?"

"What I should have done a long time ago."

"Come on, now." He took a step toward her.

I whipped my phone from behind my back. I typed 911 on the keypad and ducked it behind my back again.

"Are you feeling all right, Corinne? Should I get you one of your pills?" Bill said.

"Stop walking," she warned. "Or I'll shoot you in your left ventricle."

"What?" he said. "But, why?"

"You killed my baby." Her hands quivered. "My one and only baby!"

"No, honey, you have it all wrong." He looked over his shoulder at me and then back at her. "Don't you see? *She's* the one you should be shooting."

My eyes widened.

"*She's* the one who is causing all the trouble," he continued. "If *she* hadn't started stirring things up, you and I could go on with our lives."

Corinne glanced at me. "No," she said. "That's not true." She looked back at Bill, but I could see the confusion in her eyes. "It was you." She pulled the hammer back. "It was you all along."

"This is craziness," Bill said. "Why don't you let me get you a pill and a shot of scotch."

"How did you do it?" Corinne said. "I have to know."

"Corinne . . . please!" he pleaded.

"Bill," I said. "Maybe you should just answer her questions." My throat had dried. "Maybe once she understands she'll take that drink." I tried to smile. "And maybe I'll take one, too."

"Shut up," he snapped while still watching Corinne. "Now, come on, honey, please, just put the gun down. I swear I can explain everything."

I prayed someone had picked up the 911 call but didn't know for sure because I had muted my phone when I arrived. Luckily, in order to use my GPS to find the Johnstons' house, I had to allow my phone to use my current location. Surely 911 possessed the technology to figure out where I was. I checked to ensure the microphone was pointed out. If they answered the call, they may hear the conversation. "Corinne?" I said in a loud voice. "Maybe Bill is right. Maybe you should put the gun down and stop threatening to kill your husband."

"You tell me what happened," Corinne spat. She raised the gun to Bill's forehead.

"You don't even know how to use that thing," Bill said, his eyes staring down the barrel.

Corinne coughed out a laugh. "You want to find out?"

"No, of course not." He took a step back. "Now would you—"

"Tell me," she said through clenched teeth.

I inched closer.

"All right. I'll tell you." Bill lowered his hands. "It was an accident," he said. "All of it."

"*What?*" Corinne said.

"I took her out to dinner. She was very uptight, so I ordered us a bottle of wine. But she kept drinking glass after glass and I couldn't get her to stop. Then she started acting like a maniac. She was shouting horrible things at me, so I grabbed her arm and took her outside. She was still shouting, so I forced her over toward the marina so no one could hear her. It was getting dark and—"

Corinne shook her head. *No,* she mouthed.

"Maybe you should put the gun down while you listen," I suggested.

"Be quiet," she said and continued to stare at her husband.

"She was saying crazy things, Corinne," Bill said. "I'd never seen her act like that. I tried to shake some sense into her."

"What did you *do*?" Her brow knitted as if she couldn't quite take in what she was hearing.

"She was having an affair," he said. "With a professor! She told me that, right there on the dock."

"Oh, God," she said. Her arms were weakening.

"Oh, God," I echoed in a faint whisper.

"It's because *you* let her go to that awful school," he hissed. "This is all *your* fault. If she would have stayed here, I could have prevented this."

My ear cocked to the sound of a distant siren.

"Tell me," Corinne demanded.

"I don't think you need to hear—"

She pointed the gun at a spot on the wall just to the right of his head and fired. The sound was deafening. Drywall dust snowed through the air.

Bill covered his head. "Jesus, Corinne. What are you doing?"

She pointed the gun back at Bill.

Hunched in fear, he continued. "She *liked* telling me about him. She was smiling, like sleeping with this man was her way of getting back at me." Sweat dotted his forehead and upper lip. "I couldn't make her shut up," he said. "I had to make her shut up. Don't you see? She was intentionally tormenting me."

I placed my hand over my mouth.

Corinne flinched as the siren grew louder. "Then what?" she demanded.

"I . . . I grabbed a line from the dock. I put it around her neck. I didn't mean to squeeze so hard." He began to sob. "But she had to shut up." Bill's head spun around. Police lights flashed in the window. He looked at me. "What have you . . ." He turned and lunged at Corinne. Wrenching the gun from her hand, he swung around and aimed at me. The front door burst open. Bill started to squeeze the trigger just as Corinne flung the full force of her weight into him, tackling him to the ground. The bullet hit a lamp, knocking it off the table with a crash. The room went dark.

"In here!" I shrieked as I ducked behind a chair.

A flashlight blinded Bill. A police officer planted a boot on his arm and kicked the gun away with his other foot.

"Oh my God," I said and collapsed.

FORTY-EIGHT

The next day Tyler stood, hands on hips, and watched as I got out of my car. A dusting of brown dirt covered his jeans and T-shirt.

"What's wrong?" I juggled several reusable bags filled with groceries.

"What's wrong with you?"

"Me?" I stopped before him and set my bags on the stoop. "Let's just say I had a stressful day yesterday."

Sweetie Pie trotted around the corner with a goldfinch in his mouth. "Oh," I said. "No, Sweetie Pie. Drop that."

He opened his mouth and the bird plopped onto my foot.

"That's his third one today," Tyler said. "That feeder of yours is more like a cat feeder than a bird feeder."

I looked down. "Is it dead?"

"Uh, yes." Tyler tucked his hands in his back pockets. "I saw your note this morning that you had a cat called Sweetie Pie, but I've renamed him."

I reached down and scratched Sweetie's ears. "Are you supposed to do that?"

"That cat is no sweetie pie. He's a ruthless killer." Tyler gazed down at my new pet. "I'm calling him Sweeney. As in Sweeney Todd."

"He's just trying to adjust." Sweetie serpentined through my legs. I picked him up. He purred relentlessly as he kneaded my shoulder. "Maybe he's never been outside before. Give him time."

Tyler shook his head and started to walk away. He stopped when he saw a vehicle coming toward us kicking up dust.

Sheriff Wilgus climbed out of his cruiser. Tyler stood at alert.

"So, Hart," he said as he slammed the door and headed over to us, "I just spent the day with the Wilmington police."

I stole a glance at Tyler. "And?"

"Bill Johnston has been charged with second-degree murder." He looped his thumbs in his belt. "Seems they got the whole confession on the phone, thanks to you."

I smiled weakly. "That's wonderful news."

"I'm not even going to ask why you were at their house," the sheriff said.

"Corinne invited me. She was ready to know what I had learned." Our eyes met. "I felt a duty to tell her the truth."

"They may have some more questions for you." He looked at me warily.

I turned to Tyler. "This is about—"

"I know," he said.

"You know?"

"Annie told me a long time ago," Tyler said. "She wanted me to look out for you. She was worried."

"But you never said anything."

He shifted his weight. "And this surprises who?"

I looked back at the sheriff. It was a cloudy day. No reflecting sunglasses. His eyes were a deep brown, almost black, and questioning.

I thought about the sheriff's role in all of this, his agreeing to not conduct an investigation, his threatening me, throwing me in jail. "Would you like some coffee?" I said. "I think you and I need to have a conversation."

Without a word, he followed me into the house.

I filled two cups and joined him at the table. He was looking out at the river. "Sheriff Wilgus?"

"Feeling some déjà vu," he said and turned to face me.

I smiled. "Me, too."

He leaned back in his chair. "What do you want to know, Hart?"

"What happened in Delaware?"

He shook his head. "I don't know what you're getting at."

"Yes, you do."

"There's nothing to tell." He avoided my eyes.

"Are you going to be able to keep your job?"

"*What?*"

I flattened my back against my chair. The man still sent shivers down my spine. "Are they looking into what happened here in Cardigan? I mean, you know, because there was no investigation?"

"So far, no one has asked me anything about that." He narrowed his eyes. "And I don't expect them to start. You got that?"

"But . . . the things you did." I willed myself to hold his gaze. "A young woman was murdered."

"I wanted to conduct an investigation. I don't know why you think I didn't."

I huffed out a laugh. "Because you didn't actually do it."

"You already know what happened." His voice was quieter. His anger seemed to have dissipated. He took a swig of coffee.

"The college could do it again, you know. Blackmail you, use what they have over you."

He finished his coffee and stared down at the cup. "Damn, that's good coffee."

I picked up his cup, walked over to Mr. Miele, and refilled it. I set it down in front of him but remained standing behind my chair. I liked feeling taller than him at last.

"They can't do it again," he said.

"Why not?" I said. "What's to stop them?"

Our eyes met. "Because that problem is fixed."

"It is?" I shook my head. "How?"

His chin lifted. "Twelve steps. How else?"

"That's wonderful!" I squeezed the top of the chair, feeling thrilled at the news. "So this means David Carmichael can't control you anymore."

"It does."

"This is so great," I said. "You can continue being the sheriff and you and I don't have to hate each other anymore." I smiled broadly. "So, Sheriff, can I call you 'Joe' now?"

"You may not."

"Oh." I stepped back. Just when I thought we were making progress. I stared at the floor, feeling confused by the myriad of feelings swirling around inside. I looked up. "Since we're being honest with one another, I have a question. Did you shoot through my window on Thanksgiving?"

He stirred more sugar into his coffee, the spoon clanking against the sides. "I already told you. It was a hunter tracking a deer. It happens more often than you think."

My mouth fell open. "You mean it wasn't you?"

He shrugged. "You were lucky, that's all."

"Doesn't sound like me," I said.

"Actually . . ." He said and set the spoon on a napkin. "It sounds a lot like you."

Forty-nine

Glenn B	I finished my memoir!!! By the way, that's the first time I've inserted the overused '!' in a Facebook post. :)
Rosalie Hart	That's wonderful Glenn!!!!!!!!!!!!!!!!!!!!! Haha
Tony Ricci	Nice going, Pops. When will I see it on the shelves?
Glenn B	Now that's an LOL.

The Washington Post ran a four-part series about corruption in a small town on the Eastern Shore. Headlines above the fold read

"Cardigan, Maryland: Sleepy Eastern Shore Town or Bed of Corruption? The first segment in a series of articles by Pulitzer Prize winner Richard Burke."

Tom Bestman represented the owners of the row houses and they were compensated properly for their land. The college offered to help finance some low-income housing for the tenants. The row houses wouldn't be razed until the apartments were complete.

Once President Carmichael had agreed to the deal, the spotlight shifted away from him and blazed on the county commissioners. In addition to trying to force out the uneducated owners of the row houses, it was discovered that they were accepting bribes from a big-box store trying to weasel its way into the small county. The county commissioners had been busy bending zoning laws and smart growth legislation in order to bring in the discount store that would have put most of the shops on Main Street out of business. Sheriff Wilgus personally escorted them out of the municipal building.

I worried that people would blame me for all the uproar, but the next time I saw Doris Bird she came out from around the counter and grabbed me in a bear hug. Turns out people were relieved. The corruption was rampant, but no one had quite figured out how to expose it while keeping their necks. "It took a couple of outsiders," she said, "to put things right."

The What Ifs planted a tree in Megan's memory on the banks of the river. A Russian olive—my mother's favorite tree—with silver leaves that fluttered delicately in the breeze, catching the light and sparkling like tinsel.

I felt as if I should thank Megan somehow—for what she gave me—waking me from my complacency, from my solitude and victimization. She struggled hard, I now know, to break free from a life of tyranny. She did not make it. But I could carry on her cause, through my daughter's life and my own.

Glenn B	I'm thinking of running for county commissioner.
Rosalie Hart	I hear there are a few openings.
Sue Ling	Need a campaign manager?
Tony Ricci	You got my vote. Hey Suzy, what's with the name?
Sue Ling	Things have changed for me. I don't want to hide out anymore.
Tony Ricci	Spill, baby.
Sue Ling	It's a long story and I'll tell you all over a drink but in a nutshell, I used to work for a social media company designing software. Things happened and I filed a lawsuit. I won and got a pretty big settlement. The company wasn't happy. Let's just put it that way. And they wanted to come after me.
Rosalie Hart	So why now?
Sue Ling	This investigation has made me stronger. I don't want to be afraid of my own shadow anymore. And it feels wonderful.

FIFTY

A few weeks later, Ed called. He had ended things with Rebecca. Apparently, she had an affair with someone richer. He began calling me nightly, wanting to chat about everything from what I was eating for dinner to his business plan. He had been trying to connect with Annie, but she was still rebuffing him. She's hurt, I told him, and he agreed. When I suggested he friend her on Facebook, he scoffed at the idea. But then a few days later he opened an account, sent her a friend request, and slowly but surely eased back into her life.

Edward Hamilton Hart has sent you a friend request.

Janice Tilghman has sent you an event invitation.

Janice Tilghman
You're coming to the party, Rose Red, just so you know.

Rosalie Hart
Oh, no you don't. Been there, done that.

Janice Tilghman
Our dentist is engaged.

Rosalie Hart
Good for him. So who is it then?

Janice Tilghman
Who said there was anyone? Just come. It'll be an awesome party—outside with a whole bunch of grills going. What do you think about some jerk chicken, a Caribbean theme, maybe some fireworks over the water and a marimba band? Good times. Hey, you ever play corn hole?

I started to type a response, but stopped. Someone once asked me if I felt more or less connected now that I was a member of the Facebook community. It was a hard question to answer. On the positive side, I was much more in tune with the people closest to me. I could share Annie's daily thoughts and activities despite the physical distance between us. And I'm up to date on what people are doing, including those who I wouldn't otherwise have contact with. I even had another friend request from an old boyfriend the other day, although not the one in the denim jacket. Of course, Corinne

Johnston had tracked me down on Facebook and I'd almost gotten shot in her study. That's a little too connected for my taste. So . . . do the benefits outweigh the costs? A definite yes. You've got to put yourself out there if you want connection, adventure, and maybe even love.

Rosalie Hart
Yes! Of course I'll come. What can I bring?

A few evenings later, Tyler walked into the kitchen with an ostentatious amount of flowers. Bearded irises, yellow roses in full bloom, and blue-tinged hydrangeas poked and preened out of a glass vase. I couldn't see his face until he set them on the counter. "From you? Really, Tyler?"

"No," he said and crossed his arms in a tight grip. "They were on the stoop."

I plucked the envelope from its plastic talons, removed the card, and stared down.

> *Please marry me all over again.*
> *I love you with all my heart.*
> *Your husband, Ed.*

"Oh." I covered my open mouth.

Tyler stared at me hard.

"It's from—"

"I know who it's from," he said.

I placed the card back in the envelope, bent down, and smelled an unfurled lily. I reared back. "Whoa."

"I never cared much for the smell of groveling, either," Tyler said.

I looked up at him. I could read the pain straining his eyes. "Tyler . . ."

"I'm finished for the day," he said and left the room. His book was still on the counter. *Omnivore's Dilemma.* I guess he'd moved on from the classics.

After placing the flowers in my aunt's Waterford vase, I poured a glass of chardonnay and returned to the porch. I kicked off my peep-toe pumps and put my feet on the ottoman. I was getting pretty good at walking in heels. This pair had a two-inch heel and I hadn't stumbled or tottered all day.

I had changed very little while living here. The cushions still held that musty smell. I cooked with an old heavy, cast-iron kettle and ate from Aunt Charlotte's chipped plates. Annie and I had grown fond of drinking from her delicate Spode teacups. Every time we sat down to coffee, it felt as if we were having a tea party.

I lit the votives I kept on an old tray table and sat back. Stars littered the sky. The first crickets of the year, eager to find their mates, had begun a loud symphony of chirps. The spring peepers were at it again, joining the crickets, trilling in earnest like balladeers hoping to attract a female. I had named the loudest one Lionel. Sing away, Lionel, I thought. She'll come. We gals are suckers for the show.

"Rosalie?"

I looked up. Tyler was standing in the doorway with a wineglass and the chardonnay bottle. "Mind if I join you?"

"I would love you to." I slipped my feet from the ottoman.

He filled his glass, topped off mine, and sat in the adjacent chair. Dickens padded in after him and dropped at his feet. Tyler stared out at the river. "I know what you're thinking."

I looked over at him. Shadows from the flickering candles contoured his handsome face. "You do?"

"What I meant to say earlier was congratulations." His eyelids were heavy, his jaw clenched. "It's good your husband finally came to his senses. It's what you wanted all along."

"Tyler . . ." I gave him a puzzled expression, my forehead creased, lips turned down. "All this time I've been convinced you could read my mind."

"Excuse me?"

"Your green eyes—they're laser beams, right? I thought you could x-ray my thoughts."

He frowned. "Rosalie . . ."

"I wasn't thinking about Ed."

"But I thought you were going back to Chevy Chase." Sweeney sashayed onto the porch, puffed up at Dickens, then rubbed his chin on Tyler's jeans. Tyler reached down and scratched his ears. "Okay, so what were you thinking?"

"I'm sitting here wondering where we're going to put the chickens."

SAVORY LEMON MUFFINS

This is a basic recipe for delicious lemon muffins. They are great on their own or can be enhanced with a trace of finely chopped fresh herbs such as chives, rosemary, thyme, oregano, or even a pinch of lavender. I added rosemary to the lemon muffins I sold at Birdie's shoe store.

2 cups flour
½ teaspoon baking soda
1½ teaspoons baking powder
1 teaspoon salt
1 cup sugar
½ cup (1 stick) melted and cooled sweet cream butter
2 eggs
1 teaspoon vanilla (Mexican, if you can find it)
2 Tablespoons freshly squeezed lemon juice
2 Tablespoons lemon zest
1 cup milk
1–2 teaspoons washed and finely chopped fresh herbs (optional)

Makes 12 large muffins.

Preheat oven to 325 degrees F. Grease a muffin tin or line with paper cups.

Whisk dry ingredients together in a large bowl. In a medium-size bowl, whisk wet ingredients together. Make a well in the dry ingredients and pour in the wet. Mix lightly, stirring only until combined. Gently stir in herbs, if using. Pour batter into muffin cups.

Bake 15 to 20 minutes or until inserted toothpick comes out clean. Let rest 5 to 10 minutes before removing from tin. Cool on a wire rack.

Tips from my test kitchen: Make sure you have removed all of the paper from the butter before melting. It's also good to try and keep the cat off the counter while preparing the muffins, although I realize this is not always possible.

DOUBLE DARK CHOCOLATE MUFFINS

2 cups unbleached flour

¾ cup sugar

⅓ cup special dark cocoa

½ teaspoon baking soda

1 teaspoon baking powder

1 teaspoon salt

½ cup (1 stick) melted and cooled unsalted butter

1 cup milk

2 eggs

1 teaspoon vanilla (Mexican, if you can find it)

½ cup chopped and lightly toasted walnuts

1 cup dark chocolate morsels

Makes 12 large muffins.

Preheat over to 325 degrees F. Grease a muffin tin or line with paper cups.

Chop walnuts and toast in toaster oven for 1 minute or sauté in a small, ungreased frying pan on stovetop until just beginning to brown.

Whisk together dry ingredients in a large bowl. In a medium-size bowl, whisk wet ingredients together. Make a well in the dry ingredients and add wet ingredients. Stir until just combined. Add walnuts and chocolate morsels and gently blend into batter. Spoon batter into muffin cups and bake 15 to 20 minutes or until inserted toothpick comes out clean. Let rest 5 to 10 minutes before removing from tin. Cool on a wire rack.

Tips from the test kitchen: It is not always a good thing to have a half bag of dark chocolate morsels left over. Especially when you get a sleepy spell midafternoon. But it is advisable to have a portable spot remover pen handy while preparing and/or eating the muffins.

HOMEMADE BREAD

I first started making bread not long after Ed and I married. I was a vegetarian at the time and we received *Laurel's Kitchen* as a wedding gift from Aunt Charlotte. The recipe for one-hundred percent whole-wheat bread continues to be a staple of mine. When Annie was still living at home, I designated Sundays as soup and homemade bread night. I have fond memories of Ed, Annie, and I lingering at the table on those evenings, the room softened by candlelight, our bellies full from a delicious batch of lentil soup and warm, healthy bread.

Aunt Charlotte's five-grain bread recipe can be made by hand or with a breadmaker. As much as I love the process of kneading bread, I am practical enough to realize there isn't always time. Fortunately, almost any recipe can be adapted to a bread machine. Simply start with the required amount of warm water, add the rest of the wet ingredients, followed by the dry. Make a hollow in the center and add the yeast. If you want to shape the dough yourself, set the machine to the dough cycle, remove when finished, mold the dough, cover with a clean dish towel, and put it in a warm place for the second rising. After the second rising, customize your bread before baking. Try sprinkling the dough with herbed sea salt, slathering it with an egg wash, dividing it into several baguettes, or rolling it into a pizza. If you use the dough cycle for Aunt Charlotte's recipe, brush the surface with melted butter, then sprinkle steel-cut oats over the top before popping it into the oven.

For all three recipes, I highly recommend using organic ingredients. Most grocery stores and farmers' markets carry organic milk, butter, flour, eggs, and produce. Not only is it healthier to eat organic ingredients because of the absence of pesticides and hormones, it also (in most cases) involves a more humane treatment of the animals. Additionally, buying organic helps to sustain a demand for these products and keeps organic farmers busy and employed.

AUNT CHARLOTTE'S FIVE-GRAIN BREAD

 1 cup warm water
 1 packet of yeast
 sprinkle of sugar
 ¼ cup rolled oats
 ½ cup boiling water
 ½ cup milk
 3 Tablespoons melted butter
 1 Tablespoon molasses
 2 Tablespoons vegetable oil
 1 Tablespoon honey (local honey is great for building
   immunities to the pollen and other allergens specific to
   your environment)

2 teaspoons salt

2 cups whole-wheat flour

1 cup unbleached white flour

⅓ cup coconut flour

⅓ cup spelt flour

⅓ cup flax seed meal

⅓ rye flour

½ cup sunflower seeds

extra whole-wheat flour for kneading, ¼ cup at a time

First, remember, I warned you—it's complicated.

Sprinkle sugar over warm water in a large bowl, stir, then add yeast. Let sit until the yeast begins to bubble, around 10 minutes. Pour boiling water over oats and let stand for 10 minutes. Melt butter in a saucepan with the milk. Remove from heat. Add oil, honey, and molasses to the milk mixture. When the yeast is ready, stir the milk mixture into the water and yeast.

Whisk together the next 7 ingredients. Begin adding the flour mixture to the wet ingredients one cup at a time, stirring with a wooden spoon until combined. When all the flour is added, it is time to knead. If the mixture is still very sticky and wet, stir in an additional ¼ cup of flour. Sprinkle a bread board with flour and a handful of sunflower seeds. Begin to knead the bread, adding flour and sunflower seeds as needed. The flour should be dusted onto the board. The bread should absorb the flour and sunflower seeds from the bottom as you knead.

Time-saving tip: Once you have added the flour, before kneading, you can put the bread into a mixing bowl and use the bread paddle of a heavy-duty mixer to get the dough to the right consistency—moist and elastic—adding ¼ cup of whole-wheat flour at a time. When thoroughly mixed, put the dough on a bread board and knead with your hands for at least 5 minutes. Bread tastes better when it has a human touch.

Knead with flips, turns, and punches. Put all of your weight into the heels of your hands and push and flip again. Knead until the bread is smooth and elastic. Put in a bowl, cover with a cloth, and let rise until doubled in size—1½ to 2 hours.

Punch down dough and either put in a loaf pan or mold into desired shape. Cover and put in a warm, dark place until it rises again, about 45 minutes to 1 hour.

Preheat oven to 375 degrees F. Bake bread around 45 minutes or until an inserted toothpick or skewer comes out clean. Bread should be slightly brown on top. Let rest 10 minutes before removing from loaf pan.

This is a hearty, stand-alone bread that can be a filling meal with just a slather of butter. But it makes a wonderful sandwich or panini and will hold its own dunked into a thick bowl of soup.

It is hard to describe when you have just the right amount of flour, but a few trials and errors will eventually lead to a wonderful loaf of bread. You may want to start with a basic whole-wheat recipe and work your way up to Aunt Charlotte's fiber-packed loaf. Eating bread may go against the grain in our no-carb, gluten-free culture, but if you are using organic, whole ingredients, I can't imagine eating anything healthier or more wholesome. I have always said I was a peasant in a past life. I would be quite happy eating only stews, soups, beer, and bread. And of course a pat of butter or two.

Bread machine adaptation:

Mix oatmeal and boiling water and set aside for 10 minutes. Begin by pouring the hot water, followed by all wet ingredients (no yeast yet) into the bread machine insert. Follow with oatmeal, salt, and flours. Make a small well in the top and add 2 ¼ teaspoons yeast. Set container in the bread machine and put it on the whole-wheat setting for a 2-pound loaf. Press start. Then wait while your house fills with the mouth-watering aroma of freshly baked bread.

Tips from the test kitchen: Kneading is most enjoyable while listening to your favorite soul-filling music—opera, rock, or a good old country ballad. Singing along is encouraged. Again, no cat on the counter. They are all about the kneading.

ACKNOWLEDGMENTS

Thank you to my daughters, Elizabeth and Madeline. You ground me every day and make the world a brighter, better place just by being you.

A heartfelt thanks to my amazing friends and family. Your unfailing support through hard times and good has sustained me.

Thanks to Mom, whom I miss every day. Your wonder, curiosity, and knowledge continues to guide and inspire me. And to Dad, for sharing your love of the arts and encouraging your children to pursue their talents.

Thanks to my agent, Ken Atchity, for everything, but most importantly, for believing in my book. And to Michael Neff for the great ideas that nudged me closer to getting published.

To my amazing critique group friends: Denny, Susan, Mary, Terese, Greg, Jon, Vicki, and Joe. Thanks for the commas, smiley faces, and belly laughs.

Thanks to all the hard working folks at Thomas Dunne Books. And most especially to my editor, Anne Brewer, for your kindness, talent, and professionalism. I am so lucky to be working with you.